"We have to talk."

"No, we really don't." Isabelle wasn't going to give an inch. She wasn't even sure why Wes was there, and if he didn't know the whole truth, then she wasn't going to give him any information. The only important thing was getting rid of him before he could see Caroline.

"That's not gonna fly," he said and moved in, putting both hands on her shoulders to ease her out of the way.

The move caught her so off guard, Isabelle didn't even try to hold her ground. He was already walking into the house before she could stop him. And even as she opened her mouth to protest, his arm brushed against her and she shivered. It wasn't fear stirring inside her, not even trepidation. It was desire.

The same flush of need that had happened to her years ago whenever Wes was near. Almost from the first minute she'd met him, that jolt of something more had erupted between them. She'd never felt anything like it before Wes—or since.

"I think I deserve an explanation," he said tightly.

"You *deserve*?" she repeated, in little more than a hiss. She shot a quick look down the hall toward the kitchen where Caroline was.

"You should have told me about our daughter."

* * *

The Tycoon's Secret Child
is part of the series Texas Cattleman's Club:
Blackmail—No secret—or heart—
is safe in Royal, Texas…

THE TYCOON'S SECRET CHILD

BY
MAUREEN CHILD

First Published in Great Britain 2017
By Mills & Boon, an imprint of HarperCollins*Publishers*
1 London Bridge Street, London, SE1 9GF

© 2017 Harlequin Books S.A.

Special thanks and acknowledgement are given to Maureen Child for her contribution to the Texas Cattleman's Club: Blackmail series.

ISBN: 978-0-263-92803-7

51-0117

Printed and bound in Spain
by CPI, Barcelona

Maureen Child writes for the Mills & Boon Desire line and can't imagine a better job. A seven-time finalist for a prestigious Romance Writers of America RITA® Award, Maureen is an author of more than one hundred romance novels. Her books regularly appear on bestseller lists and have won several awards, including a Prism Award, a National Readers' Choice Award, a Colorado Romance Writers Award of Excellence and a Golden Quill Award. She is a native Californian but has recently moved to the mountains of Utah.

To the world's greatest editors,
Stacy Boyd and Charles Griemsman—
in the world of writers and editors,
you two shine. Writing isn't always easy
but you guys bring out the best in all of us.

One

Wesley Jackson sat in his corporate office in Houston, riding herd on the department heads attending the meeting he'd called. It had been a long two hours, and he was about done. Thankfully, things were winding down now and he could get out of the city. He didn't mind coming into town once in a while, but he always seemed to breathe deeper and easier back home in Royal.

Didn't appear to matter how successful he became, he'd always be a small-town guy at the heart of it. Just as, he thought with an inner smile as he set one booted foot on his knee, you couldn't take Texas out of the businessman.

"Am I keeping you from something important?" Wes asked suddenly when he noticed Mike Stein, the youngest man on his PR team, staring out a window from the other side of his wide mahogany desk.

Mike flinched. He was energetic, usually eager, but

a little distracted today. Not hard to understand, Wes thought, considering it was January 2 and everyone in the office was probably nursing the dregs of a hangover from various New Year's parties. And Wes could cut the kid a small break, but that was done now.

"What?" Mike blurted. "No, absolutely not. Sorry."

Tony Danvers snorted, then hid the sound behind a cough.

Wes's gaze slid to him, then to the woman sitting on the other side of him. Mike was new, but talented and driven. Tony knew his way around the company blind-folded, and Donna Higgs had her finger on the pulse of every department in the building. The three of them exemplified exactly what he expected from his employees. Dedication. Determination. Results.

Since everything else he'd wanted discussed had been covered in the last two hours, Wes finally brought up the most important item on his agenda.

"The Just Like Me line," he said, flicking a glance at Tony Danvers. "Any problems? We on track for spring delivery to outlets?"

This new doll was destined to be the biggest thing in the country. At least, he told himself, that was the plan. There were dolls that could be specially ordered to look like a child, of course. But Wes's company had the jump on even them. With the accessories available and the quick turnaround, the Just Like Me doll was going to smash all sales record previously set for...*anything*. He smiled to himself just thinking about it. A line of dolls that looked like their owners. Parents could find a doll that resembled their child, either online or at retail locations. Or they could special order one with accessories to make it even more like the child in question.

Wes once considered bringing the doll out early, to

catch the Christmas shopping frenzy. But he'd decided against it, banking on the fact that by February children would already be tired of their Christmas toys and looking for something new.

He was counting on making such an impact that by *next* Christmas, the dolls would be on every kid's wish list. And every child who had already received one would be looking for another. Maybe one in the image of a best friend or a sibling.

The possibilities were endless.

Tony sat back in his brown leather chair, hooked one ankle on a knee. "We're right on schedule, boss. We've got dozens of different designs of dolls. Every ethnicity, every hair type I've ever heard of, and a few that were news to me."

"You're so male," Donna Higgs, the marketing director, muttered with a shake of her head.

Tony winked at her. "Thanks for noticing."

Wes grinned but not at the two friends' byplay. His company, Texas Toy Goods Inc., was going to be the most talked-about toy company in the country once these dolls hit. Marketing, under Donna's steady hand, was already set for a huge campaign, he had the PR department set to flood social media, and a test group of kids had already proclaimed the doll a winner. After ten years of steady growth, Wes's company was poised for a jump that would change Wes from a multimillionaire to a billionaire practically overnight.

He'd started his company on not much more than a shoestring. He had had ideas, a partner he'd managed to buy out several years ago and a small inheritance from his father. With that, and his own driving ambition, Wes built a reputation for coming up with new ways of doing things in a centuries-old industry. He was known for his innovation and creativity. Thanks to him, and the best employees in the business, they'd built on their early successes until TTG was a presence in the toy industry. And the Just Like Me doll was going to give them that one last push over the top.

Each doll was unique in its own way and was going to appeal to every child on the planet. He had visions of European distribution as well, and knew that soon Texas Toy Goods was going to be an unstoppable force in the industry. And that wasn't even counting the upcoming merger he was working on with Teddy Bradford, the current CEO of PlayCo, or his other ventures under the Texas brand umbrella.

"So," Wes said, bringing them back on topic, "if the parent doesn't find exactly what they're looking for, we're set up for them to order specifics."

"Absolutely." Tony straightened up then leaned forward, bracing his forearms on his knees. "There'll be a kiosk in every toy department. The computer will link them to us and they can put in an order for any specific detail they need. Say, if the child has a prosthetic, we can match it. If the child has a specific disability, we're prepared for everything. From wheelchairs to braces, we can give every child out there the feeling of being special. Having a doll in their own image. Naturally, specific orders would take a little longer…"

Wes frowned. "How much longer?"

"Negligible," Donna put in. She checked something on her iPad and looked up at him. "I know Tony's production, but in marketing, we've been working with turnaround time so we can advertise it. With the wide array of dolls already available, we can put out a special order in a couple of days."

"That works." Nodding now, Wes leaned back in his

own chair. "Make sure the factory floor is up to speed on this, and I want a centralized area devoted *only* to this project."

"Uh, boss?" Mike Stein held up one hand as if he were in class. But then, he was young and enthusiastic and would eventually get used to the more wide-open discussions Wes preferred during meetings.

"What is it?"

Mike glanced at the others before looking back at Wes. "We've got the ads lined up and the social media blast is ready to roll on the day."

"Good."

"But," Mike added, "I know it's not my department—"

"Doesn't matter," Wes told him. He liked his people being interested in *all* departments, not just their specialties.

"Okay. I was thinking, having a dedicated area at the factory could be problematic."

Tony actually leaned a little toward the left, putting some distance between himself and the new guy. At least the others knew better than to tell Wes something couldn't be done.

"Why's that?" Wes asked calmly.

"Well, it means pulling people off the line and setting them up to handle *only* these special orders."

"And?"

"Well," Mike continued, clearly unwilling to back off the track he found himself on. Wes could give him points for having guts. "That means we have people who are standing there *waiting* for something to do instead of working on the line and getting actual work done."

"What changes would you suggest?" Wes asked coolly.

Tony cleared his throat and gave a barely there shake

of his head, trying to tell the kid in code to just shut up and let this one go. But Mike had the bit in his teeth now and wouldn't drop it.

"I would leave them working on the line and pull them out when a special order came in and then—"

"I appreciate your idea," Wes said, tapping his fingers against the gray leather blotter on his desk. "I want my people to feel free to speak up. But you're new here, Mike, and you need to learn that at TTG, we do things a little differently. Here, the customer is always number one. We design toys and the delivery system to facilitate the people who buy our toys. So if that means we have a separate crew waiting for the special orders to come in, then that's what we do. We're the best. That's what breeds success."

"Right." Mike nodded, swallowed hard and nodded again. "Absolutely. Sorry."

"No problem." Wes waved the apology away. He'd either learn from this and pick up on the way things were done at TTG, or the kid would leave and find a job somewhere else.

But damn, when did he start thinking of guys in their twenties as *kids*? When did Wes get ancient? He squashed that thought immediately. Hell, at thirty-four, he wasn't old. He was just *busy*. Running his company ate up every moment of every damn day. He was so busy, his social life was a joke. He couldn't even remember the last time he'd been with a woman. But that would come. Eventually. Right now, TTG demanded and deserved his full concentration.

Of course, his brain whispered, it hadn't always been that way. There'd been one woman—

Wes cut all thoughts of her off at the pass. That was done. Over. He hadn't been interested in long-term and she'd all but had *marriage and children* tattooed across her forehead. He'd had to end it and he wasn't sorry. Most of the time.

Having a relationship with one of his employees hadn't been a particularly smart move on his part. And sure, there'd been gossip and even resentment from some of his staff. But Wes hadn't been able to resist Belle. What the two of them had shared was like nothing he'd ever known. For a time, Wes had been willing to put up with whispers at work for the pleasure of being with Belle.

But it was over. The past.

"We've got the accessories covered, I think," Donna said. "When the special orders come in, we'll be able to turn them around in a flash."

"Good to hear. And if you don't have it?" Wes asked.

"We'll get it." Donna nodded sharply. "No problem on this, boss. It's going to work as smoothly as you expect it to. And it's going to be the biggest doll to hit the market since the vegetable patch babies back in the '80s."

"That's what I want to hear." Wes stood up, shoved both hands into his pockets and said, "That's all for now. Keep me in the loop."

Tony laughed. "Boss, everybody runs everything by you."

One corner of Wes's mouth quirked. "Yeah. Just the way I like it. Okay, back to work."

He watched them go, then told his assistant, Robin, to get him some fresh coffee. He'd need it once he started going through business emails. Inevitably, there were problems to walk through with suppliers, manufacturers, bankers and everyone else who either had a piece—or wanted one—of the Texas Toy Goods pie. But instead of taking a seat behind his desk, he walked across the wide office to the corner windows. The view of Houston was familiar, impressive. High-rises, glass walls reflecting sunlight that could blind a man. Thick white clouds sailing across a sky so blue it hurt the eyes.

He liked the city fine, but it wasn't somewhere he wanted to spend too much time. At least twice a week, he made the drive in from Royal, Texas, and his home office, to oversee accounts personally and on-site. He believed in having his employees used to seeing him there. People tended to get complacent when there was an absentee boss in the picture. But if he had a choice, he'd pick Royal over Houston.

His hometown had less traffic, less noise and the best burgers in Texas at the Royal Diner. Not to mention the fact that the memories in Royal were easier to live with than the ones centered here, in his office. Just being here, he remembered late-night work sessions with the woman he refused to think about. All-night sessions that had become a blistering-hot affair that had crashed and burned the minute she whispered those three deadly words—*I love you*. Even after all this time, that moment infuriated him. And despite—maybe *because* of—how it ended, that one woman stayed in his mind, always at the edges of his thoughts.

"What is it with women?" he asked the empty room. "Everything was going fine and then she just had to ruin it."

Of course, a boss/employee relationship wasn't going to work for the long haul anyway, and he'd known that going in. And even with the way things had ended, he couldn't completely regret any of it. What bothered him was that even now, five years later, thoughts of Belle kept cropping up as if his mind just couldn't let go.

A brisk knock on the door had him shaking his head

and pushing thoughts of her to the back of his mind, where, hopefully, they would stay. "Come in."

Robin entered, carrying a tray with a single cup, a thermal carafe of coffee and a plate of cookies. He smiled. "What would I do without you?"

"Starve to death, probably," she said. Robin was in her forties, happily married and the proud mother of four. She loved her job, was damn good at it and kept him apprised of everything going on down here when he was in Royal. If she ever threatened to quit, Wes was prepared to offer her whatever she needed to stay.

"You scared the kid today."

Snorting a laugh as he remembered the look of sheer panic on Mike's face, Wes sat down at his desk and poured the first of what would be several cups of coffee. "He'll survive."

"Yeah, he will. A little fear's good. Builds character."

One eyebrow lifted as Wes laughed. "Your kids must be terrified of you."

"Me?" she asked. "Nope. I raise them tougher than that."

Wes chuckled.

"Harry called. He's headed into that meeting in New York. Said he'd call when he had it wrapped up."

Harry Baker, his vice president, was currently doing all the traveling around the country, arranging for the expedited shipping the new doll line would require. "That's good. Thanks."

After she left, Wes sipped at his coffee, took a cookie, had a bite, then scrolled to his email account. Idly, he scanned the forty latest messages, deleting the crap. He scanned the subject lines ruthlessly, until he spotted Your secret is out.

"What the hell?" Even while a part of his mind was

thinking *virus or an ad for timeshares in Belize*, he clicked on the message and read it. Everything in him went cold and still. The cookie turned to ash in his mouth and he drank the coffee only to wash it down.

Look where your dallying has gotten you, the email read.

Check your Twitter account. Your new handle is Deadbeatdad. So you want to be the face of a new toy empire? Family friendly? Think again.

It was signed, Maverick.

"Who the hell is Maverick and what the hell is he talking about?" There was an attachment with the email, and even though Wes had a bad feeling about all of this, he opened it. The photograph popped onto his computer screen.

He shot to his feet, the legs of his chair scraping against the polished wooden floor like a screech. Staring down at the screen, his gaze locked on the image of the little girl staring back at him. "What the—"

She looked just like him. The child had Wes's eyes and a familiar smile and if that wasn't enough to convince him, which it was, he focused on the necklace the girl was wearing. Before he and Belle broke up, Wes had given her a red plastic heart on a chain of plastic beads. At the time, he'd used it as a joke gift right before giving her a pair of diamond earrings.

And the little girl in the photo was wearing that red heart necklace while she smiled into the camera.

Panic and fury tangled up inside him and tightened into a knot that made him feel like he was choking. He couldn't tear his gaze from the photo of the smiling little girl. "How does a man have a daughter and not know it?"

A daughter? How? What? Why? *Who?* He had a *child*. Judging by the picture, she looked to be four or five years old, so unless it was an old photo, there was only one woman who could be the girl's mother. And just like that, *the* woman was back, front and center in his mind.

How the hell had this happened? Stupid. He knew *how* it had happened. What he didn't know was why he hadn't been told. Wes rubbed one hand along the back of his neck and didn't even touch the tension building there. Still staring at the smiling girl on the screen, he felt the email batter away at his brain until he was forced to sit, open a new window and go to Twitter.

Somebody had hacked his account. His new handle was, as promised, Deadbeatdad. If he didn't get this stopped fast, it would go viral and might start interfering with his business.

Instantly, Wes made some calls, reporting that his account had been hacked, then turned the mess over to his IT guys to figure out. He reported the hack and had the account shuttered, hoping to buy time. Meanwhile, he was too late to stop #Deadbeatdad from spreading. The Twitterverse was already moving on it. Now he had a child he had to find and a reputation he had to repair. Snatching up the phone, he stabbed the button for his assistant's desk. "Robin," he snapped. "Get Mike from PR back in here *now*."

He didn't even wait to hear her response, just slammed the phone down and went back to his computer. He brought up the image of the little girl—his *daughter*—again and stared at her. What was her name? Where did she live? Then thoughts of the woman who had to be the girl's mother settled into his brain. Isabelle Gray. She'd disappeared from his life years ago—apparently with his child. Jaw tight, eyes narrowed, Wes promised himself he was going to get to the bottom of all of this and when he did...

For the next hour, everyone in PR and IT worked the situation. There was no stopping the flood of retweets, so Wes had Mike and his crew focused on finding a way to spin it. IT was tasked with tracking down this mysterious Maverick so that Wes could deal with him head-on.

Meanwhile, Wes had another problem to worry about. The merger with PlayCo, a major player in the toy industry, was something Wes had been carefully maneuvering his way toward for months. But the CEO there, Teddy Bradford, was a good old boy with rock-solid claims to family values. He'd been married to the same woman forever, had several kids and prided himself on being the flag bearer for the all-American, apple pie lifestyle.

This was going to throw a wrench of gigantic proportions into the mix. And so far, Teddy wasn't taking any of Wes's calls. Not a good sign.

"Uh, boss?"

"Yeah?" Wes spun around to look at one of the PR grunts. What the hell was her name? Stacy? Tracy? "What is it?"

"Teddy Bradford is holding a press conference. The news channel's website is running it live."

He stalked to her desk and only vaguely noticed that the others in the room had formed a half circle behind him. They were all watching as Bradford stepped up to a microphone and held his hands out in a settle-down gesture. As soon as he had quiet, he said, "After the disturbing revelations on social media this afternoon, I'm here to announce that I will be taking a step back to re-evaluate my options before going through with the much anticipated merger."

Wes ground his teeth together and fisted his hands at his sides. Teddy could play it any way he wanted to for the press, but it was easy to see the merger was, at the moment, dead. All around him, his employees took a collective breath that sounded like a gasp.

But Teddy wasn't finished. The older man looked somber, sad, but Wes was pretty sure he caught a gleam of satisfaction in the other man's eyes. Hell, he was probably enjoying this. Nothing the man liked better than sitting high on his righteous horse. Teddy hadn't even bothered to take his call, preferring instead to call a damn press conference. Bastard.

"Here at PlayCo," Teddy was saying, "we put a high priority on family values. In fact, you could say that's the dominant trademark of my company and it always will be. A man's family is all important—or should be. After this morning's revelations, I have to say that clearly, Wes Jackson is not the man I'd believed him to be, and so I have some thinking to do in the next few days. As things stand now, it would take a miracle to persuade me to believe otherwise." Questions were fired at him, cameras chattered as shutters clicked over and over again. But Teddy was done.

"That's it. That's all I've got to say." He looked out over the crowd. "You have more questions, I suggest you throw them at Wes Jackson. Good day." He left the podium in the midst of a media circus and Wes rubbed his eyes, trying to ease the headache crouched behind them.

Stacy/Tracy turned the sound off on the computer, and silence dropped over everyone in the room like a damn shroud. Inside Wes, irritation bubbled into anger and then morphed quickly into helpless rage. There was nowhere to turn it. Nowhere to focus it and get any kind of satisfaction.

As of now, the merger was in the toilet. And yeah, he was concentrating on the business aspect of this nightmare because he didn't have enough information to concentrate on the personal. Furious, Wes watched his PR team scramble to somehow mitigate the growing disaster. His assistant was already fielding calls from the media and this story seemed to be growing by the minute. Nothing people liked better than a scandal, and whoever this Maverick was, they obviously knew it.

For the first time ever, Wes felt helpless, and he didn't like it. Not only was his company taking a hit, but somewhere out there, he had a child he'd known nothing about. How the hell had this Maverick discovered the girl? Was Isabelle in on all of this? Or was someone close to her hoping for a giant payout along with pay-*back*? Whatever the reason, this attack was deliberate. Someone had arranged a deliberate assault on him and his company. That someone was out to ruin him, and his brain worked feverishly trying to figure out just who was behind it all.

Running a successful business meant that you would naturally make enemies. But until today he wouldn't have thought that any of them would stoop to something like this. So he went deeper, beyond business and into the personal, looking for anyone who might have set him up for a fall like this. And only one name rose up in his mind. His ex-girlfriend, Cecelia Morgan.

She and Belle had been friendly for a while back in the day. Maybe Cecelia had known about the baby. Maybe she was the one who had started all this. Hell, she might even be Maverick herself. Cecelia hadn't taken it well when he broke up with her, and God knew she had a vicious temper. But if she was behind it all, *why*? Her company, To the Moon, sold upscale merchandise for kids. They weren't in direct competition, but she was as devoted to her business as Wes was to his, and maybe that was the main reason the two of them hadn't worked out. Or, he told himself, maybe it was the mean streak he'd witnessed whenever Cecelia was with her two best friends, Simone Parker and Naomi Price. He knew for a fact that people in Royal called the three women the Mean Girls. They were rich, beautiful, entitled and sometimes not real careful about the things they said to and about people.

He didn't know if she'd had anything to do with what was happening, but there was one sure way to find out. Leaving his employees scrambling, Wes drove home to Royal to confront his ex and, just maybe, get some answers. The drive did nothing to calm him down, since his brain kept focusing on the photo of that little girl. His daughter, for God's sake.

He needed answers. The only one who could give them to him was Belle, so finding her was priority one. His IT staff was now focused on not only mitigating his business disaster, but also in finding Isabelle Gray. But until he did locate Belle, Wes told himself, at least he could do *something*. Knowing Cecelia could always be found at the Texas Cattleman's Club for lunch, he headed there the moment he hit town.

Cecelia was in the middle of what looked like a lunch meeting with a few of her employees. And though breaking it up would only encourage gossip, Wes wasn't interested in waiting for her to finish. The TCC was a legend in Royal, Texas. A members-only club, it had been around forever and only in the last several years had started accepting women as members—quite a few of the old guard still weren't happy about it. The dining room was elegant, understated and quiet but for the hush of conversation and the subtle clink of silverware against china.

On the drive from Houston, Wes's mind had raced with the implications of everything that had happened. A child he didn't know about. A merger in the toilet. His reputation shattered. And at the bottom of it all, maybe a vengeful ex. By the time he stood outside that dining room, he was ready for a battle.

"Mr. Jackson." The maître d' stepped up. "May I show you to a table? Are you alone for lunch or expecting guests?"

"Neither, thanks," Wes said, ignoring the man after a brief, polite nod. Wes speared Cecelia with a cold, hard gaze that caught her attention even from across the room. "I just need a word with Ms. Morgan."

Once she met his cool stare, she frowned slightly, then excused herself from the table and walked toward him. She was a gorgeous woman, and in a purely male response, Wes had to admire her even as his anger bubbled and churned inside. Her long, wavy blond hair lay across her shoulders and her gray-green eyes fixed on him, curiosity shining there. She wasn't very tall, but her generous figure and signature pout had brought more than one man in Texas to his knees.

She gave him a smile, then leaned in as if to kiss his cheek, but Wes pulled back out of reach. He caught the surprise and the insult in her eyes, but he only said, "We need to talk."

There were already enough people talking about his

business today, so he took her forearm in a tight grip and led her away from the dining room to a quiet corner, hoping for at least a semblance of privacy. Cecelia pulled free as soon as he stopped and hissed, "What is going on with you?"

"You know damn well what," he said in a gravelly whisper. "That email you sent."

Those big, beautiful eyes clouded with confusion. "I have zero idea what you're talking about."

He studied her for a long minute, deciding whether she was lying or not. God knew he couldn't be sure, but he was going with instinct here. She didn't look satisfied with a mission accomplished. She looked irritated and baffled.

"Fine," he said grimly and dug his cell phone out of a pocket. Pulling up his email, he handed the phone to her and waited while she read it.

"Maverick? Who the heck is Maverick?"

Her expression read confusion and a part of him eased back a little. But if she wasn't Maverick, who was?

"Good question. I got an email this morning from a stranger. They sent me a picture of a daughter I never knew existed." He opened the attachment and showed her the picture of the smiling little girl. That's when he saw the flash of recognition in her eyes and he realized that Cecelia knew more than she was saying. Her face was too easy to read. His daughter's existence hadn't surprised her a bit.

"You knew about the girl." It wasn't a question. His chest felt tight.

Taking a deep breath, Cecelia blew out a breath and said, "I knew she was pregnant when she left. I didn't know she'd had a girl."

"She?"

Cecelia huffed out a breath. "Isabelle."

He swayed in place. He'd known it. Seeing that necklace on a little girl with his eyes had been impossible to deny. Isabelle. The woman he'd been involved with for almost a year had been pregnant with *his* daughter and hadn't bothered to tell him. More than that, though, was the fact that apparently Cecelia had known about his child, too, and kept the secret. Belle had left town. Cecelia had been right here in Royal. Seeing him all the damn time. And never once had she let on that he had a child out there. He couldn't rage at Belle. Yet. So it was the woman in front of him who got the full blast of what he was feeling. Every time she'd seen him for the last five years, she'd lied to him by not saying anything. She'd *known* he was a father and never said a damn word. What the hell? And who was Maverick and how did he know?

"You knew and didn't say anything?" His voice was low and tight.

She tossed a glance over her shoulder toward the table where she'd left her friends, then looked back at him. "No, I didn't. What would have been the point?"

He glared at her. "The point? My kid would be the point. And the fact that I didn't even know she existed."

"Please, Wes. How many times have you said you don't want kids or a family or anything remotely resembling commitment?"

"Not important."

"Yeah, it is." She was getting defensive—he heard it in her voice. "She was pretty sure you wouldn't be happy about the baby and I agreed. I just told her what you'd said so many times—that you weren't interested in families or forever."

Having his own words thrown back at him stung, but worse was the fact that *two* women he'd been with had conspired to keep his child from him. No, he'd never planned on kids or a wife, but that didn't mean he wouldn't want to know.

"Then what?" he asked, his voice sounding as if it was scraping along shattered glass. "You wait a few years, find this Maverick and tell *him*? Help him slam me across social media? For what? Payback?"

Her head snapped back and her eyes went even wider. "I would never do that to you, Wes," she said, and damned if he didn't almost believe her. "I wouldn't hurt you like that."

"Yeah?" he countered. "Your rep says otherwise."

She flushed and took a deep breath. "Believe what you want, but it wasn't me."

"Fine. Then where is Isabelle?"

"I don't know. She only said she was going home. A small town in Colorado. Swan…something. I forget. Honestly, we haven't stayed in touch." Tentatively, she reached out one hand and laid it on his forearm. "But I'll help you look for her."

"You helped enough five years ago," Wes ground out, and saw her reaction to the harsh tone flash in her eyes.

Too bad. He didn't have time to worry about insulting a woman who very well might be at the heart of this Maverick business. Sure, she claimed innocence, but he'd be a fool to take her word for it. When he rushed out, he barely noticed the waiter hovering nearby.

Wes's entire IT department was working on this problem, but he should be researching himself. His own tech skills were more than decent. He could have found Isabelle years ago, if he'd been looking. Yeah, he'd have to sift through a lot of information on the web, but he'd find her.

And when he did, heaven better help her, because hell would be dropping onto her doorstep.

Isabelle Graystone sat at the kitchen table working with a pad and pen while her daughter enjoyed her post-preschool snack.

"Mommy," Caroline said, her fingers dancing as she spoke, "can I have more cookies?"

Isabelle looked at the tiny love of her life and smiled. At four years old, Caroline was beautiful, bright, curious and quite the con artist when it came to getting more cookies. That sly smile and shy glance did it every time.

Isabelle's hands moved in sign language as she said, "Two more and that's it."

Caroline grinned and helped herself. Her heels tapped against the rungs of the kitchen chair as she cupped both hands around her glass of milk to take a sip.

Watching her, Isabelle smiled thoughtfully. It wasn't easy for a child to be different, but Caroline had such a strong personality that wearing hearing aids didn't bother her in the least. And learning to sign had opened up her conversational skills. Progressive hearing loss would march on, though, Isabelle knew, and one day her daughter would be completely deaf.

So Isabelle was determined to do everything she could to make her little girl's life as normal as possible. Which might also include a cochlear implant at some point. She wasn't there yet, but she was considering all of her options. There was simply nothing she wouldn't do for Caroline.

"After lunch," Isabelle said, "I have to go into town. See some people about the fund-raiser party I'm planning. Do you want to come with me, or stay here with Edna?"

Chewing enthusiastically, Caroline didn't speak, just used sign language to say, "I'll come with you. Can we have ice cream, too?"

Laughing, Isabelle shook her head. "Where are you putting all of this food?"

A shrug and a grin were her only answers. Then the doorbell rang and Isabelle said, "Someone's at the door. You finish your cookies."

She walked through the house, hearing the soft click of her own heels against the polished wood floors. There were landscapes hanging on the walls, and watery winter sunlight filtering through the skylight positioned over the hallway. It was an elegant but homey place, in spite of its size. The restored Victorian stood on three acres outside the small town of Swan Hollow, Colorado.

Isabelle had been born and raised there, and when she'd found herself alone and pregnant, she'd come running back to the place that held her heart. She hadn't regretted it, either. It was good to be in a familiar place, nice knowing that her daughter would have the same memories of growing up in the forest that she did, and then there was the added plus of having her three older brothers nearby. Chance, Eli and Tyler were terrific uncles to Caroline and always there for Isabelle when she needed them—and sometimes when she didn't. The three of them were still as protective as they'd been when she was just a girl—and though it could get annoying on occasion, she was grateful for them, too.

Shaking her long, blond hair back from her face, she opened the door with a welcoming smile on her face—only to have it freeze up and die. A ball of ice dropped into the pit of her stomach even as her heartbeat jumped into overdrive.

Wes Jackson. The one man she'd never thought to see

again. The one man she still dreamed of almost every night. The one man she could never forget.

"Hello, Belle," he said, his eyes as cold and distant as the moon. "Aren't you going to invite me in?"

Two

Isabelle felt her heart lurch to a stop then kick to life again in a hard thump. *Invite him in?* What she wanted to do was step back inside, slam the door and lock it. Too bad she couldn't seem to move. She did manage to choke out a single word. "Wes?"

"So you do remember me. Good to know." He moved in closer and Isabelle instinctively took a step back, pulling the half-open door closer, like a shield.

Panic nibbled at her, and Isabelle knew that in a couple more seconds it would start taking huge, gobbling bites. As unexpected as it was to find Wes Jackson standing on her front porch, there was a part of her that wasn't the least bit surprised to see him. Somehow, she'd half expected that one day, her past would catch up to her.

It had been five long years since she'd seen him, yet looking at him now, it could have been yesterday. Even in this situation, with his eyes flashing fury, she felt that bone-deep stir of something hot and needy and oh, so tempting. What was *wrong* with her? Hadn't she learned her lesson?

Isabelle had loved working for Texas Toys. They were open to new ideas and Wes had been the kind of boss everyone should have. He encouraged his employees to try new and different things and rewarded hard work. He was always hands-on when it came to introducing fresh products to his established line. So he and Isabelle had worked closely together as she came up with new toys, new designs. When she'd given in to temptation, surrendered to the heat simmering between them, Isabelle had known that it wouldn't end well. Boss/employee flings were practically a cliché after all. But the more time she spent with him, the more she'd felt for him until she'd made the mistake of falling in love with him.

That's when everything had ended. When he'd told her that he wasn't interested in more than an affair. He'd broken her heart, and when she left Texas, she'd vowed to never go back.

It seemed though, she hadn't had to. Texas had come to *her*.

"We have to talk." His voice was clipped, cold.

"No, we really don't." Isabelle wasn't going to give an inch. She wasn't even sure why he was here, and if he didn't know the whole truth, she wasn't going to give him any information. The only important thing was getting rid of him before he could see Caroline.

"That's not gonna fly," he said and moved in, putting both hands on her shoulders to ease her back and out of the way.

The move caught her so off guard, Isabelle didn't even try to hold her ground. He was already walking into the house before she could stop him. And even as she opened her mouth to protest, his arm brushed against her breast and she shivered. It wasn't fear stirring inside her, not even panic. It was desire.

The same flush of need had happened to her years ago whenever Wes was near. Almost from the first minute she'd met him, that jolt of something *more* had erupted between them. She'd never felt anything like it before Wes—or since. Of course, since she came back home to Swan Hollow, she hadn't exactly been drowning in men.

After Wes, she'd made the decision to step back from relationships entirely. Instead, she had focused on building a new life for her and her daughter. And especially during the last year or so, that focus had shut out everything else. Isabelle had her brothers, her daughter, and she didn't need anything else. Least of all the man who'd stolen her heart only to crush it underfoot.

With those thoughts racing through her mind, she closed the door and turned to face her past.

"I think I deserve an explanation," he said tightly.

"You *deserve*?" she repeated, in little more than a hiss. She shot a quick look down the hall toward the kitchen where Caroline was. "Really? That's what you want to lead with?"

"You should have told me about our daughter."

Shock slapped at her. But at the same time, a tiny voice in the back of Isabelle's mind whispered, *Of course he knows. Why else would he be here?* But how had he found out?

One dark eyebrow lifted. "Surprised? Yeah, I can see that. Since you've spent *five years* hiding the truth from me."

Hard to argue with that, since he was absolutely right. But on the other hand... "Wes—"

He held up one hand and she instantly fell into silence

even though she was infuriated at herself for reacting as he expected her to.

"Spare me your excuses. There *is* no excuse for this. Damn it, Isabelle, I had a right to know."

Okay, that was enough to jolt her out of whatever fugue state he'd thrown her into. Keeping her voice low, she argued, "A right? I should have told you about *my* daughter when you made it perfectly clear you had no interest in being a father?"

Wanting to get him out of the hall where Caroline might see him, she walked past him into the living room. It was washed with pale sunlight, even on this gloomy winter day. The walls were a pale green and dotted with paintings of forests and sunsets and oceans. There were books lining the waist-high bookcases that ran the perimeter of the room and several comfortable oversize chairs and couches.

Oak tables were scattered throughout and a blue marble-tiled hearth was filled with a simmering fire. This room—heck, this *house*—was her haven. She'd made a home here for her and Caroline. It was warm and cozy in spite of its enormous size, and she loved everything about it. So why was it, she wondered, that with Wes Jackson standing in the cavernous room, she suddenly felt claustrophobic?

He came up right behind her and she felt as if she couldn't draw a breath. She wanted him out. Now. Before Caroline could come in and start asking questions Isabelle didn't want to answer. She whipped around to face him, to finish this, to allow him to satisfy whatever egotistical motive had brought him here so he could leave.

His aqua eyes were still so deep. So mesmerizing. Even with banked anger glittering there, she felt drawn to him. And that was just…sad. His collar-length blond hair was ruffled, as if he'd been impatiently driving his fingers through it. His jaw was set and his mouth a firm, grim line. This was the face he regularly showed the world. The cool, hard businessman with an extremely low threshold for lies.

But she'd known the real man. At least, she'd told herself at the time that the man she talked, laughed and slept with was the real Wes Jackson. When they were alone, his guard was relaxed, though even then, she'd had to admit that he'd held a part of himself back. Behind a wall of caution she hadn't been able to completely breach. She'd known even then that Wes would continue to keep her at a safe distance and though it had broken her heart to acknowledge it, for her own sake, and the sake of her unborn child, she'd had to walk away.

"That was a hypothetical child," he ground out, and every word sounded harsh, as if it was scraping against his throat. "I never said I wouldn't want a child who was already *here*."

A tiny flicker of guilt jumped into life in the center of her chest, but Isabelle instantly smothered it. Five years ago, Wes had made it clear he wasn't interested in a family. He'd told her in no uncertain terms that he didn't want a wife. Children. *Love*. She'd left. Come home. Had her baby alone, with her three older brothers there to support her. Now Caroline was happy, loved, settled. How was Isabelle supposed to feel guilty about doing the best thing for her child?

So she stiffened her spine, lifted her chin and met Wes's angry glare with one of her own. "You won't make me feel bad about a decision I made in the best interests of my daughter."

"*Our* daughter, and you had no right to keep her from me." He shoved both hands into the pockets of his black leather jacket, then pulled them free again. "Damn it, Isabelle, you didn't make that baby on your own."

"No, I didn't," she said, nodding. "But I've taken care of her on my own. Raised her on my own. You don't get to storm into my life and start throwing orders around, Wes. I don't work for you anymore, and this is *my* home."

His beautiful eyes narrowed on her. "You lied to me. For five years, you lied to me."

"I haven't even spoken to you."

"A lie of omission is still a lie," he snapped.

He was right, but she had to wonder. Was he here because of the child he'd just discovered or because she'd wounded his pride? She tipped her head to one side and studied him. "You haven't even asked where she is, or how she is. Or even what her name is. This isn't about her for you, Wes. This is about *you*. Your ego."

"Her name is Caroline," he said softly. He choked out a laugh that never reached his eyes. "I'm pretty good at research myself. You know, you're something else." Shaking his head he glanced around the room before skewering her with another hard look. "You think this is about ego? You took off. With *my* kid—and never bothered to tell me."

Was it just outrage she was hearing? Or was there pain in his voice as well? Hard to tell when Wes spent his life hiding what he was feeling, what he was thinking. Even when she had been closest to him, she'd had to guess what was going through his mind at any given moment. Now was no different.

She threw another worried glance toward the open doorway. Time was ticking past, and soon Caroline would come looking for her. Edna, the housekeeper, would be home from the grocery store soon, and frankly,

Isabelle wanted Wes gone before she was forced to answer any questions about him.

"How did you find out?" she asked abruptly, pushing aside the guilt he kept trying to pile on her.

He scraped one hand across his face then pushed that hand through his hair, letting her know that whatever he was feeling was in turmoil. Isabelle hadn't known he was capable of this kind of emotion. She didn't know whether she was pleased or worried.

"You haven't seen the internet headlines today?"

"No." Worry curled into a ball in the pit of her stomach and twisted tightly. "What's happened?"

"Someone knew about our daughter. And they've been hammering me with that knowledge."

"How?" She glanced at her laptop and thought briefly about turning it on, catching up with what was happening. But the easiest way to discover what she needed to know was to hear it directly from Wes.

"I got an email yesterday from someone calling themselves Maverick. Sent me a picture of my daughter."

"How did you know she was yours?"

He gave her a cool look. "She was wearing the princess heart necklace I once gave you."

Isabelle sighed a little and closed her eyes briefly. "She loves that necklace." Caro had appropriated the plastic piece of jewelry, and seeing it on her daughter helped Belle push the memory of receiving it from Wes into the background.

"You liked it once too, as I remember."

Her gaze shot up to his. "I used to like a lot of things."

Nodding at that jab, Wes said, "The same person who sent me the picture also let me know my Twitter account had been hacked. Whoever it was gave me a new handle. Real catchy. Deadbeatdad."

"Oh, God."

"Yeah, that pretty much sums it up." He shook his head again. "That new hashtag went viral so fast my IT department couldn't contain it. Before long, reporters were calling, digging for information. Then Teddy Bradford at PlayCo called a press conference to announce the merger we had planned was now up in the air because, apparently," he muttered darkly, "I'm too unsavory a character to be aligned with his family values company."

"Oh, no..." Isabelle's mind was racing. Press conferences. Reporters. Wes Jackson was big news. Not just because of his toy company, but because he was rich, handsome, a larger-than-life Texas tycoon who made news wherever he went. And with the interest in him, that meant that his personal life was fodder for stories. Reporters would be combing through Wes's past. They would find Caroline. They would do stories, take pictures and, in general, open her life up to the world. This was fast becoming a nightmare.

"The media's been hounding me since this broke. I've got Robin fielding calls—she'll stonewall them for as long as she can."

Wes's assistant was fierce enough to hold the hordes at bay—but it wouldn't last. They would eventually find her. Find Caroline. But even as threads of panic unwound and spiraled through her veins, Isabelle was already trying to figure out ways to protect her daughter from the inevitable media onslaught.

"So." Wes got her attention again. "More lies. You're not Isabelle *Gray*. Your real last name is Graystone. Imagine my surprise when I discovered *that*. Isabelle Gray didn't leave much of a mark on the world—but while typing in the name you gave me, up popped Isabelle *Graystone*. And a picture of you. So yeah. Surprised. Even more surprised to find out your family is all over the business world. As in Graystone shipping. Graystone hotels. Graystone every damn thing.

"You didn't tell me you were rich. Didn't tell me your family has their fingers into every known pie in the damn country. You didn't even tell me your damn name. You lied," he continued wryly. "But then, you seem to be pretty good at that."

She flushed in spite of everything as she watched his gaze slide around the room before turning back to her. Fine, she had lied. But she'd done what she'd had to, so she wouldn't apologize for it. And while that thought settled firmly into her brain, Isabelle ignored the niggle of guilt that continued to ping inside her.

"Why'd you hide who you were when you were working for me?"

Isabelle blew out a breath and said, "Because I wanted to be hired for *me*, for what I could do. Not because of who my family is."

Irritation, then grudging respect flashed across his face. "Okay. I can give you that one."

"Well," she said, sarcasm dripping in her tone. "Thank you so much."

He went on as if she hadn't said a word. "But once you had the job, you kept up the lie." His eyes narrowed on her. "When we were sleeping together, you were still lying to me."

"Only about my name." She wrapped her arms around her middle and held on. "I couldn't tell you my real name without admitting that I'd lied to get the job."

"A series of lies, then," he mused darkly. "And the hits just keep on coming."

"Why are you even here, Wes?" She was on marked time here and she knew it. Though it felt as if time was crawling past, she and Wes had already been talking for at least ten minutes. Caroline could come into the room any second. And Isabelle wasn't ready to have *that* conversation with her little girl.

"You can even ask me that?" he said, astonishment clear in his tone. "I just found out I'm a father. I'm here to see my daughter."

Damn it. "That's not a good idea."

"Didn't think you'd like it." He nodded sharply. "Good thing it's not up to you."

"Oh, yes, it is," Isabelle said, lifting her chin to meet his quiet fury with some of her own.

Funny, she'd thought about what this moment might be like over the years. How she would handle it if and when Wes discovered he had a child. She'd wondered if he'd even *care*. Well, that question had been answered. At least, partially. He cared. But what was it that bothered him most? That he had a child he didn't know? Or that Isabelle had lied to him? At the moment, it didn't matter.

"You don't want to fight me on this, Belle." He took a step closer and stopped. "She's my daughter, isn't she?"

No point in trying to deny it, since once he saw Caroline, all doubts would disappear. The girl looked so much like her dad, it was remarkable. "Yes."

He nodded, as if absorbing a blow. "Thanks for not lying about it this time."

"Wes…"

"I have the right to meet her. To get to know her. To let her know me." He stalked to the fireplace, laid one hand on the mantel and stared into the flames. "What does she know about me?" He turned his head to look at her. "What did you tell her?"

His eyes were gleaming, his jaw was set and every

line of his body radiated tension and barely controlled anger.

"I told her that her father couldn't be with us but that he loved her."

He snorted. "Well, thanks for that much, anyway."

"It wasn't for your benefit," she said flatly. "I don't want my daughter guessing that her father didn't want her."

"I would have," he argued, pushing away from the mantel to face her again. "If I'd known."

"Easy enough to say now."

"Well, I guess we'll never know if things would have been different, will we?" he said tightly. "But from here on out, Belle, things are going to change. I'm not going anywhere. I'm in this. She's mine and I want to be part of her life."

Isabelle was so caught up in the tension strung between them, she almost didn't notice Caroline walk quietly into the room to stand beside her. Her first instinct was to stand in front of her. To somehow hide the little girl from the father who had finally found her. But it was far too late for that.

Instantly, Wes's gaze dropped to the girl, and his features softened, the ice melted from his eyes and a look of wonder crossed his face briefly. Of course he could see the resemblance. Isabelle saw it every time she looked at her daughter. She was a tiny, feminine version of Wes Jackson and there was just no way he could miss it.

"Hi," he said, his voice filled with a warmth that had been lacking since the moment he arrived.

"Hi," Caroline said, as her fingers flew. "Who are you?"

Before he could say anything, Isabelle said, "This is Mr. Jackson, sweetie. He's just leaving in a minute."

He shot her one quick, hard look, as Isabelle dropped one hand protectively on her daughter's shoulder.

"We're not done talking." His gaze was hard and cold, his voice hardly more than a hush of sound.

"I guess not," she said, then looked down at her baby girl. Using her hands as well as her voice, she said, "I heard Edna's car pull into the driveway a minute ago. Why don't you go help her with the groceries? Then you can go upstairs and play while Mommy talks to the man."

"What about the ice cream?" Caro asked.

"Later," she signed. Sighing a little, she watched Caroline smile and wave at Wes before turning to head back to the kitchen.

Once the little girl had hurried out of the room, Wes looked at Isabelle. "She's deaf?"

"Good catch," she said and instantly regretted the sarcasm. No point in antagonizing the man any further than he already was. "Yes. She has progressive hearing loss."

"And what does that mean exactly? For her?"

"That's a long conversation better suited to another time," Isabelle said, in no mood whatsoever to get into this with Wes right this minute.

She wouldn't have thought it possible, but his features went even icier. "Fine. We'll put that aside for now." He lowered his voice. "You should have told me. About her. About everything."

Fresh guilt rushed through her like floodwaters spilling over a dam, but she fought it back. Yes, she remembered what it had been like to discover that Caroline was losing her hearing. The panic. The fear. The completely helpless feelings that had swamped her for days. Now she could look into Wes's eyes and see the same reactions she'd once lived through. He had been hit with a lot of information in a very short time, and if it had been her, she probably wouldn't have been as controlled as he was managing to be.

For some reason, that really irritated her.

Isabelle was willing to live with the consequences of the decision she'd made so long ago. Besides, in spite of being faced with Wes now, she was still sure that not telling him had been the right choice. "I did what I thought was right, Wes. You more than anyone should appreciate that."

"What's that supposed to mean?"

"Oh, please." She laughed shortly and wished tears weren't starting to pool behind her eyes. "You go through life making split-second decisions. You trust your gut. And you go with it. That's all I did, and I'm not going to apologize for it now."

He moved in on her until she swore she could feel heat radiating from his body and reaching out to hers. She caught his scent and helplessly dragged it into her lungs, savoring the taste of him even as she knew that going down this road again would lead to nothing but misery.

Besides, she reminded herself wryly, that wasn't passion glittering in his eyes. It was fury.

"We're not done here, Belle."

She gulped a breath, but it didn't help the sudden jolt to her heart. No one but Wes had ever called her Belle, and just hearing him say it again brought her back to long nights on silk sheets, wrapped in his arms. Why was it that she could still feel the rush of desire after so long? And why *now*, for heaven's sake?

It had taken her years to get past those memories, to train herself to never relive them. To push her time in Texas so far back in her mind that she could almost believe it never happened. Until she looked into her baby girl's face and saw the man she couldn't forget.

"I can't talk about this now. Not with Caroline here. I don't want her—"

"Informed?" he asked. "Can't take the chance of her finding out her father is here and wants to be with her?"

"It's a lot to put on a little girl, Wes, and I'm not going to dump it all on her until you and I come to some sort of agreement."

"What kind of agreement?" His tone was cautious. Suspicious.

"Like I said, not here." She took a breath to steady herself and wasn't even surprised when it didn't work. How could she find her balance when staring into the aqua eyes that had haunted her dreams for years? "Once you get back to Texas, call me and we'll talk everything out."

A half smile curved his mouth then disappeared, leaving no trace behind. "I'm not going back to Texas. Not yet."

"What? Why? What?" Her brain short-circuited. It was the only explanation for the way she was stumbling for words and coming up empty.

"I've got a room at the Swan Hollow Palace hotel," he said. "I'm not going anywhere until I get some time with my daughter. So that agreement you want to work on? We'll be doing it here. Up close and personal."

Her heart was racing, and breathing was becoming an issue. As if he could read exactly what she was thinking, feeling, he gave her that cold, calculated smile again, and this time, Isabelle's stomach sank.

"What time does she go to bed?"

"What?" God, she sounded like an idiot. "Eight o'clock. Why?"

"Because I'll be here at eight thirty." He headed out of the room, but paused at the threshold and looked back at her. Eyes fixed on hers he said, "Be ready to talk. I'm staying, Belle. For as long as this takes, I'm staying. I'm going to get to know my daughter. I'm going to catch up on everything I've missed. And there's not a damn thing you can do about it."

Swan Hollow, Colorado, was about thirty miles south-west of Denver and as different from that bustling city as it was possible to be. The small town was upscale but still clearly proud of its Western roots.

Tourists, skiers and snowboarders visited and shopped at the boutiques, antique stores and art galleries. Main Street was crowded with cafés, restaurants, bars and a couple of B&Bs, along with the shops. There was even a small mom-and-pop grocery store for those who didn't want to make the drive to the city.

The buildings on Main Street were huddled close together, some with brick facades, others with wood fronts deliberately made to look weather-beaten. Tall iron streetlamps lined the sidewalks and gave the impression of old-fashioned gas lights. Baskets of winter pines with tiny white lights strung through their branches hung from every lamppost. Every parking spot along the street was taken, and hordes of people hustled along the sidewalks, moving in and out of shops, juggling bags and exhaling tiny fogs of vapor into the air.

If he were here on vacation, Wes might have been charmed by the place. As it was, though, his mind was too busy to pay much attention to his surroundings. Amazing how a man's world could crash and burn within forty-eight hours.

The Palace hotel stood on a corner of Main Street, its brick facade, verdigris-tinged copper trim and shining windows making a hell of a statement. He'd already been told by the hotel clerk that the place had been in business since 1870. It had had plenty of face-lifts over the years, of course, but still managed to hold onto its historic character, so that stepping into the hotel was like moving into a time warp.

He walked into the lobby, with its scarlet rugs spread out across gleaming wood floors. Cream-colored walls were decorated with paintings by local artists, celebrating the town's mining history and the splendor of the mountains that encircled Swan Hollow on three sides. The lobby was wide and warm, with wood trim, a roaring fire in the stone hearth and dark red leather sofas and chairs sprinkled around the room, encouraging people to sit and enjoy themselves. He was greeted by muted conversations and the soft chime of an elevator bell as the car arrived. The quiet, soothing atmosphere did nothing to ease the roiling tension within him.

He avoided eye contact with everyone else as he walked past the check-in desk, a long, shining slab of oak that looked as if it had been standing in that spot since the hotel first opened. Wes took the elevator to the top floor, then walked down the hall to his suite. After letting himself in, he shrugged out of his jacket, tossed it onto the dark blue couch and walked across the room to the French doors. He threw them open, stepped out onto his balcony and let the icy wind slap some damn sense into him.

January in Colorado was freezing. Probably beautiful, too, if you didn't have too much on your mind. There was snow everywhere and the pines looked like paintings, dripping with layers of snow that bowed their branches. People streamed up and down the sidewalks, but Wes ignored all that activity and lifted his gaze to the mountains beyond the town limits. Tall enough to scrape the sky, the tips of the mountains had low-hanging gray clouds hovering over them like fog.

Wes's hands fisted around the black iron railing in front of him, and the bite of cold gave him a hard jolt. Maybe he needed it. God knew he needed something.

He had a *daughter*. There was no denying the truth even if he wanted to—which he didn't. The little girl looked so much like him, anyone would see the resemblance. His child. His little girl.

His stomach twisted into knots as the enormity of this situation hit him. He huffed out a breath and watched the cloud of it dissipate in the cold air. That beautiful little girl was *his*. And she was deaf.

He should have *known*.

He should have been a part of all of this. He might have been able to do something—anything—to help. And even if he couldn't have, it was his *right* to be a part of it. To do his share of worrying. But his daughter's mother hadn't bothered to clue him in.

As furious as he was with Isabelle, as stunned as he was at being faced with a *daughter*, he couldn't deny it wasn't only anger he'd felt when he was in that house.

"She looks even better now than she did five years ago," he muttered. Isabelle had always had a great body, but now, since having a child, she was softer, rounder and damn near irresistible.

Instantly, her image appeared in his mind and the grip he had on the icy railing tightened until his knuckles went white. That long, blond hair, those eyes that were caught somewhere between blue and green, the mouth that could tempt a dead man. He hadn't seen her in five years and his body was burning for her.

"Which just goes to prove," he mumbled, "your brain's not getting enough of the blood flow."

He shivered as the wind slapped at him, and he finally gave up and walked back into his suite. With everything else going on, he didn't need a case of pneumonia. Closing the doors behind him, he went to the fireplace and flipped a switch to turn on the gas-powered flames.

It was quiet. Too damn quiet. He stared at the fire for a minute or two, then dropped onto the couch, propping his boots up on the sturdy coffee table. Late afternoon sunlight came through the windows in a pale stream, the fire burned, and his brain just shut down. He needed to think, but how the hell could he when he was distracted by his own body's reaction to the woman who'd lied to him since the moment he met her?

"Isabelle Gray." How had she managed to get hired under a false name? Didn't his damn personnel department do a better job of checking résumés than that? "And she's rich," he exclaimed to the empty room. "Why the hell was she working for me anyway?"

But the "rich" part probably explained how she'd gotten away with changing her name to get a job. She'd been able to pay for whatever she'd needed to adopt a different name. Closing his eyes, Wes remembered the slap of shock he'd felt when looking for Isabelle Gray online only to find Isabelle *Graystone*. The names were enough alike that the search engine had hooked onto her real identity. Seeing her picture, reading about who she really was had been yet another shock in a day already filled with them.

He had no explanation for any of this, and checking his watch, Wes saw that he had several hours before he could go back and demand she give him the answers he needed. What was he supposed to do until then?

He dragged his cell phone out of his pocket and turned it back on. He'd had it off during his visit to Belle's house since he hadn't needed yet another distraction. Now, the message light blinked crazily and he scrolled through the list of missed calls.

Starting at the top, he hit speed dial and waited while his assistant's phone rang.

"Hi, boss," Robin said.

"Yeah, you called. Anything new?" He got up and walked to the bar in the far corner of the room. He opened the fridge, saw the complimentary cheese plate and helped himself before grabbing a beer. Twisting off the cap, he took a long drink to wash the cheese down and gave Robin his attention.

"IT department reports they're no closer to discovering who this Maverick is or even where he sent that email from."

"I thought they were supposed to be the best," he complained.

"Yeah, well, IT's pretty impressed with Maverick," she said wryly. "Seems he bounced his signal all over hell and back, so they're having a time pinning it down." She took a breath and said, "You already know that email account's been closed, so the guys here say there isn't much hope of running him to ground."

Perfect. He had his own computer experts and they couldn't give him a direction to focus the fury still clawing at his throat.

"What else?" Another swallow of beer as he plopped back onto the couch and stared at the flames dancing in the hearth.

"Personnel did a deeper check on the name you gave them, and turns out Isabelle Gray's name is really Graystone. Her family's got holdings in pretty much everything. She's an heiress."

He sighed. "Yeah, I know that."

"Oh. Well, that was anticlimactic. Okay. Moving on."

She forced cheer into her voice. "On the upside, IT says the Twitter trend is dying off. Apparently you're down to number ten today instead of number one."

"Great." Wes made a mental note to check with his IT guys on the status of his Twitter account when he got off the phone. What he really needed was for some celebrity to do something shocking that would be enough to push him off the stage entirely.

"And the warehouses are set up for delivery of the doll. Everything's ready to roll out on time."

"Good." He set the beer on the coffee table and rubbed his eyes in a futile attempt to ease the headache pounding there. "Keep on top of this stuff, Robin, and make sure I'm in the loop."

"Boss," she said, "you *are* the loop."

He had to smile and he was grateful for it. "Right. Did you hear from Harry today?"

"Yep, he's on it. He's working with PR to put a spin on all this, and when he's got the ideas together, he says he'll call you to discuss it."

"Okay. Look, I'm going to be staying in Colorado for a while."

"How long?"

"Not sure yet." However long it took to make sure the mother of his child understood that she was living in a new reality. "You can always get me on my cell. I'm at the Swan Hollow Palace hotel—"

"Swan Hollow?" she asked.

"Yeah." He smiled to himself again. "Weird name, but nice town from what I've seen."

"Good to know. I still can't believe you made the reservations yourself rather than let me handle it as always."

"I was in a hurry," Wes said and wondered why he was almost apologizing to his assistant for usurping her job.

She paused, then went on. "Fine, fine. When the final drawings on the PR campaign are turned in, I'll overnight them to you at the hotel. If you need anything else, let me know and I'll take care of it."

"Robin," he said with feeling, "you are the one bright spot in a fairly miserable couple of days."

"Thanks, boss," she said, and he heard the smile in her voice. "I'll remind you of that when I want a raise."

"I know you will," he said and was still smiling when he hung up.

Alone again, he drank his beer, and still facing hours to kill before speaking to Isabelle again, Wes had an idea. Grabbing the remote that worked both the flat-screen television and the computer, he turned the latter on. In a few minutes, he was watching an online video to learn ASL.

American Sign Language.

Three

Wes could have walked to Isabelle's house, since it was just outside town, but at night, the temperature dropped even farther and he figured he'd be an icicle by the time he arrived. The five-minute drive brought him to the long, winding road that stretched at least a half mile before ending in front of the stately Victorian. His headlights swept the front of the place and he took a moment to look it over.

The big house was painted forest green and boasted black shutters and white gingerbread trim. Surrounded as it was by snow-covered pines, the old house looked almost magical. Lamplight glowed from behind window glass, throwing golden shadows into the night. Porch lights shone from what used to be brass carriage lanterns and signaled welcome—though Wes was fairly certain that welcome wasn't something Belle was feeling for him.

"Doesn't matter," he told himself. He turned off the

engine and just sat there for a minute, looking up at the house. He'd been thinking about nothing but this moment for hours now, and he knew that this conversation would be the most important of his life. He had a child.

A daughter.

Just that thought alone was enough to make his insides jitter with nerves. He didn't even *know* her, yet he felt a connection to this child. There were so many different feelings running through him, he couldn't separate them all. Panic, of course—who could blame him for being terrified at the thought of being responsible for such a small human being? And whether Belle wanted to admit it or not, he *was* as responsible for Caroline as she was.

But there was more. There was…wonder. He'd helped to create a person. Okay, he hadn't had a clue, but that child was here. In the world. Because of *him*. He smiled to himself even as a fresh wave of trepidation rose up inside him.

Nothing in his life had worried him before this, but at least internally, Wes had to admit that being a father was a damn scary proposition. What the hell did he know about being a parent?

His own mother had died when Wes was six months old. His father, Henry Jackson, had raised him single-handedly. Henry had done a good job, but he'd also managed to let his son know in countless different ways that allowing a woman into your life was a sure path to misery. Though he'd made it clear it wasn't *having* a woman that was the problem—it was losing her.

He'd loved Wes's mother and was lost when she died. Once when Wes was sixteen, Henry had finally talked to him, warning him to guard his heart.

"Wes, you listen good. A woman's a fine thing for a man," Henry had mused, staring up at the wide, Texas sky on a warm summer night. "And finding one you can love more than your own life is a gift and a curse all at once."

"Why's that?" Wes held a sweating bottle of Coke between his palms and leaned back in the lawn chair beside his father. It had been a long, backbreaking day of work on the ranch, and Wes was exhausted. But he and his dad always ended the day like this, sitting out in the dark, talking, and it didn't even occur to him to give it up just because he was tired.

"Because once you give your heart to a woman, she can take it with her when she leaves." Henry turned and looked his son dead in the eye. "Your mama took mine when she died, and I've lived like half a man ever since."

Wes knew that to be true, since he'd seen the sorrow in his father's eyes ever since he was old enough to identify it.

"Love is a hard thing, Wes, and you just remember that, now that you're old enough to go sniffing around the females." He sighed and focused on the stars as if, Wes thought, the old man believed if he looked at the sky hard enough, he might be able to peer through the blackness and into Heaven itself.

"I'm not saying I regret a minute of loving your mother," Henry said on a heavy sigh. "Can't bring myself to say that, no matter how deep the loss of her cut me. Without her, I wouldn't have you, and I don't like the thought of that at all. What I'm trying to tell you, boy, is that it's better to not love too hard or too permanent. Easier to live your life when you're not worried about having the rug pulled out from under your feet." He stared into Wes's eyes. "Guard your heart, Wes. That's what I'm telling you."

Wes had listened well to his father's advice. Oh, he

loved women. All women. But he kept them at arm's length, never letting them close enough to get beyond the wall he so carefully constructed around his heart. All through school, he'd been single-mindedly focused on building a business he started with his college roommate.

Together, they'd bought up hundreds of tiny, aerodynamically perfect toy planes at auction, then sold them at a profit to bored college students at UT. Within a week, planes had been flying from dorm windows, classrooms, down staircases. The students set up contests for flight, distance and accuracy. Seeing how quickly they'd sold out of their only product, Wes and his friend had put the money they made back into their growing business. Soon, they were the go-to guys for toys to help fight boredom and mental fatigue. By the time they graduated, Wes had found his life's path. He bought out his friend, allowing him to finance his way through medical school, and Wes took Texas Toy Goods Inc. to the top.

Along the way, there had been more women, but none of them had left a mark on him—until Belle. And he'd fought against that connection with everything he had. He wasn't looking for love. He'd seen his own father wallow in his sorrow until the day he died and was able to finally rejoin the woman he'd mourned for more than twenty years. Wes had no intention of allowing his life to be turned upside down for something as ephemeral as *love*.

Yet now here he was, out in front of Belle's house, where his *daughter* slept. The world as he knew it was over. The new world was undiscovered country. And, he told himself, there was no time like the present to start exploring it.

He got out of the car, turned the collar of his black leather jacket up against the wind, closed the car door and headed up the brick walk that had been shoveled clear. Funny to think about all the times he'd avoided the very complication he was now insisting on. Still, he thought as he climbed the steps to the porch, he could take the easy way out, go along with what Belle wanted and simply disappear. His daughter wouldn't miss him because she wasn't even aware of his existence.

And that was what gnawed at him. His little girl didn't know him. She'd looked up at him today and hadn't realized who the hell he was. Who would have thought that the simple action would have hit him so hard? So yeah, he could walk away, but what would that make him?

"A coward, that's what," he grumbled as he stood before the front door. Well, Wes Jackson was many things, but no one had ever accused him of cowardice, and that wasn't going to change now.

He might not have wanted children, but he had one now, and damned if he'd pretend otherwise. With that thought firmly in mind, he rapped his knuckles against the door and waited impatiently for it to open.

A second later, Belle was there, haloed in light, her blond hair shining, her eyes worried. She wore faded jeans and a long-sleeved, dark rose T-shirt. Her feet were bare and boasted bloodred polish on her nails.

Why he found that incredibly sexy, he couldn't have said and didn't want to consider.

"Is she asleep?" he asked.

"She's in bed," Belle answered. "Sleep is a separate issue." Stepping back to allow him to enter, she closed the door, locked it and said, "Usually, she lies awake for a while, talking to herself or to Lizzie."

Wes stopped in the act of shrugging out of his jacket and looked at her. "Who's Lizzie?"

"Her stuffed dog."

"Oh." Nodding, he took his jacket off and hung it on the coat tree beside the door. For a minute there he'd actually thought maybe he was the father of twins or something. Looking at Belle, he said, "I half expected you to not open the door to me tonight."

"I thought about it," she admitted, sliding her hands into the pockets of her jeans. "Heck, I thought about snatching Caro up and flying to Europe. Just not being here when you showed up."

He hadn't considered that possibility. Now Wes realized he should have. He'd done his research and knew that Belle was wealthy enough to have disappeared if she'd wanted to, and he'd have spent years trying to find her and their daughter. Anger bubbled but was smoothed over by the fact that she hadn't run. That she was here. To give him the answers he needed.

"I would have found you."

"Yeah, I know." She pulled her hands free, then folded her arms across her chest and rubbed her upper arms briskly, as if she were cold. But the house was warm in spite of the frigid temperatures outside. So it must be nerves, he told himself and could almost sympathize. "That's just one of the reasons I didn't go."

Curious, he asked, "What're the others?"

Sighing a little, she looked up at him. "Believe it or not, you showing up here like this isn't the only thing I have to think about. My daughter comes first. I couldn't tear Caro away from her home. She has friends here. The uncles who love her are here. Secondly, this is my place, and I won't run. Not even from you."

He looked down into her eyes and saw pride and determination. He could understand that. Hell, he could *use* it. Her pride would demand that she listen to him whether she wanted to or not. Her pride would make sure she caved to his demands if only to prove she didn't fear him becoming a part of their daughter's life.

Belle had always been more complicated than any other woman he'd ever known. She was smart, funny, driven, and her personality was strong enough that she'd never had any trouble standing up for herself. Which meant that though he'd get his way in the end, it wouldn't be an easy road.

As they stood together in the quiet entryway, iron-clad pendant lights hung from the ceiling and cast shadows across her face that seemed to settle in her eyes. She looked…*vulnerable* for a second, and Wes steeled himself against feeling sympathy for her. Hell, she'd cheated him for five long years. He'd missed her pregnancy, missed the birth of his daughter, missed every damn thing. If anyone deserved some sympathy around here, it was *him*.

As if she could sense his thoughts, that vulnerability she'd inadvertently shown faded fast. "Do you want some coffee?"

"I want answers."

"Over coffee," she said. "Come on. We can sit in the kitchen."

He followed her down the hall, glancing around him as he went. The house was beautiful. There were brightly colored rugs spread everywhere on the oak floors so that the sound of his footsteps went from harsh to muffled as he navigated through the house. The dining room was big, but not formal. There was a huge pedestal table with six chairs drawn up to it. Pine branches jutted up from a tall porcelain vase and spilled that rich fragrance into the air.

He couldn't help comparing her home to his own back

in Royal. Though Wes's house was big and luxurious, it lacked the warmth he found here. Not surprising, he supposed, since he was only there to sleep and eat. The only other person who spent time in his house besides himself was his housekeeper, and she kept the place sparkling clean but couldn't do a thing about the impersonal feel. Frowning a little, he pushed those thoughts aside and focused on the moment at hand.

Isabelle didn't speak until they were in the kitchen, then it was only to say, "You still take your coffee black?"

"Yeah," he said, surprised she remembered. The kitchen had slate-blue walls, white cabinets, black granite on the counters and a long center island that boasted four stools. There was a small table with four chairs in a bay window, and Isabelle waved him toward it.

"Go sit down, this'll take a minute."

He took a chair that afforded him a view of her, and damned if he didn't enjoy it. He could be as angry as ever and still have a purely male appreciation for a woman who could look *that* good in jeans. Hell, maybe it was the Texan in him, but a woman who filled out denim like she did was the stuff dreams were made of. But he'd already had that dream and let it go, so there was no point in thinking about it again now.

He narrowed his gaze on her. She was nervous. He could see that, too.

Well, she had a right to be.

"So," he said abruptly, "how long have you lived here?"

She jolted a little at the sound of his voice reverberating through the big kitchen, but recovered quickly enough. Throwing him a quick glance, she set several cookies on a plate, then said, "In Swan Hollow? I grew up here."

He already knew that, thanks to the internet. "So you've always lived in this house?"

She took one mug out of the machine, reset it and set the next mug in place. "No, my brother Chance lives in the family home now."

One eyebrow lifted. Truth be told, as soon as he'd discovered who Belle was and where she lived, he hadn't looked any deeper. "You have a brother? Wait. Yeah. You said *uncles* earlier."

She gave him a wry smile. "I have three older brothers. Chance, Eli and Tyler. Fair warning, you'll probably be meeting them once they find out you're here."

Fine. He could handle her brothers. "They don't worry me."

"Okay. The three of them live just up the road. My parents had a big tract of land, and when they died, Chance moved into the big house and Eli and Tyler built homes for themselves on the land."

"Why didn't you? Why live here and not closer to your family?"

She laughed shortly. "In summer it takes about five minutes to walk to any of their houses. It's not like I'm far away." She carried a plate of cookies to the table and set them down. Homemade chocolate chip. When she turned to go back for the coffee, she said, "I wanted to live closer to town, with Caroline. She has school and friends..." Her voice trailed off as she set his coffee in front of him and then took her own cup and sat down in the chair opposite him.

"Big house for just the two of you," he mused, though even as he said it, he thought again about his own home. It was bigger than this place and only he and his housekeeper lived there.

"It's big, but when I was a girl, I loved this house."

She looked around the kitchen and he knew she was seeing the character, the charm of the building, not the sleek appliances or the updated tile floor. "I used to walk past it all the time and wonder about what it was like inside. When it went up for sale, I had to have it. I had it remodeled and brought it back to life, and sometimes I think the house is grateful for it." She looked at him and shrugged. "Sounds silly, but…anyway, my housekeeper, Edna, and her husband, Marco, my gardener, live in the guest house out back. So Caro and I have the main house to ourselves."

Outside, the dark pressed against the windows, but the light in the room kept it at bay. Wes had a sip of coffee, more to take a moment to gather his thoughts than for anything else. He was at home in any situation, yet here and now, he felt a little off balance. It had started with his first look at Belle after five long years. Then seeing Caroline had just pushed him over the edge. He really hadn't taken in yet just how completely his life had been forever altered. All he knew for sure was that things were different now. And he had to forge a path through uncharted territory.

When he set the mug back on the table, he looked into her eyes and asked, "Did you tell Caroline who I am?"

She bit at her bottom lip. "No."

"Good."

"What?" Clearly surprised, she stared at him, questions in her eyes.

"I want her to get to know me before we spring it on her," Wes said. He'd had some time to think about this, during his long day of waiting, and though he wanted nothing more than to go upstairs and claim his daughter, it wasn't the smart plan. He wanted Caroline to get used to him, to come to like him before she found out he was her father.

"Okay," she said. "That makes sense, I guess."

She looked relieved and Wes spoke up fast to end whatever delusion she was playing out in her head. "Don't take this to mean I might change my mind about all of this. I'm not going anywhere. Caroline is *my* daughter, Belle. And I want her to know that. I'm going to be a part of her life, whether you like the idea or not."

Irritation flashed on her features briefly, then faded as she took a gulp of her coffee and set the mug down again. "I understand. But you have to understand something, too, Wes. I won't let Caroline be hurt."

Insult slapped at him. What was he, a monster? He wasn't looking to cause Caroline pain, for God's sake. He was her father and he wanted her to know that. "I'm not going to hurt her."

"Not intentionally. I know that," she said quickly. "But she's a little girl. She doesn't know how to guard her heart or to keep from becoming attached. If she gets used to having you around, having you be a part of her world, and then you back off, it will hurt her."

He was used to responsibility, but suddenly that feeling inched up several notches. Wes couldn't have a child and ignore her. But at the same time, he was about to break every rule he'd ever had about getting involved with someone. There was danger inherent in caring about anyone, and he knew it. But she was his daughter, and that single fact trumped everything else.

"I'm here because I want to be," he said, then tipped his head to one side and stared at her. "I'm not dropping in to get a look at her before I disappear. Yes, I have an important product launch coming up and I'll have to return to Texas, but I plan on being a permanent part of Caroline's life, which you don't seem to understand. It's interesting to me, though, that suddenly I'm the one defending myself when it's *you* who has all the explaining to do."

"I didn't mean that as an attack on your motives," she said quietly. "I just want to make sure you understand exactly what's going to happen here. Once Caroline gives her heart, it's gone forever. You'll hold it and you could crush it without meaning to."

"You're still assuming I'm just passing through."

"No, I'm not." She laughed shortly, but it was a painful sound. "I know you well enough to know that arguing with you is like trying to talk a wall into falling down on its own. Pointless."

He nodded, though the analogy, correct or not, bothered him more than a little. Was he really so implacable all the damn time? "Then we understand each other."

"We do."

"So," he said, with another sip of coffee he really didn't want. "Tell me."

"I'm not sure where to start."

"How about the beginning?" Wes set the coffee down and folded his arms across his chest as he leaned back in his chair. "If you have family money, why the hell did you come to work for me?"

"Rich people can't have jobs?" Offended, she narrowed her eyes on him. "You have money, but you go into the office four days a week. Even when you're at home in Royal, you spend most of your free time on the phone with PR or marketing or whatever. That's okay?"

He squirmed a little in his chair. Maybe she had a point, but he wouldn't concede that easily. "It's my company."

She shook her head. "That's not the only reason.

You're rich. You could hire someone to run the company and you know it. But you *enjoy* your job. Well, so did I."

Hard to argue with the truth. "Okay, I give you that."

"Thank you so much," she muttered.

"But why did you lie to get the job? Why use a fake name?" He cupped his hands around the steaming mug of coffee and watched her.

"Because I wanted to make it on my own." She sighed and sat back, idly spinning the cup in front of her in slow circles. "Being a Graystone always meant that I had roads paved for me. My parents liked to help my brothers and I along the way until finally, I wanted to get out from under my own name. Prove myself, I guess."

"To who?"

She looked at him. "Me."

He could understand and even admire that, Wes realized. Too many people in her position *enjoyed* using the power of their names to get what they wanted whenever they wanted it. Hell, he saw it all the time in business— even in Royal, where the town's matriarchs ruled on the strength of tradition and their family's legacies. The admiration he felt for her irritated hell out of him, because he didn't *want* to like anything about her.

She'd lied to him for years. Hidden his child from him deliberately. So he preferred to hold onto the anger simmering quietly in the pit of his stomach. Though he was willing to cut her a break on how she'd gotten a job at his company, there was *no* excuse for not telling him she was pregnant.

Holding onto the outrage, he demanded, "When you quit your job and left Texas, you didn't bother to tell me you were pregnant. Why?"

"You know why, Wes," she said, shaking her head

slowly. "We had that *what if* conversation a few weeks before I found out. Remember?"

"Vaguely." He seemed to recall that one night she'd talked about the future—what they each wanted. She'd talked about kids. Family.

"You do remember," she said softly, gaze on his face. "We were in bed, talking, and you told me that I shouldn't start getting any idea about there being anything permanent between us."

He scowled as that night and the conversation drifted back into his mind.

"You said you weren't interested in getting married," she said, "had no intention of *ever* being a father, and if that's what I was looking for, I should just leave."

It wasn't easy hearing his own words thrown back at him, especially when they sounded so damn cold. Now that she'd brought it all up again, he remembered lying in the dark, Belle curled against his side, her breath brushing his skin as she wove fantasies he hadn't wanted to hear about.

He scraped one hand across his face but couldn't argue with the past. Couldn't pretend now that he hadn't meant every word of it. But still, she should have said something.

"So you're saying it's my fault you said nothing."

"No, but you can see why I didn't rush to confess my pregnancy to a man who'd already told me he had no interest in being a father." She rubbed the spot between her eyes and sighed a little. "You didn't want a child. I did."

"I didn't want a hypothetical child. You didn't give me a choice about Caroline."

"And here we go," she murmured with a shake of her head, "back on the carousel of never-ending accusations.

I say something, you say something and we never really *talk*, so nothing gets settled. Perfect."

She had a point. Rehashing old hurts wasn't going to get him the answers he was most interested in. He wanted to know all about his little girl. "Fine. You want settled? Start talking, I'll listen. Tell me about Caroline. Was she born deaf?"

"No." Taking a sip of coffee, she cradled the mug between her palms. "She had normal hearing until the summer she was two."

Outside, the wind blew snow against the window and it hit the glass with a whispering tap. Wes watched her and saw the play of emotions on her face in the soft glow of the overhead lights. He felt a tightness in his own chest in response as he waited for her to speak.

"We spent a lot of time at the lake that summer, and she eventually got an ear infection." Her fingers continued to turn the mug in front of her. "Apparently, it was a bad one, but she was so good, hardly cried ever, and I didn't know anything was wrong with her until she started running a fever.

"I should have known," she muttered, and he could see just how angry she still was at herself for not realizing her child was sick. "Maybe if I'd taken her to the doctor sooner…" She shook her head again and he felt the sense of helplessness that was wrapped around her like a thick blanket.

Wes felt the same way. The story she told had taken place nearly three years ago. He couldn't change it. Couldn't go back in time to be there to help. All he could do now was listen and not say anything to interrupt the flow of words.

She took a breath and blew it out. "Anyway. Her fever

suddenly spiked so high one night, I was terrified. We took her to the emergency room—"

"We?" Was she dating some guy? Some strange man had been there for his child when Wes wasn't?

She lifted her gaze to his. "My brother Chance drove us there, stayed with us. The doctors brought her temperature down, gave her antibiotics, and she seemed fine after."

"What happened?"

She sighed and sat back in her chair, folding her arms across her chest as if comforting herself. "When she healed, she had hearing loss. We didn't even notice at first. If there were hints or signs, we didn't see them. It wasn't until the following summer that I realized she couldn't hear the ice cream truck." She smiled sadly. "Silly way to discover something so elemental about your own child, but oh, she used to light up at the sound of those bells."

She took a breath and sighed a little. "The doctors weren't sure exactly what caused it. Could have been the infection itself, the buildup of water in her ears or the effects of the antibiotics. There was just no way to know for sure."

"Wasn't your fault." He met her gaze squarely.

"What?"

"It sounds to me like you couldn't have done anything differently, so it wasn't your fault."

Horrified, he watched her eyes fill with tears. "Hey, hey."

"Sorry." She laughed a little, wiped her eyes and said, "That was just…unexpected. Thank you."

Wes nodded, relieved to see she wasn't going to burst into tears on him. "Will her hearing get worse?"

"Yes." A single word that hit like a blow to the chest.

"It's progressive hearing loss. She can still hear now, and will probably for a few more years thanks to the hearing aids, but eventually…"

"What can we do?"

Her eyebrows lifted. "As much as I appreciate you being kind before, there is no *we*, Wes. I am doing everything I can. She wears hearing aids. She's using sign language to expand her conversational skills, and get familiar with it before she actually has to count on it. And I'm considering a cochlear implant."

"I read about those." He leaned his forearms on the table. He'd been doing a lot of reading over the last several hours. There were dozens of different theories and outlooks, but it seemed to him that the cochlear implants were the way to go. Best for everyone. "They're supposed to be amazing. And she's old enough to get one now."

"Yes, I know she is." Belle looked at him and said, "You know, her doctor and I do discuss all of this. He's given me all of the information I need, but it's not critical to arrange surgery for Caro right this minute. It's something I have to think about. To talk about with Caro herself."

Astonished, he blurted, "She's only four."

"I didn't say she'd be making the decision, only that I owe it to her to at least discuss it with her. She's very smart, and whatever decision I make she'll have to live with." She pushed up from the table and carried her unfinished coffee to the sink to pour out. "I'm not foolish enough to let a little girl decide on her own. But she should have a say in it."

"Seriously?" He stood up, too, and walked over to dump his own coffee. He hadn't really wanted it in the first place. "You want to wait when this could help her now? You want to give a four-year-old a vote in what happens to her medically?" Shaking his head, he reached for his cell phone. "I know the best doctors in Texas. They can give me the name of the top guy in this field. We can have Caro in to see the guy by next week, latest."

She snatched the phone right out of his hand and set it down on the counter. "What do you think you're doing?"

"What you're too cautious to do," he said shortly. "Seeing to it that Caro has the best doctor and the best treatment."

Both hands on her hips, she tipped her head back to glare up into his eyes. "You have known about her existence for two days and you really think you have the right to come in here and start giving orders?"

Those green-blue eyes of hers were flashing with indignation and the kind of protective gleam he'd once seen in the eyes of a mother black bear he'd come across in the woods. He'd known then that it wasn't smart to appear threatening to that bear's cubs. And he realized now that maybe trying to jump in and take over was obviously the wrong move. But how the hell could he be blamed for wanting to do *something* for the kid he hadn't even known he had?

"All right." Wes deliberately kept his voice cool, using the reasonable tone he wielded like a finely honed blade in board meetings. "We can talk about it first—"

"*Very* generous," she said as barely repressed fury seemed to shimmer around her in waves. "You're not listening to me, Wes. You don't have a say here. My daughter's name is Caroline *Graystone*. Not Jackson. I make the decisions where she's concerned."

His temper spiked, but he choked it back down. What

the hell good would it do for the two of them to keep butting heads? "Do I really have to get a DNA test done to prove I'm now a part of this?"

Her mouth worked as if she were biting back a sharp comeback. And she really looked as if she were trying to find a way to cut him out of the whole thing. But after a few seconds, she took a breath and said, "No. Not necessary."

"Good." Something occurred to him then. "Am I named as her father on the birth certificate?"

"Yes, of course you are." She rinsed out her coffee cup, then turned the water off again. "I want Caro to know who you are—I'd just rather have been the one to pick the time she found out."

"Yeah, well." He leaned against the counter. At least the instant burst of anger had drained away as quickly as it came. "Neither of us got a vote on that one."

The problem of Maverick rose up in his mind again, and he made a mental note to call home again. Find out how the search for the mystery man was going. And it seriously bugged him that he had no idea who it might be. Briefly, he even wondered again if Cecelia and her friends behind it, in spite of Cecelia's claim of innocence. But for now, he had other things to think about.

"Why does anyone care if you have a child or not? Why is this trending on Twitter?" She sounded as exasperated as he felt, and somehow that eased some of the tension inside him.

"Hell if I know," he muttered and shoved one hand though his hair. "But we live in a celebrity culture now. People are more interested in what some rock star had for dinner than who their damn congressman is."

She laughed a little, surprising him. "I missed that. Who knew?"

"Missed what?" Wes watched the slightest curve of her mouth, and it tugged at something inside him.

"Those mini rants of yours. They last like ten seconds, then you're done and you've moved on. Of course, people around you are shell-shocked for a lot longer…"

"I don't rant." He prided himself on being calm and controlled in nearly all aspects of his life.

"Yeah, you do," she said. "I've seen a few really spectacular ones. But in your defense, you don't do it often."

He frowned as his mind tripped back, looking for other instances of what she called rants. And surprisingly enough, he found a couple. His frown deepened.

"You've got your answers, Wes," she said quietly. "What else do you want here?"

"Some answers," he corrected. "As for what I want, I've already told you. I can't just walk away from my own kid."

"And what do you expect from fatherhood? Specifically."

"I don't know," he admitted. "I just know I have to be here. Have to be a part of her life."

She looked into his eyes for a long second or two before nodding. "Okay. We'll try this. But you have to dial it back a little, too. You're the one trying to fit yourself into *our* lives—not the other way around."

He hated that she had a point. Hated more that as confident as he was in every damn thing, he had no clue how to get to know a kid. And he *really* didn't like the fact that he was standing this close to Belle and could be moved just by her scent—vanilla, which made him think of cozying up in front of the fire with her on his lap and his hands on her—damn it, this was *not* the way he wanted this to go.

"If you can't agree to that," she said, when he was silent for too long, "then you'll just have to go, Wes."

Fighting his way past his hormones, Wes narrowed his eyes, took a step closer and was silently pleased when she backed up so fast she hit the granite counter. Bracing one hand on either side of her on that cold, black surface, he leaned in, enjoying the fact that he'd effectively caged her, giving her no room to evade him.

"No," he said, his gaze fixed with hers. "You don't want to take orders from me? Well, I sure as hell don't take them from you. I'll stay as long as I want to, and there's not a damn thing you can do about it."

She took a breath, and something flashed in her eyes. Anger, he was guessing, and could only think *join the club*. But it wasn't temper alone sparking in her eyes—there was something more. Something that held far more heat than anger.

"You lied to me for years, Belle. Now I know the truth and until I'm satisfied, until I have everything I want out of this situation, I'm sticking."

She planted both hands flat on his chest and pushed. He let her move him back a step.

"And what is it you want, Wes? What do you expect to find here?"

"Whatever I need."

Four

Whatever I need.

Wes's words echoed in her mind all night long. Even when she finally fell asleep, he was there, in her dreams, taunting her. It was as if the last five years had disappeared. All of the old feelings she'd had for him and had tried so desperately to bury had come rushing back at her the moment she saw him again.

She had three older brothers, so she was used to dealing with overbearing men and knew how to handle them. Isabelle wasn't easily intimidated, and she wasn't afraid to show her own temper or to stand up for herself, either. But what she wasn't prepared for was the rush of desire she felt just being around Wes again.

He was the same force of nature she remembered him being, and when his focus was directed solely at her, he wasn't an easy man to ignore. Old feelings stirred inside her even though she didn't want them and the only thing that was keeping her sane at the moment was the fact that it wasn't just her own heart in danger, it was Caroline's. And that Isabelle just couldn't risk. She had to find a way to appease Wes, avoid acting on what she was feeling for him and protect Caroline at the same time. She just didn't know yet how she would pull it off.

"Well," Edna said when Isabelle walked into the kitchen. "You look terrible."

Isabelle sighed. Makeup, it seemed, couldn't perform the miracles all the TV commercials promised. "Thanks. Just what I needed to hear."

Edna was in her sixties, with short silver hair that stood up in tufted spikes. Her brown eyes were warm and kind and a little too knowing sometimes. Today she wore her favored black jeans, black sneakers and a red sweatshirt that proclaimed, *For Most of History, Anonymous Was a Woman.—Virginia Woolf.*

"Seriously, did you get *any* sleep?" Edna pulled a mug from under the single-serve coffeemaker and handed it over.

It was gray and cold outside, typical January weather in Colorado. But the kitchen was bright and warm and filled with the scents of coffee and the breakfast Edna insisted on making fresh every morning.

Grateful for the ready coffee, Isabelle took the cup and had her first glorious sip. As the hot caffeine slid into her system, she looked at her housekeeper and gave her a wry smile. "Not much."

Sipping her own coffee, Edna gave her a hard look. "Because of Wes?"

She jolted and stared at the other woman. "How do you know about him?"

"Caro told us this morning. She says he's pretty and that you said he's a friend." Edna tipped her head to one side. "Marco told me to butt out, but who listens to husbands? So, Wes is more than a friend, isn't he?"

Before answering that question, Isabelle looked around and then asked, "Where's Caro?"

"Outside with Marco. She wanted to make sure the snowman they made last weekend was still standing." She paused. "So? Who is he?"

"We've known each other way too long."

Edna laughed. "That's what happens when you grow up in a town of twelve hundred people. We all know too much about each other. Probably keeps us all on the up and up. Can't do a damn thing wrong around here and get away with it." She narrowed her eyes. "And you're stalling."

"I know." Pulling out a stool at the island counter, Isabelle dropped onto it and reached out to grab a biscuit she knew would be stuffed with ham and scrambled eggs. It was Caroline's favorite breakfast, so naturally the indulgent Edna made them a lot. Taking a bite she chewed and said, "He's Caro's father."

"Whoa." Edna's eyebrows shot up. "Wasn't expecting that." She leaned on the countertop. "What does he want?"

"Caro." She took another bite and chewed glumly.

The other woman straightened up in a blink. "Well, he can't have her."

It was good to have friends, Isabelle told herself with a quiet sigh. She'd known Edna and Marco her whole life. They'd both worked for her family since Isabelle was a child. And at an age when they could have retired, instead, they'd come to work for Isabelle, to help raise Caro. And she knew that she would never be able to pay them back for their friendship or their loyalty.

Smiling, Isabelle said, "No, he can't. But to be fair,

he doesn't want to take her away, he just wants to be a part of her life."

"That's a bad thing?" Edna pushed the plate of biscuits closer to Isabelle. "Talk and eat. You're too thin."

Isabelle knew it was useless to argue, so she dutifully took another one. "It's not bad necessarily," she said, breaking off a piece of biscuit and egg to pop into her mouth. "But it's…complicated. Caro doesn't know who he is and I don't know how much he's going to push for. Plus, he's so angry that I never told him about her that he's not even trying to be reasonable…"

"Are you?"

Isabelle's gaze shot to Edna's. "Hey. Whose side are you on, anyway?"

"Yours. Absolutely." Reaching over for a dishcloth, Edna wiped up a few crumbs. "But come on, sweetie. The man's a father and you never told him. Most men like to know if their sperm scores a goal."

She snorted a laugh even while she nodded. "True. But he said he didn't want kids."

"That's before he had one." Edna sighed and leaned on the counter again so she could look directly into Isabelle's eyes. "Even Marco didn't want kids till we had our first one."

"That's hard to believe." Frowning, Isabelle remembered how Marco had devoted himself to Edna and their three kids. Even now, he spent most of his free time with their grandchildren. A more family-based man she'd never known.

"Well, it's true." Edna shook her head and grinned. "When I told him I was pregnant the first time, the man went pale—and with that Italian olive complexion of his, it wasn't easy."

Isabelle laughed a little. True.

"My point is, he completely freaked," Edna admitted. "I think he was scared, though God knows a man will never admit to *that*. But once he came around to the idea of being somebody's daddy, he was all for it, and the man is the best father in the world."

"He is," Isabelle murmured.

"So why not cut this Wes guy a break and see what happens?" Edna shrugged. "You two might find a way to work through this."

"Anything's possible, I suppose." But at the moment, Isabelle was having a hard time believing that. She could remember, so clearly, how it had felt to have him looming close to her last night. She'd felt the heat of him reaching for her. And when she'd pushed him away, she'd come very close to grabbing him instead and pulling him closer.

Really irritating that she could be furious with him and *still* want him so badly.

"Is there more going on here than just worry for Caro?" Edna asked quietly.

Isabelle looked at the other woman. "Too much and not enough all at the same time."

Edna took a sip of coffee. "I hate when that happens."

Room service brought him coffee and toast. Wes ate and drank while he ran through the latest stream of emails clogging up his inbox. Deleting as he went, he kept expecting to see another message from Maverick. Why, he didn't know. The damage had already been done. But wouldn't he want to gloat? Wes really hoped so, because just one more email from the mystery man might be enough to help Wes's IT department nail the bastard.

Until that happy day, Wes focused on what he *could*

do. The TV was on, the local news channel a constant murmur of sound in the room. One part of Wes's mind paid attention to the reporters, wondering if he'd hear more about this Maverick mess. Meanwhile, he concentrated on answering business emails, then made a call to his VP. When Harry answered, Wes smiled. Good to know his employees were up and working as early as he was.

"Morning, Wes," Harry said. "Sorry to say, if you're calling for an update on Maverick, I don't have one for you yet."

Scowling, Wes rubbed his forehead and walked to the French doors of his suite. It was too damned cold to throw them open, so he settled for holding back the drapes and staring out at Swan Hollow as the small town woke up. The clouds were low and gray—no surprise, and yet more snow was forecasted for today.

"How is it no one can nail this guy—or woman?" Wes grumbled, not really expecting an answer. "Is Maverick some kind of technical ninja or something?"

Harry laughed shortly. "No. So far, he's just been lucky. He got in and out of your account so fast, the IT guys couldn't track him. But Jones in IT tells me he's rigged it to let him know if anyone tries to breach again."

"Well, that's something." It was a lot, really, just not enough. Wes didn't function well with helplessness. Because he'd never accepted it before. Always, he'd been able to do *something*. He'd never been in the position of standing on the sidelines, watching other players make moves he couldn't.

And he didn't like it.

"Not enough, I know," Harry said, as if he knew exactly what Wes was thinking. "But we're still working it. On the downside, Teddy Bradford won't take my call, so if you want to try to do CPR on that merger, you'll have to reach out to him yourself."

"Yeah, I tried before I left Texas. He blew me off, too."

"It may just be over, boss."

"No, I won't accept that," Wes said. "We spent nearly two years putting that merger on the table and I'll be damned before I let some cowardly rumormonger ruin it. There's a way to save us taking over PlayCo, and I'll find it."

"If you say so," Harry told him, but disbelief was clear in his tone.

Fine, he'd proved people wrong before, and he could do it again. Turning away from the view, Wes voiced a suspicion that had occurred to him only late last night. "You think maybe Teddy's working this from both angles?"

A pause while Harry thought about it. "What exactly do you mean?"

Wes had been turning this over in his mind for hours now, and though it sounded twisted, he thought it could just be true. "Well, we had a deal and he's backed out— what if he and Maverick were in on it together?"

"For what reason?" Harry asked, not shooting down the theory right away.

Any number of reasons, really, Wes told himself, but the most likely one had slipped into his mind last night and refused to leave. "Maybe he's lined up a deal with a different toy company and needed a way to get out of our merger without looking bad."

There was a long pause as Harry considered the idea. "Anything's possible," he said, his voice slow and thoughtful. "I'll put some feelers out. I've got some friends over at Toy America. I'll talk to them. See what I can find out."

"Good. Let me know ASAP if you discover anything." Wes picked up the coffee carafe from the dining table and poured himself another cup. If Bradford was working with Maverick to try to ruin Wes and his company's reputation, heads were going to roll. "I'm going to be here at least a few more days—"

"Yeah." Harry sighed. "Okay, I promised myself I wouldn't ask why you were in Duck Springs, Colorado…"

Unexpectedly, Wes laughed. "Swan Hollow."

"What's the difference?" Harry asked. Then before Wes could speak, he said, "Just tell me. Is everything all right?"

Wes's smile faded slowly. Things were as far from all right as they could get, he thought, but he didn't bother to say anything. Harry and the rest of the company had probably figured out that Maverick's email about Wes's daughter had been nothing but the truth. But that didn't mean he was ready to discuss it with everyone. Not even his friend Harry.

"Yeah," he said, gulping coffee. "Everything's fine. I just have a few…personal issues to work out."

Understatement of the century. There was so much rushing through his mind, he hadn't gotten more than a couple of hours of sleep all night. And this morning, Wes felt like his eyeballs had been rolled around in sand. In those long sleepless hours, his brain had raced with images, ideas. A daughter. The dead merger. A saboteur—perhaps even his ex—trying to take down his business. And then there was Belle. A woman he should know better than to want—yet apparently his body hadn't gotten that memo.

"If you say so." Harry didn't sound convinced, but

then he added, "When you're ready to talk about it, I'm here. And if I can do something, let me know."

"Find Maverick," Wes said. "That's what I need you to do. Keep everyone on it. I want to know who and where this guy is."

"We're working it, boss. Do what you have to do and don't worry about what's going on back in Houston. We'll find him. I'll be in touch."

After Harry hung up, Wes tossed his phone onto the couch and grabbed the remote when he saw the stock report flash onto the television screen. Draining his coffee cup, he punched up the volume and then cursed as the anchor started speaking.

"Things are not looking good for TTG Inc.," the man said in a low, deep voice. "Texas Toy Goods' stock has taken a hard dip over the last couple of days. CEO Wes Jackson has not yet commented on the short-lived scandal that apparently was behind Teddy Bradford of PlayCo announcing the end of their much-anticipated merger."

The stocks reporter then turned to the digital screen behind him and tracked the TTG stock on a downward slide. Meanwhile Wes's temper inched up in an opposite trajectory.

"TTG Inc.," the man said, "is down five points, and my sources say there are no immediate plans to put the merger back in play. PlayCo, the anticipated merger partner, on the other hand, has ticked up two points in the last twenty-four hours."

Disgusted, Wes hit the mute button and wished fervently that his thoughts were as easy to silence. One thing he knew for sure. Once a stock started slipping, the whole thing took on a life of its own. People would worry and sell off their stock and his price would dip even lower.

He had to put a stop to this before he lost everything he'd worked for. Stalking to the carafe of coffee, he re-filled his cup and carried it with him to the door when a knock sounded.

Who the hell could that be? Room service had already come and gone. He doubted very much that Belle would be dropping in for a visit. And he was in no mood to talk to anybody else. Riding on temper, he yanked the door open and demanded, "What?"

A tall man in a heavy brown coat with a sheepskin collar stood on the threshold. He had narrowed blue eyes, short, light brown hair and a neatly trimmed beard. Two men with a slight resemblance to the first man stood right behind him, and not one of them looked happy to be there. Wes braced himself for whatever was coming.

"You Wes Jackson?" The first man spoke while the other two continued to glare at Wes.

"Yeah, I am." He met that flat cool stare with one of his own. "Who're you?"

"Chance Graystone."

Damn it. Well, Belle had warned him about her older brothers. Looked like he was going to meet the family whether he wanted to or not.

Chance jerked a thumb over his shoulder. "My broth-ers, Eli and Tyler. We're here to talk to you."

"That's great." They didn't give Wes an opportu-nity to shut the door on them. Instead, all three of them pushed past him into the room. Each of them somehow managing to give Wes an accidental shove as they did.

"Well, sure," he said. "Come on in."

All three men stood in the living room of the suite, waiting for him. Their stances were identical. Feet braced wide apart, arms across their chests, features cold, mouths tight. They could have stepped right out of an old Western movie—three sheriffs ready to face the outlaw. Who would, he told himself, be *him*.

There was no avoiding this. Slowly, Wes closed the door then glanced down into the cup he held. "This is not gonna be enough coffee."

Still, he took a sip to steel himself then deliberately took his time as he strolled out to meet Belle's brothers. He had no idea what was coming. Did they want to talk? Fight? Ride him out of town on a rail? Who the hell knew? Setting his coffee cup down on the closest table, he faced the three men. Wes guessed Chance was the oldest, since he took the lead in the conversation.

"We're here to set you straight on a few things."

"Is that right?" Wes wasn't intimidated, though he had the feeling the Graystone brothers were used to putting the fear of God into whoever happened to be standing against them at the time. Well, they were going to have a hard time with him. He didn't scare easily, and he *never* backed down when he knew he was right.

"That's about it," Chance said in a flat, dark voice. "Isabelle's our sister. Caro's our niece. You do anything to hurt either one of them and we're going to have a problem."

Wes shifted his stance to mock the three men facing him. Arms across his chest, he glared at each of them in turn before settling his gaze back on Chance. "I'd say that what happens between Belle and me is our business."

Chance took a single step forward. "Then you'd be wrong. You made your choice. You let her walk out of your life five years ago."

Though he might have a point, Wes didn't acknowledge it. "She didn't tell me about our daughter."

The two brothers behind Chance exchanged a quick look. "He's right about that," one of them said.

Chance nodded. "Yeah, she should have told you. I give you that."

"Thanks," Wes said wryly.

"We told her so when she first came home. It wasn't right, her keeping it from you."

"Agreed."

"But Isabelle does things her way. Always has. She doesn't take advice well."

"Yeah," Wes said. "Me neither. Who knew she and I would have that in common?" One of the brothers—Eli or Tyler, he didn't know which—smiled at that. "Just how did you guys know I was here? Did Belle send you to scare me off?"

"This is a small town, man. Word started spreading the minute you drove up to Isabelle's house, and the talk hasn't slowed down since." Chance laughed shortly. "Besides, there is no way Isabelle would have come running to us. Our little sister doesn't need a man to protect her."

Wes waved one hand at the three of them. "And yet…"

Chance smiled slightly. "Just because she doesn't need it doesn't mean she won't get it."

He could understand that. Family standing for family. But knowing that didn't mean he liked being warned off or threatened.

"Fine." Wes nodded and met Chance's steady gaze with his own. "I'm not here to hurt Belle. I'm here to connect with my daughter. And," he added, "there's no way you can stop me."

A long, tension-filled silence followed as the men took each other's measure. Wes didn't flinch. He'd faced down adversaries before. He'd been in his share of fistfights growing up, and he'd won them all. He'd looked across boardroom tables at competitors aching to take him down, and he hadn't folded to anyone. Damned if he'd start now. A part of him admired Belle's brothers. Loyalty was everything to him, and maybe that's why Belle's lies had cut so deeply. But he could understand these men standing up for their sister even as he knew it wouldn't stop him from doing what he'd come to Swan Hollow to do.

Finally, Chance nodded. "Can't say that I blame you for coming here. Actually, under other circumstances, I might even like you for it."

Wes laughed.

"But we'll be watching," Chance promised. "You make Isabelle or Caroline unhappy—it won't be pretty."

"Seems fair," Wes agreed. "As long as you three understand I'll be staying in town as long as I please. I'll see my daughter and your sister as often as I can manage it, and I don't want any of you interfering. This is between Belle and I."

Chance's gaze locked with Wes's for a long moment. Then he nodded. "I think we have an understanding."

"And you're not going to have an easy time of it," one of the other brothers quipped, a half smile on his face. "Isabelle's got a head like a rock when her mind's made up. And she's probably not real happy that you're here."

Wes frowned, and Chance laughed at his expression.

"Yeah," the man said a second later. "I'm thinking Tyler's right and you've got bigger problems with Isabelle than you do dealing with us."

Belle's brothers silently filed out of the room. Wes stayed where he was and didn't watch them go.

He'd been alone since his father's death a few years earlier. No siblings, no extended family, and since he'd never known anything different, he hadn't really missed it, either. Until just now. But even he could see that the Graystone siblings were tight. Close-knit. And a part of him he hadn't even been aware of was almost jealous of it.

Then his mind started clicking. Thoughts, ideas, possible plans flashed through his brain so quickly he couldn't separate them all. But somewhere in the chaos of his thoughts there was a single notion that began to shine brightly. If he could make it work, it might solve everything.

Yes, he wanted Maverick caught. Dealt with. The man—or whoever—had cost him a merger Wes had spent two years setting up. On the other hand, if not for Maverick, he might never have known about his daughter's existence. Wes didn't want another relationship with Belle—she'd lied to him for five years. But he did want to be a part of Caroline's life.

And as his mind worked, he realized there might be a way to salvage that merger after all. As long as he was here, in Colorado, spending time with Caro and Belle anyway, he might be able to use this time to convince the CEO of PlayCo that he, Belle and Caroline were a happy little family. Teddy Bradford wanted family values? Well, Wes might be in a position to offer that. *If* Bradford wasn't behind the Maverick mess himself.

It was a thought. Something to look at, maybe plan for. Making the best of a situation was what Wes did. And that damn merger meant too much to just walk away from it.

The key to all of this came down to one word. A word Wes had avoided for years, but now it had caught him, held him and wouldn't let go.

Family.

Five

An hour later, after leaving Caro in her pre-K class-room, Belle found Wes waiting for her in the parking lot. He was leaning against a huge black SUV, watching her, and he looked…dangerous. Okay, maybe that was just her. The day was bright and freezing, with high clouds studding a deep blue sky. Pine trees were layered with snow, and high barriers of the white stuff lined the parking lot where it had been pushed by the maintenance crew.

She'd like to think Wes looked out of place at the school in his black jeans, forest green sweater and black leather jacket. The truth was, he fit in everywhere. His blond hair ruffled in the wind, and as he pulled his sunglasses off to look at her, she noted his eyes were narrowed against the glint of the sun off the snow.

He looked dark, edgy, and her heart gave a hard thump she couldn't deny. Having Wes come back into her life was throwing everything off balance. Thoughts of him had kept her awake all night as her brain replayed memories she'd tried to bury for the past five years.

Working with him had been challenging, but fun. As focused as he was on his own vision, Wes had always been the kind of boss to welcome other ideas besides his own. That made for a great working environment, and Isabelle had loved being a part of it—until she fell in love with the boss. Then, everything had changed for her.

She'd let herself believe that the partnership she felt with him at work could extend to the personal, too. But even when they were alone together, at their most intimate, Isabelle had felt Wes pulling back. And the harder she tried to reach him, the more elusive he became. Finally, she'd had to realize that he wouldn't change. Would never be able to love her as she loved him and that waiting and hoping would slowly wear her heart away like waves against rock, until there was nothing left.

Now, he was back. Pushing himself into her life whether she liked it or not. Refusing to go away. It seemed, she thought, that Wes would always do the opposite of what she wanted him to.

All around her, the sidewalk and parking lot was alive with people. Parents soothing toddlers, folks starting cars, rushing off to the rest of their days. But all she could see was Wes.

She headed toward him. "What are you doing here?"

"Wanted to see her school." He pushed away from what was probably a rental. "Wanted to see you."

Just five years ago, those words would have turned her heart inside out. Now, she was worried. Why did he want to see her? Before she could find out, someone called her name.

"Isabelle!" She turned and smiled tightly at the woman hurrying toward her.

"Hi, Kim. What's up?" From the corner of her eye, Isabelle saw Wes approaching. Kim's reaction was instantaneous and completely predictable. The woman's eyes widened in appreciation, and a soft, speculative curve lifted her mouth.

Typical.

"What can I do for you?" Isabelle asked, drawing the woman's attention back to her.

"Oh. Right." She smiled at Wes again as he walked up to stand beside Isabelle. "Sorry. I just wanted to remind you that you volunteered to provide refreshments for the girls' dance recital next week."

"Sure. Thanks for the reminder," Isabelle said, "I've been so…busy, I'd forgotten."

"I don't blame you for being…*busy*," Kim said, shifting her gaze to Wes again. "Hello. I'm Kim Roberts."

He took her hand in his. "Wes Jackson."

She never took her eyes from his as she said, "Isabelle, you've been keeping this gorgeous man all to yourself? Selfish."

Kim was doing everything but drooling, and Isabelle had to squelch a flash of irritation. Just like the old days, she told herself. Even when Isabelle was standing right beside him, women would coo and practically purr at him, completely ignoring Isabelle's presence.

"Wes is an old…friend of mine from Texas," she said and scowled when he smiled at her explanation. "He's here visiting."

"Well," Kim said, her smile brightening enough that she looked like an actress in a toothpaste commercial, "maybe we could get together while you're in town. I'd love to show you around."

"Thanks," Wes said, "but I think Isabelle's got that covered." He turned his back on Kim and asked Isabelle, "Are you ready to go?"

"What? Oh. Yes." Surprised that he had turned down Kim's oh-so-generous offer, Isabelle looked up at him and wondered, not for the first time, what he was thinking. He tugged at her arm and she'd actually started walking with him until she realized he was escorting her to his car. Then she stopped. "My car's here."

"We'll come back for it later." He helped her into the oversize Suburban, then closed the door.

Kim was staring after them, a look of shock on her features. It had probably been years since a man had shown such a lack of interest in her. Sadly, Isabelle knew that Kim would only react to his response as a challenge. She liked Kim, but the woman was always on the prowl for her next ex-husband.

"She's interested in you, you know," Isabelle said as Wes drove through the parking lot and out onto the street.

He snorted. "That type's interested in everything male."

"That was rude," Isabelle muttered. "True, but rude. Anyway, where are we going?"

"I don't know," he said, aiming the car for Main Street. "Why don't you tell me? What do you usually do after dropping Caroline at school?"

Frowning, she half turned in her seat to look at him. Even his profile looked hard, implacable. Why was it she liked that about him even as it drove her crazy? Okay, fine, he was here to see Caroline. But why was he spending time with *her*? "What's this about, Wes? Do you plan to just follow me around town?"

He shrugged. "Would you rather we go back to your place and talk?"

"No." Being alone with him wasn't a good idea. Even knowing better, she might be tempted to—nope.

"There you go. So where are we headed?"

She sighed. The man was nothing if not determined. Rather than argue with him, she surrendered. "Business supply store," she said. "I need a new laser printer and some other supplies."

One eyebrow winged up. "Still working? What do you do now?"

"What I always did. I design toys, only now I free-lance," she said, turning her face to look out the window at Swan Hollow as it flashed past.

"For who?"

She thought about not telling him, but the minute she considered it, she let it go. The man could find out the truth easily enough if he did a little digging online. So really, it was pointless to try to keep it a secret even though she didn't love the idea of allowing him even deeper into her life.

"Myself," she said, keeping her gaze focused out the side window so she didn't have to look at him.

"Right," he said wryly, "because rich people can work, too."

She whipped her head around to glare at him. "Why is it when *you* have your own company that's okay, but when I do, I'm a rich dilettante just killing time?"

"I didn't say that."

"You didn't have to." She took a breath and let it out again. "Besides, my life is not your business."

"If that life concerns Caro, then you're wrong. It is."

"Where is this coming from?" She squirmed in her seat and wished she were on her feet so she could pace off the nervous energy pulsing inside her. "You never wanted kids, so why are you so fixated on involving yourself with Caro?"

"Because she's *mine*," he said and stepped on the brake for a red light. Turning to meet her eyes, he said, "I protect what's *mine*."

"So it's just a pride thing?" she asked, trying to read his features, his eyes, hoping she'd see something that would reassure her. That would let her know they'd find a way to work all this out. But as usual, Wes hid what he was thinking, feeling, locking it all down behind an impenetrable wall.

"You hid my daughter from me, Belle. That's not a pride thing, that's a damn fact."

His eyes flashed, a muscle in his jaw flexed and his hands fisted on the steering wheel. Staring into those intense eyes of his, Isabelle knew that he would be a formidable enemy. But was that really what they'd come to? Were they so obviously on opposite sides of this one issue that there would be no way to reach some kind of accord?

He couldn't use his money against her, because she had plenty of her own. But she couldn't use hers against him for the same reason—there, at least, they were on equal ground.

But what would a court say, she suddenly wondered. If he got a lawyer and sued for custody, would the judge punish her for keeping Caroline from him for years? Would he order her daughter turned over to her father? A way to make up to him for all the time he'd lost with Caro? God, that thought opened up a hole inside her.

"I did what I thought was the best thing for me," she said softly. "For Caroline."

"Well," he snapped as the light turned green and he stepped on the gas again, "you were wrong."

But she hadn't been wrong at all, Belle thought. The only thing she'd done wrong was get caught.

"Your brothers came to see me this morning."

"They what?" The change in subject was so startling, it completely threw her off. But a second later, Isabelle gritted her teeth and rolled her eyes. This was her own fault. She had planned to tell her brothers today about Wes being in town. She should have known that they would hear the town grapevine buzzing long before that. Rubbing her fingers against her forehead, trying to fight a headache that seemed to have settled in permanently, Isabelle reminded herself that Chance, Eli and Tyler loved her. They were just being protective. They were looking out for Caroline.

Nope, trying to calm herself down wasn't working, she thought. She was still furious. "What did they do?"

One corner of his mouth quirked in response to the tone of her voice.

"You think this is amusing?" she asked, stunned at the sudden shift in his attitude.

"I didn't this morning," he admitted. "When they pushed their way into my hotel room, my first instinct was to go a few rounds with them. But now, seeing how them interfering really frosts you, yeah. It's amusing."

"That's great," she said, nodding as her world tipped even farther off balance. "You're bonding with my brothers. I should have expected that. You're all so much alike."

"Excuse me?"

She glanced at him. "Now you're offended. That's what I find funny." Shaking her head, she said, "You don't even see it. You, Chance, Eli and Tyler are all pushy, domineering, know-it-alls. You think you know what's best for *everyone* and none of you are willing to listen to reason."

"Reason?" he repeated. "I think I've been pretty damn reasonable so far."

"Ah," she said, lifting one hand. "*So far* being the key words in that sentence. How do I know you're not going to suddenly decide to sue me for custody of Caro?" she asked, blurting out her deepest fear. "How do I know you're not already planning to take her away from me?"

"Because I just found out about her two days ago?" he asked. "I'm good, but even I need more time than that."

He parked the car in the lot and shut off the engine, and Isabelle shifted in her seat to look at him. "How much time, Wes? How long do I have before you come after me with all of your lawyers?"

Wes shifted in his seat, too, until they faced each other in the closed-off silence of the big car. Outside, people wandered in and out of the store and a few more clouds filled the sky, threatening more of the snow that still covered the parking lot. "Who said anything about lawyers?"

"I've been waiting for *you* to say it," she admitted. "But just know, if you bring lawyers into it, so will I."

"Yeah, I know." He nodded grimly. "So no lawyers. We do this between us."

Isabelle released a breath she hadn't realized she'd been holding. For now, at least, she didn't have to worry about Wes taking her to court. He might change his mind later, but she'd be grateful for today. "Okay, good. So how do we settle this?"

"To start? You get used to me being here. Being with Caroline. I'll jet back and forth to Texas as needed for business, but I plan on being here. A lot. Don't fight me on it, Belle," he warned. "We'll figure the rest out as we go."

She didn't like it. But why would she? Still, she liked

this better than the idea of a protracted courtroom drama where they ended up at each other's throats. That wouldn't be good for Caro—or for any of them. It went against every instinct she had to let him into her and her daughter's lives. But the way she saw it, she just didn't have a choice.

Staring into those beautiful eyes of his, she felt that near magnetic pull that she'd always experienced around him. That was dangerous, but only to her. Isabelle knew she would have to be on guard—and never let him know what he could do to her with just a look. Her reawakened feelings aside, it would be easier all the way around if she could just get through this situation with Wes without slipping back into dangerous feelings.

Wes hadn't wanted a family—kids. Finding out that she had kept Caroline from him had hit him in his pride, so naturally he'd had to come here. Had to get answers. But it wouldn't last, she told herself. He'd spend some time here and then he'd go back to his real life and she could return to normal. All she had to do was hang on until Wes remembered that he liked being unencumbered by a family.

"So are we good?" he demanded.

He was watching her, waiting.

"Yes," she said. "We're good. For now." And that was the best she could give him.

"That's a start," he said and opened the car door.

Much later, bedtime was a little crazier than usual. Caroline was fascinated with Wes, and Isabelle couldn't blame her. When Wes smiled, the female heart melted. Didn't matter if you were four or eighty-four, the man had a power. For the last five years, Isabelle had assured herself that she was immune to Wes's charms.

It was a hard thing to discover that she'd been lying to herself, too.

"Another story!" Caroline said, grinning up at Wes. The two of them were sitting on the floor in front of her bed.

Isabelle leaned one shoulder against the doorjamb and folded her arms across her chest. She couldn't tear her eyes off the man and his daughter. Just like she couldn't help wondering where they would all be right now if she had told Wes about Caroline from the beginning. Would he have changed? Would he have wanted the three of them to be a family?

Had she cheated all of them out of what they might have had? God, that was a terrible thought and one that couldn't do the slightest bit of good. What she had to do now was concentrate on the moment at hand and not get lost in memories or dreams of *what if*.

Wes had a book on his lap, and while he read the story out loud, he also tried to use sign language. The movements were a little clumsy, and he got quite a few of the hand signs completely wrong. Isabelle noticed Caroline giggling a little when Wes read the word *bear* and signed something entirely different. But making mistakes wasn't important. The fact that he was trying, that he was going to the trouble to learn ASL tugged at Isabelle's heart.

"Wes," Caro said and signed, "read the one about Christmas."

He feigned dramatic shock. "Christmas is over."

"Not *next* Christmas," Caro argued, with a little giggle that rippled through Isabelle's heart.

"Three stories is enough, Caroline," Isabelle said from the doorway, and the girl and her father both turned to look at her. Two sets of eyes the color of the sea in the

Caribbean studied her. She saw Wes in her daughter every day, but seeing the two of them together like this, the resemblance was heartbreaking.

She wasn't blind here. Not only was Wes enjoying this time with Caroline, but her little girl already adored him. Once she found out Wes was her father, that affection would be sealed forever. And again, Isabelle felt that twinge of guilt for keeping them apart.

"Mommy..." Caro dipped her head, looked up and let her bottom lip jut out just enough for a really good pout.

Isabelle laughed in spite of herself. "Not a chance, kiddo. Now get into bed and I'll tuck you in."

Dragging herself to her feet, Caro sighed heavily, turned and crawled under the covers, tugging them up to her chin. "Can Wes tuck me in tonight?"

Wow. Arrow to her heart. Shifting a glance to Wes, she saw the pleasure shining in his eyes, and that actually took a bit of the sting out of Caro's request. She'd never had to share her daughter with another parent before. The joys, the worries, the sleepless nights had all been for her alone. But standing in the bedroom with Wes, both of them looking at the child they'd created together, Isabelle could almost see what she'd been missing. It was more than sharing the responsibilities. It was sharing those secret looks of pride and understanding when their child did something cute. Or silly. Or tender.

So Isabelle took a step forward, into that joint custody world. Bending down, she gave Caro a kiss and whispered, "Sleep tight. I love you."

Then she stepped aside and let Wes be the one to smooth the sheet and blanket, to sweep soft, silky hair back off their girl's forehead. He kissed her cheek and said, "Good night, Caroline."

"G'night," she said on a yawn. "Will I see you some more tomorrow?"

Wes straightened up and glanced at Isabelle meaningfully before looking back at his daughter. "You sure will."

For the next week, Isabelle felt like a caged tiger in the zoo. Someone was always watching her—and that someone was Wes. Every time she turned around, there he was. At the grocery store. At Caro's school—where he'd charmed the little girl's teacher until the woman was practically a puddle of goo in front of him.

He showed up at her house nearly every evening, bringing dinner with him—which endeared him to Edna, who enjoyed the time off from cooking. He helped Marco pull a tree stump from the backyard, and now Isabelle had to listen to Marco's glowing remarks about a "city man" who knew how to put in a real day's work.

But the worst, she thought, as she pulled into the school parking lot, was Caro herself. The little girl was completely in love with her father.

Wes had plenty of charm when he wanted to use it, as Belle was in a position to know. But she'd never really stood back and watched as he made a conquest. The women in town, Edna, they were one thing, but seeing Caro respond to her father's determination to win her over had been both touching and worrisome. The harder Caro fell for Wes, the easier it would be for him to eventually break the girl's heart. Though to be honest, she hadn't really seen any sign of Wes pulling away. Instead, he seemed focused on being an integral part of Caro's life.

And all of it worried Isabelle. Sooner or later, he would return to Texas. What then? Would he want to take Caroline back with him? Would they end up in a bitter custody fight after all? Or would he have his fill of playing daddy and just leave—breaking Caroline's heart? Even a best-case scenario was filled with possible misery. Say she and Wes worked it out together and he didn't get tired of being a father? Wouldn't he want Caro with him in Texas for at least part of the year?

Isabelle's head hurt, and she didn't see any relief in her near future. So she pushed all of those thoughts out of her mind and tried instead to focus on her work.

She went over the last of her digital drawings, adding a touch of color here, smoothing a sharp line there, until she was completely satisfied. Well, *completely* was a stretch. She was never truly satisfied with her work, and invariably, once she'd sent the drawings off, she would think of dozens of things she could have done differently.

But the most important thing here was getting her latest designs to the manufacturer who could get started on production. Isabelle sent off a quick email, attaching the designs, and then shifted her attention to the paperwork that had been mounting over the last few days.

"You work from home?"

Isabelle jolted in her chair, glanced at the open doorway to her home office and slapped one hand to her chest when she saw Wes standing there. "How did you get in?"

"Edna let me in. Told me you were up here."

Traitor, Isabelle thought. Her housekeeper was clearly indulging her inner matchmaker. Too bad the woman didn't know that Wes wasn't interested in a match of any kind. Isabelle's heart ached a little at that internal reminder. It would be so much easier for her if she could just get past the feelings for him that kept resurfacing.

He strolled into the room, hands in his pockets, and wandered the perimeter, invading her space, looking at everything. She bit her tongue, because telling him to get out of her office would only make him that much more determined to look around. He took long, slow strides, moving with a sort of stealthy grace that made her insides quiver completely against her will.

Taking a deep breath, Isabelle watched as he checked out the full-color digital printouts of her latest sketches she had taped to a wall and the easel where one of her charcoal sketches was on display. Then he moved onto the dry erase board, with her schedule laid out, and finally to the corkboard where she'd affixed dozens of pictures of children holding toys.

Her office was at the front of the house on the second floor. Caroline called it the tower room. The windows looked out over a landscape that included the woods full of snow-covered pines, a lake, and in the distance, mountains that looked tall enough to scrape the sky.

The room wasn't very big, but she didn't need a massive office since there was no one to impress. She had a desk with a computer, an easel and paints, and space enough to pace when she needed to think. But right now, Isabelle wished for a much bigger space, because her office seemed to have shrunk the moment Wes walked into it.

"What is all this?" he asked quietly, turning at last to look at her.

"My work. It's what I do now," she told him and stood up from behind her desk. She didn't want to be seated while he loomed over her. "I set up a nonprofit that provides toys to hospitalized children. I call it Caro's Toybox."

She didn't look at him, instead focusing on the pictures of the smiling kids she kept in her office as inspiration. "I do the design work and the manufacturer produces the toys, then we distribute them."

He looked at those smiling faces in the photographs, too, and asked, "How'd you get into this?"

Isabelle walked up to stand beside him so that both of them were looking at those happy faces staring back at them. "When Caro was so sick, and then diagnosed, we spent a lot of time in the local hospital. We saw ill, scared children, and I realized that stuffed animals, or dolls, or even a toy plane could bring comfort to those kids when no one was around."

She sighed as memories rushed into her mind—sharing waiting rooms with other worried mothers, hearing the muffled cries of children, punctuated by an occasional wail of pain.

"I held Caro on my lap as doctors poked and prodded her. She was scared, but she had me there to try to comfort her," she said sadly. "But there were a lot of kids on the ward who spent too much time alone in their beds. Their moms and dads had other kids to take care of, and jobs, too. Nurses are amazingly great, but they're frantically busy and can't always take the time to try to ease a child's fear."

"I wish I'd been there. For Caro. For you." His voice was low, soft and tinged with regret.

Isabelle looked at him and saw his features soften and felt closer to him than she ever had. Whether he'd been there or not, he was Caroline's father, and only the two of them could really understand what it was like to have a sick child you couldn't help.

"I wish you had been, too." She looked up at him. "I know it's my fault that you weren't, and for that, I'm really sorry."

He looked down at her, and his clear aqua eyes shone with emotion that he couldn't hide. "Thanks. For saying that. For meaning it."

Isabelle's heart thumped hard in her chest. Her stomach swirled with anticipation, expectation and a jolt of nerves that only increased with every breath she drew. "I do, Wes," she said. "If I could do it all over…"

He shook his head, reached out and laid one hand on her shoulder. "We can't do any of it over. But we can do it differently from here on."

The heat of his touch drifted down, sliding into her chest and filling her with a kind of warmth she hadn't known in five years. Staring into his eyes, she was drawn in by that magnetic pull she'd always felt around him. It took everything she had to keep from moving into him, wrapping her arms around his neck and kissing him. But that would only make this moment even more confusing than it already was.

So she only reached up to cover his hand with her own. "We can do that."

He released her as his eyes warmed and a half smile curved his mouth. "Good." He shifted his gaze back to the faces on her board. "So you decided to try to take care of all of those kids," he said.

"To do what I could, yes." She too looked at the board where smiling children were caught in a moment of time. "We set up a toy room on the pediatric floor—" She broke off and chuckled. "Nothing fabulous, of course, usually a maintenance closet that we take over. We add shelves, paint and stock it with toys. Then every new patient gets to choose a toy for themselves."

She smiled a little, remembering the excitement of the kids when they were given the chance to go toy shopping right in the hospital. "It's a good feeling, watching children go into the room and inspect everything there before making their choice."

"Yeah," he said softly, "I bet it is."

She felt him looking at her, and she turned her head to meet his gaze. He was giving her a quizzical look, as if he was trying to figure her out. "What is it?"

He shook his head. "Nothing. I'm just…impressed."

"And surprised?"

"No, not really," he said, tipping his head to one side to look at her more deeply. "You always had a big heart."

Now *she* was the one shocked. And a little off balance. These few moments with Wes had fundamentally changed how they were dealing with each other. Which was good for Caroline, but dangerous for Isabelle. Old feelings were awakened and new ones were jolting into life. "Well, it's getting late, and I need to pick up Caro at school."

"Yeah," he said. "I'll go with you. But first…" He paused, looked down at her and said, "I'd like to help you. With this."

"What?"

"If you had more toys available, you could get into more hospitals, right?" He studied each smiling face on the board as if committing them each to memory.

"Well, yes," she said, watching him. "We've been moving slowly, running on donations and what we can produce. It's taking longer than I'd like."

"Then let me help," he said, and this time he turned to her and reached out to hold her upper arms in a soft, firm grip. "What you're doing is something special. Something important, and it makes me proud that you started it all. So let me in, Belle. Let me be a part of what you do."

Her heart jumped into a fast, heavy rhythm. His eyes on hers, she saw his sincerity. Saw how much he wanted this and what it meant to him. She was touched more deeply than she'd expected. With Wes's help she could grow her program faster than ever before. They could reach more children. Offer more comfort. That he wanted to do this meant more to her than anything else he could have done.

"I'd like that very much," she said.

A slow, satisfied smile curved his mouth, and his eyes gleamed. He rubbed his hands up and down her arms, creating a friction that kindled the heat already building inside her.

"Thanks for that," he said. "I think we'll make a great team."

Isabelle smiled, but her heart hurt a little, since five years ago, she'd thought the same thing.

Six

If anyone had told Wes a month ago that he'd be sitting front row center at a four-year-old's dance recital, he would have called them crazy. Yet, here he was. And most amazing of all, he was having a good time.

Isabelle sat beside him, and next to her were Edna and Marco. On Wes's right, Chance, Eli and Tyler sprawled in the too-small chairs, trying to get comfortable. The elementary school auditorium was packed with parents, grandparents and kids of all ages. The room was big, the chairs were uncomfortable and in the corner beside the stage, an elderly woman was playing a piano that looked as if it could have been one of the first ones ever made.

Smiling to himself, he shook his head and leaned in when Isabelle whispered, "Look over there."

He followed her gaze and spotted Caro, standing in the wings, peeking around the stage curtain. When she saw him, she grinned and her little face brightened. She waved, then made the sign for *thank you*. His heart did a slow, hard roll in his chest as he signed back *you're welcome*.

Of course she didn't have to thank him for coming. There was literally nowhere else he'd rather be than here, waiting to see his little girl take part in a dance recital. With the help of the hearing aids she wore, Caro could hear the music well enough to participate in the dancing she loved. Wes frowned thoughtfully to himself as Caro ducked back behind the curtain to join her class.

How long, he wondered, would the hearing aids work? How long before she entered a completely silent world? He'd been doing research on the cochlear implant, and the more he read the more certain he was that he wanted to get Caroline to a specialist as soon as possible. Yes, he knew that there were many, many happy, healthy deaf people and he knew that Caro would no doubt have a fulfilled life no matter which path she took. But was it so wrong for a father to do everything he could to try to make his child's life a little easier?

He glanced at Isabelle, who had the look of a nervous mom. Her blond hair waved and curled across her shoulders, and as she listened to Edna, she laughed quietly and her greenish-blue eyes shone. She wore a red silk shirt and black slacks, and just looking at her sent a jolt of desire whipping through Wes that he fought like hell to tamp down.

Ever since their talk in her office a couple of days ago, the tension between them had eased in one way and tightened in another. Though there was less anger, more understanding now, the sexual buzz they shared was stronger than ever. Hell, it had been five years since he'd been with her, and sitting beside her now, it was all he could think about.

But he had to move carefully. Slowly. He couldn't give

in to what he wanted if his desires were going to make everything else harder. He needed to get his daughter to a specialist. He needed to save the merger, though right now that looked impossible. And soon, he was going to have to be back in Texas to take care of the business he couldn't handle over the phone. And he wanted Belle and Caroline to go with him. Sex would just complicate everything.

Damn it.

"Oh, hell," Chance muttered from beside him. "Hide me."

Frowning, Wes looked up and saw Kim Roberts headed their way, her gaze fixed on the oldest Graystone brother. Wes was so pleased her laser focus was on someone other than *him*, he couldn't even feel sorry for Chance.

"They're starting!" Isabelle reached over, grabbed Wes's hand and squeezed as the piano music got louder and the lights in the hall were dimmed.

"Thank God," Chance mumbled as Kim had to retreat and find a seat. "Saved by tiny dancers."

Wes grinned, then everything in the room faded away but his daughter, one of a dozen little girls dressed as butterflies as they pranced across the stage. Brightly colored tissue paper wings fluttered, pigtails bounced and nervous giggles erupted in more than a few of the performers. In the darkness, he and Isabelle held hands, linked together by one beautiful little girl and the heat threatening to engulf them both.

After the performance, Wes stood apart from the group of parents, siblings and relatives. He was watching them all as his mind raced. His gaze fixed on Belle, behind the refreshment counter, laughing, talking and serving punch, cookies and cupcakes. And he thought he'd never seen anything more beautiful.

Wes wasn't kidding himself. He had no more interest in love than he ever had. But he could admit he wanted Belle. And that he needed her. In more ways than one. If he could convince Teddy Bradford that he, Belle and Caroline were really a happy little family, then he might be able to salvage the merger that meant so much to his company.

If he felt a twinge of something that could have been guilt, he denied it. He wasn't planning to use Belle and Caroline. But it was hardly his fault if being with his daughter and Belle helped solve a major problem.

He wandered toward the table and stepped up in time to listen in as Caro began a step-by-step description of the performance they'd just seen. Words rushing, fingers flying, his little girl was quivering with excitement, and Wes loved every second of it. Seeing his daughter with her blond hair in pigtails, big aqua eyes wide with happiness, made him smile. She was so small that her butterfly wings really did look as if they could lift her into the sky, but it was her tiny pink ballet shoes that for some reason struck his heart like an arrow.

She'd gotten to him, he realized. In little more than a week, Caroline had become so important to him, he couldn't imagine a life without his daughter. He'd never expected, or wanted, to be a parent, and now he couldn't imagine why. He wanted to tell Caroline he was her father. But he wasn't going to do that then disappear back to Texas and only be involved in her life in the most peripheral way.

He wanted more. Wanted to be there every damn day to watch her grow up. To be a part of her world. But Belle and Caro were a package deal—so he had to somehow convince Belle that the three of them belonged together.

He glanced at Belle, standing behind the refreshment

counter, helping Caro take the paper off her cupcake. He smiled to himself. The two of them were so beautiful it was hard not to look. The buzz of conversations, the ripples of laughter seemed to drift away. He was so caught up in watching them, he didn't even notice Chance walking up alongside him.

"You're making plans, aren't you?" he asked.

"What?" Caught, Wes looked at him.

"It's all right," Chance said, shoving his hands into his pockets. "See, there's a look in your eye when you look at my sister that tells me I should back off. Let you two figure this out. So that's what I'm going to do."

"Glad to hear it," Wes said wryly, though he hadn't been the least bit worried about Chance Graystone or his brothers.

"Don't make me sorry." The man wandered over to Caro, scooped the girl up in his arms and gave her a spin that had giggles erupting and floating in the air like soap bubbles.

Wes watched and continued to plan. That little girl was his. Her mother was his, too. She just didn't know it yet.

But she would, soon.

By the time they got back to Belle's house, Caro was wired on sugar and excitement and getting her ready for bed was a challenge Wes was happy to leave to Belle. While they were upstairs, he went out to his car to get the surprise he'd had sent in from Texas. He'd called his company three days ago to order it, and tonight was the perfect time to give it to Caroline.

The now familiar house was quiet when he went back inside and headed up the stairs to his daughter's bedroom. But as he approached the open door, he heard

Belle and the little girl talking. Shadows thrown from the night-lights plugged in at intervals along the hall crouched in corners. The old house sighed in the cold wind whipping under the eaves. Moving quietly, he stopped in the doorway and blatantly eavesdropped.

"Is Wes gonna kiss me good-night?"

"He'll be here in a minute, sweetie."

"He's nice," Caro said, and though he couldn't see her, he imagined her small hands moving with every word, and his heart swelled.

"Yes, he is nice," Belle said, and Wes couldn't help but wonder if it had cost her to agree with her daughter.

"He's funny, too, and pretty and I think he should stay here now."

"Here?" Belle asked. "In Swan Hollow?"

"Here with us, Mommy," Caro answered and Wes went perfectly still, waiting to hear the rest. "He likes me and he should be here so we can play some more."

"Wes lives in Texas, honey," Belle said gently. "He's just visiting us."

"He's gonna *leave*?" There was a catch in Caro's throat that Wes felt as well.

"Not right away," Belle reassured her daughter, "but yes, he'll have to go home soon."

"But he can be home here, Mommy."

"It's not that easy, baby."

"Why?"

"Because…" She paused, clearly searching for an explanation that would make sense to a little girl. "…because his house is in Texas."

"Why?"

"Because that's where he lives."

"But *why*?"

He muffled a snort. He really shouldn't be enjoying

so much how Belle squirmed, Wes thought. Still, he couldn't help the deep pang of regret he felt at making his little girl unhappy. It only strengthened his resolve to stay in her life permanently.

"Can we go to Texas?" Caro asked, trying a new tack.

Another long pause, and Wes imagined that Belle was wishing he would hurry and show up to dig her out of the conversation.

"No, we really can't."

"Why?"

He heard Isabelle sigh.

"What about your uncles? They all live here. Wouldn't you miss them?"

"Yes. But they could come, too!"

Wes felt a surge of pride. It seemed his daughter was as hardheaded as he was.

"Baby girl," Belle said, "how about we just enjoy Wes while he's here, okay?"

"But I don't want him to leave."

Wes's heart filled and he had to gulp in a breath to steady himself.

"I know, sweetie," Belle said softly. "Neither do I."

And he smiled. There it was. She didn't want him to leave any more than Caro did. So maybe it wouldn't be hard to convince Belle to come back to Texas with him. To try being together—not just for the sake of their daughter.

And on that happy thought, he stepped into Caroline's room. It was a little girl's dream, he imagined. Everything from a canopy bed to a play table and chairs and bookcases filled with stories to be read over and over again. There were stuffed animals, a child's learning computer and, in the corner, a dollhouse as tall as Caro herself.

"Wes!" Caroline scooted out of bed, ran to him and threw her arms around his legs.

There went that twist to his heart again. While he hugged his daughter, his gaze caught Belle's, and he knew she was wondering how much of their conversation he'd overheard.

"Did you bring a present?" Caro squealed, her fingers moving as fast her voice. "For me?"

"It's a present for the best dancer in the whole show," he said, tapping his finger against his mouth. "Now who was that?"

"Me!" Caroline shouted. "It was me. Wasn't it me?" she asked, now sounding a little less confident.

"You bet it was you," Wes told her and handed her the red ribbon–wrapped white box.

"Mommy, look!" Caro staggered toward her mother, balancing the box awkwardly but refusing to put it down.

"I see," Belle said, laughing. "Why don't you put the box down so you can open it?"

"I will!" Caro set it on the floor, plopped down beside it and yanked at the ribbon until it fell away. Then she lifted the lid, pushed back the white tissue and said, "Ooh…"

One small word drawn out into a sigh of pleasure so rich and deep. Wes had to grin. She liked it.

"Mommy, *look*!" Caroline pulled the doll out of the box and inspected every inch of her. "She's like me, Mommy. Her hair and her eyes and, Mommy, she gots *hearing aids* like me!"

"You like her?" Wes asked unnecessarily.

"I *love* her," Caro said and handed the doll to her mother so she could run at Wes again. This time, he scooped her up and held her so she could throw her small arms around his neck and hang on. He'd never felt anything as wonderful as a freely given hug from his child. Her warm, soft weight in his arms, the scent of her shampoo, her grip on his neck and her whisper of "Thank you, Wes" made his heart fill to bursting.

Then he looked at Belle and saw her beautiful eyes shining with unshed tears and he was lost completely. He felt the ground beneath his feet shift as if he were standing in an earthquake. These two females had shattered him without even trying. And he wasn't entirely sure it bothered him.

Once Caroline was tucked in with her new doll clutched tightly to her chest, Isabelle led Wes from the room and pulled the door almost closed behind them.

In the dimly lit hallway, she turned to look up at Wes and said softly, "She loves that doll. Thank you."

"You don't have to thank me. But I'm glad she loves it." He smiled and threw a quick glance at the door separating them from their daughter. He looked back at Isabelle. "It's from our new Just Like Me line. We're set to launch in a few weeks, so Caro got one of the very first."

The fact that he'd thought of it, arranged to have the doll sent here, touched Isabelle so deeply, her heart ached. "It meant so much to her. To me, too. You could have told her then. That you're her father."

He shook his head slowly. "No. I don't want to give her a present and a responsibility all at once. When I tell her who I am, I want it to be the right time."

Tears still brimmed in her eyes, remembering her daughter's excitement and the wonder on her face when she realized the doll had hearing aids just like she did. Wes could not have given her anything that would have meant more. It was hard on a child, being different from all of the other kids, but Caro was so much a force of nature, that even at four, she was completely sure of herself. And yet, having a doll with hearing aids had suddenly given Caro a boost of even more self-confidence.

Wes had given their daughter more than a doll. He'd given her acceptance. Now, with his simple truth that he wanted to wait for the right time to admit to Caroline who he was, Isabelle's heart was lost. Again.

She took a breath, grabbed Wes's hand, pulled him along the hallway and said, "Come with me."

"Where we going?"

"Where we were always headed," she said and tugged him into her bedroom. No point in lying to herself, Isabelle thought. This had been inevitable from the moment he arrived in Colorado. She'd known it, felt it. As if seeing him again had fanned every ember inside her into life, now that banked fire was a raging inferno and she didn't want to try to quench it anymore.

Moonlight on snow reflected into the room through the wide windows, giving the bedroom a soft, pale glow. She took a quick glance around the familiar space, the mountains of pillows stacked against the curved brass headboard, the thick, dark green comforter, the cozy chairs in front of the bay window and the brightly flowered rug across the gleaming wood floors. Reaching out, she flipped a wall switch and the gas fireplace in the sky blue–tiled hearth leaped to life.

This was her sanctuary. She'd never invited a man into this space before—not only because she hadn't been interested, but because she hadn't wanted Caroline to watch men coming and going. Not that there would have been a parade of men or anything. Yet tonight, it somehow seemed inevitable that Wes would be the first. Isabelle wasn't nervous, because it felt too right to her to second-guess herself. She'd made her decision and wouldn't back down now.

"Belle?" Wes looked down at her, desire warring with questions in his eyes.

"No talking," she said and went up on her toes. She hooked her arms around his neck, tipped her head to one side and kissed him with everything she had.

Surprised, it took him a second to react, but then he was kissing her back, making Isabelle's head spin when he deepened that kiss, stealing her breath. He parted her lips with his tongue, dipping into her mouth to taste, explore with a hunger that matched her own.

His arms came around her, pressing her body tightly to his. Isabelle felt like she was on a roller coaster. Her stomach pitched wildly, her heartbeat thundered in her chest and everywhere he touched her, her skin burned.

One of his big hands caught the back of her head and his fingers speared through her hair, holding her still for the wild plundering of her mouth. She felt every inch of his body along hers and moaned at the hard length of him pushing against her abdomen. She wanted him, maybe more now than she ever had before.

She hadn't been with a man since Wes. Isabelle had told herself that she simply wasn't ready. That one day she would be and then she would move on. Find a life. But the simple truth was, she hadn't been able to be with another man because it was always Wes that she wanted. Everything she'd once felt for him came rushing back in an undeniable wave, knocking her sideways while she struggled to find balance.

Wes walked her forward a few steps, eased her onto the bed and then followed her down. He never let go of her, only adjusting his grip so that his hands could slide over her body with a fierce possessiveness that thrilled

Isabelle. Finally, he tore his mouth from hers and she gasped and gulped for air.

Tipping her head back into the mattress, she felt him tugging at the buttons of her shirt and wished wildly for Velcro closing. It would be so much faster. At that last thought, the fabric parted and his hand came down on one of her breasts. Even through the silky lace of her bra, she felt the heat of him, and when his thumb rubbed across her nipple, she whimpered.

"Wes…"

"No talking," he whispered. "Remember?"

"Right. No talking. All I'll say is…*more*."

"Right there with you," he muttered and flicked open the front clasp of her bra, freeing her breasts so that he could lower his head and take first one nipple and then the other into his mouth.

Everything inside her exploded. Isabelle arched into him as his lips, tongue and teeth pulled at her sensitive nipples. A kaleidoscope of sensation shattered inside her mind. While he tortured her with his mouth, he slid one hand down her body to the waistband of her slacks, and in seconds he had the button and zipper undone. His fingers slipped beneath her panties to stroke her center.

And just like that, she was wearing too many clothes. Isabelle's mind struggled for clarity, even as her body shrieked at her to stop thinking and just feel. But she needed more of him. The hot slide of skin to skin, the feel of his hard, muscular body pressed to hers. The amazing sensation of him pushing into her depths and filling her completely.

"I want to feel you," she whispered.

He lifted his head and grinned. "You are."

She laughed a little and felt it tremble through her. "Funny. But take your clothes off."

"Yes, ma'am," he said, bending down to plant another long, hard kiss on her mouth.

She loved the taste of him, the feel of him. And when he moved away from her to peel off his clothes, she missed his warmth, the heat of their bodies wrapped together. He stood up, and she shrugged out of her clothes, kicked her pants off and lay on the comforter, watching him. When he stopped dead, with his hands at his belt, she managed to ask, "What's wrong?"

"We can't do this."

"What?"

He pushed both hands through his hair in frustration. "No protection, Belle. I haven't kept a condom in my wallet since I was in college."

She was glad to hear it. But she laughed a little and said, "Oh. For a second there, I thought you were changing your mind."

"Not a chance," he said, "but unless you—"

"In the bedside table drawer," she said, wanting to cut this conversation short and get back to shivering and trembling.

He pulled the drawer open, then looked at her, eyebrows arched. "Quite the supply," he said. "Been busy?"

She shook her head, licked her lips and choked out a short chuckle. "No. I think of that drawer as my hope chest. I figured it's better to have them and not need them—"

"Than to need them and not have them," he finished for her.

"Exactly."

He grabbed one of the foil packets, stripped out of his clothes and said, "I do like a woman who's prepared."

"Show me."

He didn't need another invitation. He came to her,

covering her body with his, and Isabelle sighed at the first soft, warm contact of his skin to hers. She'd missed this so much. His scent, his taste, his strength. He was a businessman, but his big hands still carried the calluses he'd earned as a young man. And the scrape of his rough palms along her body created a new and even more exciting layer of sensation.

He rolled over, bringing her on top of him, and she loved looking down into those sea-colored crystal eyes. His hands cupped and kneaded her behind and she writhed on top of him in response. She kissed him hard, fast, then raised her head to watch him as she shifted, rising up, moving to straddle him.

In the moonlit room, even the air felt like magic. This moment was one she'd been thinking and dreaming of since she'd first opened her door and seen him on her porch. Slowly sitting up, she dragged the palms of her hands across his chest and loved the flash of something hot and dark that shot through his eyes.

Isabelle felt a rush of sexual power that ratcheted higher and higher inside her as she went up on her knees and slowly, slowly, lowered herself onto him. She took his hard, thick length inside, inch by glorious inch, and when he was filling her completely, she sighed and reveled in everything she was feeling.

He reached up, covering her breasts with his hands, tweaking and tugging at her nipples until she groaned and twisted her body in response. That movement sent shock waves rippling through her system and made her want to feel more, to feel it all.

Unable to wait a moment longer to experience the release clamoring inside her, Isabelle moved on him, rocking up and down in a slow, rhythmic dance that created tingles that rose up and burst and rose up again. She lifted her arms high over her head, giving herself over to what was happening, and the feel of his hands on her breasts only fed the fire that burned brightly inside her.

Then his hands dropped to her hips and guided her into a faster pace. His gaze locked on hers, they stared into each other's eyes as they claimed each other in the most intimate way possible. The tingle at her core became an incessant burn that ached and ached, pushing her toward the release she needed. And when Isabelle felt she couldn't take it a moment more, the needing, the desire, he shifted one hand to her center and rubbed that sensitive nub at her core.

"Wes!" She cried his name but kept moving on him, kept rocking, twisting her hips in a blind effort to take him higher, deeper. That bone-deep ache intensified as they moved together in a dance as ancient as time, and when her body exploded, shattering into a fusillade of color and sensation, Isabelle clung to his forearms and rode the wave to the end.

Only then, when she was shaking and shivering, did Wes let himself follow. She stared into his eyes and watched as he surrendered himself to her. Gave himself to her.

And she wished, from the bottom of her heart, that that surrender was complete.

Seven

An hour later, they were lying wrapped together beneath the comforter. There was a bottle of wine on the nightstand, thanks to Wes making a trip down to the kitchen. He'd had to wait until he was sure his legs would work—but he'd needed those few minutes away from Belle. Away from what they'd shared, to try to think. Hopeless, though, since there wasn't enough blood flow to fuel his brain. All he knew was that what he'd just shared with Belle had been so much more than he'd expected. So much more than he'd been ready for. He'd have to take the time—later—to examine it all from every possible angle. But for now, he was only hoping to experience it all again. Soon.

Outside, snow fell again in soft, white puffs that danced against the window and slid down the glass. Inside, the room was warm, the wine was cold and firelight tossed dancing shadows across the walls.

"Well," Belle said on a sigh, "that was…"

Wes smiled to himself, then took a sip of his wine. "Yeah, it was."

Belle tugged the edge of the comforter up to cover her breasts as she leaned back on the pillows propped against the brass headboard. Then she pushed one hand through her hair and sipped at her own wine. "So, do we need to talk about this?"

Why did women always want to *talk*? He grinned and shrugged. "We're both naked, lying here drinking wine, and I don't know about you, but I'm already thinking about round two. What is there to talk about?"

She shifted, sliding one leg over his. "Well, I thought I should try to explain why we had round one."

He ran his hand over her thigh and smiled when she shivered. Wes didn't want her thinking too much about any of this. Better that they simply accept what happened and build on it. Why ask too many questions? The answers might not be what either of them wanted to hear.

"Oh, no explanation necessary." He winked and said, "I understand completely. You couldn't fight off your desire for me any longer, and in a rush of lust, you surrendered to the urge to fling yourself into my manly arms."

She blinked at him, then smiled, then laughed as she shook her head. "You're crazy."

"That's been said before," he told her and moved, taking her wineglass and setting it on the table beside his. He wanted her off balance with no time to think, to consider, to second-guess the decision she'd already made. Because there was more that he wanted and now that he'd made this much headway, he didn't want to backslide.

He cupped her face in his palm, stared into her eyes and said, "I have to go back to Texas, Belle. Tomorrow. The day after, at the latest."

Surprise flickered in her eyes. She covered his hand with hers. "You're leaving?"

"I have to get back." That was true. His company was trying to fight its way out of a scandal. He had to try to save that merger. And they were getting ready for the big toy launch. And that was just dealing with TTG. He had any number of other companies he had to check on. "There are things I have to be on-site to handle. I've already stayed longer than I should have—not that I'm sorry about that. But I've got to get back."

Her eyes mirrored what she was thinking. They always had. That's why he had known five years ago that she was falling for him. Why he'd let her go. And why right now, he knew she didn't want him to leave.

"Caro will miss you."

He kissed her. "Only Caro?"

She sighed. "I will, too, damn it."

He laughed, enjoying the irritation on her face. "I can fix that. Come with me."

She blinked at him. "To *Texas*?"

"Why not?"

"How many reasons do you need?" She inched away from him, scooted higher on the pillows and pushed her hair back from her face again.

"Come for a week, Belle." He talked fast, knowing he had to drive his point home and make it count. "Come home with me. Let me show Caroline where I live, let her see some of Texas."

"I can't just pick up and go, Wes."

She wasn't saying no outright, so that gave him some wiggle room. He'd take it. "Give me a reason why not. One good one. We'll start there."

"Caro's school."

He almost laughed. "Pre-K, Belle," he said, shaking

his head at the sad attempt at an excuse. "It's not like she's in med school. You could pull her out for a week. Call it an extended field trip."

She scowled at him, clearly realizing that she hadn't offered much of a reason. A second later, she tried again. "Fine. Then there's my work. I have donations to line up, plans to finalize..."

He was prepared for that argument, too. Wes had been thinking about this for a few days now, and tonight had sealed it all in his mind. He had to go back home, and he wasn't going to leave alone.

"And in Texas, you can visit the company, meet with the PR team, and they'll help you come up with ways to drum up more donations."

"I don't need help—"

"And," he interrupted, "you can go through the toy catalog at the company and choose which toys of ours you want to add to your project."

"I hate when you interrupt me."

"I know. Maybe that's why I do it." He gave her another smile and she rolled her eyes.

Then she bit her lip and her gaze slid from his as if she didn't want him to see what she was thinking. He knew she was considering it, and he also knew enough to let his adversary work through everything without another interruption. *Adversary.* That word stuck in his brain until he mentally erased it. She wasn't an enemy. She was—hell, he wasn't completely sure what Belle was to him. He only knew that he wasn't ready to be without her.

"Say we do go with you. Then what?" she finally asked, her voice little more than a whisper.

"What do you mean?"

She half turned on the bed to meet his gaze. Firelight

played over her skin and flickered in her eyes. "I mean, say we spend the week together, all of us. What happens after that? Caro and I come back home, you stay in Texas and we all go on with our lives like before?"

He smoothed her hair back, more because he couldn't stop himself from touching her than for any other reason. His fingertips traced along her jawline then dropped to where her hand lay on the comforter. He took it in his and held on. He thought about it for a second, considered his options, then went with honesty.

"I don't know, Belle. Neither of us *can* know. All I'm sure of is that I want you and Caro to come with me. To be with me. Give me that week, Belle."

Her gaze never wavered. She looked at him for several long, tense seconds as if trying to see past his reserve to what he was really thinking. If she knew, he told himself, she would never come with him.

He wanted her in Texas not only because he wanted more time with Caro. Not only because he wanted Belle in his bed. But because if the three of them presented a united front, the scandal driven by Maverick might disappear entirely and Teddy Bradford could get back on board with the merger.

His people were no closer to finding the mysterious Maverick, but he had learned that Bradford wasn't in talks with anyone else. So the odds of him being in on the scandal eruption were really low. And that meant that the merger might still be salvageable. If he worked this right.

He swallowed his impatience and let Belle see only what he wanted her to see. A man unwilling to let go just yet.

Finally, she nodded. "Okay. A week. After that, we'll talk about what comes next."

He squeezed her hand and smiled. "We'll work something out," he promised her and meant it. No matter what else happened in his life, he knew he'd find a way to keep Caro, and maybe her mother, in his life.

She smiled, but it was barely more than a slight lifting of her lips. Wes knew she wasn't sure of this decision, but he wasn't going to give her a chance to change her mind, either.

"Good," he said, leaning in to kiss her. "Now that that's settled..." He pushed the comforter down and cupped her breast, thumb and forefinger rubbing her hardened nipple until her eyes glazed over and she gave a soft sigh. Smiling down into her eyes, he quipped, "I think it's time to think about round two. I'm feeling the need to fling myself at you. How do you feel about that?"

She held his hand to her breast and with her free hand she reached up and drew his face to hers. "Fling when ready."

He grinned. Damned if he hadn't missed her. He hadn't allowed himself to acknowledge it before now. He remembered all the nights they'd stayed awake talking, laughing, making love. He'd never had that in his life until Belle, and when she left Texas, she'd taken all of it with her.

No other woman had given him what she had. Now she was back in his life, and he wasn't going to let her go anytime soon.

He bent his head to kiss her and instantly lost all thought under the rising tide of need. Tomorrow could take care of itself. For tonight, all he wanted was *this*.

Two days later, the three of them were on Wes's private jet. Edna had urged her to go, to see where this thing with Wes would lead, and with that tiny bit of encouragement, Isabelle was going to give it a try. Of course, it didn't help anything to know that Chance, Eli and Tyler were less than thrilled at her going off with Wes. Though they'd changed their initial opinion of him mainly because of the way he was with Caro, Isabelle's brothers were still not ready to trust him not to hurt her or her daughter.

Neither was she, when it came right down to it. But if she didn't try, she'd never forgive herself. Still, Isabelle knew she had to approach this time with Wes carefully. If not to protect her own heart—then at least to guard Caroline's.

Because her little girl was thrilled with this new adventure. Caro loved the plane, loved flying above the clouds and loved the limo ride from the airport to Wes's home just west of Royal, Texas.

Five years ago, Wes had been in the process of building his home. Isabelle had seen the blueprints, they'd talked about different design features and she'd suggested quite a few changes to the original plan. Now, seeing it finished, Isabelle thought it was breathtaking.

Under the soft Texas winter sun, the massive two-story house sprawled across a beautifully landscaped property. There was a tidy lawn that seemed wider than a football field. Young trees ran the perimeter of the property with a few older live oak trees that had been left standing during construction. Flowers in wildly bright and cheerful colors hugged the base of the house and lined the brick walk that led to the long, inviting porch.

The house itself was a gorgeous blend of wood and stone and glass. Tall windows lined the front of the house and glinted in the sunlight. Stone walls made the house look as if it had been standing in that spot for decades. The porch was filled with rocking chairs and a swing that hung by thick chains from the overhead beams. A white wood railing completed that picture, along with the baskets of flowers that stood at either side of the double front doors.

Isabelle was used to seeing mountains, and the land here was flat, but for a few rolling hills in the distance. And still, it was beautiful.

It seemed strange, Isabelle thought. They'd left Colorado in the middle of the latest snowstorm. There were snowdrifts four feet high all over Swan Hollow. And here in Texas, there were winter flowers blooming under a mild sun. Kind of a culture shock for Isabelle, but Caroline didn't seem to have a problem with it.

The little girl, clutching her new favorite doll, bolted from the limo onto the grass. She spun in a circle, holding her head back and laughing. When she stopped, she looked at her mother, wide-eyed. "There's no snow, Mommy!"

"I know, baby." Isabelle tossed a glance at Wes to see him smiling indulgently. Looking back to Caro, she asked, "Do you like it?"

"I like making snowmen," she said thoughtfully, taking another slow spin to look all around her. "But I like this, too."

"I'm glad you do," Wes said, using sign language as well as speaking. "We don't have snow, but we have other fun stuff."

"Like what?" Caroline asked, eyes bright and interested.

Put on the spot, he seemed to flounder for a minute and Isabelle waited, curious to see how he'd recover. She shouldn't have doubted him.

"Oh, we've got a big zoo that has a carousel and we've got lakes. We can go out on a boat—"

"I like boats!" Caroline grinned. "Uncle Chance has a boat and it's fun!"

"Good to know," Wes said wryly. "There's an amusement park in Houston where we can go on rides, and there's a trampoline park, too." He reached out and gently tugged one of her pigtails. "Texas has a lot of great stuff."

"But no snow."

He shook his head. "Not usually."

She thought about that for a second then shrugged. "It's okay. Home has snow, so it's okay you don't."

"Well, thanks," Wes said, slanting a look at Isabelle. "You know, your mom used to live in Texas."

"Really?" She looked up at her mother. "Did you have fun with Wes, too?"

Before she answered, she saw the speculative expression on Wes's face and smiled to herself. The man was impossible. "I sure did, honey. So will you."

At least, Isabelle really hoped so. Looking at her little girl's excitement right now, she could only pray that nothing happened to dampen that enthusiasm. Shifting her gaze to Wes, Isabelle tried to see beyond the facade to the man beneath. What did this trip mean to him? Was it simply to get a little extra time with his daughter? Was he considering a future for all of them? Or was there another reason for this trip altogether? Impossible to know.

"Why don't we go inside," Wes said to Caroline. "Then you can see your room."

"*My* room?" Caro asked, her mouth wide-open in pleased surprise.

"Yep, and it's special just for you." He took Caroline's hand, winked at Isabelle, then walked to the front door, the little girl skipping and chattering happily alongside him.

Isabelle followed, shaking her head. The man never

ceased to surprise her. Of course he had a room for Caroline. He'd had two days, after all. No doubt he'd made a few calls and had everything taken care of just the way he wanted it. It probably should have bothered her that he was so obviously planning on more than just a week with Caroline. You didn't go to that kind of trouble for a child who would only be spending a few days there. But on the other hand, how could she be upset with a man who went the extra mile to make their daughter feel special?

"A dog! You gots a dog!"

Caroline's squeal of delight reached Isabelle as she stepped up onto the porch, and she couldn't quite hold back a sigh of defeat. Caro had been asking for a dog for months, and Isabelle had kept putting her off. Now Caroline would be even more determined than ever.

Isabelle stepped into the entryway and immediately noted the warm oak floors, the pale misty-green walls and the thick oak trim everywhere. There was a table near the stairs where a vase of flowers stood and several doors leading off a long hallway that stretched to the back of the house. Later, she'd have time to explore. But for right now, Isabelle's gaze was fixed on her daughter and the golden retriever currently adoring each other.

"What's his name?" Caro demanded as she buried her face in all that soft, golden fur.

"Her name is Abbey," Wes said, signing as well as speaking.

Isabelle had to admit that his signing had really come a long way in a week. Clearly he was practicing a lot.

Abbey, reacting to her name, abandoned Caroline briefly to welcome Wes home, her nails clicking on the hardwood floor. Then the big dog shifted her attention to Isabelle, coming up to her and leaning against her, giving Isabelle the opportunity to stroke that sleek golden head.

But when the hellos were done, the dog shot straight back to Caroline. She plopped to the floor in front of the little girl and rolled over to her back to allow for a good belly rub. Caro complied with a delighted laugh.

"I like dogs," Caro shouted over her own laughter when Abbey sprang up to lick the girl's face.

"She likes you, too," Wes said, then as an older woman approached, said, "I'm home, Bobbi."

"So I see." Bobbi had long, gray-streaked black hair, currently in a thick braid that hung over one shoulder. She wore jeans, a long-sleeved blue T-shirt and dark red cowboy boots. "You brought me a little girl to spoil, too, I see."

"Hi," the girl announced. "I'm Caroline."

"Nice to meet you," Bobbi said. Then, holding out a hand, she said, "You must be Isabelle."

"I am, it's nice to meet you, too." Isabelle looked around, then back to the woman who was so clearly in charge. "It's a gorgeous house."

"Needs some life in it," Bobbi pointed out with a slanted look at Wes. "But looks like it'll be a little livelier for a while anyway."

"All right," Wes said, tossing a knowing look at the older woman. "Caro, you want to see your room? It's upstairs."

Bobbi's eyebrows lifted at the sign language he used, but then she nodded as if pleased to see it.

"I do! Come on, Abbey!" Caroline headed for the stairs at a run, and the dog was only a pace behind her.

Isabelle and Wes followed, and when he took her hand, she held on, pleased at the warmth. The connection. This was a big step for her. Coming back to Royal with the man she had once run from. Odd that she'd never planned on it, but she'd ended up coming full circle. If it all worked out somehow, great. If it didn't, would she pay for this decision for the rest of her life? For her own sake, as well as Caroline's, she hoped not.

At the top of the stairs, they turned left and Wes led the way to a door halfway down the hall. When he threw it open, Caroline raced inside, then stopped dead and sighed, "Oh, boy."

Isabelle had to agree. Wes had gone all out. The room was a pale, dreamy blue, with white curtains at the windows and a blue-and-white coverlet on the bed. There was a table and chairs in one corner, bookshelves filled with books and a child-size blue couch covered in white pillows, just made for curling up and daydreaming. There was a mural on the wall of butterflies, fairies and storybook castles and a thick blue rug spread across the wood floors.

How he'd managed all of this in just a couple of days was amazing. Unless, Isabelle thought with a sideways glance at him, he'd been planning to get her and Caro to Texas all along. Good thing? Bad? She couldn't be sure yet.

Caroline whipped around, still clutching her doll in the crook of one arm, and threw her free arm around Wes's knees. Tipping her head back, she said, softly, "Thank you, Wes."

He cupped the back of her head and smiled down at her with a gentleness that touched Isabelle's heart. There were so many layers to the man that she doubted she would ever learn them all. But this man, the gentle, loving man, was the one she'd fallen so deeply in love with years ago. It was a side of him she'd rarely seen, and it was all the more beautiful now because of it.

And Isabelle was forced to admit, at least to herself, that she *still* loved him. Watching him with their daughter had only solidified the feelings that had never faded away. She'd known five years ago, even when she left him, that she wouldn't be able to run far enough to outdistance what she felt for him. She'd tried. She'd buried herself in work she believed in, in caring for her daughter and in being a part of her town and her family.

But in spite of everything, for five long years, Wes had remained in the back of her mind, in a corner of her heart. And even as she tried to fool herself, she'd known somehow that what she felt for him was still alive and well. Today just proved that.

As her heart ached and her throat tightened, he lifted his head, catching her eye, and everything inside her melted. Isabelle had risked a lot by coming here with him, staying with him. But it was too late to back out now. She had to see this through. See where it would take her. Love didn't disappear just because it was inconvenient. But if she walked away a second time with a broken heart, Isabelle wasn't sure she'd survive it.

"You're welcome," he said to the little girl still beaming at him as if he were a superhero.

Caroline gave him another quick grin, then climbed onto her couch to try it out and Abbey crawled up right beside her, laying her big head in the little girl's lap. Clearly, a mutual adoration society had been born.

"Now," Wes said to Isabelle, "I'll show you your room." He took her hand again to lead her directly across the hall.

The moment he opened the door, she knew it was the master bedroom. It was massive. Far bigger than her own bedroom at home, this one boasted a stone fireplace on one wall, with a flat-screen TV mounted over the mantel. There were two comfy high-back chairs and a small table in front of the hearth, and on either side of the fireplace, floor-to-ceiling bookcases. A bank of windows on the far wall was bare of curtains and displayed a view of the trees, grass, a swimming pool and those hills she'd spotted before, off in the distance. There was also what looked like a barn. Or a stable.

She wondered idly how many acres he owned, but then her thoughts were scattered by a glance at his bed. It was *huge*. A dark blue duvet lay atop the mattress, and the head and footboard were heavy golden oak. Dark red rugs were tossed across the shining floor, and all in all, it was a beautiful, masculine space. But it was the bed that kept drawing her gaze. Finally she forced herself to look away, to meet Wes's gaze.

In his eyes, she saw the glint of desire and the determination of a man who knew what he wanted and had no trouble going after it. "You don't have another guest room?"

He gave her a half smile, reached out and stroked one hand down her back. Isabelle took a breath, then steeled herself against her reaction. The ripple of goose bumps along her arms, mixed with the heat building at her core, was enough to shatter any woman's defenses.

"Sure," he said, voice a low rumble of need, "but we can't pretend we didn't sleep together. Can't go back, Belle." His gaze locked on hers. "And I wouldn't even if we could. Don't think you would, either."

She shook her head. No point in denying it.

"Do you really want us to be sneaking up and down the hallway in the middle of the night?"

The image his words painted was both pitiful and funny. She sighed. "With Caro right across the hall…"

Wes chuckled. "She won't think anything of it, Belle. Heck, with Abbey around, she probably won't *notice*." He moved in and wrapped both arms around her. "We already crossed this bridge back in Colorado, you know. You're not going to try to tell me you're sorry about it, are you?"

No, she really wasn't. Maybe she should have been, but she wasn't. Five years without him had been long and lonely. Having him back in her life might be dangerous to her heart, but Isabelle knew that loving him was no longer a choice for her. It just *was*.

As for sharing his bed here… Isabelle would be going to bed long after Caro. And she'd be up before her daughter in the morning, so her little girl would probably never realize where her mother was spending the night. And honestly, Isabelle admitted silently, she wanted to stay with Wes. She was here for a week. Why not enjoy what she had while she had it? Risk be damned. If this time with him was destined to end, Isabelle at least wanted *now*.

"No," she said, "I'm not sorry." She watched pleasure dart across his eyes, then she lifted one hand and cupped his cheek, just because she wanted to. "I'll stay here. With you."

"Good." He caught her hand and held onto it. "Now that we've got that settled…come on."

Frowning at his abrupt shift, she asked, "Where are we going?"

"Outside. Let's find out if Caro likes her pony."

"What?" She laughed as he pulled her along behind him and wondered how she'd ever made it through the last five years without him.

Eight

"Boss?" Robin's voice was a little loud, which made Wes think this wasn't the first time she'd spoken to him.

Whatever the situation going on at home, he had to focus here at work. "Sorry. Yeah. What were you saying?"

She frowned at him. "Everything all right?"

"Sure." He pushed up from his desk, stood straight and shoved his hands into his pockets. "So what's going on?"

She didn't look like she believed him, but since he was the boss, she went with it. "Okay, the news from Texas Tech is good," she said. "They've got the next line of tablets ready to roll before summer, with the new bells and whistles you ordered."

"Good." He moved out from behind his desk and walked to the window overlooking the city of Houston. While the PR and IT teams were still working on uncovering the mysterious Maverick, Wes was concentrating on the other arms of Jackson Inc. He had majority interest in Texas Tech; Texas Jets, a charter jet service; and a few other smaller yet growing companies. He'd been building his empire for decades, and getting to the bottom of Maverick's deliberate sabotage of Texas Toy Goods was important. He couldn't risk the man going after any of his other companies as well.

"I want to talk to Sam Holloway at Texas Jets sometime today," he said, never taking his gaze from the cityscape sprawled out below him. "And then get me Andy at Texas Tech. I want to hear details on those bells and whistles."

"Got it."

He half turned from the window. "Are Belle and Caroline still in the PR department?"

"Isabelle is, yes," Robin told him. "But Maggie from PR took Caroline down to the cafeteria for a chocolate shake." She sighed and smiled. "That little girl is just adorable, boss. I gotta say, makes me miss my own kids' younger days."

"Yeah, she's pretty great," he said, thinking, as he had been for days now, about how Caroline had wormed her way straight into his heart, and no matter what happened between him and Isabelle, nothing for him would ever be the same again.

"She showed me how to say hello in sign language." Robin shook her head. "Smart kid. Just like her daddy."

His eyebrows lifted.

"Please." Robin waved one hand at him. "No, you didn't make some grand announcement, but I'd have to be blind to not notice the child has your eyes. Right down to the unusual color."

"It's not a secret," he said, then half laughed at himself. "At least, not since Maverick blasted it all over the internet. But I haven't told Caro who I am yet."

"For heaven's sake, *why*?" Robin asked.

She sounded completely exasperated, and Wes realized that for some reason, his assistant and his housekeeper shared the same attitude. Neither of them was intimidated by him and both of them continually seemed to forget just who was really in charge. "You know, I could fire you," he pointed out wryly.

She waved that away with a flick of her hand. "That'll never happen and we both know it. So why haven't you told that child you're her father?"

"Because I want her to know me. To—" it was humiliating to admit "—*like* me."

Robin gave him an understanding smile. "She already does, boss. You can see it in the way her face lights up when you walk into the room."

He pushed his hand through his hair. Robin was right. He'd seen that look. It had made him feel ten feet tall. So why then was he waiting to tell his daughter who he really was? He hated to think it was fear. Hell, nothing had scared Wes in…well, ever. But the thought of that little girl turning from him could bring him to his knees.

"Robin," he said abruptly, "I'm taking the rest of the day off."

"I'm sorry. I think I must have had a stroke. What was that?"

"Surrounded by sarcasm," he said with a nod. "I'm taking the day off."

"Yesterday, you took Caroline to the aquarium, the day before it was ice-skating and the day before that you and Isabelle had her riding roller coasters." Robin tipped her head to one side and looked at him. "I'm beginning to think you might be looking for a life, boss."

"I'm beginning to think you may be right." He grinned

and shrugged into his jacket. "Just forward my calls to my cell. I'll check messages later."

He caught up to Isabelle in PR. The room was bustling, people typing on keyboards, sketching on whiteboards and huddled around desks, arguing and discussing. The noise level was high, so Wes decided to try out some sign language. He caught her eye and from across the room, she smiled at him. Then she flushed and chuckled when he started signing.

At another desk, a guy named Drake laughed, too, then ducked his head and pretended he hadn't.

"Something funny?" Wes asked him.

"Um, no, sir," the kid answered quickly, his gaze darting from side to side to avoid making direct contact with Wes's. "It's just that, um, my mother's deaf. I speak sign language, and, well…"

"Perfect." Wes sighed and shook his head. "What were the odds," he muttered. Then he bent low and whispered, "I expect you to forget everything you just saw."

"Didn't see a thing," Drake assured him and deliberately went back to work with a frenzied attack on his keyboard.

Nodding, Wes was satisfied that the kid wouldn't be telling anyone that the boss had just signed, *You look incredible. I want you in bed. Now.*

Isabelle walked toward him, still smiling. He took her hand and led her from the room. Out in the hall, he said, "Well, that was unexpected. I didn't think there'd be someone here who understands sign language."

She squeezed his hand and let him see her smile grow. "It's okay. I don't think he's going to be telling anyone that you want me in bad."

He stopped. *"Bad?"*

Laughing, she nodded. "You're getting better at signing every day, but it's pretty tricky."

No wonder the kid had laughed. "Still, having you wrapped up in bed and bad on top of it isn't a bad idea, either. I could eat my way down to you and then just keep going."

Her eyes flashed and she licked her lips, sending a jolt of heat straight down to the one area of his body that hadn't relaxed since he'd first seen her. Shaking his head, he murmured, "I came to get you so we could take Caro to the zoo. But now..."

She tipped her head to his shoulder briefly, then looked up at him. "Zoo first. Bad later."

"Deal."

They must have walked for miles, Isabelle thought. She and Wes and Caroline had spent hours at the zoo, and she wouldn't have thought that Wes would enjoy it. But he had. Just as much as he'd enjoyed the amusement park and the ice-skating. Maybe it was the magic of seeing things through the eyes of a child, but he'd been more relaxed and happy in the last few days than she'd ever seen him. In a gray suit, now minus the red power tie, he should have looked out of place at the zoo. But she'd learned that Wes wasn't a man easily defined. Despite the suit, he carried Caro on his shoulders and didn't seem to mind when her ice cream cone dripped all over him. On the ride home to Royal, it took only seconds for Caro to be sound asleep in her car seat. After checking on her, Isabelle sat back and turned her head to look at Wes. Her heart did a quick tumble as she stared at his profile. "Caro had a wonderful time today."

He glanced at her and gave her a half smile. "So did I.

Until this week, I hadn't taken a day off in years. I think Robin is shell-shocked."

Isabelle laughed. She'd always liked Wes's no-nonsense assistant. "She'll recover."

"How did it go in the PR department?" He paused. "You know, before I got there. You get anything you can use?"

"Absolutely." In the couple of hours she'd been with PR that morning, Isabelle had found new and clever ways to hit people up for donations. "Mike actually suggested that I sort of adopt out hospitals."

"You lost me." He steered the car into the passing lane to go around a truck.

"Well—" she turned in her seat to face him even though he had to keep his eyes on the road "—it's like, I print up information on specific hospitals. The kids— first names only—their health issues, how long they'll be there in that sterile environment. Let potential donors see these kids as real people rather than just another random charity."

"Good idea." He nodded. "And you'd send these flyers or newsletters or whatever out to your mailing list?"

"To start, yes, but I could also make more of a splash on my Facebook page. And get more involved in social media. Honestly, I get so busy with the actual work that I forget I also have to get out there and promote what the charity does, too. Social media is so hot right now—"

"Believe me," Wes said with a tight groan, "I know."

"Right." She winced, remembering suddenly that it had been a Twitter attack that had brought them back together. "Sorry. Sore spot."

"It's okay," he said, shaking his head. "Go ahead."

"All right. So Mike suggested I start a public Facebook page detailing what the nonprofit is about. Pictures of the toys we give to these kids. Maybe pictures of the toy closets in the hospitals themselves. I'd like to add pictures of the kids with their toys, but I'd have to get their parents to sign releases..."

"They probably would," he said.

"You think so?"

"You should know better than me what a parent of a sick kid would be feeling. What would you have done if someone had given Caro a brand-new doll or stuffed animal when she was miserable in the hospital?" He looked at her briefly.

"I'd have kissed them," she admitted. "So, okay, maybe you're right about that. I can check with some of the parents at the hospital when we go home next week and—"

"About that..."

She looked at him for a long second or two before saying, "What?"

"Well," he said, shifting position slightly in his seat, "I was just thinking that maybe one week here won't be enough time. I mean, for Caroline. To get to know me, my place—hell, Texas."

Isabelle frowned, and her stomach jumped with a sudden eruption of nerves. "We agreed on a week, Wes. I have work. Caro has school. We don't live here."

"You could."

"What are you saying?" Her heart jumped into her throat and the hard, rapid beat thundered in her ears. Was he saying what she thought he might be saying, because if he was, driving down the freeway doing eighty miles an hour was an odd time to be saying it. "You want us to *live* here?"

"Sure. The house is huge, plenty of room, Caro could go to school in Royal and—"

He kept talking, but Isabelle had stopped listening. There was no mention of love or commitment or anything else in that little speech. He wanted them in his house, her in his bed, but he was no closer to intimacy than he had been five years ago, so Isabelle did them both a favor and interrupted him. "Wes, it's really not the time to talk about this."

His mouth worked as if he were biting back words clamoring to get out. Finally though, he said, "Okay. But you can think about it."

She could practically guarantee she wouldn't be thinking about anything else. The fact that he could just bring up the idea so casually, though, told Isabelle more than she wanted to know. He wasn't looking for family. For love. He wanted her and Caro to be a part of his life without strings. Without the ties that would make them a unit.

Maybe she'd been fooling herself from the beginning.

"Okay," he said, still frowning, "we'll table that discussion for now. Instead, you can tell me if you got a chance to look through the toy catalog I gave you yesterday."

He went from frowning to facile in the blink of an eye. She'd forgotten he could do that. Isabelle used to be fascinated by the way he could switch gears so easily. If he saw himself losing one argument, he'd immediately change tacks and come at it from a completely different direction, and pretty soon, he had exactly what he'd wanted all along.

Now, he was doing it to *her*. Isabelle was going to keep her guard up around him, because he was her weakness. She couldn't let him see that she loved him, because one of two things would happen—he'd either back off as he had five years ago. Or, worse yet, he'd look at her with pity.

She wasn't interested in either.

"I did," she said, deliberately cheerful. "You've got some great things, Wes. If you're serious about donating, we'd love to add anything you can spare."

He reached over and took her hand, holding it in his much larger one. The heat of him swept up her arm to puddle in the center of her chest, wrapping her heart in the warmth of him. God, she wasn't going to be able to protect her heart, because it was already his.

"Just tell Robin what you need. She'll take care of it."

"Thanks." She couldn't stop looking at him. Maybe she was storing up memories, Isabelle thought. Maybe a part of her knew that this couldn't last and was instinctively etching him into her mind so that years from now, when she was still missing him, she could pull these images out and remember.

She only hoped it would be enough.

The following evening, Wes realized that he was in the middle of the very situation he'd been avoiding for years. He had a woman and a child in his home, and instead of feeling trapped, he felt…good.

But then, this wasn't permanent, was it? That thought didn't bring him the rush of happiness he would have expected. When he'd suggested to Belle that she and Caroline could stay with him, she hadn't jumped at it, had she? So he was still looking at saying goodbye to them all too soon. His guts twisted into knots. Isabelle had only agreed to be here for a week, and four of those days were already gone.

And instead of being at home with them right now, he was here at the Texas Cattleman's Club for a meeting. Shaking his head, he lifted the crystal tumbler in front of him and took a small sip of his scotch. Usually, he enjoyed coming into town, sitting in the lounge, talking with friends, joining in on plans for the future of the club. But tonight, he knew Isabelle and Caroline were back at the house, and he caught himself constantly wondering what they were up to while he was stuck here.

"Your head's not in this meeting," an amused voice noted.

Wes looked at Clay Everett and gave him a nod. "Good catch." Clay was a local rancher with brown hair, green eyes and a permanent limp due to a bull-riding accident. Like Wes, Clay was a driven, stubborn man.

"So what's more fascinating than painting the club restrooms?" Tom Knox asked.

"Oh, I don't know," Toby McKittrick said wryly. "*Everything*, maybe?"

Wes grinned and gazed at each of the men in turn. Tom looked the part of the ex-soldier he was, with broad shoulders, lots of tattoos and the scars he carried as a badge of honor. He was a man to be counted on.

Toby was taller, leaner and just as stubborn as the rest of them. A rancher, he was loyal to his friends, tough on his enemies and didn't take crap from anyone.

"Yeah, got better things to do than sit here and listen to a lot of nonsense," Wes said, idly turning the scotch glass in damp circles on the tabletop.

"So I heard," Tom said with a knowing smile. "Isabelle's back. How's that going?"

"The word is," Clay offered slyly, "our boy Wes here is practically domesticated."

"No way," Toby put in with a laugh. "The woman who could put a leash on this man hasn't been born yet."

"Not what I hear," Clay said, taking a sip of his beer.

Great. Even his friends were talking about him, wondering about what was going on. He supposed bringing

Isabelle and Caro back to Royal had been inviting the gossip, but what the hell else could he have done? Eventually, he knew, the talk in Royal would move on to some fresh meat and he and his problems would fade away. All he had to do was make it that long without popping someone in the mouth.

And he didn't have a damn leash around his neck.

Wes nodded as he lifted his glass to the other men. "Good to be with friends who know just how to aim their shots."

They all took a drink and Toby said, "Damn straight. What're friends for, after all? And since we're such good friends, maybe we should go back to your place with you. Let Isabelle know that when she gets tired of dealing with you, we stand at the ready."

Giving him a smile, Wes shook his head. "Yeah. That'll happen. I don't think so."

Clay grinned. "Worth a try. When do we meet your daughter, then?"

Wes shot him a look. He shouldn't have been surprised, since half the country had been talking about him, thanks to Maverick and Twitter. Still, it seemed weird to have someone ask about his *daughter* so easily.

"Soon," he said. "Hopefully. Her mother and I have some things to work out first. Which I could be at home doing if I wasn't here listening to the old-timers gripe about too many changes."

"The girl's a cutie," Clay told him. "Saw pictures of you three in the grocery store."

"What?" Wes just looked at his friend and waited.

"Yeah, those tabloids by the cash registers? There you all were at the ice-skating rink." Clay shrugged. "Headline was something like hashtag Deadbeatdad No More."

"Great. That's terrific."

"Hey," Toby said, "it's better than saying you're *still* a crappy father."

"I didn't know I was a father," Wes pointed out.

"Yeah, we know," Tom said, holding both hands up in mock surrender. "We're just saying that everybody else seeing the three of you looking like a family is going to take the sting out of that whole Twitter nonsense."

He had a point, Wes told himself. And if the pictures were in the tabloids, they'd be showing up other places, too. Magazines, newspapers, online. Teddy Bradford would see them and maybe rethink his position on the merger. One of the reasons Wes had brought Isabelle and Caroline back to Texas with him was to take the pressure off the scandal.

So why was he feeling a little guilty about all of this now?

Wes scanned the room, noting the members who were here and wondering about those who weren't. Hell, it was a pain in the butt to have to come to redecorating meetings, but if you were a member you should damn well show up and do what needed doing.

The club had been the same for more than a hundred years. Typical of the wealthy, men-only clubs of the day, the TCC had mostly been decorated with masculine comfort in mind. Hunting trophies along with historical Texas documents and pictures dotted the walls. Dark beams crossed the ceilings, which were higher now, thanks to the renovations done after damage incurred by the last tornado. The furniture was dark leather, a blaze burned in the stone fireplace and the thick rugs that were spread across the gleaming wood floor were a deep red.

Of course, since female members were admitted to the club several years ago, there'd been some changes, too. The child care facility was the most monumental, but there were smaller, less obvious changes as well. The walls were a lighter color, there were fresh flowers in the meeting rooms and the quiet hush that used to define the old place had been replaced with an abundance of feminine voices.

Wes had no problem with female members and neither did his friends. But the old guard still wasn't happy and usually fought the women on every change they tried to institute. Even something as stupid as what they were dealing with tonight—the color of the restrooms.

Wes focused on a trio of women across the room who were even now arguing with two older men whose faces were practically purple with suppressed rage. Shaking his head, Wes looked at his ex, Cecelia Morgan, and her pals Simone Parker and Naomi Price. The three of them together were surely annoying, but he'd always thought of them as benign, somehow. Now though, he had to wonder if the trio of Mean Girls were behind the Maverick business. Yet even as he thought it, Cecelia spouted off about the color of the walls in the women's restroom as if deciding on Springtime Peach was the most important thing in the world. Could she really be behind the devious attack on him?

While she propped her hands on her hips and glared at the older man in the leather chair, Wes could hardly believe that once upon a time, he'd been involved with Cecelia. What the hell had he ever seen in her? Sure, she was gorgeous, but she and her friends still seemed to be locked into high-school behavior, living up to their nickname, the Mean Girls.

As he watched, Simone Parker, with her bold blue eyes, long black hair and body built to wake the dead, leaned into old man McGuire, shaking her finger in his face. Right beside her was stunning Naomi Price, with brown eyes and long reddish-brown hair. Naomi had a self-satisfied look on her face as she watched Simone battle with the old man. Cecelia, though, gave a glance around as if she were looking for a way out.

Briefly, her gaze met Wes's, and she must have read the disgust on his face, because damned if she didn't look embarrassed to be a part of the scene playing out in front of her. But thankfully, Cecelia was no longer Wes's problem.

As if he could read Wes's mind, Toby sighed and said, "Those three should have grown out of that nonsense after high school." He paused, then added, "Especially Naomi. That's just not who she is. Not really."

"I don't know," Tom put in. "The three of them have been bothering people in Royal for years. Maybe it's just become a habit for all of them."

"Then it's one they should break," Wes said, taking another sip of scotch.

"Agreed," Toby muttered darkly.

"All right now." Parker Reese, pediatrician at Royal Memorial hospital, spoke up loudly enough to be heard over everyone else. "Can we cut to the chase here? Let's get the decisions done so we can get out of here."

Normally, Parker was quiet, approachable, but not overly friendly. The crowd quieted, the club's president, Case Baxter, took over and the Mean Girls subsided into silence.

"Well, damn," Wes muttered. He might actually get out of this meeting in time to tuck Caroline in and read her a story. "It's a miracle."

"Yeah," Toby said, "I'm thinking we owe Parker a beer."

A couple hours later, he was home in bed, waiting for the woman he couldn't get enough of. When the bedroom door opened and Belle slipped inside, he smiled. "Caro asleep?"

"Out like a light," she said, "still clutching her doll to her chest. She hasn't come up with the right name for her yet, but she's working on it." Belle eased under the covers and moved in close to Wes, laying her head on his shoulder.

The big bed faced the fireplace, where a nice blaze was going, sending out flickering light and shadow around the room. He tucked his arm around her and held her close, thinking this just couldn't get much better.

A shame he had to shatter it. Holding on to her, just in case she tried to pull away, Wes said, "I spoke to a specialist in Houston today."

She stiffened in his arms, but only tipped her head back to look at him. "About…?"

Wes scowled. "You know what about. Caroline."

"Wes, we agreed that we'd decide on specialists *together*."

"I just talked to him, Belle," Wes said, stroking one hand up and down her back. "I didn't sign our girl up for surgery."

Seconds ticked past, and he watched as anger drained away to frustration, then to simple curiosity. "Okay, fine. What did he say?"

"That he couldn't tell me anything without examining Caro," Wes admitted, "which I knew already. I was just asking some general questions. To satisfy my own curiosity."

"And did you?"

"Yeah." He smoothed one hand through her hair, letting the silky tendrils slide through his fingers. "I wondered, what do you think about getting her a cochlear implant in only one ear?"

She frowned up at him and waited, so he continued.

"We could start out with one, let her go for a few years, see if there are more advancements made in the meantime, and then later on we can include her in the decision making. If she wants to get a second one, then we do that. If not, we don't."

He looked into her eyes and hoped she saw that he was only trying to figure out the best thing for Caroline. It wasn't easy to know what to do, and he figured all parents felt the same. Different issues, maybe, but no one had a game plan that would let them see the future. To *know* which path was the right one to take.

"When she's older, Caroline can tell us what she wants to do. But meanwhile, we make sure she doesn't lose too much ground."

Isabelle was quiet for so long, Wes half wondered if she'd just zoned out. But then she reached up and ran the tip of her finger across his lips. "You surprise me, Wes."

"Yeah?" He kissed her fingertip. "How?"

"That's an excellent compromise from a man not known for making them."

He gave her a wink. "I'm a great businessman. I know how to make deals that everyone can live with. Ask anyone."

"I don't have to ask." She gave him a wry smile. "I've seen you convince people to do things they had no intention of doing, and it looks like you've done it again."

"Yeah?" He smiled. Wes wasn't trying to fast-talk Belle into anything, but he couldn't pretend he wasn't going to do everything he could to help his child, either.

"Yeah," she repeated, and turned, bracing one arm across his chest as she looked at him. "I don't know why I didn't think of it myself. Somehow I convinced myself it was all or nothing, but it's not. We can ease into the implant situation and see how Caro responds."

"Exactly." Wes pulled her over to lie on top of him and skimmed his hands down her back to her behind. She sighed and briefly closed her eyes before looking at him again, and he thought he'd never seen anything as beautiful as this woman.

"We can't get into the specialist until next week." He stared up into her eyes and watched as a layer of frost dazzled their surface. Belle never had been an easy woman, and he could see clearly that she was willing to dig her heels in.

"We won't be here next week," she said quietly.

"You could be. Stay." His hands gripped her hips to hold her in place, because he could tell she wanted to slide off him. Hard to argue with a man when you were both naked and pressed together. Which was exactly why he was keeping her right where she was.

"We've been through this already, Wes," she said. "Why should we stay?"

He watched those eyes of hers, felt himself drowning in them, and every instinct he possessed warned him to take a huge mental step back. To ease away. Let her slide off his body and put some distance between them. But he couldn't do it.

He knew he had to give her a reason to stay, and so he offered the only one he had. "I'm not ready for you to go."

She went still, her hands on his shoulders, her mouth no more than a breath away from his. He waited what felt like forever for her to speak. When she did, he released a breath he hadn't realized had been caught in his chest.

"Okay," she said softly. "We'll stay a few more days. To see the specialist."

A few more days wasn't forever, but it would do for now.

"Deal," he said, then rolled over, taking her with him, holding her body beneath his as he bent to take her nipple into his mouth.

She trembled and he felt like a damn king. She sighed and it was like music. Night after night, they came together, and it was always good. Always right. Always better than the time before. He couldn't get enough of her and didn't think he ever would.

Five long years without her had taught him that no other woman could compare to her. And he wasn't ready to lose her again just yet.

Her hands slid from his shoulders down his arms, and Wes felt every stroke like a line of fire dissolving into his bones. Sliding his hands along her body, he laid claim to her in the most intimate, ancient way. Every line and curve of her body became his as he tasted, touched, caressed.

Moonlight speared through the windows, bathing the room in a pale, silvery light. Her eyes caught that light, reflected it and shone like beacons, drawing Wes in closer, deeper. He felt himself falling and couldn't seem to stop it. Didn't know if he *wanted* to stop it.

At this moment, all he knew was that he needed to lose himself in the woman with him. She brought him confusion, laughter, warmth and the near constant need to be inside her. Wes ached for her night and day. The longer he was with her, the more that need intensified. That alone should have worried him, he knew. But the simple fact was, he didn't care what, if anything, it meant. All he could think about was *her*.

She arched into him, and Wes smiled against her skin. She moved against him, shifting her hips, letting him know that the ache inside was building. He loved that she felt what he did, that she wanted as desperately as he did. *Loved.* He blanked his mind at that wayward thought and gave himself up to the moment.

Wes skimmed one hand down to her core and cupped the heat nestled there. Instantly, she lifted her hips, rocking helplessly beneath his touch.

"Wes," she said on a sigh, "don't tease me..."

"Teasing's half the fun," he murmured and took first one nipple then the other into his mouth, tugging, suckling, relishing the tiny gasps and groans she made. He dipped one finger into her center, then another. He stroked her inside and out, while his thumb traced lazy, relentless circles over that most sensitive bud at the heart of her. She twisted in his grasp, moving her hips, arching her back, as her breath came faster, faster. He suckled at her breast, felt her tremble and knew it wasn't enough. He wanted her mindless, defenseless.

Sliding down the length of her body, he knelt between her thighs, scooped his hands beneath her bottom and raised her high off the mattress.

"Wes—" Her eyes were burning. Her hands fisted in the sheet beneath her as her legs dangled off the bed.

Keeping his gaze locked with hers, he bent his head to her center and covered her with his mouth. Instantly, her head tipped back into the bank of pillows behind her and her grip on the sheets tightened until her knuckles went white.

He smiled to himself as he used his lips, tongue and teeth to drive her to the brink, only to keep her from going over. He held her on the edge deliberately, feeling her shake and shiver, knowing what her body wanted, knowing how she craved it, because he did, too.

Again and again, his tongue laid claim to her and Wes

knew he'd never hear anything more beautiful than the whimpering sighs sliding from her throat.

"Wes, please. Please."

He laid her down and reached for the bedside drawer. Grabbing a condom, he sheathed himself, then leaned over her to sheathe himself again…inside her. He entered her on a whisper, and she sighed at the sense of completion when he filled her. Wes closed his eyes and stayed perfectly still for a long moment, savoring the sensation of being held inside her body. The heat, the slick feel of her surrounding him. Then he opened his eyes, looked down into hers and murmured, "Enough."

"Now, Wes," she said, gripping his hips even as she lifted her legs to wrap them around him. *"Now."*

"Yes," he murmured and lowered his head to kiss her. His body rocked into hers, and he fell into a frantic rhythm, his hips pounding against hers, pushing them both faster, higher until release hung just within reach in the darkness. They lunged for it together and together they shattered, holding onto each other as they took the fall.

And with her wrapped in his arms, Wes closed his eyes and held her tight.

...

Nine

The following night, they left Caroline in Bobbi's care and went to dinner at the Texas Cattleman's Club. Isabelle had always loved the place, for its history, its meaning to the town of Royal. It had never bothered her that it had traditionally been an all-male private club. Heck, she figured women liked time to themselves, too. But now that women were welcome as members, she loved the changes that had only been started the last time she was in Royal.

There was a different feeling to the place. Not exactly feminine, but at least a few of the rough edges seemed to have been smoothed over.

"It's been a while since you've been here," Wes said, tucking her hand through the crook of his arm.

"Five years," she said, glancing up at him. He looked gorgeous, of course, but then Wes Jackson would have to work at looking anything less than amazing. His black suit was elegantly tailored, and the deep red tie against the white dress shirt looked great. His hair was ruffled—she didn't suppose it would ever look anything but. And she liked it that way.

She was wearing a long-sleeved navy blue dress with a full skirt and a scooped neckline that just hinted at the cleavage beneath. Her black heels added three inches to her height, and she still had to look up to meet Wes's gaze. But she saw approval and desire in his eyes, so it was worth it. "Do you still come here for lunch every week?"

"Usually." He nodded to the waiter and headed for his favorite table. Wes seated Isabelle then sat down opposite her. "It's a good spot to get together and talk business."

Wine was served after a moment or two, and Isabelle's eyebrows arched. "Ordered ahead of time, did you? Think you know me that well?"

"Yes, I do." He leaned across the table and smiled. "Your favorite here is the chicken marsala and a side salad, blue cheese dressing."

"I don't know whether to be flattered that you remembered or appalled that I'm so predictable."

"Be flattered," he said. "You've never been predictable, Belle. You always did keep me guessing. Still do."

"I'm glad to know that," she said and took a sip of her wine. Setting the glass back down again, she looked at him, sitting there with all the quiet confidence of a king. He was in his element here, and she was on his turf. She'd have done well to remember that, but sadly, it was too late now. Isabelle had tumbled right back into love with the man, and there didn't seem to be a way out that didn't include a lot of pain.

"Thank you," he said, throwing her off balance again. "For what?"

"For agreeing to stay into next week. To talk to the specialist with Caro."

They hadn't spoken about that since the night before, but then really, what was there to say? He'd caught her in a weak moment, Isabelle told herself. Naked and wrapped up in his arms, she might have agreed to anything. So she could hardly be blamed for putting off leaving for a few more days. Besides, Caroline loved it here.

Her little girl spent hours in the stable with the head groom, Davey. He was teaching her about horses and had already taught her how to brush her pony, Sid, named after her favorite character in the *Ice Age* movies, and feed him. Caroline was thriving, with both of her parents at her side, with Bobbi and Tony. Not to mention Robin and everyone at the Houston office.

She was a sweet girl and people responded to that, making Caroline feel like a princess wherever she went. In fact, Caro hadn't once asked about going home. Which should, Isabelle thought, worry her. When they did eventually leave, it would be a hard thing for Caroline. It was going to be nearly impossible for Isabelle.

"You're welcome," she said, shoving those dark thoughts down into a corner of her mind. "I'm interested in what the specialist has to say, too."

"Good." He lifted his glass, looked past her and sighed. "Damn it."

"What is it?" She made to turn around, but he stopped her.

"Don't look. It's Cecelia Morgan, and it looks like she's coming over here."

Wes's ex-girlfriend. When she was in Royal before, Isabelle and Cecelia had been friendly, but never friends. The last time she'd spoken to Cecelia, the woman had happened upon her while Isabelle was indulging in a good cry. After hearing her out, Cecelia had urged Isabelle to leave Royal, insisting that Wes would never be interested in a child or commitment or any of the other things that Isabelle had wanted so badly.

"Hi, Wes," the woman said with a cautious smile as she stopped at their table. "Isabelle."

"Hello, Cecelia," Isabelle said, wondering why the woman looked so uncomfortable. "It's nice to see you again."

The other woman smiled wryly, clearly not believing the platitude.

Cecelia was beautiful, with her blond hair, long legs and a figure that would make most women incredibly jealous. But right now her green eyes were filled with regret that had Isabelle curious.

"Look," Cecelia said softly, giving a quick look around the room to make sure she wasn't being overheard. "I don't mean to interrupt, so I won't be long. I just had to stop and say something to both of you."

"What is it, Cecelia?" Wes asked, his deep, curt voice anything but welcoming.

The other woman heard the ice in his voice and stiffened in response. "I just wanted to apologize to you. Both of you. I should have told you about your daughter, Wes. And Isabelle, I never should have said that Wes wouldn't want his child. I feel terrible for my part in all of this and I just wanted to say I'm really sorry."

"Cecelia—I don't blame you for that." Isabelle reached out to her, but the other woman shook her head and held up one hand for quiet.

"It's okay. I just saw you both here and I wanted to say that I've got some regrets over things I did in the past.

That's all." She took a step back. "So, just…enjoy your dinner." And she was gone.

"That was weird," Wes said. "I don't think I've ever seen her so thoughtful."

"It was unexpected," Isabelle agreed. She wouldn't have believed that Cecelia would ever apologize like that. The woman had never been concerned with anyone beyond herself and her two best friends. But maybe, Isabelle thought, as her gaze settled on Wes, people really could change.

The next morning, Wes was at the Houston office for a few hours before heading home to take Belle and Caroline to a park. He laughed to himself at the thought. Hell, even with the upcoming launch, he'd taken more time off lately than he had in years. And though he'd never been one to delegate important duties, he'd been doing just that more and more lately—and feeling his priorities shift as if they'd taken on a life of their own. Business had always been his joy. His passion. Growing his companies had been the focus of his life—until he'd discovered he was a father. One little girl—and her mother—had changed everything for Wes.

He leaned back in his desk chair and stared out the window at the steel-gray winter sky. January in Texas didn't mean snow like Colorado, but the weather could change on a dime and usually did. The park might not be the best destination for today.

"Boss?"

He turned his head to Robin in the open doorway. "What is it?"

"You're not going to believe this," she said, worrying her bottom lip, "but Teddy Bradford is on video call for you."

Frowning, Wes straightened up. Teddy hadn't taken Wes's calls since all of this started. Granted, Wes had been focused more on damage control than in trying to reach out to Teddy—especially after the press conference the man had held. Still, the CEO of PlayCo had been silent up until now, so what had changed?

"Put him through." Wes turned to the monitor on his desk and waited. Teddy's face appeared on the screen moments later.

The older man was in his sixties, with salt-and-pepper hair and shrewd green eyes. He was in good shape and in person was an imposing figure. But Wes wasn't so easily intimidated.

"Bradford," he said, with a nod of greeting.

"Jackson." Teddy gave him a benevolent smile and folded his hands together, laying the tips of his index fingers against his chin. "I thought it was time we talked."

"Why now?" Best to play his cards close to the vest. Wes had learned early on when people were caught up in casual conversation, they made slips. So he watched what he said and tried to make the other man give away his secrets instead.

Teddy leaned back in his oversize maroon leather chair. "I've seen the pictures of you with your daughter and her mother. You're making quite the splash, publicity-wise."

Understanding dawned. Hell, this was just what Wes had originally hoped for. He'd known that photographers would be following him around hoping to get more dirt to feed the scandal that had erupted almost two weeks ago. Instead, the pictures were of him, Belle and Caro together. Happy. Enjoying each other. And he had known that people would assume they were the family they appeared to be.

The plan had worked great. Except that Wes no longer felt as if he were pretending. Things had changed for him, he realized. It wasn't a subterfuge anymore. The situation felt real to him, and he couldn't imagine living without Belle and Caro. That was an unsettling thought for a man who'd spent his entire life avoiding commitment, love and any semblance of family.

Putting all of that aside for the moment, he asked, "Why exactly are you calling, Teddy?"

The older man's face creased in an avuncular smile that instantly rubbed Wes the wrong way.

"That takeover could be back on the table for you," Teddy said, dropping his hands to rest on his desktop. "As a family man myself, I can appreciate when a man makes a mistake and sets it right. You getting things straight with the mother of your child has made me look at you in a new light."

Pompous old bastard. What Wes really wanted to do was hang up. Teddy Bradford as the arbiter of family values was annoying enough. Knowing that he had somehow gotten the old goat's approval really stuck in his craw.

"You should know, though," Teddy continued, in that oh-so-confidential tone, "that we've had another offer for the company. I wanted to give you a heads-up before I make any decisions. Maybe we can still work something out on the merger."

Wes's expression didn't give away what he was thinking. Mainly because he wasn't sure how he felt about any of this. Taking over PlayCo, blending it into his own company had been his purpose for a couple of years now. A part of him was eager at the chance to seal the very deal that had been shattered so completely by the mysterious Maverick. Yet there was another part of Wes that was standing back, wary of this sudden magnanimous burst from the other man.

"Shame about that little gal of yours," Teddy was saying with a sad shake of his head. "Saw she's got a set of hearing aids. Looks like she'll have some challenges ahead."

Wes gritted his teeth. Caroline was the most amazing kid he'd ever met. Hearing or not, she was way better than this man's version of *challenged*.

"I appreciate the phone call," Wes said, somehow managing to hide the guilt nearly choking him. "But like you said in that press conference, I've got a lot of thinking to do."

"Is that right?"

"Teddy," Wes said, "there's a lot going on right now, so I'll have to get back to you on this."

"See that you do," Teddy said, then stabbed a finger at the disconnect button and the screen went dark.

For a second or two, Wes just sat at his desk as fury ebbed and flowed inside him. At Bradford. At the situation he'd found himself in. At himself for dragging Belle and Caro into this mess. The merger with PlayCo was huge. He was being offered the very merger he'd been working toward for two years. But taking it, he might have to swallow more than he was willing to. And Wes didn't know if he could do it. Or even if he was interested in trying.

Still, there was more to think about here than just himself. Expanding the company meant hiring more people, and that was good for everyone. And hadn't this been exactly what he'd been aiming for all along? So what was he waiting for? Why was he easing back from the very thing he'd been counting on?

He scrubbed both hands over his face. "Robin!"

Seconds later, his assistant appeared in the doorway.

"Gather the heads of every department," he said. "I want them here in an hour, discussing that call from Bradford."

"Yes, boss."

When she left, Wes was alone with his thoughts again. And he didn't much like them.

Isabelle stopped by the Royal Diner to pick up the lunch she'd ordered. Amanda Battle, the diner's owner, was at the counter, waiting with Isabelle's takeout bag. Inside that bag were Wes's favorites—grilled ham-and-cheese sandwiches and fresh onion rings. Not the healthiest lunch in the world, Isabelle thought, but a spontaneous office picnic required more than raw veggies and a salad.

Wes was supposed to come home early and take her and Caro out for the afternoon. But Isabelle had received such great news from home, she hadn't wanted to wait to see him. So an office picnic sounded like fun. Besides, Wes had been devoting so much time to her and Caro, Isabelle knew he had a lot of work to catch up on. The new toy launch was still a few weeks away, but he had to be on-site to handle any problems that might crop up.

She couldn't wait to tell him that the toys she'd selected from Wes's company had already arrived in Swan Hollow. And they'd sent so much more than she'd expected, Isabelle was sure she could supply two or three children's wards with those toys alone.

But as good as the news was, it also meant she had to leave for home soon. The distribution of toys was always a logistical nightmare, and she had to be there to supervise it all. She hated the thought of leaving, which was silly since that had been the plan all along. But things had changed, hadn't they? Wes had changed. So maybe after the work was done in Swan Hollow, she and Caro could come back. Maybe.

"Well, it's about time you came in to see me."

Isabelle cleared her mind, slid onto one of the counter stools and smiled at Amanda. "Sorry, I've been busy."

"So I heard." Amanda slid a cup of coffee toward her. "In fact, the whole town's been talking about you and Wes and your daughter almost nonstop. And you know the diner is the unofficial clearinghouse for information."

Isabelle winced, knowing that she was the subject of gossip and speculation. But honestly, she'd expected nothing less. Royal's lifeblood was gossip, and if you wanted to find out the latest news, you came to the Royal Diner.

"Bobbi had your daughter in here yesterday for a milkshake," Amanda said. "She's a cutie."

"Thanks." Isabelle glanced around the familiar diner and was glad to see it hadn't changed. Black-and-white floors, red vinyl booths, and the delicious scent of cheeseburgers cooking on the grill. She was also happy to see there weren't many customers this early in the day.

"How's Wes taking being an instant daddy?" Amanda asked, leaning against the counter.

Back when Isabelle was living in Texas, she'd spent a lot of time in Royal. She and Amanda had become friends, and it was really good to see her again. Actually, she'd enjoyed a lot about being back in Royal and hadn't really expected to, since she'd left Texas so abruptly, thinking to put it all behind her.

"It's been a little iffy," Isabelle said honestly. "He's crazy about Caroline and the feeling's mutual."

"But…?"

She smiled and sighed. Amanda always had been too intuitive. "But I have the same problem I did five years ago," she admitted. "I love him and he likes me. And just how fifth grade does that sound?" She sighed and gave in to her inner worries. "I just don't know if this is going to work or not."

"Sweetie," Amanda said softly, "nobody ever knows that going in. With Nathan and I, it was touch and go from the beginning. But it was worth it. So don't give up. Just ride it out and hope for the best."

Good advice, she thought, and if it was just *her*, maybe she would. But she had Caroline to worry about now, too. And she couldn't justify risking her little girl's heart on the off chance that Wes would see how good they all were together and want it to be permanent.

Although… "Wes has been…different," Isabelle said, keeping her voice low, confidential, just in case there were any big ears listening in. "He's warmer than he was. More reachable somehow. Less obsessed with his business. Sometimes I look at him and I think, it could work. And then I worry that I'm seeing what I want to see. Basically," she said on a choked laugh, "I'm going a little crazy."

Amanda laughed and patted her hand. "Isabelle, we're *all* a little crazy."

Smiling ruefully, she admitted, "I hate that I'm getting pulled in, but Amanda, I keep thinking that this time Wes and I might have the chance to build something."

Amanda sighed in commiseration. "Sweetie, if he has a brain in his head, he won't mess this up."

"I hope you're right."

When Isabelle reached the office in Houston, Robin wasn't at her desk, but the door to Wes's inner sanctum was partially open. Thinking he and Robin were going over some work, she approached quietly and listened, not wanting to interrupt.

"It worked perfectly." A man's voice spoke up. "Bradford was so impressed seeing pictures of you, Isabelle and Caroline together, he's giving you everything you wanted."

Isabelle took a breath and held it as she stood, rooted to the spot.

Another man spoke up. "Maybe Maverick did you a favor, bringing this all out into the open."

Isabelle sucked in a breath.

"Maverick, whoever he or she is, wasn't trying to help me. And I still want the IT department working on finding out just who the hell he or she is."

"Right. Sorry, boss."

Isabelle's throat was tight and her stomach was alive with nerves.

"Back to Bradford," Wes said. "He's still talking about another offer on the table."

"Yes," a woman answered, "but he called you. Clearly he prefers selling out to us."

The man spoke up again, and Isabelle was pretty sure she recognized the voice as Mike from the PR department. "If you can just make the whole family thing work for another couple of weeks, we could seal the deal."

Family thing. Had it all been an act? A performance for Teddy Bradford? Had any of what she'd felt in the last week or more been real?

"I'm not waiting two weeks to give Bradford my decision," Wes said.

Heart dropping to her feet, Isabelle backed away from the door. No, she told herself. Nothing was real. It was all for show. All to help Wes nail down the merger that was, in spite of what she'd believed, still all important to him. Clutching the takeout bag, she bumped into the edge of Robin's desk and staggered. She felt as though the world was tipping beneath her feet. Everything she'd thought, hoped for, was a lie. How could she have been so stupid?

Wes had only been using her and Caroline to fight back against that Twitter attack and the crashing of his business plans. How could she have believed even for a second that he'd meant any of it? That he'd suddenly learned how to love?

Furious with him but even more with herself, Isabelle turned to leave, then stopped at Robin's voice. "Oh, hi, Isabelle. Are you here to see the boss?"

Panicked, desperate to escape, she forced a smile and shook her head. "It's not important. He's busy. Here." She handed the bag of food to the other woman and left, this time at a sprint.

Robin came back into the office carrying a Royal Diner takeout bag, and Wes frowned. "You called in for takeout from *Royal*?"

"Nope," she said. "Isabelle was in the outer office. She brought this for you, but she left because she could see you're busy."

Busy. Wes's brain raced, going back over everything that had been said in the last few minutes. Had Isabelle heard it? Was that why she left? *Damn it.* He jumped up from behind his desk and hit the door at a dead run. "I'll be back."

He didn't bother with the elevator—it would have taken too long. Why the hell had she chosen *today* to surprise him? If she'd heard any of what was being said in his office, she had to be furious. But she'd calm down once he explained. He bolted down the stairs and hit the parking garage just as the elevator arrived and Isabelle stepped out. She took one look at him and her features iced over.

Explaining wasn't going to be as easy as he'd hoped. "Belle—"

"Don't." She hurried past him. "I don't want to talk to you right now."

He took hold of her upper arm and didn't let go when her gaze shifted meaningfully to his hand on her. The parking garage was cold, dark, and their voices were echoing through the structure. Overhead lights fought the darkness and squares of watery sunlight speared in through the entrance and exits.

"Damn it, you don't understand."

"I understand everything," she countered, yanking her arm free. "Maverick messed up your plans."

"Damn right he did."

"And everything with me, with Caro, was all a lie. You *used* us to get that stupid merger that's so important to you."

Insulted, mostly because her accusation held a hell of a lot of truth, Wes swallowed his own anger before speaking again. "That merger was important. Something I've been working toward for years. But I wasn't using you. Either of you."

"Sure." She nodded sharply, her eyes narrowed on him. "I believe you."

"Yeah, I can see that." Helplessness rose up in him and nearly choked his air off. Wes hated this feeling and could honestly say that until he'd met Isabelle, he'd never really experienced it. "I don't know what you heard—"

She sneered at him. "I heard all I needed to."

He thought back fast, recalling what everyone was saying in the minutes before he'd found out she'd run off. Gritting his teeth at the memory, he said, "It was out of context."

"Right."

His anger burst free. "Are you going to listen to me about this or just keep agreeing with me to shut me up?"

"Which will get me out of here the fastest?" She folded her arms over her chest and tapped the toe of her shoe against the concrete in a staccato beat.

Irritating, fascinating, infuriating woman.

Scowling, he said, "Did it hurt that pictures of the three of us were in the news? No. But did I arrange it? No. I didn't lie to you, Belle."

"Really." She tipped her head to one side. "Explain Caro's bedroom."

"What?"

"Murals on the wall. Rugs. Chairs. New bed. Toys." She ticked them all off, then said, "You started preparing for our arrival long before you asked me to come to Texas. This was all a plan from the beginning."

"Yeah," he said, refusing to deny this much, at least. "When I found out I had a daughter—after her mother had lied to me about it for five years—I had a room set up for her. That makes me a bad guy?"

She shook her head. "You don't get it. But then, you never did." She started walking again.

"What the hell? You don't finish an argument? You just walk off."

"This argument *is* finished," she called back, and the click of her heels on concrete sounded out like beats of a drum.

He let her go. No point chasing her down to keep

arguing here. He'd give her time to calm down. Let her get back home, think everything through.

Wes listened to her car door slam and the engine fire up. "Once she settles a bit, it'll be fine," he told himself. "I'll fix all of it tonight."

Ten

Belle wasn't there when he got home.

At first, he couldn't believe it. He'd expected to find her in the great room, quietly stewing. Wes had arrived, flowers in hand, ready to smooth out every rut between them and charm her into seeing things his way. The reasonable way.

Now, he stood in the empty room, a bouquet of lavender peonies gripped in one tight fist. There was no sign of either his wife or his daughter.

Wife?

That word had popped into his head from God knew where, and Wes rubbed his forehead as if trying to erase it. But it wouldn't go. When had he started thinking of Belle as a wife? About the time, he figured, that he'd realized he had no interest in living his life without the two people who meant everything to him. Staggered, he shook his head and kept looking around the room.

None of Caroline's toys were lying abandoned in the middle of the floor. Belle's electronic tablet wasn't on the coffee table, and the house *felt* empty.

His heart fisted in his chest, and a soul-deep ache settled over him. Why the hell would she leave? He pushed one hand through his hair and turned a fast circle, checking every damn corner of the empty room as if somehow expecting Isabelle and Caroline to simply appear out of thin air. "She was supposed to *be* here," he muttered. "We're supposed to straighten this out. She's supposed to *listen* to me, damn it."

Refusing to believe that she would simply leave without a word, without even a damn note, he headed for the stairs and was stopped halfway across the hall.

"They're gone."

He stared at Bobbi and ground out, "When?"

"A few hours ago." She leaned one shoulder against the doorjamb and crossed her arms over her chest.

Hours? They'd left hours ago?

"Why the hell didn't you call me at work?" he demanded. "Let me know?"

"Because she asked me not to," Bobbi snapped, her gaze drilling into his.

Looked like Belle wasn't the only woman he'd pissed off today. His housekeeper was clearly disgusted with him. But that didn't excuse her keeping this from him.

"You realize that you don't work for Belle, right?"

"And you realize that I'm on her side in this, right?"

When had he lost complete control of his world? This kind of thing just didn't happen to Wes Jackson. "You're fired," he said tightly.

"No, I'm not," she retorted and pushed off the wall. Wagging one finger at him, she added, "You can't fire me, because you *need* me. Just like you need Isabelle and your daughter."

He felt the punch of those words as he would have a fist. She was right. He was alone and she was right. He did need them. Wes scowled more fiercely, not knowing whom he was more angry with. Bobbi? Or himself?

"That little girl was *crying* when they left."

Himself, he thought. He was definitely most angry at himself. And yet, Belle hadn't had to leave. She should have stayed. Talked this out. Wes swallowed back a fresh tide of anger rising up from the pit of his belly. Sure, he'd screwed up. But Belle had walked out. Caro had been crying. Had Belle cried, too? Regret shattered the anger, and guilt buried what was left. So many emotions were charging around inside him, it was a wonder Wes could draw a breath at all.

"You should have called me." Turning his back on Bobbi, he took the stairs three at a time and headed straight to the master bedroom.

No sign of Belle there, either. Somehow, he'd wanted to believe that his housekeeper had been lying to him. That she was trying to make him wise up before facing Isabelle. But she hadn't lied. He threw the walk-in closet door open and stared at the empty rack where Belle's clothes had been hanging only that morning.

Hell, her scent was still there, lingering in the still air. Haunting him until her face rose up in his mind and he couldn't see anything else. But she was gone.

He left his bedroom, stalked across the hall to Caro's room and felt his heart rip when he found it as empty as the rest of the house. A soft whining sound caught his ear and he looked around the door to the child-size couch. Abbey was stretched out, as if waiting for Caro to come back. The dog lifted her head when he entered, then seeing him alone, whined again and dropped her head to her paws.

Wes knew just how she felt.

He glanced down at the peonies he still held in his clenched fist. Then he dropped them to the floor and stepped on the fragile petals on the way out of the room.

Grabbing his cell phone, Wes walked across his bedroom until he was staring out over the yard. He hit speed dial, and while he waited, he looked at the stables, then the corral, where Caro's pony was wandering alone. His daughter should be there right now. Waving at him. Signing to him. But no, her mother had taken her away. *Again.*

He was so wrapped up in his own thoughts, it startled him when a voice came on the line and said, "She doesn't want to speak to you."

"What?" Wes yanked the phone from his ear and glanced at the number he'd dialed, making sure it was Belle's. But there was no mistake.

"Edna?" he asked, realizing Belle's housekeeper was running interference for her. She couldn't even talk to him on the *phone*? "Where's Belle?"

"She's here at home where she belongs," Belle's housekeeper informed him. "And she asked me to tell you she's got nothing more to say to you. She says that everything that needed saying was said this morning."

He held the phone so tight, it should have shattered in his grasp. Taking one long, deep breath, Wes reached down deep for patience and came up empty-handed. He couldn't believe that she was going to such lengths to avoid him.

"So her answer is to run away?" he countered.

"She didn't run. She flew."

Was he paying off some terrible karma from a past life? Why else would every woman he knew be giving him such a hard time? Couldn't they all see that there were two sides to this?

"Damn it, Edna, put her on the phone."

"Don't you curse at me. And I don't take orders from you."

He was beginning to wonder if *anyone* did. Taking another deep breath, he held it for a second, then released it to calmly ask, "Can I speak to my daughter then?"

"Nope."

A fresh rush of anger surged through him at the nonchalant attitude. He'd never been more frustrated in his life. Separated from his family by hundreds of miles and an emotional chasm that appeared too deep to cross. "You can't keep her from me."

"I can't, no," she said flatly. "But Isabelle can, and good for her, I say. You had a chance at something wonderful and you threw it away. You threw *them* away. I know what you did, so if you're looking for understanding, you dialed the wrong damn number."

Then she hung up.

Stunned, Wes stared at his phone for a long second. *Nobody* hung up on him! "What the hell is wrong with everybody?"

There was no answer to his strangled question. His cell didn't ring; the blank screen taunted him. So he threw his window open, pitched the phone into the yard, then slammed the sash down again.

And he still didn't feel better.

"What did he say?" Isabelle looked at Edna.

"I think it's fair to say that his cookies are completely frosted." Handing the phone back, Edna picked up a plate of brownies and set it in front of Isabelle. "He's mad, of course, and I think a little hurt."

"I doubt it." Edna was too nice, too optimistic. Wes wasn't hurt—just frustrated that she hadn't fallen in line with his plan. You couldn't hurt Wes Jackson with a sledgehammer. A person had to *care* to be hurt.

Like her daughter cared. Just as Isabelle had feared, leaving Texas had been a misery for Caroline. The drama from earlier that day was still playing through her mind.

"But I don't want to go," the little girl had wailed, bottom lip jutting out in a warning sign of a meltdown approaching.

"I know you don't," Isabelle told her. "But it's time we left. We have things to do at home, baby girl."

She sniffled dramatically. "Like what?"

"School."

"I can go to school here. Wes says so."

Oh, thanks so much for that, Isabelle thought with a new burst of anger at the infuriating man. "You already have a school. And Edna and Marco and your uncles miss us."

"But I will miss Wes. And Abbey! Abbey sleeps with me, Mommy. She'll be sad if I go away."

Isabelle sighed. "The dog is not supposed to be sleeping in your bed."

"We sleep on my couch."

"Perfect," she muttered and threw the rest of Caro's clothes into the suitcase. A cab would be there to pick them up in twenty minutes, and the charter jet was waiting on the tarmac. Sometimes, she thought, it was good to be rich. At least she didn't have to wait for a commercial flight and chance having to deal with Wes again. "Go get your doll, sweetie."

"I don't want to leave Wes. And Abbey. And Tony. And Bobbi. And Sid."

Isabelle sighed. She hated putting Caro through this.

Hated even more that it was all her fault for coming to Texas in the first place. For risking so much. For wanting to believe that she and Wes could share a future as well as a past. She should have known better. But apparently, one heartbreak in a lifetime just wasn't enough for her.

"Mommy, I don't wanna go!" Hands were flying and Isabelle wondered how her daughter managed to shout in sign language.

"We have to go." My God, Isabelle could actually feel her patience dissolving. She understood what Caro felt, but there was nothing she could do to ease any of it. The best thing for all of them was to leave Texas as quickly as possible. Get back to normal. So she stooped to what all parents eventually surrendered to. Bribery. "When we get home, we'll get you the puppy you wanted, okay?"

Caro's little hands flashed like mad as her features twisted and her eyes narrowed. "Don't want another dog. Want Abbey."

Things had not improved from there. Caro had cried and pleaded and begged, then at last had resorted to not speaking to her mother at all. By that point, Isabelle had been grateful for the respite. But she knew that tomorrow morning when her darling daughter woke up, there was still going to be trouble.

"God, I'm an idiot," she muttered and sipped at the tea Edna had made for her. Not only was her daughter miserable, but Isabelle's own heart was breaking. How could she have been so stupid to love Wes again? To hope again?

"Oh, honey, you're in love," Edna said with a wave of her hand. "That makes idiots of all of us."

She lifted her gaze to the other woman. "I never should have let Caro's heart get involved. How could I have done that to my daughter?"

"She's *his* daughter, too, honey." Sighing, Edna added, "I know you don't want to hear it right now, but the fact is, he has a right to know her and a right for Caro to know him."

Disgusted with herself, Isabelle muttered, "Well, if you're going to use logic…"

Laughing now, her old friend said, "Take the tea up to your room. A couple brownies wouldn't hurt, either. Get a good night's sleep. There'll be plenty of time tomorrow to worry yourself sick over all this."

"Maybe I will," Isabelle said and stood up. She'd go to her room, but she knew she wouldn't be sleeping. Instead, she'd be lying awake, remembering the last time she'd seen Wes and the flicker of guilt she'd read in his eyes.

"Where the hell did it all go sideways?" he asked the empty room and then actually paused to see if the universe would provide an answer.

But there was nothing. Just his own circling thoughts and the relentless silence in the house. He'd never minded it before. Hell, he'd relished it. Having this big place all to himself—but for Bobbi—had been like an island of peace.

Now it was more like a prison.

And he paced the confines of it all night as any good prisoner should. He went from room to room, staring out windows, listening to his own footsteps on the wood floor. He let Abbey out and stood in the cold January night, tipping his head back to look at the ink-black sky with the bright pinpoints of stars glittering down at him. Then he and the dog, who was yet another female ignoring him, went back into the house and were stuck with each other.

And in the quiet, Wes remembered the meeting that morning. Remembered everyone talking about the merger and how the pictures of him and his family had saved the situation with PlayCo. Recalled that even he had talked about it.

Mostly though, he remembered the look on Belle's face when he caught up with her in the parking garage. The hurt. The betrayal. He took a breath, looked around his empty bedroom and knew what he had to do. Dawn was just streaking the sky when he picked up the phone.

"More news out of Texas this morning," the stock reporter on the TV said. "Renewed talks of a merger between Texas Toy Goods Inc. and PlayCo have ended. Again." The reporter smiled, checked her notes and continued. "This time though, it's Wes Jackson, CEO of Texas Toy Goods, who's backing away. Mr. Jackson confirmed the news earlier today. So far, Teddy Bradford hasn't been available for a comment."

Isabelle stared at the television as if she couldn't believe what she'd just heard. "Why would he do that? Why would he call off the merger?"

Chance stood in the middle of the room and shrugged. "Maybe he finally realized there are other things more important."

She looked at her oldest brother and wondered. About this time yesterday, she'd walked into Wes's office for a surprise picnic only to have the world fall out from beneath her feet. Now, it felt like it was happening all over again. What was she supposed to think? Why did he stop a merger that he'd been so determined to pull off? Did he expect her to see that report and come running back to him? Oh, God, what did it say about her that she *wanted* to?

The doorbell rang, and since Chance was up already, he said, "I'll get it. You stay here."

Her brothers had circled the wagons as soon as she came home. While Chance kept her company, Eli and Tyler were with Caro in the kitchen while she had lunch. It was good to have family. Especially when everything seemed to be going so wrong.

"Okay, thanks," she said, curling up on the couch to watch the financial reports, hoping for more of a clue as to what Wes was up to.

When she heard the argument from the front hallway, though, Isabelle jolted to her feet, one hand slapped to her chest, as though she could soothe her suddenly galloping heart. Two voices, raised.

"What're you doing here?" Chance demanded.

"I'm here to see Belle. And my daughter."

Wes's voice. Hard. Implacable. Her heart jumped again, and the pit of her stomach came alive with what felt like thousands of butterflies. She couldn't believe he was here. He'd come to her. Why? Isabelle turned to the doorway and stood completely still. Waiting.

"Get out of my way, Chance," Wes grumbled.

"I warned you once what would happen to you if you made either my sister or my niece cry."

"Don't try to stop me."

"You don't deserve them, you know."

"You're probably right," Wes said. "But they're my family and no one can keep me from them."

For a moment, Isabelle held her breath, shocked to the bone by what Wes had said.

"Don't blow this again," Chance warned.

A moment or two later, Wes was there, staring at her, and what she saw in his eyes stunned her. He'd always been so locked down. So emotionally distant that he was practically unreadable. But today, everything she'd ever dreamed of seeing was there, in his beautiful sea-green eyes.

Drawn by the loud argument, Eli and Tyler marched into the room, too, and Isabelle's three brothers formed a half circle behind Wes. Supportive? Threatening? She couldn't be sure, and at the moment, she didn't care. All she could see was Wes and all she felt was a rising sense of hope that fluttered to life in the center of her chest.

Wes didn't care about her brothers, either. He'd known before he arrived that he'd have to force his way past the Graystone wall of protection, and he'd been prepared for it. The brothers had given him a welcome as icy as the Colorado weather, but it didn't matter. He'd been willing to face anything to reach Isabelle.

Looking at her now, his heart thrummed in his chest and he took his first easy breath since the night before, when he'd found her gone and the world as he'd known it had ended. He crossed the room to her in a few long strides and stopped when he was within touching distance. God, he wanted to reach out to her, but there were things he had to say first. Things she needed to hear. Ignoring her brothers, he focused on the only woman he'd ever loved and started talking.

"I was wrong."

She blinked at him, and he read the surprise on her face.

Smiling sadly, he went on in a rush. "I know. I don't say that often. But I was stupid. Shortsighted. Stubborn. I never should have let you leave me five years ago. And I can't let you go now."

"Wes—"

"No," he said, quickly interrupting her. "Let me say this, Belle. Say what's needed saying for way too long."

She nodded, and he felt a wild flicker of optimism in his chest. He couldn't stop looking at her. Her beautiful eyes were wide with a mixture of disbelief and expectation. Her blond hair fell loose to her shoulders and the blue sweater she wore over jeans made her eyes look deeper, as if they held every secret in the universe.

Shaking his head, he began, "See, when my mother died, my father lived the rest of his life in misery. He never recovered, because he'd loved her too much." He reached out, laid both hands on her shoulders and smiled because he was there, with her again. This was the most important speech he'd ever make and he hoped to hell he'd find the right words. "I promised myself I'd never let a woman mean that much to me. It was a kid's reaction. A kid's vow—and it guided me most of my life. Yesterday though, I realized that I had never looked beyond my Dad's pain. But now I see that the happiness my father had before he lost my mom was worth the risk. Worth everything."

God, it sounded pitiful, even to him. He'd lived his life in fear. Love had had him running for years. And he'd never realized that by evading it, he'd been missing out on the best part of life. Well, no more.

"I love you, Isabelle," he said. "I loved you five years ago. I love you now. I will always love you."

She took a breath and swayed slightly in place, lifting one hand to her mouth. Absently, Wes heard her brothers leave the room, and he was grateful. He wanted privacy for this. For the most important moment of his life.

"I want to believe," she said, and he could see the truth of that in her eyes. "But how can I risk Caro's heart? She was devastated when we left yesterday. She cried herself to sleep last night."

He closed his eyes briefly and silently cursed. If he

hadn't been so stupid, he never would have hurt his child. Hurt the woman he loved. Created such a damn mess out of everything.

"It tears at me to hear that," he said. "But you can trust me, Belle." He looked into her eyes and willed her to see the truth. "You'll never be rid of me again. Even if you tell me to go away today, I'll just come back. I'll keep trying for however long it takes to convince you that you're all I want. All I need."

She bit her bottom lip, and tears welled in her eyes. Feeling hope lift like a helium balloon in his chest, Wes kept talking. "I called off the merger."

"I know. I saw it on the news. I couldn't believe it."

"Yes, you can. I put Teddy off. None of that matters to me anymore. The only merger I'm interested in is the one between us. Marry me, Belle. You and Caroline come home with me. Build a future and a family with me."

"Oh, Wes…"

He smiled now, because he could see that she believed. That she was going to say yes. "You can design toys for the company, and together, we'll make sure Caro's Toybox is big enough that every child around the world has a toy to play with and a stuffed animal to cuddle."

A short, choked laugh shot from her throat.

Now that he was on a roll, he just kept building on the future he could see so clearly. "I want more kids, Belle. Brothers, sisters for Caroline. I want us to build a family so strong, not even your hardheaded brothers could tear it down."

She laughed again, louder this time, and reached up to cup his face between her palms. He closed his eyes briefly and released the last of his worries. The heat of her touch sank into him, reaching down into the darkest, loneliest corners of his heart, and left him breathless.

"It's not my brothers you have to worry about, Wes," she said, with a slow shake of her head. "It's *me*. Because once I say yes, I'm never letting you go."

Wes grinned. "That is the best news I've ever heard. So are you saying yes?"

"How could I not? I love you, Wes. I always have. So yes, I'll marry you and have babies with you and build a future filled with family."

"Thank God," he whispered, then reached into his pocket. Showing her the small blue velvet box, he opened it to reveal a square-cut emerald surrounded by diamonds.

"It's beautiful," she whispered.

He slid it onto her finger. "*Now* it's beautiful."

Then he kissed her, and she melted against him while Wes gave silent thanks for whatever gods had blessed him with a second chance at the love of a lifetime.

"Hey, you two," Eli called out. "Come up for air. There's a little girl here who wants to say hi."

They broke apart, and Wes looked down into the shining face of his daughter. Caro was staring up at him with pleasure in her eyes and a delighted smile on her face. She wore the red plastic heart that had first started him out on the journey that had led him here to this amazing moment. Shooting a quick look at Belle, he grinned. "I can't believe you saved that necklace."

Her smile was soft, tender. "It was the first thing you ever gave me. And Caro loves it. She loves you too, Wes. It's time she knows who you are."

Nodding, Wes went down on one knee in front of his daughter. Weirdly, nerves rattled the pit of his stomach. "I missed you," he said and signed.

"Me too," she answered, then threw her arms around his neck.

The force of that hug freely given shook Wes to his

soul. Tears burned his eyes, so he closed them, reveling in the knowledge that he would never lose Belle and his daughter again. Then he pulled back, looked into her eyes and said softly, "I'm your father, Caro, and I love you very much."

Her eyes went wide and her mouth dropped open. She shifted her gaze to her mother and asked, "Really?"

"Really, baby," Belle said through her tears.

The little girl looked at Wes again and gave him a bright, happy smile. Her fingers flying along with the words pouring from her, she asked, "You're my daddy?"

"Yes," Wes said and signed.

"I wished that you were," she said, grinning now. "And my wish came true! I love you, Wes. I mean, *Daddy*."

His heart burst in a sweet blast of love and joy as Wes reached out to scoop her up and stand, still holding her close. Balancing his daughter on one arm he draped the other around Belle's shoulders and knew he'd never been more complete.

Completely shattered still as his daughter's simple words made him feel like the luckiest man on the face of the planet, he paid no attention to Belle's grinning brothers, still watching. He simply handed Caroline to her mother to free his hands and then he carefully signed, "I love you, too, baby girl."

Caroline clapped, Belle laughed and sighed all at once, and the Graystone brothers were applauding.

Wes wrapped his arms around his girls and told himself he was never letting go.

Back in Royal...

Brandee Lawless left her foreman in charge of the mare and her new foal and walked through her ranch house with a smile on her face. Though the birth had gone well, she wanted to email her vet, Scarlett McKittrick, to come give the new mother and baby a once-over.

She snatched her Stetson off, letting her long, wavy blond hair tumble free to the middle of her back. Shrugging out of her jacket as she walked toward her ranch office, Brandee grinned to herself. How could she not?

Everything was going great for her. After the tornado that had caused so much damage to the town of Royal and so many ranches—including her own—things were looking up. She'd rebuilt and now was bigger and better than ever, with plans for even more.

"Basically," she said aloud as she walked into her office and hit the light switch, "everything's coming up Brandee."

She laughed a little, sat down behind her desk and booted up the computer. A couple minutes later, she had her email open and scanned her inbox. But one particular email had her frowning as she read the subject line.

ARE YOU READY TO PLAY?

Wary, because she didn't recognize the sender—who the heck was Maverick? She opened the email and read the brief, yet somehow threatening missive.

You're next.

* * * * *

***

"You could show me your room."

She knew it was a bold thing to say, but she didn't care. She needed to convey her feelings, especially with how easily they were touching each other. "I've been wondering what your bedroom is like."

"That's a dangerous thought, Meagan."

"I can't help it." She looked into the depths of his eyes, nearly losing herself in them. They were the deepest, darkest, richest shade of brown, with tiny amber flecks that she hadn't noticed before now. "What have you been wondering about?"

"What it would feel like to kiss you."

"That's easy to find out." Meagan lifted her chin, inviting him to satisfy his curiosity.

Garrett hesitated, but only for a moment. Clearly, his willpower was at the brink. He tugged her even closer, lowered his head and put his lips warmly against hers.

Holy. Heaven. On. Earth.

Everything inside her went wonderfully weak.

* * *

Single Mum, Billionaire Boss
is part of the Billionaire Brothers Club series—
Three foster brothers grow up, get rich…
and find the perfect woman.

SINGLE MUM, BILLIONAIRE BOSS

BY
SHERI WHITEFEATHER

First Published in Great Britain 2017
By Mills & Boon, an imprint of HarperCollins*Publishers*
1 London Bridge Street, London, SE1 9GF

© 2017 Sheree Henry-WhiteFeather

ISBN: 978-0-263-92803-7

51-0117

Our policy is to use papers that are natural, renewable and recyclable products and made from wood grown in sustainable forests. The logging and manufacturing processes conform to the legal environmental regulations of the country of origin.

Printed and bound in Spain
by CPI, Barcelona

Sheri WhiteFeather is an award-winning, bestselling author. She writes a variety of romance novels for Mills & Boon and is known for incorporating Native American elements into her stories. She has two grown children who are tribally enrolled members of the Muscogee Creek Nation. She lives in California and enjoys shopping in vintage stores and visiting art galleries and museums. Sheri loves to hear from her readers at www.sheriwhitefeather.com.

One

At twenty-seven, Meagan Quinn was starting her life over. People often said they were going to, especially screwups like herself, but she meant it.

Really, truly meant it.

She'd spent nearly three years in prison for a crime she'd stupidly committed. She'd only been out for a week, and now here she was at the Ocean Cliff Hotel and Resort, preparing to finalize the details of her employment.

She exited her car and smoothed the front of her skirt, anxious about her appearance, hoping that she looked more composed than she felt. As she crossed the parking lot, a Southern California breeze stirred her long, straight dark hair and rustled the scarf attached to her blouse.

One of the terms of her release was that she had to have a job lined up, but this one hadn't come easily. The parole commission had considered the job carefully before they'd approved it because Garrett Snow, the billionaire who owned the resort and had offered to hire her, was one of Meagan's victims. She'd embezzled sixty thousand dollars from Garrett and his equally rich foster brothers. Basically, she'd nabbed twenty grand from each man from the accounting firm where she used to work.

A portion of her wages from this job would be used for restitution so she could pay back what she'd stolen. Her victims had arranged for it to go to their foster care charity, instead of it being returned directly to them. Regardless, Meagan wanted to make amends, to prove that she was reformed.

When Garrett had offered her this job, it had been through a written correspondence, simply stating that he was willing to give her a fresh start, if the parole commission agreed that she was ready to be released. But she still wasn't sure why Garrett had decided to help her to begin with. That part wasn't quite clear to her.

She just wished that she wasn't so darned nervous about coming face-to-face with him again. She'd done him wrong, and now she was at his mercy, trying to keep her heart from blasting its way out of her chest and splattering her pretty new blouse.

Meagan entered the hotel, clutching her purse and a manila envelope that contained her paperwork. She would be working here as a stable hand. The resort offered all sorts of luxuries, including horseback riding along the beach.

As she passed through the lobby, her boots sounded on the colorfully tiled floor. The overall decor consisted of painted woods, breezy fabrics and Native American accents. Garrett was a half blood from the Northern Cheyenne Nation. Meagan had the same tribal affiliation.

She headed down the hallway that led to Garrett's office and came to two big double doors. After taking a deep breath, she opened them and approached the male receptionist seated at a circular desk. He was young and trendy, maybe a college student, with buzz-cut blond hair and a neatly trimmed beard. He greeted her with a smile, and she gave him her name. He checked her appointment on the computer and instructed her to wait.

Meagan glanced around. The waiting area was big and bright, with magazines scattered on glass-topped tables. She sat on the edge of a printed sofa and placed the envelope on her lap, trying not to fidget. She was the only person there.

About ten minutes later, the receptionist escorted her to Garrett's private office and left her alone with him, closing the door with a soft and scary click.

Garrett gazed across the room at her, but neither of them spoke. He was standing beside his desk, dressed in a sharp gray suit and Western-style boots. His short black hair was combed straight back, making the angles of his handsome face more prominent. He was a well-built man, tall in stature, with wide shoulders. By now, he would be thirty-two years old.

The last time she'd seen him in person had been at her sentencing, and that was almost three years ago. She'd broken down and cried that day, apologizing for what she'd done, but he'd been unmoved by her tears. She remembered how stoic he'd looked then. He looked stoic now, too. She wasn't even sure why he was helping her now.

Finally he said, "Have a seat."

She thanked him and took the proffered chair.

He walked behind his desk. After a moment of silence, of squaring his shoulders and straightening his tie, he sat down, too. "Did you bring the forms?"

"Yes." She handed him the envelope, hating how awkward this was.

While he sifted through the papers, she thought about

how they'd become acquainted. On occasion, she'd caught sight of his foster brothers at the firm, slipping in to meet with their accountant. At the time, she hadn't yet seen Garrett, who was rumored to have a hard-edged nature. But she'd preferred it that way. By then, Meagan had already been stealing from all three men, and the last thing she'd wanted was to grow fond of any of them.

She and Neil, her longtime boyfriend, had plotted every aspect of the embezzlement, with Meagan taking the money so they could live a more glamorous life. But, in actuality, it was Neil who craved fancy things. Meagan, idiot that she was, just wanted Neil to love and adore her in the same blind-faith way that she'd loved and adored him.

Then, one day during her lunch hour at work, she came into contact with Garrett. She was sitting on the curb outside of the building, crying, on the heels of a telephone argument with Neil.

Garrett had approached her and asked if she was okay. She'd insisted that she was, but he'd plopped down beside her anyway, introducing himself and giving her the handkerchief from his pocket. It had seemed like something out of a movie, so gallant, so old-fashioned. The hard-edged billionaire was more human than she could have imagined.

He'd walked her back inside, and while they were saying goodbye in the lobby, he'd pilfered a daisy from one of the flower arrangements and presented it to her. She remembered clutching the fragile bloom and feeling horribly guilty about the money she'd already taken from him. And when she went home that night to Neil, Garrett Snow had been all she could think about.

She'd seen him a number of times after that, and every time he came to the accounting firm's office, he stopped by her desk to talk to her, treating her like a friend.

But she wasn't his friend. She'd stolen from him and allowed Neil to burn through the money, telling herself that she'd done it because she loved Neil. Yet, even in the midst of that supposed love, she'd been fighting warm and stirring feelings for Garrett.

He glanced up from the documents in his hands. "I'll send these over to HR later today, and you can start next Monday."

"Thank you." She tried for a smile, wishing that he would smile, too. Then again, maybe it was better that he was being so detached. His smile used to make her knees watery and weak. "I really need this job."

"I'm aware of your situation." He returned the paperwork to the envelope. "I heard that you had a baby while you were in prison, and that she's about two now."

"Yes, I have a sweet little daughter." Meagan had discovered that she was pregnant soon after she was incarcerated, throwing her already-damaged world for a loop. "Her name is Ivy."

"One of your brothers took custody of her, didn't he?"

Meagan nodded. "Yes. Tanner, and his fiancée, Candy, raised her while I was in prison. There was no one else who was willing or able to take her." Feeling ashamed, she paused before explaining, "Neil wasn't an option. He walked out on me before she was born. He's never even met her."

Garrett frowned. "Why didn't you implicate Neil in the crime when the cops suspected that he'd been involved?"

She answered as honestly as she could, hating how naive it was going to make her sound. "When I first got arrested, I thought that he would remain loyal to me if I protected him. I truly believed that he would wait for me."

Garrett didn't reply. Did he think she was a fool for trusting Neil? Or did he think she deserved it?

She explained further. "I told the police that Neil was under the impression that I'd come into the money through an inheritance. That was a lie, of course. He knew I'd embezzled it. He was involved from the start. But since there was no evidence against him, he was never charged with anything." She quickly added, "I'm grateful that Tanner was there. After Ivy was born, he and Candy used to bring her to visit me. It wasn't the same as seeing her every day, but it was better than not seeing her at all." Meagan had battled her insecurities, clinging to the future, desperate to form a stronger bond with her child. "I'm trying to make up for lost time and be the best mom I can be. My baby girl is just the most amazing kid."

Once again, Garrett didn't say anything.

But she prattled on. "Tanner was nervous about taking her at first because he was single then. He didn't become engaged until later. Of course now Ivy is really close to him and Candy. I even…" She stopped midsentence.

"You what?" he asked, prodding her to finish.

"Nothing." She couldn't bring herself to admit that she'd been so distraught and depressed in prison that she'd tried to talk Tanner and Candy into adopting Ivy. But thankfully they'd encouraged her to hold tight, knowing that she didn't really want to give up her baby.

Garrett leaned back in his chair, watching her with a taut expression. Whatever he was thinking or feeling didn't seem favorable.

She gazed across the desk at him. "I'm so sorry for what I did to you. And to your foster brothers."

His expression didn't change. "You already apologized at the sentencing."

"I know. But I wanted to say it again. Here and now."

She paused, a lump catching in her throat. "I was sorry at the sentencing, too, but I didn't understand who I was then." She was a different person today. Meagan had been to hell and back. "I've grown up. I've learned from my mistakes, and if I could take it back, I would."

"Yes, but you can't. What's done is done."

She sensed that he wasn't talking about the money but the callous way he'd been treated as the entire scenario unfolded. As wrong as they were, she couldn't explain her actions, not without delving into deeper issues, including her mixed-up attachment to him.

"You're right," she said. "I can't change it."

He nodded, and they both went quiet, the past stirring uncomfortably between them.

Then, after another beat of heart-shredding silence, she asked, "Why did you offer me this job?"

He shifted in his seat. "I stated the reason in the letter I sent to you. The same letter I submitted to the parole commission."

"Yes, I know. You claimed that you wanted to give me a second chance. But you don't seem like you really want to."

"Truthfully, none of this was my idea. My mom suggested it. She's the one who convinced me to hire you."

"Your real mom or one of your foster moms?" Meagan knew that he'd once been a foster child. But she didn't know much more than that.

"My real mom. She's always been part of my life, even when she wasn't able to take care of me. But that's a whole other story."

And one he seemed reluctant to share. "Why would your mom want to go to bat for me?"

"She saw you at the sentencing and felt bad for you, with the way you were crying and whatnot."

"Was she the lady who was sitting next to you?" Now that Meagan thought about it, she recalled an older woman who could have been related to him.

"Yes, that was her. So, anyway, later on, when you were coming up for parole, she did a little research on you. I guess you could call it a background check of sorts. She was curious to know more about you, and that's when she found out that you'd had a baby."

"So this is because of Ivy?"

"Your child's welfare is part of it."

So what was the rest of it? she wondered. Apparently, there were a lot of things he wasn't inclined to discuss. Regardless, she appreciated his mother's support. Meagan's mom had died a while back, and she missed her terribly. "Do you know that my mother is gone? That I lost her before any of this happened?"

"Yes." He didn't offer his condolences, but he spoke a little more softly. "It came up in the background check."

She struggled to blink away her emotions. "Will you tell me how I can contact your mom? I'd like to thank her for convincing you to hire me." Without this job, Meagan wouldn't have gotten paroled. "Maybe I can send her a card or something?"

Garrett shook his head. "I'll relay the message."

Clearly, he didn't want her associating with his mom, even if it was just to say thanks. But she could hardly blame him. Meagan was fresh out of prison, trying to prove that she could be trusted. She certainly wasn't going to press the issue.

"We have a day care center and an after-school program here for the children of our employees," he said, changing the subject.

"Is that something that will be available to Ivy?"

"Yes, absolutely. It's free, so it won't affect your income." He removed a sheet of paper from his desk drawer and handed it to her. "Here's more information about it. If you want to bring your daughter to the day care, just call them directly to arrange for her enrollment."

"Thank you." She folded the paper and slipped it into her purse. And when she glanced back up at Garrett, she noticed how intently he was gazing at her. Sometimes she used to wonder if he'd been as attracted to her as she'd been to him. If some of those confusing feelings had been mutual.

But none of that mattered now, she reminded herself. Meagan was only here to make a living and pay back the money she owed, not to rekindle her crush on Garrett.

"I'll be a good employee," she said, needing to reaffirm her intentions out loud. "I'll work hard."

A muscle in his jaw flexed. "I'm counting on it."

Yes, of course. He was expecting her to toe the line. Her parole officer was expecting the same thing. So was Meagan's family. She had a lot of people counting on her to make the right choices from now on.

She contemplated the position he'd offered her. "Can I ask you something?"

He nodded warily. Did he think her question was going to be personal?

She closed the latch on her purse, realizing that she'd left it open. Then she asked, "What made you decide on me being a stable hand? Is it because both of my brothers work in the horse industry, and you figured that I had knowledge of it, too?"

"That's pretty much it." He squinted at her. "Why? Do you have reservations about the job? Because you told the parole commission that you were qualified for it."

"My experience with horses was a long time ago, when I was a kid. I can still do the job, though. It won't be a problem."

He angled his head. "Are you sure?"

"I'm positive." She would be feeding, grooming and saddling the animals, as well as cleaning and maintaining the stalls and equipment. "I know what it entails." And she would bust her hump if she had to. "But I just thought I should tell you that my experience was limited to when I was younger."

While she waited for him to respond, she tried not to get intimidated. Especially with how drawn to him she'd once been. And still was, she thought.

"All right," he said. "I can give you a tour of the stables now if you'd like."

"Thank you. That would be great. I'm looking forward to seeing them."

He stood and removed his jacket, and her pulse zipped a bit too quickly. She needed to focus on her job and not on how he made her feel. She was going to work here, but she wasn't going to fall for Garrett again. She'd hurt him—and herself—enough already.

The stables were located on a grass-topped hill that overlooked the resort, with brush-lined trails leading to the beach. There were public paths that went into the hills, and beyond those trails, even higher up, on a private and gated road, was Garrett's house. This was his world, his sanctuary, and now he was lending it to a woman who'd played him for a fool.

According to his mother, he needed to forgive Meagan, to give her a chance to prove herself. Mom had all sorts of do-gooder reasons for believing it was the right thing to do.

Garrett had spent months thinking it through, and even now, he wasn't sure why he'd given in. Maybe it was because somewhere deep down, he wanted to believe that Meagan was capable of being reformed. Or maybe it was because she had a child to care for, and Garrett had a soft spot for kids.

He just wished that his mom had never dragged him into this mess. But she didn't know that he'd had romantic feelings for Meagan. No one knew, not even his foster brothers. To them, she was just someone who'd worked at their accountant's office.

But, to Garrett, she was someone he'd wanted to explore on a deeper level. If she'd been single, he would have asked her out. But since she was tied up with Neil, he'd been careful not to overstep his bounds. Of course, he'd been hoping that she was on the verge of leaving her loser boyfriend, the jerk who'd made her cry on the phone that first day, giving Garrett a chance to dash in like the knight he'd imagined himself to be.

A knight who'd gotten his armor crushed.

As they entered the barn, he glanced over at her. She was as beautiful as he remembered, with her almond-shaped eyes and long silky hair. She did seem more mature, though, far less flighty than before. Prison had changed her. Motherhood, too, he supposed. But were those changes he could trust? She might have become more conniving over the years, more charming, more of a seductress. Her sweet little apologies could be an act, and a damned good one at that.

He intended to keep a close eye on her. There was no way he was going to let her screw him over again.

Garrett spotted Tom Lutz, the barn manager, and motioned for him to come over and meet Meagan. Tom was a friendly old cowboy, short and stocky, with a big bushy mustache like the one Wyatt Earp used to wear. Once Meagan started working here, Tom would be her supervisor.

The introduction went well. Tom was his usual pleasant self, and Meagan was as sweet and humble as she'd been with Garrett back in his office. He sure as hell hoped it wasn't an act.

After a bit of chitchat, the old cowboy returned to work, leaving Garrett and Meagan alone once again.

"Tom seems really nice," she said.

"Yeah, he's as loyal as they come. He knows about your criminal history. I discussed it with him ahead of time. But he isn't going to hold it against you. The only thing that matters to him is that you do your job."

"Do the other employees at the stables know?"

"I haven't told them and neither has Tom. Nor do we plan to." Garrett didn't want it getting around. "But it's public record. So they might find out on their own. Or someone in HR might mention it and get tongues wagging. People gossip, even if they've been warned not to."

They stopped in the breezeway of the barn, and Garrett rolled up his shirtsleeves. He'd left his jacket back at his office, but he was still wearing his tie. He had a huge collection of them. He kept them in his closet, organized by color, the same as his suits.

Meagan's skirt was flowing softly around her ankles. Everything about her looked soft and touchable. Not that he ever intended to touch her.

She turned to pat the neck of a big bay gelding poking his head over his stall.

"That's Ho-Dad," Garrett told her.

She smiled. "That's an interesting name for a horse."

"It's an old surf term. It refers to anyone who pesters them when they're on their boards, and Ho-Dad likes surfers, sometimes a little too much. He would probably go surfing himself, if he could."

"Oh, that's cute." Her smile widened. "Can't you just see him out there?"

"In a wet suit? That wouldn't be a pretty sight." Garrett just wished that Meagan wasn't so damned pretty. He didn't need the distraction.

She gave the bay another affectionate pat, and he noticed how gently she handled the animal. Ho-Dad was enthralled with her already.

"Do you like to ride?" Garrett asked.

"Surfboards?" She laughed a little. Ho-Dad was craning his neck to get closer to her. "Oh, you mean horses? I haven't ridden since I was a kid. Ivy loves being in the saddle, though. Tanner puts her up on his horses with him. It's been good for me to see her enjoying it so much. It was tough for me when I was little."

"What was? Being around horses?" He was curious, far more than he should be. But he still wanted to know exactly what she meant.

She turned away from Ho-Dad, giving Garrett her full attention. "Yes, being around horses became difficult, especially after my baby sister died and my parents got divorced."

"You had a sister?" As far as he knew, his mom hadn't uncovered that bit of information. If she had, she would've mentioned it to him, particularly with how determined she was in this whole forgive-Meagan affair.

She took an audible breath. "It was a terrible time for my family. Mom fell apart, and Dad got even meaner." She glanced at the gelding. "Dad never appreciated horses the way Mom did. In fact, he hated that she and us kids shared the interest. So after the divorce, I took less of an interest in horses, hoping that Dad would be nicer to me. But it didn't make a difference. On occasion I still rode with Mom, just so she didn't feel so neglected. Then, as time went on, I stopped riding altogether because Dad was still trashing us for it."

Garrett had never really thought about the kind of childhood Meagan might've had. But it wasn't his concern. Still, it bothered him that her dad seemed like such a prick. "Your old man sounds like a piece of work."

"I never should've tried to be a daddy's girl. Not after how he treated my mother."

Garrett debated whether to tell her that his mom and her mom had been loosely connected, that they'd actually belonged to the same Native American women's group when they were younger, even if they'd barely known each other.

No, he thought. He wasn't going to say anything. His mom was already making too big of a deal out of it, and he didn't want Meagan blowing it out of proportion, too.

She cleared her throat. "None of us have anything to do with Dad anymore. Not me or my brothers. I'm not even sure if he knows that I went to prison or that I have a daughter. But he probably wouldn't care, anyway."

"You should start riding again and stick with it this time."

"That's what Tanner said. But he's biased, especially with how much Ivy loves it."

"I keep my horses here. They're on the other side of the barn. I ride nearly every day, so you'll be seeing me around, sometimes in the mornings, other times in the afternoons, depending on my schedule. You can ride here, too, if you want to take it up again. That's a perk that comes with working at the stables. You can use any of the horses that belong to the hotel."

"Thank you. I'll think about it." She smiled at Ho-Dad. He was pestering her to pet him again.

After the tour ended, Garrett and Meagan went back outside, with the grass beneath their feet and the sun shining through the trees.

She glanced around. "It's so pretty here." She looked

higher up the hill. "Oh, wow. There's a house up there, all by itself."

Well, hell, Garrett thought. He couldn't very well leave his home out of this. She would find out sooner or later that he resided on the property. "That's where I live. I had it custom-built."

She glanced at him and then back up the hill. "I should have guessed it was yours. It's like a castle that overlooks your kingdom."

He downplayed her words. He didn't like to think of himself that way. "It's just a beach house."

"Well, it looks spectacular, even from here."

Garrett didn't thank her for the compliment. Someday he hoped to have a wife and kids to live there with him. Only he'd yet to find someone who loved him for himself and not his money.

But that was the last thing he wanted to think about, especially while he was in the presence of the beautiful young woman who'd ripped him off. He wasn't going to let her sad story sway him, either. So she'd had a troubled childhood. So had he, but he hadn't become a criminal. Or an ex-con or whatever the hell she was now.

He took her back to the hotel, and they parted ways, with Garrett doing his damnedest to forget about her.

But when he returned to his office, she was still on his mind, burning a fiery hole right through it.

Two

What a day, Meagan thought. But she'd gotten through it. She'd seen Garrett and secured her new job. Still, she was feeling the aftereffects of having been in his company.

And now she needed to go home and decompress. These days, she lived in a guesthouse on Tanner's property, a far cry—thank goodness—from the correctional institution.

She climbed into her car and pulled out of the parking lot. Once she got on the main road, the traffic was heavy, the sights and sounds quick and noisy. Meagan had grown up in LA, but, since she'd gotten out of prison, she felt like a tourist, gawking at the city that surrounded her. Being free was a strange and wondrous feeling. But it was confusing, too. Everything felt different, somehow.

When she arrived at her destination, she parked in front of the main house, a bungalow built in the 1930s, where her brother and Candy resided. With its stucco exterior, brick chimney and stone walkway, it had tons of curb appeal.

Meagan's place, a guesthouse in the back, was just as charming. She even had her own little courtyard that included a patch of grass, a smattering of flowers and a fountain with a naked putto, a Cupid of sorts, who appeared to be peeing in the water. Most people would call it a cherub, but she knew the difference. Cherubs were angels, hailing from heaven, and putti were mythical beings who misbehaved. In that respect, Meagan could relate.

She noticed that Candy's car was missing from the driveway, which meant she was still out and about. She'd taken Ivy grocery shopping with her this afternoon. Tanner was at work and wouldn't be home until later.

For now, Meagan was all alone. She took the side entrance to her house and opened the gate.

She unlocked the front door, went inside and placed her purse on the kitchen table. Next she wandered into Ivy's room. It was fully furnished and decorated in a fairy-tale theme, but Ivy wasn't occupying it yet. Although Ivy had gotten to know Meagan from the prison visits, she'd thrown a panicked fit when they'd tried to move her in with Meagan. Bedtime was the worst. Her daughter absolutely refused to sleep there. So, for the time being, Ivy was still living with Tanner and Candy.

It made Meagan feel like a failure as a mother. But she needed to be patient and give her child time to adjust. It had only been a week.

Meagan went into her own room and heaved a sigh. She sat on the edge of the bed and pulled off her boots.

Barefoot, she returned to the kitchen and checked the microwave clock. To keep herself busy, she brewed a cup of herbal tea and sat in the courtyard. The water from the fountain flowed from tier to tier, making rain-like sounds.

After a short while, she heard a car pull into the driveway. Meagan hopped up and headed over to it.

Candy was just getting out of the driver's side, looking as gorgeous as ever. She was a long, leggy brunette, a former beauty queen and model who'd become a yoga teacher. She and Tanner used to date when they were teenagers. At the time Meagan was only eight, but she'd adored Candy, impressed that her brother was seeing someone so sweet and pretty.

Then, after their baby sister died and their parents started going through the divorce, Tanner couldn't handle having a girlfriend anymore, so he'd broken up with Candy.

Now all these years later, they were back together and engaged to be married. Who knew it would turn out this way? Meagan certainly hadn't seen it coming, especially the part where she ended up in prison while the couple helped raise her child.

Candy walked around to the passenger's side of the vehicle and removed Ivy from the safety seat. Meagan had one in the backseat of her car, too. Tanner had bought two of them, so they didn't have to switch the same one out all the time.

Ivy was dressed in a bright red romper with her silky brown hair fastened into fancy pigtails sitting high atop her head, twisted and parted in clever ways. Meagan didn't have a clue how to fix her baby's hair like that. It was all Candy's doing.

Ivy glanced over and grinned, waving at Meagan. She wanted to melt on the spot. She waved back, excited by the acknowledgment. Her daughter was the most precious person on earth.

Candy turned and saw Meagan, and they exchanged a smile. Then Candy asked, "How'd the job meeting go?"

"Good. I'll fill you in later, when we're able to sit and talk." Meagan came forward and reached for Ivy. "I can take her now."

"Sure." Candy passed the toddler off. "I'll get the groceries."

"I can help with those, too." Meagan balanced her daughter on her hip, took one of the bags and headed for the back door of the main house.

Once they were inside, she set Ivy down and Candy's dog, a yellow Labrador named Yogi, came into the room.

"Yoey!" Ivy raced toward her canine friend. "See, Mommy? Yoey?"

"Yes, sweetheart, I see her." She loved hearing her daughter mispronounce the dog's name, but she loved hearing her say "Mommy" even more. Ivy had been taught from the beginning who Meagan was. She was too young to grasp it completely, but she liked looking at pictures of animals with their offspring. She knew there were all types of mommies. And daddies, too. That much, she understood.

"Where Tanny?" Ivy asked, using the name she'd learned for Tanner. For Candy, she used Canny.

"Your uncle is at work," Meagan replied.

"Horsey," the child confirmed.

Meagan nodded. "Yes, he works with horses." Tanner owned a riding academy and stables near Griffith Park. He also leased horses to the movie industry. He rode Western and English styles, and Ivy was fascinated with his job.

"I work with horses now, too," Meagan said.

Ivy cocked her head. "Mommy horsey?"

"I'll be taking care of them." At the resort owned by one of the men she'd embezzled from, she thought. But that wasn't something she could tell her daughter. Ivy didn't know that the place where she used to visit Meagan was a prison, and even if she did, it wouldn't have meant anything to her. Someday it would, though. Once Ivy got older, it would be a discussion they were destined to have.

After the groceries were put away, Candy gave Ivy a sippy cup with milk in it, and the child sat on the floor with Yogi, drinking her beverage and pretending to do yoga. Or maybe she was actually doing it for real, to the best of her ability. The dog got into some poses with her.

Besides regular yoga, Candy also taught doga, yoga for dogs, where the animals exercised with their owners, and Yogi knew her stuff.

Meagan watched her daughter, smiling as Ivy concentrated on her task. She was proud of her little girl but intimidated by how strong Candy's influence was on her. Ivy mirrored the other woman's mannerisms, not Meagan's.

Then again, did she really want Ivy to emulate her? Meagan was still working on becoming the kind of person who would make her daughter proud, and Candy was already an elegant role model. Even as casually as she was dressed, in leggings and an oversized T-shirt, she exhibited grace and style. As a child, Meagan had wanted to grow up to be just like her. Boy, had she missed the mark on that one.

Candy removed a pitcher of lemonade from the fridge. "Want some?"

Meagan nodded. "Sure. Thanks." There was a lemon tree on the property, so it was fresh-squeezed juice.

Candy poured two frosty glasses. Meagan accepted hers, and they sat in the living room, where Ivy and Yogi played.

"You can fill me in now," Candy said.

"Yes, of course. It turned out fine, but I was super nervous seeing Garrett again. He admitted that it wasn't his idea to hire me. His mother convinced him to give me a chance."

"Really?" Candy angled her head. "She must be a nice lady."

"I've never met her. I got a glimpse of her at the sentencing, though. He said that she felt bad for me then, and me having a baby while I was in prison was part of it, too. I guess that affected her somehow. I asked Garrett if I could send her a thank-you card, but he's going to relay the message instead."

"What about the other men? Did you see them?"

"His foster brothers? No. They weren't at this meeting. They don't own the hotel with him. They have their own businesses. One of them is a real estate mogul, and the other one is an internet entrepreneur."

"What type of person is Garrett?"

Meagan drew a breath. "He's…" She couldn't think of the right adjectives to describe him, not without her heart going a little haywire. She'd never told anyone that she used to have feelings for him. Finally she settled on, "He used to be really kind to me."

Candy frowned. "He isn't being kind to you now?"

"He was proper and professional. A bit cautious, I suppose. But he used to go out of his way to treat me like a friend."

"That's confusing."

"What do you mean?"

"Why, of all people, did you embezzle from a man who was good to you? Not that you should steal from anyone, but to choose him? I don't get it."

"I took the money before I met him."

"And afterward?"

"I didn't take any more money, but it was already too late by then. He was really nice to me until he found out what a traitor I was. He even gave me a daisy." She explained how she'd first met him, reciting the details. She left out the part about being attracted to Garrett, though. She didn't think it was wise to mention that. Besides, she didn't want anyone figuring out that she was still having those types of feelings for him. Nonetheless, she admitted how important the daisy had been to her. "I kept the flower for a while. I wrapped it in plastic and tucked it away in my drawer. Neil didn't pay attention to stuff like that. But I finally got rid of it, because every time I looked at it, it made me feel worse about what I'd done."

Candy had a sympathetic expression. "Have I ever told you about the language of flowers?"

Meagan shook her head. "Not that I recall."

"It's called floriography, and it's a method that was used in the Victorian era when people would exchange flowers in lieu of written greetings. I became really fascinated with it, and I taught your brother about it, too. Each flower has a meaning, so you can give someone a single bloom or an entire bouquet to express a certain sentiment or have conversations. I studied a book about it."

"That does sound fascinating." Curious, Meagan asked, "Do you know what daisies mean?"

"Yes, but it depends on what kind they are. English daisies are the most recognizable. They're sometimes called common daisies. But there are other kinds, too."

"I don't know what type it was, except that it was bigger than the usual ones."

"Here." Candy reached for an iPad sitting on a nearby table and gave the device to Meagan. "See if you can find it."

She did an internet search, scrolling through the different varieties until she found the right kind. She noticed how bright and pretty the flowers were and how many colors they came in. Hers had been yellow with double florets. She turned the screen around. "It was a gerbera, like this."

Candy looked at the picture and said, "Those embody

friendship. But they can mean sadness and someone need-ing protection, too."

"All of that works." The sadness Meagan had been feel-ing that day, the friendship Garrett had offered, the pro-tection she'd needed from her crazy life with Neil. She doubted that Garrett knew any of this. Still, the fact that he'd given her a flower with those meanings gave her goose bumps.

Candy took back the iPad and set it aside. "Isn't it funny how things like that present themselves?"

"Yes." A strange kind of funny. Now she wished that she hadn't disposed of the daisy. If she'd held onto it, it would have been stored with the rest of her belongings. Tanner had kept Meagan's things for her, along with items that had belonged to their mother.

Feeling far too emotional, she glanced at her daughter. Ivy was still playing with the dog, stretching out on the floor and lifting her stubby little legs in the air.

Candy watched the child, too. Then she said, "Tanner and I are going to set the date for the wedding. As you know, we've been waiting to get married so you could be there, and now that you're home, we figured we should start planning it. I want you to be one of my bridesmaids, and I promise I won't make you wear an ugly dress." The bride-to-be smiled. "We'll choose something that you feel glamorous in."

Meagan hadn't felt glamorous in a very long time. "What about a dress for you? It's going to be your special day. That's the dress that really matters."

"Will you help me shop for it?"

"Yes, of course. I'd love to. And I'm honored that you want me to be in your wedding."

"Ivy and Yogi are going to be in it, too. They're both going to be flower girls. I figured that they could walk down the aisle together, but if Ivy falters and runs ahead, that's okay. Tanner and I want the ceremony to be fun."

Meagan smiled, warmed by the thought. She glanced at her daughter again, overwhelmed by how beautiful she was. "That's sweet, and I'm sure Ivy will love it."

Candy sent her a comforting look. "It won't be long before she gets comfortable staying at your house, Meagan."

"Do you think so?"

"Yes, I'm sure of it. You're an amazing mother, and she's going to need you more and more as time goes on."

"Thank you. That means a lot to me."

"Do you want to stay for dinner tonight?" Candy asked. "Or would you rather go back to your place and unwind?"

"I'd like to stay." Being in a family setting felt good, and Meagan knew how important it was for her to spend as much time with Ivy as possible. "After dinner, I can bathe Ivy and read her a story and tuck her in." They weren't living together yet, but that didn't mean she couldn't be part of her child's bedtime. "I should probably start doing that every night, so she gets used to me putting her to bed."

"That's a great idea." Candy shifted her gaze, glancing in the direction of the kitchen. "I'll make a chicken-and-rice casserole for you and Tanner and Ivy."

"That sounds good. But what are you going to eat?" Her brother's fiancée was vegetarian.

"I'll whip up a spinach soufflé. Of course you guys can eat that, too."

"Does Ivy like spinach?"

"It's one of her favorites."

"That's good to know." Meagan was just learning how to interact with her daughter on a daily basis and that included becoming accustomed to her food habits. "I can help with the meal. I'm out of practice, but I like to cook."

"Did your mom teach you?"

"Yes." Meagan turned toward the fireplace, where a framed photo of her mother was, amid a grouping of other pictures. "I miss her every day."

Candy sighed. "I had a difficult relationship with my mom when I was growing up, but things are good between us now. She adores Tanner and Ivy. She can't wait for me to have kids of my own, too. Whenever she babysits Ivy, she mentions it."

"I'm glad that Ivy is inspiring her to want grandbabies." Meagan knew that Candy had been pregnant once and had miscarried, but that was years ago, when she was married to someone else—a man who hadn't treated her right.

In that respect, Meagan and Candy were alike. They'd both survived controlling relationships. But now Candy had Tanner, the love of her life and the person she was meant to be with.

If the possibility existed, Meagan hoped that someday she would find someone special, too. But at this stage of her life, she was a single mother and brand-new parolee, taking one step at a time on the road to redemption.

In the evening, when Meagan's brother came home from work, Ivy was thrilled to see him.

The instant he opened the door she dashed over to him, calling his name as she knew it. "Tanny! Tanny!"

He scooped her up and gave her a loud smacking kiss. The child giggled and looped her arms around his neck.

Meagan lingered in the background and watched the exchange. At six-three, Tanner was a striking man, with short black hair and slate-gray eyes. Today he was dressed in Western riding gear. He was a darned fine uncle. He'd earned Ivy's love and respect.

Candy heard the commotion and came around the corner, moving forward to greet her fiancé. He kissed her, as well, only it wasn't as noisy as the playful peck he'd bestowed upon Ivy.

"Hey, sis," Tanner said, when he noticed Meagan standing there. "How'd the job stuff go?"

She stepped forward, keeping her response simple. "Good. I'll be starting on Monday."

He smiled and shifted Ivy in his arms. "You're going to do great."

Putting on a brave front, she returned his smile. But deep inside, her nerves were fluttering, a reminder of how working at Garrett's resort was making her feel. "I'm certainly going to try."

"Meagan is staying for dinner," Candy said. "She helped me cook. We've got casseroles in the oven."

"Cool." Tanner sounded pleased. "We can all hang out together." He put Ivy on her feet, and the child toddled off to dig through a basket of toys that was in the living room.

Tanner disappeared, probably to shower and change, and Candy bustled around, setting the table and filling the water glasses.

"Can I help with anything else?" Meagan asked her.

"No, thanks. I've got it under control. You can just relax."

"Okay. Then I'll stay right here." Meagan sat on the floor next to her daughter, using the extra time to try to keep bonding with her.

Ivy reached into the basket and removed a pink plastic pony that had a long purple mane and a green tail. Clipped onto its back was a polka-dotted saddle.

She gave the toy to Meagan and said, "Pay." It was her way of saying, "Play."

Meagan gently obliged. She walked the pony in a slow circle, and Ivy watched it go round and round.

The two-year-old looked a lot like Meagan, with her

dark hair and naturally tanned complexion. She didn't favor blond, blue-eyed Neil, which was just as well. Meagan hadn't seen him since he'd left her, pregnant and alone. He was still somewhere in the area, she suspected. He thrived on the LA club scene. Meagan had done her fair share of partying when she was with Neil, but all she wanted was stability now.

Ivy extended her hand, asking for her pony. "Mine."

Meagan returned it, and the little girl trotted it high in the air, as if it were climbing a magical hill.

Instantly, Meagan thought about Garrett and his ocean-cliff home. She assumed that he'd never been married or had kids. But she couldn't be sure. She didn't know anything about his personal life. She wondered about him and the types of women he dated. As for herself, Neil had been her first and only lover, but she used to fantasize about Garrett something fierce.

"Is everything okay? You seem preoccupied."

She glanced up and saw Tanner staring at her with a concerned look on his face. He'd just returned to the living room, attired in sweatpants and a T-shirt.

She couldn't tell her brother what she'd been thinking. Her thoughts of Garrett were her own, particularly when they concerned sexy things.

"I'm just getting hungry," she said.

"Then you're in luck." Tanner motioned to the kitchen, where Candy was putting the finishing touches on the salad and taking the casseroles out of the oven.

They sat at the dining room table, and Meagan snapped a bib around Ivy. The toddler was raring to go. She even brought the pony with her, setting it on her high chair tray.

Ivy ate both casseroles, quite happily. Dessert, a creamy chocolate pudding, made her even happier. Meagan kept wiping her daughter's mouth and hands. She cleaned the pony, too. Ivy was making a gleeful mess feeding it, as well.

"I can bring Ivy with me when I go to work," Meagan said to Tanner and Candy. "The resort offers free day care and after-school programs for children of the employees. I'm going to check it out and hopefully get her enrolled by Monday."

"That sounds great," her brother replied. "I think it'll be good for Ivy to be in that type of setting, especially with you being nearby."

"I agree," Candy said. "I think Ivy will enjoy it. She likes playing with other kids. I'll miss having her with me every day, but you need to do what's right for yourself and your daughter."

"Thank you." Meagan was glad that everyone approved of the idea. "I appreciate your support."

"I'd like to meet Garrett sometime." Tanner took a second helping of the chicken-and-rice casserole. "He sounds like a pretty decent guy, offering something like that." He turned toward Meagan. "It was decent of him to hire you, too."

Yes, it was, she thought. Even if it had been his mother's idea, he'd still followed through and given her a job. "He told me that I can ride at the resort any time I want."

"Then you should take him up on it." Tanner spoke softly. "You know I'd like to see you get back on a horse. You're always welcome to ride at my stables, too."

"I know. It might be easier at the resort, though, since I'll already be there for work. And I like the atmosphere." She'd always loved the sand and surf. When she was a teenager, like a slew of other California girls, she used to go the beach with her friends. "If I'm going to ride again, maybe I should start there."

Her brother encouraged her. "So go for it."

Would she come across Garrett on the trail? Would she pass him along the shore? "I'm considering it." Before her nerves ran away with her, she added, "But I don't want to jump into anything too soon."

"You'll be ready when the time comes."

"I hope so." Especially if it involved seeing Garrett. Already she was anxious about their next encounter and how it would unfold. He'd told her that he spent a lot of time at the stables. So one way or another, she had to get used to seeing him.

Tanner went quiet, returning to his food. Meagan lifted her fork and raised it to her mouth, trying to concentrate on her meal, too. But above all else, she needed to clear her troubled mind.

And stop worrying about Garrett.

Three

Garrett headed toward the child care center at the resort. He promised himself that he was going to keep an eye on Meagan, to see what type of person she truly was, so he decided to be there when she dropped her kid off.

Today was Meagan's first day on the job, and he'd learned from HR that she'd enrolled her daughter in the day care. So why shouldn't he be curious to see her with her child, especially on this very first day?

Besides, it wasn't as if he'd never popped over to the day care before. He actually did it quite often. This was his resort, his place of business, and he was a hands-on CEO. He made a point of checking on every department to make sure that things were running smoothly, to speak to everyone employed there. He knew the day care teachers by name. He liked being around the kids, too. When he was in foster care, some of the younger children used to come to him for comfort and support. Sometimes it was for something as simple as a skinned knee. On occasion, it was far more serious, like bullying. He used to look out for Max, his tech-geek foster brother, when Max had been too small and skinny to fend for himself. Garrett was good at protecting the rights of others. He handled his own rights just fine, too.

He sat on a bench in the atrium where the day care was located and sipped his coffee out of a disposable cup. Every workday morning, he got a medium-bodied roast with a dash of milk from the coffee vendor in the food court in the hotel.

Here we go, he thought. His timing was impeccable. He spotted Meagan entering the atrium and holding her daughter's hand. He couldn't help smiling to himself. Her kid was a cute little tyke, toddling along in a denim outfit and pink cowboy boots. In her free hand, she clutched a heart-shaped purse with cartoon characters on it, swinging it as she moved. She walked with a bounce in her step, a ribbon-wrapped ponytail exploding from the top of her head. Meagan was in denim, too, but she looked far more serene in her Western wear. Her long thick hair was plaited into a single braid that hung down her back, and her boots were a neutral shade of brown. She had a hell of a figure. Her jeans cupped her rear like nobody's business.

She glanced over, and their gazes met across the open space. Garrett stood and tossed his empty cup into a recycle bin.

He walked over to her, and they faced each other, with sunlight spilling down over them, courtesy of the glass roof above their heads.

"I wanted to be here when you brought your daughter to the day care," he said, being as honest as the moment would allow.

Meagan seemed taken aback. Clearly, she hadn't expected his intrusion to be so deliberate. But she recovered quickly and focused on her child. She said to the little girl, "Ivy, this is Garrett. He gave me my job. The one I told you about before, where I'll be working with horses."

The toddler released her mother's hand. Puckering her tiny face, she stared up at Garrett and made an empty gesture, like an actress playing to an audience. "Where horsies?"

Instantly amused by her, he motioned toward a window. "They're outside in the stables." He got down on one knee, putting himself at her level, and asked, "Do you like horses?"

She nodded vigorously and tugged at the Velcro on her purse. Once she got it open, she removed a toy pony and showed it to him. The purse was given to Meagan to hold on to.

Garrett studied the pony and smiled. It looked like a rainbow had thrown up on it, spewing all sorts of colors. "That's the fanciest mare I've ever seen."

"Horsie mine." She pointed to herself. "Iby."

He smiled again and then exchanged a glance with Meagan.

Her mother said, "She can't quite say her name yet. She mispronounces other things, too. But mostly, she has really good language skills for a child her age. She comprehends well, and she's learning new words every day."

"She's beautiful," he replied. "Aren't you, Ivy?"

Proving how much she loved her pony, the animated toddler held it a few inches from her lips and made a kissy sound. Then she brought it about the same distance from Garrett's lips, so he could air-kiss it, too. He laughed and mimicked the sound she'd made. He was totally smitten with this kid.

She pulled the pony away from him and said, "Horsie

eat." She pretended the toy was wolfing something down. "See, Mommy?" She looked back at her mother.

"Yes, I see. And I remember that the pony had dinner with you last night." Meagan turned to Garrett and said, "The pony got a bubble bath afterward, too. She had chocolate pudding on her face."

"That's my kind of horse." He tugged Ivy's ponytail and got to his feet, coming to his full height.

Garrett and Meagan made direct eye contact again. He was doing his damnedest not to be as smitten with the mother as he was with the child. To keep his priorities in check, he reminded himself that this was the woman who'd acted all sweet and innocent, even after she'd ripped him off.

"You're good with kids," she said.

"I've always liked children."

"You don't have any, do you?"

He shook his head. He wasn't about to admit that he wanted a houseful. That wasn't anything she needed to know.

"I didn't think so, but I wasn't sure. I guess it's safe to assume you've never been married, either."

"Yes, that's a safe assumption." He'd been looking for the right mate, but so far he hadn't found her. Sometimes he got burned out believing it would happen. His last relationship had ended badly, with his former lover storming out of his life because he wouldn't invest in a half-baked business venture of hers. "Jake is married now, though, with a baby on the way." He added, "You remember Jake," saying it as a not-so-subtle reminder that she'd stolen from him, too.

"Yes, of course." Meagan looked guilty as charged. "He's one of your foster brothers."

Garrett felt something poke his leg. It was Ivy, jabbing

him with the pony as she waved the toy around. He relaxed his posture, not wanting the child to absorb the tension he'd just created between himself and her mom.

He softened his voice. "Jake and his wife are having a girl."

"When is the baby due?"

"I'm not sure of the exact date. It's still a few months away. They're over the moon about it. Jake is excited about being in the delivery room. He wants to cradle his daughter the moment she's born."

"That's nice." Even though Meagan smiled, her eyes were edged with pain. "That's how it should be."

Was she thinking about the way in which she'd given birth to her own child? Garrett didn't know if Ivy had been born at the prison itself or if Meagan had been taken to a hospital. Whichever way it happened, he couldn't fathom it. He was sorry if she'd had a rough time of it, but he couldn't bring himself to say those words out loud. Yet he couldn't stay completely silent, either. He felt compelled to say something, if just to keep the conversation going.

He settled on "Jake was a little freaked out at first. He never expected to get married or have kids. He understood what was at stake, that being a parent is the most important job in the world. But I'm sure you already know that."

"Yes, I do." She reached down and scooped up her daughter, holding her close.

Ivy put her head on her mother's shoulder and grinned at Garrett. Then she dropped her pony and said, "Uh-oh."

Little devil. He could tell that she'd done it on purpose. He picked up the toy and handed it to her. Already she had a way with men. No doubt she'd gotten it from her mother.

The kid made an impish face and dropped it again.

"Ivy," her mom gently scolded.

He retrieved the toy a second time. He just couldn't seem to resist.

"Sorry." Meagan set Ivy on her feet.

"It's okay." He gave the child her pony. She was just too damned clever for her own good. They both were.

"Thank you," Meagan said. She urged her daughter to say it, as well. "Tell Garrett thank you."

Ivy obliged with "Tank you, Garry."

His heart melted, all the way to his toes. "You're welcome." He gazed at Meagan, laughed a little and said, "I guess I'm Garry now."

"She calls my brother Tanny and his fiancée Canny. A friend of theirs has a son who called them that when he was first learning to talk, so they taught Ivy to refer to them that way, too." She smiled. "But you just got your nickname all on your own."

"Like a guy who's been knighted?" He made a sweeping bow. "Well done, Princess Ivy."

The toddler stared up at him, and Meagan said, "Oh, that's so sweet, you calling her that. I named her after a princess in a children's book. I read the book when I was in elementary school, and I always remembered the name."

"It suits her." She was a regal kid, with her pink boots, painted pony and long, spiky eyelashes.

"I better get her to the day care." Meagan took Ivy's hand. "Do you want to go inside with us?"

"Sure. Why not?" He could have made an excuse to dash off, but he'd come here to observe Meagan with her daughter, so he might as well see it through to the end. "I like visiting the center."

It went well, with Ivy's teacher showing her around. The toddler seemed excited until she realized that she was going to be left there, without Meagan. She cried and clung to her mother's leg. Both Meagan and the teacher attempted to reassure her, but she wasn't having it. She kept bawling.

Garrett intervened, asking Ivy if she wanted to play blocks with him. She refused, but he didn't give up. He sat on a carpeted section of the floor with some of the other kids, hoping she would get curious and join the party.

Eventually, her sniffles and tears subsided and she wandered over to him. He handed her one of the blocks, which he'd saved exclusively for her, and her eyes grew big and wide. The block had a picture of a horse on it. A lot of them had images of animals. Some had numbers and letters, too.

Meagan stood off to the side and watched him as if he were some sort of hero. He could have kicked himself for it.

He didn't need her admiring him, or getting close to him, or using her beautiful charms and pulling him under her spell.

Finally, when Ivy was chattering with another little girl and stacking the blocks like an architect, Garrett got up from the floor.

"That was wonderful of you," Meagan said to him. "I never anticipated her crying like that."

"She seems okay now."

"Thanks to you."

He shrugged, making light of it, even if there was heaviness inside him. "It's all in a day's work."

"I hope she's going to be okay for the rest of the day."

"She'll be fine." He almost offered to come back and check on her, but he'd already taken this further than he should have. "You can stop by on your lunch hour to see her. Lots of the other parents do that."

"I definitely will. Thank you for everything, Garrett."

"You don't have to keep thanking me."

"You've just done so much to help, with the job and now with Ivy."

Garrett didn't reply. Her daughter's tears had affected him more than he cared to admit. It reminded him of the younger kids who used to cry in foster care.

Ivy turned and waved at her mother, giving her permission to leave, and he and Meagan walked out of the day care together.

"Oh, my goodness," she said, as soon as they were free of the place. "My first experience with taking my baby to school."

Garrett merely nodded. He could tell she was struggling not to break down, but her eyes had turned teary nonetheless. He considered giving her his handkerchief, the way he'd done when they'd originally met. But he refrained from making the gesture. By now, he was supposed to know better.

While he steeled his thoughts, she dabbed at the corners of her eyes with the tips of her knuckles, as if she were trying to wipe away the evidence of her emotions and look stronger than she felt. Only it wasn't working. She still seemed fragile.

But Meagan's vulnerability wasn't his concern. Nor was he going to be sitting on the floor with a bunch of kids for the rest of the morning. He had grown-up meetings to attend. He was leaving tomorrow on a business trip and had a lot to do before then. "I should go."

She quit fussing with her eyes. "Maybe I'll see you later."

"Yeah," he replied, intending to escape with his indifference intact. "Have a good first day of work."

"Thank you. I'll try."

She was clutching her daughter's cartoon character purse as if the bag contained magic. And maybe in some sort of storybook way it did. He could almost imagine stars and moons and bits of glitter coming from it.

They said a quick goodbye and exited the atrium, going in different directions. But being separated from Meagan didn't stop Garrett from thinking about her. Once again, he couldn't seem to shake her, no matter how hard he tried.

Meagan hadn't seen Garrett since he'd soothed Ivy at the day care, and that was a week ago. Time was moving on already. Today was her second Monday on the job, and she was doing well at work. But she couldn't help wondering why he hadn't come by the stables. She'd expected to catch sight of him at the barn, hanging out with his horses or going for a ride. But he was nowhere to be seen, at least not while Meagan was present.

Was it a coincidence that he hadn't been there? Or was he staying away on purpose, distancing himself from her?

She spoke to the gelding she was grooming. "What do you think, Ho-Dad?"

The horse blew out a breath as if to say she was jumping to conclusions.

She laughed. "You're right. Why would he go out of his way to avoid me? If he wanted to ride, he would come here and saddle up. He's probably just had a heavy schedule."

Ho-Dad bobbed his head, and she decided, a bit foolishly, that he actually understood what she was saying. Still, she wished that Garrett would appear, just so she could get accustomed to being around him. Otherwise, her stomach would keep tying itself up in little knots. Or tangled butterflies, or whatever they were.

The gelding stood there patiently as she continued grooming him. When she was finished, she gave him a carrot, offering it to him from the flat of her hand.

As Ho-Dad chewed and dropped tiny orange bits from his mouth, she heard a man say, "Are you spoiling that surfer boy?"

Meagan's heart pounded like a drumbeat in her chest. She recognized Garrett's voice. She'd wished that he would appear, and now he was here.

Preparing to face him, she turned all the way around. He was standing on the other side of the stall, dressed in jeans, a casual Western shirt and boots. Obviously, he was planning on riding this afternoon.

"Ho-Dad is my favorite," she said, trying to keep herself calm.

Garrett nodded. "I figured he would be."

She struggled to act normally. The horse was chomping his treat in her ear, and her heart was thumping just as loudly. "Have you been busy?"

"Why do you ask?"

"You haven't been at the barn."

Garrett raised his eyebrows. "You've been keeping tabs on me?"

Meagan nearly winced. She wasn't doing a very good job of seeming normal. "I just noticed that you haven't been here. You told me that you ride nearly every day and that I would see you at barn, but you haven't been around. So I wondered about it."

"I was in Las Vegas at a hospitality convention. I'm leaving again in a few days, so I'll be gone again."

"For how long?"

"Another week. It's for business, too."

"Do you travel a lot for work?"

"Not necessarily. I prefer staying home and running the resort, but sometimes it can't be helped." He shifted his stance. "I'm here now, though, and ready to ride."

Yes, he most definitely was. She was used to cowboys, both of her brothers being that type. But Garrett was altering her perspective. With the sexy goose bumps he was giving her, she was seeing Western men in a far less brotherly way. Or this man, anyway. But she'd always had a hot and dizzying thing for him, so she'd been doomed from the start.

Ho-Dad nudged her shoulder, bugging her for another carrot. Normally she gave him two. Already they'd established a routine.

"Go ahead," Garrett said.

"Go ahead and what?" she asked.

"Give him the other one. I can tell that's the pattern between you."

Either Garrett was highly observant or she and the horse were ridiculously transparent. She removed the second carrot from her pocket and offered it to Ho-Dad, and the gelding took it eagerly.

Meagan stayed inside the stall, even though she didn't need to. She was done with Ho-Dad. But for now, the stall seemed like the safest place to be, acting as a barrier and keeping her from getting too close to Garrett.

He said, "Tom told me you're doing a great job."

Ah, yes, Tom. Her kindly old boss. "I appreciate him saying that."

"He also said that you hardly ever take breaks."

"I take a lunch every day. That's when I go to the day care to see Ivy."

"He was referring to breaks in-between. He thinks you work harder than anyone else here."

"That's not a bad thing, is it?"

"No, of course not. But you're allowed to have a moment to yourself, Meagan."

"I'm used to living by someone else's time clock."

"What do you mean? When you were locked up?"

She nodded. "I was a level-one inmate, the least dangerous type of offender, so I lived in an open dormitory with a low security perimeter. But it was still regimented."

She added, "In the beginning when I was pregnant with Ivy, I was considered special needs and was kept in a unit with other pregnant women."

"Where did you give birth?"

"In a hospital. They transported me there from the prison, but I was lucky they didn't put me in waist chains or leg irons or handcuff my hands behind my body. That's been outlawed in California."

"Damn," he said. "Did you get to see Ivy or hold her?"

"Yes, but not for very long. Thankfully, the hospital staff was nice to me. It's not always like that. Some pregnant inmates have had horrendous experiences, with the doctors and nurses being mean or indifferent to them. But I was still really scared. I wasn't allowed to have a birthing coach. Or see my family. By the time Tanner was notified, and he and Candy picked Ivy up from the hospital, I was already gone, back at the prison."

"That sounds terribly lonely."

"It was, but it's my own fault. I'm the one who committed a crime. You know better than anyone what I did."

"Yes, but having a baby shouldn't be like that." He looked like he wanted to touch her, to comfort her in some way, but he gripped the stall door instead. Neither of them spoke again, until he said, "I still want you to take breaks while you're here."

"All right." She didn't want to make waves, even if it was for working too hard. "I'm taking a break right now, talking to you."

"I suppose you are." He swept his gaze over her. "So how are your lunch visits with Ivy? Is she enjoying the day care?"

"Yes, she's settling in beautifully. She's excited to go to work with me and play with her new friends at school.

But she keeps asking me about the horses. She wants to see them."

"Then bring her here and show her around."

"That would be okay?"

"Sure. You can bring her here today, if you want to, after your shift."

"She would love that." Meagan dusted her hands on her jeans, debating whether to tell him how interested her daughter was in him. But for her child's sake, she went ahead and said it. "Ivy hasn't just been asking me about the horses—she's also been asking me about you."

"She has?" He sounded surprised. "What did she say?"

"She's been wondering why you haven't come back to the day care to see her."

"Really?" He squinted, but he smiled a little, too. "I thought about checking up on her, but I didn't think it was my place."

"Are you kidding? She would be thrilled. She keeps asking, 'Where Garry?' Apparently, you made quite an impression with how attentive you were to her. I also think you remind her of Tanner. Your hair is the same color as his, and you have a similar height and build. She's really close to him, so it would stand to reason that she would feel comfortable around you, too."

"If you bring her here after you get off work, I'll probably be here anyway, finishing up my ride, as late in the day as it is now. Then we can all look at the horses together."

"Okay. Sure." Meagan's heart hadn't quit pounding, and now it was really racing up a storm. Doing something "together" with Garrett and Ivy seemed sweetly intimate. Her fantasies about him had begun to progress in ways she'd never expected. "I want Ivy to meet Ho-Dad most of all."

"He certainly likes you." Garrett glanced at the horse

and then back at her. "I'm going to go for my ride now. I'll catch you and Ivy later."

"Yes, later." She watched him walk away, much too excited about seeing him again.

Four

When Garrett returned to the barn, Meagan wasn't there. But he figured she was probably picking up her daughter and would arrive soon. He gave his horse to one of the other stable hands and waited out front.

He was flattered that Ivy had been asking about him, but should he really be doing this?

No, he thought, he shouldn't be. But he couldn't ditch Meagan or her kid. That would be cruel to the child. And to Meagan, too.

But he wasn't supposed to give a damn about Meagan. He was only doing this for Ivy, he told himself. She deserved all the breaks she could get.

And Meagan didn't? His mother would argue the point. Even Jake and Max weren't as pissed about the embezzlement as he was. But his foster brothers hadn't wanted to date Meagan, either. They'd barely even known her. It was different for Garrett. She'd tricked him into liking her.

Was she tricking him again? Or was he just overreacting to the past? He honestly didn't know.

Meagan arrived and pulled into the parking lot. While she parked her car, he stood in the dirt, releasing the air in his lungs and gearing up for this little get-together he'd initiated.

Meagan exited the vehicle and removed Ivy from the backseat. As soon as the toddler saw him, she shot him a chubby-cheeked smile. She was wearing the same frilly pink boots he'd seen her in before.

"Garry!" she said, as he moved closer to her.

"Hello, Princess Ivy," he replied.

She extended both arms, and he assumed that she wanted him to pick her up. He looked at Meagan, making sure it was all right with her. She nodded, and just like that, he was holding Ivy, as if he'd been doing it ever since she was an infant.

"See horsies?" she asked him.

"Yes. We're going to see them."

They entered the barn, and Ivy oohed and ahhed over everything. Even horse turds excited this kid. She squirmed a lot, like children her age typically did. Garrett had to keep a secure hold on her. He even danced her around a bit, making her laugh.

As they stopped at Ho-Dad's stall, he wondered what it would be like to get this close to Meagan, to dance with her, too, which was about the worst thought he could've had.

Dancing with Meagan was off the table. Way off the table. No way in hell was he going to put himself in a situation like that. He was supposed to be over his interest in her.

"This is Ho-Dad," she told her daughter. "He's my favorite."

"Him a daddy?" Ivy asked, leaning forward in Garrett's arms to check out the big bay.

"No, that's just his name," Meagan replied.

Ivy made a perplexed face. "Him no daddy?"

"No, sweetheart, he's not. Geldings are boys, but they aren't daddies."

Ivy decided otherwise. "Yes, him is."

Garrett exchanged a glance with Meagan, and they both smiled. Ho-Dad was as low-key as it got, a far cry from the stud Ivy was making him out to be.

"Do you want to pet him?" Garrett asked her.

She nodded, and he explained how to stroke the horse's neck, but she already knew. Her uncle Tanner must have taught her. She was cautious and gentle, which was a valuable lesson. Some horses spooked when you came at them. Ho-Dad, however, loved being touched. You could go right for his nose, and he wouldn't care. He thrived on any kind of affection.

She called the gelding "Daddy" while she petted him.

And suddenly Garrett thought about the man who'd fathered Ivy and what a jerk he was, cutting this precious child out of his life. But he wasn't going to say that to Meagan, at least not in front of Ivy.

Yet somehow that didn't stop him from blurting out the truth about his own missing father. "I've never met my dad."

Meagan turned to look at him. "You haven't?"

"No. He was a college student at Oklahoma State, which is near the area where my mother is from. They dated for about a year, but when she got pregnant, he didn't want any part of it. He left town soon after that, and she never saw him again."

"Does she know where he went?"

Garrett shook his head. "She didn't try to track him

down, but she assumed that he transferred to another school somewhere. It's tough to say where he is now or if he ever got married or has any other kids. But I don't care. I'm not interested in knowing him."

"I don't blame you." Meagan crinkled her forehead. "Do you think your mother loved him or was it more of a casual relationship?"

"I have no idea. She never talked about it, and I never asked."

"My mom loved my dad, far more than she should have. She used to cry about the divorce, even years later, wishing he would come back to her." She paused. "I think her desperation influenced me in the way I took to Neil and all of the crazy stuff I did for him."

Garrett was curious to know more about her relationship with Neil, but he didn't question her about it, not while he was holding the other man's child.

Ivy stopped petting Ho-Dad and put her head on Garrett's shoulder. He adjusted her to a more comfortable position, letting her use him as a pillow.

Meagan watched how gently he handled her daughter and smiled. Garrett felt her admiration all the way to the pit of his stomach.

"Why were you in foster care?" she asked after a pause.

He quietly replied, "My mother was sick when I was a kid, and there were times that she couldn't take care of me." He gave her the condensed version, keeping the painful details to himself. He'd spent a good portion of his childhood worrying that his mom was going to die.

"Oh, I'm sorry. Is she well now?"

"As well as can be expected. She has an autoimmune disease, so sometimes she still suffers from it."

"Does she live with you?"

"No. She lives at the hotel. She likes it there." He frowned. "I shouldn't be telling you all of this about her."

"Why? Because you're concerned I might contact her? I promise that I won't. But did you relay my message to her?"

"Not yet." He had too much else going on. "I'll do it after I get back from this next trip."

"I appreciate that. I really want your mom to know how grateful I am to her for her involvement in all of this."

"Yeah, I know." But "all of this," as she put it, was getting more complicated than he'd bargained for. Already he was sharing details about himself that he hadn't intended to reveal.

He changed the subject to something less personal. "Have you given any more thought to getting back on a horse?"

"I'm still considering it."

"You should ride Ho-Dad. You've already established a rapport with him, and he's a gentle old soul. He'd be a great mount for you, starting over the way you would be."

"That's good to know. Because he would be my first choice, too." She gazed at Ivy nuzzled against Garrett. "She looks content."

He warned himself, for the umpteenth time, that he was getting closer to Meagan and her daughter than he should be. "Yes, she does. But maybe you should take her now." He transferred Ivy into her mother's arms, hoping the separation would help.

But it didn't. When it came time for them to leave, he didn't want them to go.

He walked Meagan back outside. By now, the child was nodding off, her head drooping forward.

"It must be nap time," he said.

Meagan nodded. "She can nap just about anywhere.

She's fussier at bedtime. She cries if she's not in her crib at Tanner and Candy's. I live in a cottage in the back, but Ivy hasn't moved in with me yet." When they got to Meagan's car, she double-checked the buckle on the car seat, making sure it was latched. "For now, I'm tucking her in each night at their house, so she gets used to me being the one who reads her a story and puts her to bed."

He glanced at Ivy. Her eyes were completely closed. "She sure is a sweet kid."

"Thank you." Meagan smiled. "And thank you for spending this time with us. It meant a lot to Ivy, and to me, too."

Damn. This goodbye was drilling a cozy little hole inside his heart. "Be safe on your way home."

"We will."

She got behind the wheel and started the engine. After she drove away, he remained at the stables, immersed in a stream of warmth he didn't want to feel.

Meagan spent Saturday afternoon with Candy at a bridal salon, where Candy was hoping to find a wedding dress. Dana Reeves was there, too. She was a happy-go-lucky blonde, a self-proclaimed "bohemian" with a fresh and fun nature. She was also Candy's best friend and the matron of honor.

The date had been set for three months from now, and there was a lot of preparation in the works. The ceremony would be held at Tanner's stables and riding academy, where there was plenty of outdoor space, as well as a banquet hall that had been built for special events.

Meagan and Dana were waiting for Candy to come out of the fitting room. A salesgirl—or consultant, as they were called here—had gone in there with her and was helping with all of the buttons, lace and bows. Candy had already tried on a batch of gowns and none of them had been quite right, so she was trying on another round of dresses for them to view.

"I've never been to a bridal shop or participated in a wedding before," Meagan said.

"Really?" Dana smiled, her blues eyes sparkling. "How exciting this must be for you." She shifted in her seat. "Did you know that Candy hosted my wedding?"

"No, I didn't." All Meagan knew was that Dana's husband's name was Eric, and they had a young son they called Jude. He was the kid who'd come up with the Canny and Tanny nicknames that Ivy used. "Was it at the house where she and Tanner are now?"

"Yes, in the garden. But it was before she sold the place to him or they started seeing each other again."

Meagan nodded. Tanner had purchased the property from Candy when he was looking for a house with a guesthouse that would accommodate Meagan after she got out of prison. At the time, Candy had been going through a financial struggle and couldn't afford to keep her home.

Dana smiled once again. "I like thinking of you being in the guesthouse. I used to live there, too. I was Candy's tenant way back when. That's how we met."

"I wasn't aware of that." Meagan hadn't considered how Candy and her BFF had gotten to know each other.

"For me it was a magical place, like an enchanted cottage."

"It does have that vibe." Meagan couldn't deny that she felt that way about it, too. She just wished that Ivy was staying there with her. But in time she would be. Then it would be even more enchanted.

"I brought Eric there on our first date." Dana all but swooned. Beneath the store's bright lights, her pale yellow hair was shining. Her fair skin seemed almost iridescent, too. "It was one of the most romantic nights of my life." Dana leaned closer. "Maybe some of it will rub off on you."

Meagan felt the other woman's shoulder brush hers, as if the "rubbing off" was happening already.

Naturally, her mind drifted to Garrett. Every time she thought about the paternal way in which he held Ivy, she could barely breathe. Exchanging glances with him left her breathless, too. She used to wonder if he was as attracted to her as she was to him, but now she was pretty darned sure that he was.

Maybe it was better that he was going to be gone this coming week. Maybe she could use that time to start riding again and try to free her mind. Of course, once he returned, she would probably get all fluttery over him again.

Dana watched her for a second and then said, "I hope Candy finds just the right dress."

Grateful for the change of topic, Meagan asked, "Did you wear a traditional gown at your wedding?"

"No. But Candy helped me shop for it. We went to vintage stores because I wanted to keep the cost down. And I love those old styles. It was a cocktail dress from the 1970s, with multicolored jewels on it in the shapes of daisies."

Meagan's heart bumped in her chest. "Daisies?"

"Yes. I got these really cool hairpins to match, too. And then Eric surprised me with an Edwardian daisy-cluster ring." Dana held out her left hand. "See? It goes with my wedding band. He had them soldered together."

"It's beautiful." The ring consisted of a series of natural-cut diamonds forming a single daisy, reminding Meagan of the flower Garrett had given her. Only the ring looked to be an English daisy, whereas the variety she'd received had been a gerbera. "Candy taught me a little bit about the floriography she's been studying."

"It's interesting, isn't it?"

"Yes." Meagan had discovered that Candy was going to use white roses in her wedding. They represented unity and love.

A few minutes later, the bride-to-be emerged from the fitting room. She stepped up onto the platform to show them the silk dress she was wearing, and Meagan and Dana gasped in unison.

The strapless gown had a mermaid silhouette, with a sweetheart neckline, a keyhole design in back and lace embellishments. The design was stunning on Candy: classic elegance with a court train.

"I love it," Dana said.

"Me, too," Meagan chimed in.

"So do I." Candy swirled, making the hem swish. "I just found my dress."

"You most definitely did." Dana got teary eyed.

Meagan's eyes misted, too. "You're going to be the most gorgeous bride ever. My brother is going to love how you look in it."

"Thank you." Candy gazed at herself in the three-way mirror. "It needs a nip here and tuck there." She glanced at the consultant, who stood nearby, ready to help. "But you'll take care of that."

"Yes, we most certainly will" came the woman's reply. "And you can order a matching jacket for it, if you want."

"I should probably do that, with it being a winter wedding." Candy turned back around. "I'm so excited."

"As you should be." Dana approached the platform, gazing up at her friend. "Now all you need is something borrowed and something blue."

Candy seemed to think about it for moment. Then she replied, "I can slip a blue rose into my bouquet. All white roses, except for one blue one."

"I've never seen a blue rose," Meagan said. Not that she

was an authority on what colors they came in. She was just learning about flowers only now.

"They're not found in nature," Candy told her. "Horticulturists have been working on it for years, but the results always look sort of purplish, rather than a deep, rich blue. So if I want that type of pigment, it'll have to be dyed."

Curious to know more, Meagan asked, "Do they have a floriography meaning?"

"Not in the Victorian dictionary, but they've acquired one since then. The unattainable dream." Candy swayed in her dress. "Only I'll be realizing my dream by marrying Tanner, so adding a blue rose to my bouquet will signify something truly extraordinary for us."

"That's a wonderful sentiment." Meagan loved the idea. Everything about it just seemed so right. But it was especially exciting when Candy decided that the rest of the women in the bridal party should also carry one. It made Meagan feel as if someday something extraordinary could happen to her, too.

When Garrett returned from his trip, he stopped by his mom's penthouse to see her. She lived on the top floor of the hotel, with a view of the ocean. Her place was cluttered with knickknacks: scented candles, polished stones, glass figurines in the forms of fantasy creatures. Everywhere he looked, he saw dragons, fairies and unicorns. She practiced the old Cheyenne ways, but she dabbled in metaphysical-type stuff, too. In that regard, she was a bit of an enigma. Then again, so was he. His beliefs were as abstract as hers, but that was how she'd raised him.

"Hey, Mom." He sat beside her on her wine-colored sofa and studied her. She was fifty years old, with graying black hair, warm brown eyes and sculpted cheekbones. Even as pretty as she was, she had deep lines etched in her face. Her ill health had taken its toll, beating her up over the years. "How are you?"

"I'm fine." She smiled softly. "I missed you while you were gone. You've been so busy lately."

He shrugged. "I'm always busy."

"I know but more than usual."

"I've had a lot going on, but I'm home now and settling back into things."

"Things?"

"Running the resort."

"Did Meagan start working at the stables yet?"

"Yes." His stomach tightened. Even while he was out of town, he'd thought about Meagan, consumed with the tension of becoming reacquainted with her. "This will be her third week."

"Three weeks?" Mom's eyes went wide. "Why didn't you tell me she's been there that long?"

"Because you're just asking me about it now." When his mother shot him a calculated look, he added, "And I've been gone for most of that time."

She nodded, accepting his explanation. But he knew the conversation wasn't over. She wouldn't let it go that easily. Besides, if he was too closemouthed, that might set off alarm bells, and the last thing he wanted was for his mother to figure out how Meagan was making him feel.

He said, "Tom said that she's doing a good job. That she works hard. I met her kid, too. She's a sweet little girl. Oh, and Meagan asked me to thank you for convincing me to hire her."

"You told her the truth about why you hired her?"

"I wasn't going to lie and pretend that it was my idea."

"Are you being nice to her?"

Because he didn't know how else to respond, he said, "I'm treating her like any other employee."

"You better be."

"I just told you I am." Except that none of his other employees left him reeling the way she did. He didn't go to bed at night thinking about any of them. He was still imagining how it would feel to get close enough to Meagan to dance with her, to sweep her into his arms and spin her around.

"Did you tell her about the day care? Did she enroll her daughter?"

"Yes, she's bringing her there." He thought about how horribly Ivy had cried on that very first day. He hoped that he never had to see her bawl that way again. "I helped her get the child settled in."

"Really?" Mom seemed impressed. She even sat a little straighter, smoothing her broom-style skirt over her long, rickety legs. "I guess you really are being nice."

His heart went thick, heavy with emotion. "I'm not an ogre." He cared about being a good person.

"I know." She patted his knee. "But you were just so angry about the embezzlement. I'd never seen you that ticked off before. Carrying around all of that negativity isn't good for you."

"It isn't good getting duped by someone, either. There's no guarantee that she can be trusted."

"Has she given you a reason to believe that she would ever commit another crime?"

"No." But what the hell did he know, except that she was driving him mad? "She appears to be a nice girl, always saying how sorry she is. But I thought she was nice before I discovered that she ripped us off."

"Just keep giving her a chance, okay?"

"I'm trying to give her the benefit of the doubt." And it wasn't just that. As deeply as Meagan was burrowing into his brain, he could barely concentrate on anything else.

"Were you becoming friends with her before? Is that why you got so angry about what she did?"

"Yes, that's pretty much it." That and how insanely attracted to her he'd been. And still was, he amended. But that was a secret he was keeping to himself.

His mother peppered him with questions. "Do you think you'll ever become friends with her again?"

"I don't know. It's too early to know how it'll pan out." Nor did he want to think too deeply about that right now.

"Did you tell her that I once knew her mother?"

He squared his shoulders. "No."

"Why not?"

Bloody hell. He was more than ready for this discussion to end. But Mom was gazing at him in that persistent way of hers, waiting for him to respond. "Because I don't want her bugging you about it."

She rolled her eyes at his choice of words. "She wouldn't be bugging me. I would be more than happy to discuss it with her."

"Yeah, well, I told her not to contact you, and she promised that she wouldn't. You already got involved in this more than you should have."

"I got involved because I knew it was the right thing to do, and at some point I'd like to meet her."

"I'd rather that you didn't."

Mom set her jaw. "You can't stop me, Garrett. Sooner or later, I intend to meet her."

Rather than incite an argument, he said, "All right, we'll see how it goes. But for now, just let me handle it."

He wanted to be in control of the situation, to deal with Meagan in his own way, however he could.

Five

After Garrett left his mom's, he went for a ride, needing to unwind and enjoy the elements. The weather was refreshing, with a light breeze and the scent of the surf and sand in the air. The beach was relatively quiet, he noticed, but it usually was this time of year. Nonetheless, the resort still got plenty of business. His place was an LA hotspot, catering to a variety of clientele.

He hadn't seen Meagan at the barn when he'd saddled his horse and figured she was already gone for the day. He'd more or less planned it that way. He wanted this to be a stress-free ride, without the tension that being around her caused.

Hot and sexy tension, he thought. No, he didn't need that today.

He took his horse along the shore, and everything went splendidly until he spotted another lone figure coming toward him, also on horseback.

From this distance, he couldn't be sure who it was. But

his radar went off, anyway. Something told him it was Meagan. A feeling. A gut instinct.

As the horse and rider came closer, his intuition was confirmed. It was Meagan, and she was riding Ho-Dad.

When they were close enough to look into each other's eyes, they both reined their mounts to a stop. While he battled the feelings he'd been trying to avoid, tiny tendrils of hair escaped from her braid and fluttered around her face.

"You did it," he said, congratulating her. "You're riding again."

She nodded and smiled. "Yes, and it's been wonderful, more therapeutic than I imagined. I started last week."

During the time he was gone? Had she done that deliberately or had it just happened that way? He wasn't going to ask, not at the risk of making it sound more important than it was. Instead he inquired, "How often have you been out?"

"Nearly every day. Ivy is doing so well at the day care I either bring her early or keep her a little later, so I can ride."

"You and Ho-Dad make a good pair."

"You said that we would."

"And I was right." But damn if she wasn't killing him. When she leaned forward, patting the side of the gelding's neck, her button-down blouse gaped a bit in front, exposing a hint of flesh. "Have you gone into the hills yet?"

She shook her head and settled back into her seat. "I've been sticking to the beach. But I've been tempted to make my way up there."

"You should."

"Which trails do you think are the best?"

He motioned to the area just east of the stables. "If I were you, I'd go that way. It's nice and wide, and there's a plateau at the top, where you can picnic or relax or whatever."

"That's in the direction where you live," she replied, pointing out the obvious.

"Yes, but the road leading to my house is private." He tried not to fixate on her mouth. But he got lost in his own stupidity and wondered what kissing her would be like. Her lips looked soft and shiny, like she was wearing a glossy balm on them. Maybe one of those flavored kinds? "No one has access to that part of the property except me."

"I can see why you chose such an isolated area to build your house, with how active your work life is. You're around people at the hotel all the time."

And now he was on the beach with her, a woman he still didn't know if he could trust. "Are you going to head into the hills today?"

"I don't think I have time. I've already been out for a while, so I'll need to get back to the day care and pick up Ivy soon. Maybe I'll go into the hills tomorrow."

He took a moment to think, to get his mental bearings. Would it be a mistake to offer to accompany her? Or would it be a good way to get to know her better, to figure out who and what she really was?

He decided to make the offer. He had a right to gauge her sincerity, to pick her brain and see where it led.

"If you want some company, I can be your guide," he said.

She hesitated. Then she asked, "You'd do that for me?"

"Sure," he replied, even though he would be doing it for himself. "We can try to be friends, can't we?" *Or at least have the illusion of friendship*, he thought. For now, he didn't know if forming a genuine truce with her was possible.

Her gaze locked gently onto his. "That would be nice. And different from before, with the way I deceived you when you thought we were becoming friends."

He almost felt guilty for deceiving her this time. But he couldn't just jump into trusting her that easily. Nor could he keep fantasizing about kissing her. Whatever conclusions he came to about her character, the rest of it would be strictly platonic.

"What time of the day would be better for you?" he asked. "Morning or afternoon? I'm open to either."

"Let's do morning. I can meet you at the stables a few hours before I start my shift."

"Sounds good. I'll see you then."

"Thank you, Garrett. I'm looking forward to it." She said goodbye and headed back to the barn.

He kept going, riding along the shore, hoping that building a "friendship" with her wasn't going to be a mistake.

Meagan rode with Garrett the next morning, trying to keep from staring at him. He was riding the same horse she'd seen him on yesterday—a muscular gelding, shiny and black. Both horse and man looked strong and handsome.

The air was crisp at this early hour. Garrett was dressed for the weather, with a rugged jacket over his shirt. Meagan had a jacket on, too. Later, it was supposed to warm up.

He took her on the trails that led toward the plateau he'd told her about. They barely talked on the way. Mostly, they just absorbed the scenery—dirt and brush and rocks, along with flowering weeds shooting up through the ground, creating colorful patches of prettiness.

When they reached the plateau, she gasped at the sight. It was an open field, as beautiful as could as be, with scattered grass and plush ground cover in various shades of green. There were trees, too, branching their way to the sky.

"This is incredible," she said. It was like being in a

whole other dimension. In one direction, she could see the ocean far below. In the other, she sighted the resort and the city that surrounded it.

He watched her as she took it all in. "Do you want to dismount? Maybe kick back awhile?"

Meagan nodded. She could stay here forever.

They tied up their horses, and he spread a gray-and-maroon blanket on the ground.

She stood off to the side. "You came prepared."

He shrugged, smiled. "What kind of Cheyenne would I be if I didn't keep a blanket handy?"

"Well, I'm glad we're here, getting to do this." She was overwhelmed with him actually wanting to attempt a friendship with her. Between the beauty of the land and being here with him, she felt like she was floating. It was odd, though, how tangible he suddenly seemed. Even the tiny crow's-feet around his eyes jumped out at her. She suspected they were mostly frown lines, even if they appeared when he smiled, too.

They sat across from each other. They both had water bottles they'd packed. She sipped from hers while he took a larger swig from his.

"I never asked you about your trip," she said. "How did it go?"

"It was productive. I had meetings and luncheons and those sorts of things. It's good to be back, though. What did you do while I was gone, besides work? And ride," he added.

"That was about it." She paused to refine her answer. "I also went shopping with Candy and a friend of hers for Candy's wedding dress. She and my brother set the date for three months from now."

"Three months?" Garrett shook his head. "What's the hurry?"

"They're just anxious to make it official. They've been engaged for two years, but they've been waiting for me, so I could be part of it."

"We have lots of nuptials here, at the resort, with on-site event planners who handle the details. Typically, it takes about fourteen months to plan a wedding. The quickest one we've ever done was for Jake. He was in a bit of a rush because of the baby, but it turned out beautifully. They exchanged their vows on the beach."

Meagan glanced toward the ocean, picturing the bride's veil billowing in the wind. "Who did he marry?"

"Her name is Carol. She's his personal assistant, so he's always been really reliant on her. He just never expected to fall in love with her and certainly not to the degree he did."

"I heard that Jake was a party boy. That he was really wild and that he dated models and actresses and heiresses. Or that's what people at the accounting firm used to say about him."

"That's true. He played around a lot. But he's different now that he's with Carol. He's a great husband, and he's going to be a wonderful father, too."

"Were you his best man?" In her mind's eye, Meagan saw him in a sleek black tux, his hair combed straight back, his posture tall and straight.

"Yes, me and Max. We both stood up for him."

"People at the firm used to gossip about you and Max, too."

"Oh, yeah?" Garrett stretched out his legs. "What sorts of things did they say?"

"Max was painted as a bit of a mystery. Supersmart but sort of offbeat and reclusive, too. He was rumored to have lots of lovers, except that he didn't show them off the way Jake did. I think that was part of why people thought he was a mystery, with him keeping his women to himself."

"And me?" Garrett asked, his gaze boring into hers. "How was I portrayed?"

She toyed with a corner of the blanket, unnerved by the deep, dark way he was looking at her. "They said that you were the toughest of the three, hard-edged and difficult to get to know." She twisted the material. "I envisioned you as being really ruthless. But you weren't like that when I met you."

"I do have a hard-edged side." His voice went rough. "But it's not as bad as they made it sound. Or at least I don't think it is."

"Maybe you just confuse people."

"Do I confuse you?"

"Sometimes." She was feeling that way right now. But it was different for her, given their history.

Garrett drank more of his water. Meagan was getting thirsty again, too. Or maybe she was feeling the need to do what he did. Either way, she took a sip.

"So what was the rest of the gossip about me?" he asked.

She put down her bottle. "What do you mean?"

"Did they mention my love life? Did they have an opinion on that?"

Her pulse jumped at the line of questioning. "As far as I know, it was never discussed." But she wished it had been. Oh, how she wished. "I'm not sure why no one ever brought it up."

"I don't know whether to be relieved or offended by their lack of interest."

"I think it just makes you even more of a mystery than Max." She quickly added, "Not that it's anyone's business who either of you date." Even if she longed for answers, even if she hoped that he would reveal more about who he was.

But he didn't say a word, leaving her to her own devices.

"I started seeing Neil when I was nineteen," she said, giving him a bit of insight into who she was beyond what he already knew. "I had other boyfriends before him, but he was my first serious relationship. The only man I've ever been with."

"You mean slept with?"

She nodded, and, suddenly, there was a shift in the air between them. Garrett started roaming his gaze over her, checking her out from the top of her head to the tips of her plain and simple boots.

He was making her much too warm. She even removed her jacket. He took off his, too. Then they just sat there, steeped in the awareness of each other.

Until he asked, "What was it about Neil that you were attracted to?"

That was a loaded question, she thought. But she answered it the best she could. "I was young and insecure, and he was bold and adventurous. In some ways, he reminded me of my dad. That sounds so clichéd, but that's how he affected me. Only, unlike my father, Neil treated me like I mattered. Or he did in the beginning, anyway. Later, he expected more out of me than was right." She expelled a shaky breath. "Like asking me to commit a crime."

Garrett kept his gaze trained on her. But he didn't comment. He just listened.

"I'm not saying that what I did is Neil's fault. I should have had the common sense to say no."

"Then why didn't you?"

"I thought that taking the money would make me more exciting in Neil's eyes. And that he would love me." She hated how pathetic she'd been back then, a girl whose every action was born of desperation. "He never actually told me that he loved me, and it was the one thing I kept waiting to hear."

"Did he say it after you took the money?"

Shame coiled in her heart. "Yes, he did. But it felt hollow, especially after I met you. Before then, you and your foster brothers were just some rich guys who weren't going to miss the money. Or that's what I kept telling myself. But when you stopped to comfort me that day, all the remorse I'd been fighting came rushing to the surface." She was feeling it now, too. "I even kept the flower you gave me. But I was too guilty to keep it forever."

"I wasn't expecting you to keep it, let alone forever." His tone sounded a little raw.

Her words went raw, too. "I still wish that I had it, tucked away somewhere. It was really special to me."

He dragged a hand through his hair. He seemed troubled. Or uncomfortable. Or both.

Then he said, "I think I should check on the horses."

When he stood and stepped off the blanket, Meagan watched him walk away, his tall, broad-shouldered body creating a dark and looming shadow. He was like a gunslinger on his way to a fight.

Garrett used the horses as an excuse to clear his head. He'd spent the last three years, while Meagan was in prison, condemning her for what she'd done, and now he was trapped in a prison of his own making.

This outing was supposed to be an exercise in analyzing her character, not falling for every word she said. Yet everything she'd told him sounded painfully real. Even more disturbing was the memory she and Garrett shared. That stupid flower she'd mentioned. He remembered the moment he'd given it to her and the beautifully fractured way she'd looked at him, as if she needed him more than he could possibly know. He'd pilfered it from the arrangement in the lobby and handed it to her because he'd wanted to make her smile.

He still liked seeing her smile.

Damn, he was losing his perspective. Then again, maybe it wasn't such a stretch that he and Meagan could work toward becoming friends. They'd been drawn to each other from the start.

The sexy stuff wasn't plausible, though. That was definitely off-limits. She was the last woman on earth with whom he should get romantically involved.

He checked on the horses, as he'd said he would. They were fine, of course. But he stayed there with them a bit longer.

Finally, he went back to Meagan. She was sitting in the same spot as before.

"Is everything okay?" she asked.

"It's all good," he replied, even if it wasn't. His thoughts were still scattered.

He rejoined her on the blanket. Then he realized that there was a detail about the day they'd met that eluded him. "Not that this matters, but what kind of flower was it that I gave you?" The bloom she wished that she'd kept. "I don't remember what it looked like." All he recalled was the act itself.

"It was a daisy, and it's funny you should ask, because there's this thing Candy has been studying called the language of flowers, and I'm fascinated by it now, too."

She went on to explain that the type of daisy he'd given her had several meanings—sadness, friendship, protection—all of which felt highly significant to her.

With all the emotional vines that were tangling inside him, he was feeling the significance, too. But he said, "I didn't choose that flower specifically. It was just handy."

"Yes, but it's the one you gave me, the one that was meant to be."

He didn't want to cop to the idea, at least not out loud. "It was just a random thing, Meagan."

She pulled her knees closer to her chest and wrapped her arms around them. "So you don't believe that things can happen for a reason?"

He tried to play down her theory, without squelching it completely. "Sometimes I do, and sometimes I don't."

"Well, whatever it was, whatever the rationale, I think communicating with flowers is a captivating notion."

"It's different, that's for sure." And so was his behavior. He couldn't seem to rid himself of the hunger, the knee-jerk need inside him. He'd never gotten this twisted up over a woman before. If only he could kiss her, just to know how it would feel, just to get it out of his blood.

Was there a flower that meant *forbidden*? he wondered. If there was, he needed to plant them all over his yard, keeping those damned urges at bay.

Meagan said, "Candy is going to carry white roses in her bouquet. And a dyed blue one. They don't exist in nature, so that's why she wants to include them in the ceremony—to represent her unattainable dream coming true. I'll get to carry one, too. I'm going to be a bridesmaid, and Ivy and Candy's dog are going to be the flower girls."

He busted out a grin. "Her dog?"

She smiled, too. "Yogi is a really smart Labrador. I'm excited about the wedding." Her smile fell a little. "I missed my other brother's wedding."

Garrett assumed that meant she was in prison when her oldest brother got hitched. "His name is Kade, isn't it?"

"Yes. He lives in Montana, with his wife and twelve-year-old son. Kade didn't even know he had a son, until a few years ago. Then, when he found out, he got back together with the boy's mother. They're expecting another child now, too."

"Are they going to attend Tanner's wedding?"

"Yes, they'll be there. I was never really close to Kade when I was growing up. There's a fairly big age gap between us. He left home when I was still in elementary school and hardly ever came back to visit. But we've been working on becoming closer now that we both have children."

"That's good." Garrett didn't know much about Kade Quinn, other than he was a renowned horse trainer with celebrity clients who flocked to him. Both of her brothers were successful in their fields.

She released her hands from around her legs. "Tanner said that he wants to meet you. He really appreciates that you gave me a job here."

"Sure, maybe I can meet him sometime. And maybe you can get a bit more acquainted with my foster brothers." It might help to bring Meagan into the fold, for them to see her, too. "Especially since they're such a big part of this."

"Do they hate me for taking the money, the way you used to?"

"I never said I hated you. I just—" he searched for the right words "—hated that you pretended to be something you weren't."

"I'm not pretending now."

He was, he supposed, with how badly he wanted to kiss her. "Just for the record, Jake and Max aren't holding grudges against you. I was more affected by what you did than they were."

"I'd like to see them. It would be nice to be able to apologize to them, like I've been able to do with you."

"Jake used to steal," Garrett said, tossing out a tidbit from the past.

Meagan blinked. "What?"

"He used to shoplift when he was a kid. He was really messed up after his parents died, and he stole things to fill the hole that was inside him. So, in that respect, he understands how easy it is to do something you shouldn't do."

"Thank you for telling me that." She sighed, a soft sound of relief. "Did Jake ever get caught?"

"Yes, he did, when he was about fifteen. He didn't go to a juvenile detention center, though. He got probation instead, and he learned his lesson, because he never did it again."

She spoke quietly. "And what about Max? Did he ever do anything bad?"

"Not that I'm aware of. But a lot of bad things were done to him when he was a child."

"I'm so sorry. Is Max okay now?"

"Yeah, he's all right. But the hurt and neglect that he suffered is always there, I think, breathing down his neck. You don't get over that kind of pain. He even went on a recent sabbatical, taking time off from everything and everyone. He really is a bit of a mystery. I never really know what he's thinking or feeling."

"You seem like that, too," she replied, reminding him that she'd already put him in the mystery category.

"Yeah, but I'm different from Max. I have a parent who loves me. Jake had a good family, too, even though he lost them. Max didn't have anyone." Garrett gazed solemnly at her. "But without Max, Jake and I wouldn't be as successful as we are today. We all vowed when we were kids that we were going to become billionaires, but it was Max who clung the hardest to the dream, insisting it was possible. He's also the one who made his fortune first, then loaned us the money to start our businesses. The foster children's charity was his brainchild, too. He wanted us to create it together, and it's become vital in all our lives."

"You're good men, the three of you."

"We try to do good things."

"I'm glad the restitution I'll be paying is going to your charity. It would have broken my heart if Ivy had gone into foster care."

"My mom felt broken every time I was separated from her. But it couldn't be helped."

"You're together now."

He nodded. He was grateful that he had the resources to provide for his mother, to give her a life of leisure and pay for the best medical care available. "She used to be a hotel maid. That's what she did when I was growing up."

"That makes perfect sense, doesn't it? With you owning a resort now?" Meagan plucked a long spindly weed that was growing beside the blanket. "We're all a product of our environments, in some shape or form."

"Yes, we are. Products of the lives we've led."

She pressed the weed to her chest, as if it were the daisy he'd given her. "Mine has been mixed up."

"Mine, too." He shuddered to think of how badly he was going to want her as time forged on, with this friendship of theirs on the rise. But instead of yanking it out by its roots, he was allowing it to grow.

Six

The following week, Garrett met with his foster brothers to discuss an upcoming charity event: a big fun-filled, family-style picnic in the park. They were in his office gathered around a conference table, wrapping things up. The rest of the organizers, the people who worked for their Caring for Fosters Foundation had already left. Basically, they'd created the nonprofit to help provide financial and emotional support to foster children.

Garrett poured himself a cup of coffee, his second one that morning. He offered Jake and Max a refill, too. Jake held out his cup, but Max declined, shaking his head.

Garrett silently studied both men. In his heart, the three of them could have been natural-born brothers. They didn't look that much alike, aside from being tall and athletically built, but their bond was strong, as well as the culture they shared.

Jake was the most noticeable, with his trendy clothes,

rebellious smile and swooped-back hair. His adoring wife thought that he looked like a Native American version of James Dean. Even as a teenager, Jake had girls flocking around him. He used to say that he was never going to settle down or have children, but he'd eaten those words when he'd gotten his personal assistant pregnant. Marrying her hadn't been easy, though. She'd refused his proposal at first. But, in the end, it had worked out, and Garrett couldn't be happier for them.

Max was a whole other animal. He had been a shy, skinny kid with no social skills and a genius IQ. He hadn't beefed up until he was in his twenties and started hitting the gym. He'd become successful then, too, designing software that had earned him his fortune.

Garrett said to both of them, "There's something I want to run past you."

Max replied, "About the event?"

"No. About Meagan Quinn. You guys already know that I offered her a job and she's been working here, but I was hoping that you'd be willing to meet her. You only saw her around the accounting office. Neither of you have ever really spoken to her." They hadn't attended her sentencing, either. Only Garrett and his mother had gone. "So I'd like to get that cat out of the bag."

"Is this your mom's idea?" Jake asked. "For us to meet her?"

"No, it's mine. But they'll probably get acquainted soon, too. Mom wants to get to know her." And he couldn't keep them apart for much longer. Nor, he supposed, was there any reason to. "Meagan is a great employee. She works hard, and I'm trying to help her turn her life around."

"So you've forgiven her?" Jake asked.

"I'm doing the best I can, befriending her and whatnot." He chose his words carefully, admitting that they were becoming friends without letting on that he had the hots for her.

Max said, "I'd be willing to meet her, if that's what you want us to do."

Garrett glanced over at Jake. "How about you?"

"Yes, of course. I've always believed in second chances. I have my own delinquent history. But I'm curious about what made the difference for you, especially with how angry you were about getting ripped off. What has she done to convince you that she's changed, besides how hard she works? Because she was a valued employee at the accounting firm, too, before she hacked into our accounts. So why would her work ethic be the deciding factor for you now?"

"It's not just that. I've spent some time with her over the past few weeks, and she's been confiding in me about how messed up she used to be. She explained why she took the money and how sorry she is. She's trying to be a good mother, too, and raise her daughter right. I truly believe that she's being sincere."

"That's nice to hear," Jake said. "And I'm glad you're getting over this."

Yeah, Garrett was getting over the theft, but he was far from getting over Meagan. "I appreciate that you're both on board."

Jake nodded. "No problem."

Max nodded, too, and moved to stand near the window. Sunlight streamed through the blinds, creating jagged shards of light. Max's favorite sport was shadowboxing, and Garrett often wondered if it was his way of attacking the past and the demons that still lived inside him.

At the moment, Garrett knew the feeling. He wouldn't mind taking a few swings at his own shadow. As much as he wanted to be around Meagan, he was worried about it, too.

What if he got too attached to Ivy? Or what if he never got over his hunger for Meagan? There was a fistful of reasons why he shouldn't be hanging out with her. But, even so, he was determined to follow through on their friendship.

"When should we do this?" Jake asked.

"Do what?" Garrett asked.

Jake rolled his eyes. But he cocked a smile, too. He seemed perfectly relaxed, with his shirtsleeves rolled up and his tattoos artfully exposed. "Meet Meagan. That was what we were talking about."

"I don't know." Garrett hadn't gotten that far, which wasn't like him. Typically, he was a highly organized person.

"Why don't you invite her to the charity?" Jake said. "We'll all be there, and she can bring her kid, too."

"That's a great idea." And something Garrett should have considered, especially since this particular event was designed for families. "I'll talk to her about it."

"Sounds like a plan." Jake smiled again.

Max didn't say anything, but he'd always been the quietest of the three. He was still standing beside the window in his *Star Wars* T-shirt and time-worn jeans. He wasn't opposed to wearing business attire, in the socially acceptable manner Jake and Garrett typically did. But today he'd shown up in casual clothes, like the nonconformist he sometimes was. Garrett never really knew what to expect of Max.

"Are we good to go now?" Jake asked.

"Sure," Garrett replied. Their meeting had come to an end. "You guys can head out, and I'll stop by the day care later to see Meagan on her lunch hour. She eats with her daughter every day." Already Garrett had become accustomed to Meagan's schedule, keeping her whereabouts etched in his mind.

* * *

Meagan and Ivy sat by themselves. The other kids at their table had already finished their lunches and had dashed off to play under the supervision of a teacher's aide.

Meagan and Ivy were still eating. Meagan nibbled on a bologna sandwich, and her daughter was picking at finger foods.

Even though Ivy kept glancing around, she seemed content to stay with Meagan and make their visit last. Meagan, too, was enjoying every treasured second of their time together.

"Mommy! Look!" Ivy pointed to the open doorway that led to the patio. "Garry here!"

Meagan's pulse jumped to attention. Indeed, it was Garrett entering the lunch area. He carried himself in his usual way, like a CEO—strong and polished and confident.

Meagan's daughter wiggled in her seat while Garrett stopped to greet one of the teachers on staff.

"Him see me?" Ivy asked.

"Yes, I think he's here to see you." And to see Meagan, too, but she wasn't going to say that.

Garrett glanced in their direction, and Ivy waved at him. She loved waving at people. He smiled and came over to them.

"Hello, Princess Ivy," he said.

She grinned and stood on the bench seat to welcome him. He sat on the other side of her, steadying her so she didn't fall. Meagan was doing the same thing, and it made her feel as if she and Garrett were Ivy's parents. But they weren't, she told herself. He wasn't Ivy's father. Nor should Meagan be thinking those sorts of thoughts.

The child sat back down and offered him some of her food. He politely refused, but she insisted. So he took a slice of banana and ate it. By now, Ivy was wedged between him and Meagan, and the toddler seemed even more content than she had been earlier. But she was used to having Tanner and Candy as her guardians, so it would stand to reason that she was comfortable being with two attending adults. A couple, if you will. That was her norm. But it wasn't Meagan's. She wasn't accustomed to having a man by her side.

Garrett finally spoke to Meagan. "How are you doing?"

Aside from analyzing herself and her daughter? "I'm fine." She smiled and gestured to her lunch. "Just brown-bagging it."

He glanced at her half-eaten sandwich. "So I see." He accepted a cheese-flavored cracker that Ivy handed him. Then he continued talking to Meagan. "I can't stay long. I have a lot to do today, but I wanted to invite you and Ivy to an upcoming charity event."

"What exactly is it?" She doubted that it was a fancy gala, not if a two-year-old would be coming along.

"It's a picnic at a local park. Lots of kids will be there with their foster families, along with people who are donating to the charity and their families. I'll buy your tickets, so you and your daughter can attend."

"Will your foster brothers be there?"

He nodded. "I just talked to them this morning about it. Do you want to go?"

"Sure." This would give her the opportunity to apologize to his brothers. She also thought a picnic sounded nice. "When is it?"

"Next Saturday." He paused. "Come to think of it, maybe Tanner and Candy can join you. I'll provide their tickets, too. If they come, then everyone can meet everyone."

"What about your mom? Is she included in this?"

He shook his head. "She won't be there. She can't spend

too much time in the sun. But we'll work out another day for the two of you to get together."

Meagan felt a huge weight being lifted from her shoulders. "Thank you. Meeting her is really important to me."

"Maybe we can arrange it for later this week, if Mom is feeling up to it."

"That would be wonderful."

In the next quiet moment, Ivy drew their attention, humming to herself and playing with her food. She lined up the crackers, making them walk.

Garrett smiled, and so did Meagan. Then he said, "There are some things about my mom that I'd like to tell you. Things you should know ahead of time."

She assumed he meant about his mother's illness. "Just let me know when you want to talk about it."

"Do you want to meet tomorrow, before your shift starts? I can cook breakfast for you at my house."

Oh, wow. He was inviting her to his castle in the sky. "You cook?"

He lifted one brawny shoulder in a partial shrug. He laughed a little, too. "I manage."

"I'd love to join you for breakfast." She'd never had a man cook for her before. Neil hadn't been that kind of guy. She searched Garrett's gaze. "Should I bring anything?"

He looked back at her. "All I need is for you to be there."

Meagan sucked in her breath. His response sounded more romantic than it should have. But she knew that he wasn't inviting her to his house to make out with him. Nothing was going to happen.

Was she secretly hoping that it would? With each week that passed, she was becoming more infatuated with him. Even now, a warm hush had come over them. She couldn't stop staring at him. Neither of them had broken eye contact yet.

Thank goodness they were sitting off by themselves, without any of the teachers nearby to observe them. Ivy, of course, was too young to understand.

Garrett finally glanced away, prompting Meagan to peer off to the side, too. But when he spoke, she shifted her focus back to him.

He said, "There's a security gate before you get to my house, so I'll have to let you onto the property. Just drive up to the gate and push the buzzer."

"Will do." Meagan still hadn't finished her sandwich. She tore at the crust on her bread, and her daughter nabbed it, adding it to the crushed-up crackers she'd been playing with.

"I should go." Garrett stood and ruffled Ivy's hair. "Goodbye, princess."

"Bye, Garry." The child looked up and gave him a handful of crumbs as a parting gift.

He tucked them into his jacket pocket, and she grinned and returned to the mess she'd made.

"See you tomorrow," he said to Meagan. "Sevenish?"

"I'll be there." For a date that wasn't a date, she thought. With a man who was already making her melt.

The next morning, Meagan arrived at the gate and followed Garrett's instructions to push the buzzer. He buzzed her in, and she drove farther up the hill and parked in front of his house.

She was dressed for work since that was where she would be going afterward. But she hadn't braided her hair yet. For now, it was long and loose and flowing down her back. She'd spent nearly three years wearing a dowdy prison uniform with her hair in a no-frills ponytail. The least she could do was try to look nice, especially when she was on her way to see Garrett. She wanted to be pretty for him.

Nonetheless, she was nervous about this get-together. She'd barely slept last night thinking about it, and this morning when she'd dropped Ivy off at day care, her daughter had given her an extra-special kiss goodbye—as if the child sensed that she needed it.

Meagan took a moment to study the outside of Garrett's beach house–style mansion, with its tree-lined courtyard and enormous picture windows.

But before she could knock or ring the bell, he opened the front door and greeted her. He was dressed for the office. Or sort of dressed for it, she thought. He wore gray trousers and a pinstriped shirt, but it wasn't tucked into his pants. He didn't have a tie.

"Hey," he said.

"Hi," she replied. When she glanced down, she noticed that his feet were bare.

He gestured. "Come in."

She followed him into the entryway, where they ascended a staircase that led to the living room. From there, he took her into the kitchen.

"Your house is magnificent," she told him. She could see the ocean from nearly every window. Most of his furnishings were made from natural woods. "I love the kitchen." It was decorated in black and white, with an intricately tiled floor. "Everything is so bright and inviting."

"Thank you. Take a seat, and I'll get started on the meal."

"Okay." Meagan sat at a bar-style counter that divided the kitchen from the living room. From her vantage point, she could watch Garrett cook.

He removed a carton of eggs from the fridge. He placed

tomatoes on a cutting board, too. He also put potatoes in a colander to be cleaned and peeled.

"Do you need some help?" she asked.

"No, thanks. I've got it." Garrett turned toward her. "Do you want coffee or orange juice? Or both?"

"Juice would be nice." She'd already had coffee this morning.

He poured it from a store-bought carton and set it in front of her. "It's the kind with lots of pulp."

"I like that kind." She took a sip. "I get the sneaking suspicion that you're a better cook than you led me to believe."

"I'm just making eggs and potatoes."

"Yes, but look how good you are at it." He peeled the spuds with a paring knife, working them like a chef. He even had fresh herbs available.

"I'm just fanatical about doing things right."

He did seem like a perfectionist. "I can tell."

She enjoyed watching him move about the kitchen. He remained neat and tidy, without spilling or splattering anything on his shirt. She almost wished that he would, in hope that he would remove it.

Meagan drank more of her juice, trying to cool herself off. She didn't need to be fantasizing about Garrett without his shirt. He was sexy enough, just as he was.

He finished cooking the meal and filled her plate, giving her two poached eggs and a generous helping of pan-roasted, rosemary-seasoned potatoes. The tomatoes had been diced up, drizzled with olive oil and garnished with parsley. There was whole wheat toast, too.

She sat a little more forward in her seat. "It looks fabulous." Normally, she just had a bowl of oatmeal in the morning. Of course when she'd been in prison, she ate whatever they gave her.

He placed a tub of butter and a jar of strawberry preserves on the counter, along with clear glass salt and pepper shakers, paper napkins and sturdy flatware.

He took the bar stool next to hers. "I hardly ever use the dining room table. This is where I usually eat."

"It works for me." She liked that he was seated so close to her. He smelled like cologne. The spicy fragrance mingled with the food he'd fixed. She could've breathed him in all day.

They ate their breakfast, and it was as good as it looked. She smothered her toast in jam, and he spread butter on his.

"Did you tell Tanner and Candy about the charity event?" he asked.

"Yes, and they thought it sounded wonderful, but they can't go. They already have an appointment that day, tasting wedding cakes. If they cancel it, they'll be scrambling to get everything done. The caterer they're using is really busy. They still want to meet you, though. Hopefully, we can arrange it for another time."

"I'm sure we can figure something out."

"Okay, but will you tell me more about the event?" she asked. "And what to expect?"

"Truthfully, I don't know what to expect, other than it's going to be a picnic with games and prizes and sports activities. We've never done anything where the kids themselves would be in attendance. But we thought it would be nice to have something fun for them to do, where the entertainment was created for them. When I was in foster care, a lot of the kids felt like second-class citizens, as if nothing they said or did mattered."

Her heart went heavy. "Did you feel that way?"

"Mostly, I just worried about my mom, but it was hard for me, too, getting bounced in and out of someone else's house every time she got sick. It was a tough and lonely existence, and, without Jake and Max, it would have been even more unbearable."

"How old were you?"

"When I first went into foster care? Twelve. Jake went in when he was twelve, too, and Max had been there since he was eight, but he didn't end up in the same house with us until he was eleven. Jake thought Max was a dork at first, but we all got really close as time went on." Garrett finished his eggs and started on the rest of his food. "Jake's wife used to be a foster kid, too, an orphan like he was. But she handled her grief in more sensible ways. She didn't run wild the way he did."

Meagan could barely comprehend their childhoods. Hers had been bad, but theirs sounded far worse. "Did you all know her back then?"

"No. Jake met Carol a few years ago when she applied to work for our charity. But he hired her as his personal assistant instead. I think he was drawn to her from the start because they suffered similar tragedies."

"What a beautiful thing—them having a baby together."

"It's great to see him so happy."

"Will Carol be at the picnic, too?"

"As far as I know, she will."

"Does she know about what I did?"

Garrett nodded. "Yes, she knows the whole story."

"And now here I am at your house." She stared into his eyes and felt her heart bump her chest. "I never would have imagined it."

"Me, neither." He gazed at her in the same emotional way that she was looking at him. "We've come a long way."

"I like being your friend."

"I like it, too."

Maybe they liked it too much? Meagan felt light-headed just from being near him. To keep herself from sliding straight off her bar stool, she gripped her fork and ate every last bite of her food. By now Garrett was done, as well.

She helped him clear the dishes, and he said, "Do you want to go outside and sit by the pool?"

"Sure." She assumed that he wanted to finish their conversation out there.

"It's this way." He led her to the back of the house and through a sliding glass door, where his white-bricked patio and kidney-shaped pool awaited. The yard itself was fenced and surrounded by nature.

"It's beautiful out here," she said.

"It's my favorite spot in the house. I have access to it from my bedroom, too."

She glanced in the direction he indicated. She wanted to get a better look, but the blinds on the sliding glass doors were closed, making his sleeping quarters a mystery.

She sat across from him in a wicker chair. "You created a glittering haven for yourself."

"Glittering?"

"In the way the sun hits the water," she clarified, still thinking about his shrouded bedroom. To keep him from noticing her interest in his room, she hurriedly asked, "Where did you live when you were young? When you were with your mom and not in foster care?"

"We had a little apartment above someone's garage. He was a nice old man. He understood how it was for us and never raised the rent or kicked us out when we struggled to pay it."

"Is he still around?"

"No. He died before I was able to repay him for his kindness. I attended his funeral, though. So did Mom, even though she was feeling poorly that day. She's always had her ups and downs."

"Are you going to tell me more about her illness? So I can be prepared when I meet her?"

"Yes, but mostly I want to discuss her association with your mother."

Stunned, Meagan repeated what he said. "Her association with my mother? She knew my mom?" She leaned forward. "When?"

"A long time ago," he replied, while Meagan remained perched on the edge of her seat, waiting for him to expound.

Seven

Garrett noticed how eager Meagan was to hear what he had to say, so he got right to the point, telling her what he knew. "When Mom was researching your background, she discovered that your mother was a member of a Native American women's group that she once belonged to. This particular branch was a sewing circle."

"Was the woman who belonged to that group Mary *Aénéva*-Quinn?" Meagan asked, as if she wanted to be absolutely certain they were talking about the right person.

"Yes. That's her. *Aénéva*. Her maiden name means *Winter Time*." When she nodded, confirming the translation, he said, "My great-great-grandfather's name was *É-hestáseve*. It means *There is Snow*. So that's how my family got the surname Snow." Garrett frowned a little. "I suppose it's strange, isn't it, how your mother's people are Winter Time and mine are Snow?"

"There are a lot of strange things between us, Garrett."

She glanced at the pool and then back at him. "How well did our moms know each other?"

"Not well. They only attended a few meetings at the same time. But Mom can tell you whatever you want to know when you meet her. I don't have all the details. I didn't want to know too much about it."

"Why not?"

"Because I didn't used to think it was important."

"But now you do?"

"It's sure starting to seem that way." He couldn't deny this was affecting him now that he'd told her about it. Meagan even looked as if she were battling the urge to cry.

She said, "I nearly fell apart after my mom died. It was so sudden, her heart failure. There was no time to prepare for it." She paused. "But I'm glad that she never saw what happened to me. How I stole the money and went to prison. That would have destroyed her."

"Maybe you wouldn't have done it if she'd still been alive."

"You're right. I'm sure I wouldn't have." The tears Meagan had been fighting gathered in her eyes. "Her funeral was one of the worst days of my life."

Garrett got up and sat in the patio chair next to hers, wanting to be closer to her. "She's at peace, Meagan." In the old Cheyenne way, the souls of the departed traveled along the Milky Way to the place of the dead, where they met with friends and family who'd also passed on.

"I know. But it still hurts."

"I'm sorry." He'd never lost anyone he loved, but he'd lived on the edge of fear, wondering when it was going to happen to him. "When I was in foster care, I used to lie awake at night and worry that my mom was going to die and that I'd never see her again. Then I'd go home and, after a while, she would fall ill again. It was a vicious cycle that never seemed to end."

"You told me before that she had an autoimmune disease. But you never said what it was."

"She has lupus. It's a chronic inflammatory disease. There's no cure for it, but treatment can help control the symptoms. They can range from mild to severe."

"It sounds awful."

"Mom has always been a sickly person. But she has her good moments, too. She hasn't been symptomatic all the time. Even when I was a kid, she was able to work and go places and try to live a fairly normal life."

"So why was she hospitalized?"

"Soon after my twelfth birthday, she took me on a camping trip. She was determined to get out there and commune with nature. She wanted both of us to have that experience. But it backfired, and she got bitten by a tick and contracted Lyme disease. The combination of the Lyme disease and the lupus was too much for her. She got violently ill. Lyme disease can be severe on its own, but for someone with an autoimmune disease, it is even worse."

"No wonder you were afraid that she was going to die."

"It took years for her to recover from the Lyme disease. For her, it became chronic. She couldn't even get out of bed in the beginning. And when she finally got well, she would have relapses." His stomach tightened with the memory. "And even after she recovered, she was still weak from the lupus. It's a miracle that she survived, with the toll it took on her."

Meagan put her hand on top of his, where it was resting on the arm of his chair. "I can only imagine what you went through, seeing her like that."

Her fingertips sent a rush of heat through his body. "I guess it's why I'm still so protective of her now."

"That's understandable." She removed her hand from his and placed it on her lap. "You have a right to protect her."

He wished that Meagan would touch him again. He'd found it soothing and stirring, and he wanted more. So much more. "I'm heavily involved in a lupus foundation. And one for Lyme disease, too."

"Along with running a foster children's charity?" She smiled a little. "You're a busy man."

Not too busy to be enthralled with her, he thought. "I'll let Mom know that we're going to work out a time for you to meet her."

"I really want to hear about her experience with my mother. And I promise I'll be sensitive to her health issues. I won't do anything to wear her out."

"I trust you." In all sorts of ways, he realized.

"Thank you. Hearing you say that is..." She couldn't seem to find the words to express herself.

He understood exactly how she felt. He wanted to express himself by kissing her senseless. But he couldn't.

"It's probably time for me to go work," she said.

No doubt it was. "Maybe we can do this again."

"Have breakfast at your house?"

He looked into her eyes. "Yes."

She gazed into his. "I'd love to come back, anytime you want me to."

He would use any excuse to be alone with her, to satisfy the erotic feeling it gave him. Garrett had it bad—this crazy desire for her. "I'll walk you out."

They got up at the same time, and he escorted her through the house and back down the entryway stairs to the front door. He went outside with her, and they stood in the courtyard of his home.

"Thank you for a lovely morning," she said.

"Was it lovely, Meagan? Even with the heavy stuff we talked about?"

"Yes, it still was." She reached out to hug him.

And *bam*! he was holding her in his arms. Holding her so damned close, he never wanted to let go. He ran his hand down her back, where her long, glorious hair was falling like silk.

"You're a Winter Time woman," he whispered.

"And you're a man called Snow," she whispered back.

"A snowman?" he asked and made both of them laugh. But his silly joke didn't stop the moment from escalating. It only made it seem fresh and sweet. He noticed the scent from the evergreen trees swirling around them.

Meagan remained in his arms, clasped in the hug she'd initiated. Clearly, she didn't want to let go, either.

"You have pretty hair," he said. He was still skimming a hand up and down her back.

"I wore it loose for you." She caught her breath. "I can't believe I just told you that."

He finally released her and stepped back, so he could look at her. "It's okay that you told me." He liked knowing how strongly he affected her.

She bit down on her bottom lip. "I need to braid it before I go to work."

"I can do it for you."

She seemed nervous but excited, too, at the prospect of him doing something so personal for her. "Are you sure?"

"I'm positive." He paused. "Do you have a rubber band?"

"I have this." She reached into the pocket of her jeans and produced a red ponytail holder.

He took it from her. "Turn around, and we'll do it right here." Standing in his courtyard, surrounded by tall trees and big flowering plants.

She presented him her back, and he separated her hair into three sections and began plaiting it into a long, shiny braid. He took his time, doing it carefully. When the job was complete, he wound the ponytail holder around the end.

Meagan turned to face him once again. "Thank you, Garrett."

"You're welcome." Unable to help himself, he skimmed her cheek with his fingertip.

"Just let me know when your mom is ready to meet me," she said, with a slight shiver.

"I will." He didn't ask if she was cold. He suspected that she was feeling all too warm—that her shiver was a reaction to his touch.

She walked to her car, her braid swishing as she moved.

Garrett had no idea how long they could keep this going without being together. Only he wasn't sure what being together would entail.

All he knew was how badly he wanted her.

Meagan adored Garrett's mother. From the very instant they said hello, a bond was formed. The older woman's name was Shirley, and she was kind and gracious and warm.

It was just the two of them in Shirley's penthouse suite. Meagan felt right at home amid the little statuettes of fantasy creatures scattered about. Meagan had always loved fairy tales. As a little girl she'd immersed herself in them.

As for Shirley, she reminded Meagan of a fortune-teller, with her long, graying black hair and colorful clothes. She even had a deck of Native American–themed tarot cards that she was studying how to use. Meagan didn't ask for a reading because Shirley claimed that she hadn't mastered them yet.

They sat next to each other, drinking hot tea from floral-printed cups. There was a fruit-and-cheese platter on the coffee table, too, ordered from room service.

"Do you have a picture of your daughter that I can see?" Shirley asked.

"I have tons." Meagan smiled and removed her smartphone from her purse. "But this is my favorite." It was the image of Ivy she used as the wallpaper on her phone. Ivy was dressed in her favorite Western outfit and was waving at the camera.

"Oh, my. How sweet she is. Just so beautiful." Shirley glanced up. "She looks like you. And you look like your mother, from what I can recall."

Here it was. The conversation about Meagan's mom. She'd been waiting for this.

Shirley continued by saying, "When I saw you at your sentencing, your last name didn't ring a bell. It wasn't until I researched you later and discovered your mother's maiden name that it hit me. That I once knew a woman whose name translated to Winter Time. Your mother joined the group under her Cheyenne name, not under Quinn."

"When was this?" Garrett had mentioned it had been a long time ago, but the era wasn't clear. "Was my mom even married yet?"

"Oh, yes, she was. In fact, she was pregnant, with her tummy out to here." Shirley formed a large circle with her arms. "She was a lovely lady." A pause, then: "It was about twenty-seven years ago."

"Oh, my goodness. That was me in her stomach."

Garrett's mother gave her a big smile. "Yes, it was you."

Meagan felt a rush of sweet, sweet warmth. "I was there, inside her, when you met. Garrett didn't mention that to me, but I guess he didn't know."

"No, I didn't tell him. Up until now, he hasn't agreed

with me about how important it is that I knew your mother. He didn't want to hear the details."

"He said that you and my mother only saw each other a few times."

"That's true. She was a new member, and she only came to two or three meetings. I assumed that she took time off because she was nearing her due date and would be back later. But she never returned. I do remember how easily we talked, though. We joked about her being Winter Time and me being Snow."

Meagan nodded. She and Garrett had joked about the same thing, right before he'd braided her hair with those strong, capable hands. She would never forget the feeling it gave her.

"Your mother talked about her children," Shirley said. "She told me that she had two boys and the one in her womb was a girl."

"Did you tell her about Garrett?"

"Yes, of course. He would have been around five then. He was such a serious little boy."

Meagan tried to get a mental image of him at that age. But it was tough not to think of him as the big, powerful man he was today. "Serious suits him." She waited a beat before she asked, "Did he tell you that I had a baby sister?"

"No, he didn't."

"I was eight when Ella was born. But she died six months later, from SIDS."

"Oh, honey. I'm so sorry."

"After she died, I thought of her as an angel. But she was my mother's little fairy, too. The name Ella means *beautiful fairy.*"

"What a pretty name." Shirley reached for one of the fairies in her collection. A tiny winged girl with big brown eyes and blue-black hair. "You can keep this. For Ella."

Meagan clutched the figurine. "Are you sure?"

"Absolutely."

"Thank you." She wrapped the fairy in a napkin and slipped it carefully into her purse. "I'll put it in Ivy's room at my house. She doesn't sleep there yet. She's still spending each night with my brother and his fiancée, but at some point Ivy is going to move in with me. My family thinks it will happen soon, but I'm being careful not to push her before she's ready. It's still hard, though, not having her there."

"I know what you mean. I was lost when Garrett wasn't living with me. But I was too ill to care for him."

"He told me about the camping trip."

"Who would have seen that coming, me contracting another disease on top on what was already wrong with me? But things are so much better now. Garrett and I both weathered it."

"I'm going to meet Jake and Max at a charity event next Saturday. A picnic in the park."

"That will be nice for you. You'll be able to clear the air with them the way you have with Garrett."

Shirley didn't seem to be aware that Meagan and her son were dancing on the edge of desire, with the air getting thicker each time they saw each other.

"Did my mother tell you anything about my father?" Meagan asked.

"No, she didn't. But maybe she would have if we'd gotten to know each other better."

"They had a terrible marriage. But she loved him just the same."

Shirley watched her as the smoke from scented candles perfumed the room. "Do you love the father of your child?"

"Not anymore. I haven't loved Neil since I stole the money." Since she'd met Garrett on that very first day;

since he'd given her his handkerchief; since he'd presented her with that long-ago daisy. "But even after I stopped loving Neil, I was still being loyal to him."

"When I discovered that you'd had a baby in prison, it made me so sad for you. Especially when I learned that your boyfriend had washed his hands of it. Then, when I uncovered the connection I once had to your pregnant mother, I just couldn't get you out of my mind."

"Thank you so much for caring about my situation and convincing your son to hire me and help me get paroled. Without you, I wouldn't have such a fulfilling job." *Or be getting so close to Garrett*, Meagan thought. "I love working with the horses. And being near the beach. It's such an idyllic setting."

"I'm glad you're happy working here and that it's giving you a fresh start in life." Shirley smiled. "Everyone deserves a clean slate."

"Since we've been speaking so candidly, can I ask you something about Garrett's father?"

"If I loved him?"

"Yes." Meagan was curious to know.

"In the beginning, I thought I did. But after he left, all that mattered was the baby I was going to have."

"My daughter is my priority now, too. I'm going to show her the fairy you gave me, and I'm going to tell her its name is Ella."

"I'm glad you came to visit me. We've had such a nice talk."

"Yes, we have." They'd discussed so many vital subjects. Yet the one thing Meagan couldn't mention was how badly she was yearning for Garrett.

The next day, Meagan joined Garrett at his house once again. This time, they'd agreed on six thirty. So she dropped

Ivy off at day care, bright and early, and headed for his castle in the sky.

She'd just arrived, and so far all they'd done was embrace. A long, lingering, body-warming hug.

"Are you ready?" he whispered.

"For breakfast?" she asked, just as quietly. "I'm not really all that hungry."

"Then why are you here?"

She shifted to meet his gaze. "To be near you." She softly added, "In your company." She skimmed her fingers down his shirt, wishing she could unbutton it. Once again, he was only halfway dressed for work.

"So I shouldn't cook?"

"Not yet."

He smoothed a hand down her hair. She'd left it unbraided for him. "What should we do instead?"

"You could show me your room." She knew it was a bold thing to say, but she didn't care. She needed to convey her feelings, especially in light of how easily they were touching each other. "I've been wondering what your bedroom is like."

"That's a dangerous thought, Meagan."

"I can't help it." She looked into the depths of his eyes, nearly losing herself in them. They were the deepest, darkest, richest shade of brown with tiny amber flecks that she hadn't noticed before now. "What have you been wondering about?"

"What it would feel like to kiss you."

"That's easy to find out." Meagan lifted her chin, inviting him to satisfy his curiosity.

He hesitated but only for a moment. Clearly, his willpower was on the brink. He tugged her even closer, lowered his head and put his lips warmly against hers.

Holy. Heaven. On. Earth.

Everything inside her went wonderfully weak. The kiss started off soft and slow, like a lone leaf floating in the wind. She lifted her hands and looped them around his neck. By now, Meagan was actually teetering in her boots.

He deepened the kiss, the taste of desire rising between them. She could feel it, overflowing with every sexy swirl of his tongue.

She moaned and asked the Creator to forgive her. Because anything this good, this hot, this exciting had to be a sin.

"We shouldn't be doing this," he said, even as he kept doing it.

"I know." But she couldn't seem to control her urges any more than he could. Her body was pressed intimately against his.

He tightened his hold on her, his hands looped around her waist. "When I first got to know you, I kept hoping that you would leave Neil, so I could dash in and sweep you off your feet. But you stayed with him, and then I discovered all the craziness that was going on."

The craziness of what she'd done to him and his foster brothers. "I'm sorry."

"No more apologies, Meagan. We're getting past that."

She looked into his eyes as intently as before. The gold flecks were still there, but now she realized it was a trick of the light. A beautiful illusion. "You're sweeping me off my feet now." He was as dashing as any man could be.

He kissed her again and she let the sensation immerse her.

When he stepped back, she asked, "Are you going to show me your room?"

He ran his thumb along her jaw, as if he was memorizing the angles of her face. "I already told you that's a dangerous thought."

"And I already told you that I can't help wanting to see it." She had been memorizing him in her sleep in the hours just before dawn, when she dreamed the hardest. "I've been fantasizing about you since the day you gave me the daisy. I went home that night to Neil, but it was you who was on my mind. You, I wanted."

His voice turned rough, as gravely as she'd ever heard. "Are you seducing me, Meagan?"

Was she? She honestly didn't know. She'd never seduced anyone before. "Before now, all I've ever done was what men told me to do." She'd never been her own woman, speaking her own mind.

"If I take you to my room, all sorts of bad things could result from it."

A jolt of electricity shot through her. "Bad things?"

"I just don't want to take advantage of you."

"How can you be taking advantage of me if I'm seducing you?"

"I don't know." He kept touching her face. "But I don't usually act on impulse."

"Neither do I." Being this impulsive was new to her. "But we don't have to shout it out to the rest of the world." Her instinct was to keep it between them, to let it be theirs, and theirs alone. "No one except us has to know."

His breath rushed out. "A secret affair?"

She nodded. "As far as anyone else knows, we're just friends."

"Are we going to be able to act that convincingly?"

"I was in a school play once," she teased him. "When I was in second grade. It was a Thanksgiving production, and I played one of the Indians."

He smiled. He even laughed. "Now there's a stretch."

She cuddled up to him, close and warm. "I wanted to be the turkey."

"And get eaten?"

"It didn't get eaten in our play. It got to dance around on stage with the pumpkin pie."

He nuzzled her hair. "I love pumpkin pie."

"I'll bake one for you sometime."

"With lots of whipped cream on top?" He ran his tongue along the side of her neck.

This was the most dizzying foreplay she'd ever imagined. "Whatever you want, you can have."

"I want you."

"Then take me." For their secret affair, she thought. For the heat and passion they'd both been craving.

He reached for her hand and squeezed it. "I'm going to show you my room now." He waited a second, as if he was giving her a chance to change her mind.

But she had no intention of doing that. This was exactly what she needed, what she was desperate for.

Garrett took her down the hall, past two guest rooms and into the master suite. The door was already open, and they both stepped inside. He was still holding her hand.

His room boasted cherrywood furniture and maroon-colored accents. The curtains on the glass doors that overlooked the pool were closed, just as they'd been the other day. The paintings on the walls consisted of misty seascapes, and a carefully woven dream catcher, decorated with shiny gold beads and a red-tailed hawk feather, dangled from the headboard. The bed itself was neatly made. Meagan had left hers in a pile of blankets this morning as she'd rushed out the door.

She turned her attention back to him. "Can I unbutton your shirt?" she asked, itching to bare his flesh.

"Only if I can unbutton yours," he replied, moving forward to make the moment happen.

Eight

Garrett was living out a fantasy, right here and now. He was being seduced, but he was part of the seduction, too, taking what he wanted, what he needed.

He'd never expected Meagan to end up in his bedroom this morning, yet here she was—so soft and pretty and willing.

He undid the first button on her blouse. Then the second. Then the third. He stopped there, simply to admire her. By now, he could see the tops of her breasts. Her skin was golden brown, and her bra was white.

She went after his shirt, opening it all the way. And when she placed her hand against his chest, his heart pounded like a shaman's drum.

"Wow," she said, running the tip of an index finger down the center of his body. "Look at you and your hot-guy abs."

Garrett was too busy looking at her. "You're the hot one." He finished unbuttoning her blouse. He reached around and unhooked her bra, too.

He finished disrobing her to the best of his ability. She had to help, removing her boots and shimmying out of her jeans.

Finally, when she stood before him in her loosened bra and wispy blue panties, he pulled her closer and kissed her. She made a sound that reminded him of something wild. An exotic creature, he thought, in the midst of a forbidden mating. He suspected that she was going to be the most untamed lover he ever had. The most fulfilling, too. Already, it was an intoxicating combination.

Her bra was discarded and so was his shirt. Her breasts were full and round, her caramel-colored nipples hard and pressed against him. He kept her in the tight circle of his arms.

Once again, Meagan made *that* sound, the feral little throat rumbling, and he thought he might lose what was left of his sex-hungry mind. He backed her toward the bed, one step at a time.

"Garrett." She spoke softly. "Shouldn't we pull aside the covers first?"

Details, he thought. But she was right. He wanted to lie upon his cool, crisp sheets with her.

He released her and turned down the quilt. He removed a condom from the nightstand drawer, too. Another detail. A necessity that couldn't be overlooked.

He stripped down to his underwear, and they got into bed. He slipped his hand past the waistband of her panties, and she smiled and slid her hand straight into his briefs.

He was already aroused. So was she. But the foreplay felt good. So damned good. They messed around, rubbing and touching until their undergarments came off.

The early-morning light enhanced her appearance. Meagan's nakedness was breathtaking. Her hair was beautiful, too, fanning across the pillow and tumbling down her body. They hadn't even consummated their union yet, and already he longed to keep her there for the rest of the day. But that was impossible.

To compensate for it, he said, "Will you lie still for me?"

She furrowed her brows. "Why do you want me to do that?"

"So I can taste you." He wanted her to come before he was inside her, to watch her while she mewled and moaned, to drive her decidedly mad.

She didn't refuse his request. She even reached back to grip the rails on the headboard, as if that might help keep her still.

Kissing his way down her body, he treated her with the ultimate care. He took his time, purposely toying with her senses. Her lashes fluttered, but she didn't close her eyes. She watched him as he watched her.

Garrett used his mouth in clever ways, and as he focused on that one little spot, she let go of the headboard and delved all ten fingers into his hair. Lifting her knees, she arched her hips.

So eager. So carnal.

"Do you want more, Meagan?"

"Yes—" she kept her gaze trained on him, her voice going choppy, her limbs quavering "—more."

He kept doing what he was doing, bathing her with lust and intimacy. She was on the verge of orgasm, just seconds away from the first shudder. He felt her resolve, as sure as he felt his own rocking desire. He swirled his tongue, and her hands tightened in his hair.

She came in a feminine fever, shaking against the current and making the erotic sounds he wanted to hear.

He waited until the last shiver receded before he rose

up to kiss her forehead. She reacted just as gently, drawing her arms around him.

And holding him romantically close.

Meagan clung to Garrett, giving herself time to recover from the heat shimmering through her veins. It was like glitter, she thought, lighting up her blood.

"You okay?" he asked.

"I'm wonderful." She nuzzled closer. "How are you?"

He pressed his erection against her stomach. "How do I feel?"

Like a man in need, she thought. Ditching her sweet afterglow, she closed her hand around him. She shouldn't be getting so dreamy about him, anyway. This was just an affair, after all. A wild, glorious affair.

"Maybe I better take care of that for you," she said.

"Yeah." He kissed her, his mouth warm and stirring against hers. "Maybe you should."

Meagan stroked him, enjoying the feeling, the hardness of his body, the strength and power he emitted. She didn't ease up, not until she made him bead at the tip. She even collected the saltiness on her thumb, tasting it for her own pleasure.

In the next anxious instant, they rolled over the bed, sunlight streaming in through the windows.

Garrett took the condom off the nightstand and tore into the packet. He put on the protection and entered her.

He pushed deeper, and Meagan wrapped her legs around him.

"Damn," he said, as she squeezed tighter.

She smiled. Obviously, he liked it.

She trailed her fingers along his stomach, tracing his sinfully sculpted abs, unable to keep her hands off of him.

He looked down at the place where their bodies were joined. She did, too. It was a thrilling sight.

They moved in unison, their rhythm slick and ravenous. He shifted his position and rolled over, taking her with him and putting her on top.

She straddled him, and when she tipped back her head so he could pepper her neck with hot little kisses, her hair fell behind her, flowing to her tailbone.

He reached around and grabbed a handful, tugging on the long dark strands and tangling them however he saw fit. His roughness excited her. She almost wished that he would mar her skin, leaving evidence of his kisses. But he seemed to know better than to brand her.

"Have you done this before?" she asked.

"Done what?"

"Been with a woman you shouldn't be with?"

"No. I'm private about who I date, but I don't…"

"Have secret rendezvous?"

He nodded and sought her lips. This particular kiss was terrifying. The kind that left you wanting more than you were capable of handling.

Was he right about what he'd said earlier? Was their affair destined to go bad? She'd stolen from him, this billionaire who lived a quiet and cautious life, and now she was buck naked in his bed. Where was the logic in that?

Nonetheless, she didn't want to stop being his lover. Meagan longed to be with him, to continue what she'd started.

Once the kiss ended, she tried to catch her breath, to slow down and make the moment last. But he was still holding a fistful of her hair, urging her on.

She gave in to the frenzy, riding him hard and fast and becoming part of his thirst for completion.

When he came, she absorbed the slamming shock and pulsing friction. He even growled in her ear.

Afterward, he went into the adjoining bathroom to dispose of the condom and she remained in bed, clutching the sheet. She was still reeling from the force of his climax.

He returned and sat next to her, and she wanted to fling her arms around him and never let go. Of course there was no logic in that, either. However long this lasted, it wasn't going to be forever. But that shouldn't matter. She'd chosen to be with him. She'd acted on her desires. But she wasn't going to allow herself to get attached, at least not in a way that would involve the tattered strings of her heart. Falling for Garrett, any more than she already had, wasn't in her best interest.

Or so she kept telling herself.

"What time is it?" she asked, trying to be brave and free, like an uncommitted lover should be.

"I don't know. I don't have a clock in here."

When he leaned toward her, she waited a beat, thinking that he was going to reach out and hold her. But he didn't. Disappointment washed over her, mingled with a wave of relief. "How do you wake up without a clock?"

"I set the alarm on my phone."

"Where's your phone?" Hers was still in her car.

"In the kitchen. I took it in there before you arrived, when I thought I'd be making breakfast for you. Speaking of which, we still need to eat."

"I can't be late for work." A shot of panic set in. "What if I'm late already?"

"You don't have to be there until nine, and you got here at six-thirty. We haven't been in bed that long."

"Are you sure?" Sleeping with the owner of the resort was no excuse for being late. It would make her feel cheap and dirty, even if she wasn't taking advantage of the situation purposely.

"Yeah, I'm sure." He climbed into his underwear and then his pants. "You can get dressed and meet me in kitchen. And feel free to freshen up, if you need to."

"Thank you." She worked on calming herself down, on taking a deep breath. "But I still need to be mindful of getting to work on time."

"I know." He resumed his spot next to her. "But I can't help wanting to keep you here."

She smiled, warmed by his admission. Worrying about her feelings for him was foolish. She just needed to go with the flow.

Finally, he headed for the kitchen, and she trailed into the bathroom, carrying her clothes.

Meagan got herself ready. She rebuttoned her chambray blouse, tucked it into her cowgirl-cut jeans and braided her hair, taming the tangled mess Garrett had made out of it.

She entered the kitchen, and he greeted her with a cup of coffee, which smelled heavenly.

He said, "There's cream and sugar on the counter. Sugar substitutes, too, if you prefer those. Oh, and you've got an hour before you need to go to work."

"A whole hour?" She glanced at the microwave clock, confirming the timeline. "Who knew?"

"I did. If you want a repeat performance, we could go back to my room." He waggled his eyebrows. "Or we could do it here. I could lift you onto the sink. Or we could make use of the floor. Or bump and grind against the fridge."

She laughed. "You wish."

"Yeah, I do." Suddenly he didn't look like he was joking around anymore.

Meagan felt the steam rising from her cup. Steam could have been rising from her body, too. She changed the subject to keep herself from mauling him. If they went at it again, she would be late for work for sure. "What are you making for breakfast?"

"I thought I'd throw together something sweet. I've got pancakes in the freezer. I can warm them in the microwave, and we can smother them in syrup."

He made pancakes sound like the sexiest thing ever. And for now, they were. He quickly prepared the meal, and with every bite Meagan took, maple syrup melted in her mouth.

"So exactly when are we going to do this again?" he asked.

She added even more syrup. She couldn't seem to get enough. "As soon as we're both able."

"I'm free on Sunday."

"I might be, if Candy and Tanner can watch Ivy on that day for me. But first you and I need to get through the charity event on Saturday."

"You're right. We've got that coming up." He watched her eat. "We'll be putting our acting skills to the test."

"I don't think I should stay the whole time." Meagan chewed and swallowed, a little more slowly than before. She liked that he was watching her, but he was making her self-conscious, too. "I think it's better if we keep our public appearances to a minimum."

"That's fine. You can arrive late or leave a little early, whichever works for you. But my brothers are expecting you so don't bail out completely, okay?"

"I would never do that." She wanted to make a good impression. "I'll probably be nervous, though, especially now that we're sleeping together."

"I know. It's going to be weird." He moved closer, his face just inches from hers. "But we'll just do the best we can, keeping this secret of ours."

Before she could respond, he kissed her while the syrup was still warm and sticky on both of their lips.

When he let her go, she teetered in her chair and finished her pancakes, devouring every sweet and spongy bite.

Meagan had no idea where Garrett was. She was supposed to text him when she arrived, but she hadn't done that yet. Instead, she strolled through the park, carrying Ivy on her hip.

Along with the barbecue itself, lots of other activities were underway. While a variety of games were being played by some of the younger kids, a group of rebellious-looking teenagers opted for an aggressive match of volleyball. In another direction, Frisbees soared, with humans and dogs alike chasing them. There was a standard playground with slides and swings and such, but a bouncy castle was available, too. On the outskirts of it all was a trackless train, carrying a load of all-aged passengers.

Clearly, there was plenty to do, but Meagan had also brought along a satchel of toys to keep Ivy occupied. She figured they would come in handy when they were sitting still. At the moment, though, Ivy was craning her neck to see everything, pointing to this and that.

Finally, Meagan sent Garrett a text letting him know her whereabouts. She was near a professional face-painting booth.

Garrett quickly replied to the text: Stay there. I'll come get u.

Meagan typed: OK.

It wasn't the most scintillating exchange, but they were both behaving like friends instead of lovers. Adding a sexy emoticon to her message wouldn't do.

"We're waiting for Garrett," Meagan told her child. "We're going to meet his brothers."

Ivy angled her head. "Him brothees?"

"He has two." She wasn't going to say that they'd lived in foster care together or try to explain what that meant. She kept it simple where her toddler was concerned.

"Me no brothees."

No, her baby girl didn't have any siblings. Meagan couldn't even think about more children right now. She was still trying to be the perfect mother to this one. And it wasn't easy, not with her lack of experience.

Feeling far too reflective, she looked at her child's sweet, round face. She'd labored over Ivy's hair today because the two-year-old wanted it in a style that Candy typically fixed for her, and Candy hadn't been home to do it. But Meagan finally created a hairdo that made Ivy happy, using a host of sparkly barrettes. The fussy toddler also wanted to wear her new toy tiara, so that was fastened onto her head, too.

Ivy said, "There Garry!"

Meagan spun around. Dang, but her kid had a knack for finding Garrett. She was like a bat in that regard, honing in with her "Garry" radar.

As he walked toward them, Meagan's pulse skyrocketed. He moved with masculine grace, his shoulders strong and erect. When he smiled, she thought about how delicious he was in bed.

Ivy reached out to him. Clearly, she wanted him to hold her. Meagan understood just how she felt.

He scooped the child right up. He met Meagan's gaze, but he didn't linger. He played his part like he was supposed to, but their secret was still there, deep in his eyes.

He spoke to Ivy. "Well, look at you, princess. You have a crown."

"Me prinny."

He chuckled and asked Meagan, "Is she saying that she's pretty?"

"No. She's confirming that she's a princess."

"Indeed you are," he said to Ivy.

"Her tiara is new," Meagan told him, noticing how excited her daughter was perched in his arms. "We got it yesterday. She saw it at the pharmacy and insisted that she had to have it. She has some real tiaras that Candy has put away for her. But she isn't allowed to wear those yet."

"Real?" he asked.

"They're not diamonds or anything. But they came from Candy's old beauty pageants, so they're real in that sense."

"Someday Ivy will have lots of diamonds." He bounced her. "Won't you, princess?"

Ivy didn't respond to him. She was too busy watching a rambunctious group of boys who'd come out of the face-painting booth with superhero masks artfully painted around their eyes.

Garrett turned his attention to Meagan. "My brothers already got their food. Carol did also, but she's eating for two. She said it was an excuse to go back for seconds." He smiled and then shrugged, as if his knowledge of pregnant women was limited. "I haven't eaten yet. I was waiting for you and Ivy."

"That was nice of you." She appreciated how courteous he was. "But before we load up on barbecue, can I meet Jake and Carol and Max?" She couldn't eat until that was over.

"That's fine." He gestured to a stretch of lawn past the volleyball courts. "They're out that way. We're not using any of the picnic benches. We brought a blanket and folding chairs for our group."

Meagan noticed that lots of families had done that very same thing. People were scattered all over the grass.

Suddenly Ivy exclaimed, "Me!" and pointed to a little girl with stars and moons on her cheeks. "Me! Me!"

"Do you want your face painted?" Meagan asked her.

Ivy nodded so hard that she looked like one of those toy bobbleheads.

Meagan certainly didn't want to deny her daughter the magic of being made up. "Do you mind if we take a detour?" she asked Garrett. "Then I can meet everyone and we can eat?"

"Sounds good to me." He headed straight for the booth, hauling the little bobblehead with him. "It'll be fun."

They got in line, and Ivy squirmed in Garrett's arms, impatient for her turn.

Thankfully, there was an entire crew of makeup artists doing the work, so they didn't have to wait long. The artists themselves were dressed like fairies, their skin glowing with pixie dust.

Illustrations of the types of designs that were available for Ivy's age range were presented to her. Arms and ankles could be decorated, too. But Ivy didn't know what she wanted. She was more interested in the fairy who was going to paint her.

"Ella," the toddler said, her eyes wide with enchantment. Apparently, she thought that the young woman's costume was real.

A lump formed in Meagan's throat. Ever since she'd shown her daughter the tiny statue that had come from Garrett's mom and told her its name was Ella, Ivy had begun calling all fairies that. Meagan glanced at Garrett and a moment of silence passed between them.

Then Ivy said to the fairy, "Me Prinny Iby."

Meagan translated. "She's Princess Ivy."

The artist smiled. "How about a design with ivy leaves?" She demonstrated where they would go. "And some hearts and diamonds, too?"

Meagan approved of the suggestion. So did Garrett, it seemed, with the way he was grinning at Ivy. But he'd already mentioned diamonds earlier.

The process was quick and easy. Within no time, Ivy's face was decorated with just the right amount of shimmer to match her drugstore tiara.

The fairy held up a mirror, and Ivy gasped at her new reflection. Clearly, she was delighted with how she looked. Meagan felt great, too, seeing her daughter so happy.

Ivy waved goodbye to the makeup artist, and they were on their way. But Ivy didn't want to be carried anymore. She insisted on walking on her own between Meagan and Garrett and holding both of their hands. When she decided that she wanted them to swing her, she jumped in the air, leaving them little choice but to accommodate her.

Garrett chuckled. "She's got us right where she wants us."

Meagan laughed, as well. Her kid definitely had a superior attitude. "She's the princess, and we're her court."

"So you're the lady-in-waiting and I'm the knight?" He held tight to Ivy's hand and turned his admiring gaze on Meagan. "I'm really glad that you're here with me."

Her heart fluttered. "So am I." She was having a brilliant time, and the day had only just begun.

Nine

As Garrett steered Meagan and Ivy toward his brothers, Meagan geared up for the meeting.

She spotted Jake, looking like a modern-day rebel with his stylishly messy hair and dark sunglasses. His adoring wife, Carol, was an attractive strawberry blonde with a radiant glow. Meagan remembered how it felt to be big and round with a babe in her belly, except that she'd cried through most of her pregnancy, worrying about her child's future.

She noticed how content Jake and Carol seemed. They were seated next to each other, as cozy as could be. It appeared that they'd already finished their lunches and disposed of their plates.

On the other side of Jake, however, was a vacant chair with a paper plate of half-eaten food on it. Meagan assumed it belonged to Max, even if he wasn't anywhere to be seen. The edge of the napkin tucked beneath the plate was fluttering in the breeze, like a bird attempting to take flight—a symbol, perhaps, of Max's elusive personality.

Meagan shifted her gaze. The other vacant chairs were for her and Garrett and Ivy. The one for Ivy was smaller and designed for a child. Garrett had thought of everything.

He made the official introductions. Jake and Carol stood to shake Meagan's hand. They said hello to Ivy, too, and gushed over her painted face.

After the greeting, Meagan spoke directly to Jake, telling him how sorry she was about what she'd done.

He accepted her apology, his manner kind yet casual. They exchanged a smile, and that was that. It was over. She didn't need to mention it to him again. It almost seemed too easy. But she didn't mind. Easy was good.

"What happened to Max?" Garrett asked his brother.

Jake motioned with his chin. "He's over there, talking to Lizzie."

Curious, Meagan glanced in the direction of where Max was. He was engaged in conversation with a beautiful woman, a tall, slim redhead who looked like a socialite, a high-society type Meagan would never come across in the real world. Or a world that didn't involve Garrett and his brothers, she amended.

After a few minutes, Ivy turned restless. She climbed onto Garrett's lap and then onto Meagan's and then onto her own chair. But that didn't last long. Soon she was sitting on the blanket, dumping her toys into a pile and moving them around. One of them was a monkey with a pink bonnet on its head and a pacifier in its mouth.

Carol asked her, "May I see your baby?"

Ivy inched forward and gave it to her.

Carol rocked the stuffed monkey and said, "I'm having my own baby. For now, it's in here." She patted her ballooning belly. "It's a girl. Like you."

Ivy's little mouth formed a giant O, and she moved closer to examine Carol's stomach. Jake showed Ivy how to glide her hand around to make the baby kick. When it happened, Ivy burst into a fit of giggles, making the adults laugh, too.

"Have you chosen a name for your daughter?" Meagan asked the expectant parents.

Jake replied, "We're going to call her Nita Shivaun. Nita is a Choctaw name so we chose it to represent my family, and Shivaun has Irish origins so we picked that to honor Carol's family. Both sets of her maternal great-grandparents were from Ireland."

"It's a pretty combination." Meagan liked the way it sounded. "What does Nita mean?"

"Bear. We've been getting so many teddy bears as gifts that it just seems to fit. We had a lot of Irish names in mind, but we liked Shivaun because it's the Irish form of Joan, and Carol's mother's name was Joan."

"I named Ivy after a princess in a book I read. Her full name is Ivy Ann."

"She's beautiful," Carol said, studying Meagan's daughter, as if she were wondering what her own mixed-blood child was going to look like.

Jake's wife returned the monkey, and Ivy placed it on the blanket, putting the plush primate down for its nap. She patted its furry head and gave it a ridiculously noisy kiss. Meagan got all warm and gooey inside, watching her precious girl pretend to be a mommy.

Then, as Max came walking over to them, Ivy looked up and boldly asked, "Who you?"

The returning brother smiled, checking out her glittery ensemble. "I think the real question is, who are you?"

She leaned back on her haunches and repeated what she'd told the fairy. "Me Prinny Iby."

"In that case, I'm Mad Max." He made a funny face. She laughed and mimicked him, scrunching up her features, too. He didn't seem concerned at this point what her actual name might be. Or what his was, for that matter.

But Ivy cared. She said to Garrett, "Him Maddy," just in case he didn't know who his oddball brother was.

"He sure is." He bumped Max's shoulder. They were standing side by side.

Max certainly had an unusual charm about him, Meagan thought, with his longish hair and pitch-dark eyes. Although he was built like a runner, he had some obvious muscle on him. His arms were cut, like Garrett's. No doubt he had hot-guy abs, too. All three foster brothers were tremendously fit.

Max turned to Meagan and said, "I remember seeing you at the accountant's office, but we never actually spoke." He nodded toward Ivy. "She's rather cool—this sparkly daughter of yours."

"Thank you." She prepared for the apology. "I'm sorry for the trouble I caused. I never should have taken what didn't belong to me."

"It's all right. You did your time. And now you're friends with Garrett." Max glanced at his brother. "He used to keep me from getting my ass kicked when I was a kid. I couldn't defend myself very well back then, and he always came to my rescue."

"You can fight your own battles now," Garrett said.

"Yes, but you were there when I needed it most."

It seemed clear that Max still regarded Garrett as a man who deserved to be honored. Meagan couldn't agree more. She said to Max, "He's been kind to me and Ivy, too."

When a hush came over all of them, Garrett said to her, "What do you think? Should we get our food?"

Meagan nodded, trying to keep a casual air. She wasn't supposed to be admiring Garrett more than was necessary.

He scooped Ivy into his arms. "Come on, princess. It's time for some barbecue." To everyone else, he said, "See you in a bit."

As the three of them headed for the buffet, Meagan glanced at Garrett. "I liked hearing what Max had to say about you."

"I liked it, too. Max doesn't always say what he feels. Sometimes he just stays quiet. He does have a close friend that he confides in, though. Lizzie always lends him her ear."

"Lizzie? You mean the glamorous redhead he was talking to earlier?"

"Yep, that's her."

Meagan couldn't help but wonder precisely what that relationship entailed. "Are they friends the way we're friends?"

Garrett leaned in close and lowered his voice. "If you're asking me if they're sleeping together, then the answer is no."

"How do you know they aren't?"

"Because they've openly discussed *not* being together. They think it'll ruin their friendship if they hook up."

"How long have they known each other?"

"Since their senior year in high school. By then, Jake and I had already graduated and left foster care, so Max was more or less on his own. He tutored Lizzie for one of her classes, which is how they got acquainted. They weren't from the same social circle. She was rich and beautiful and hung out with the popular kids, and he was a poor, skinny nerd who'd never even been to a school dance. But deep inside, they had things in common." Garrett paused. "Inner turmoil. Secrets they shared."

"We're sharing a secret."

He stopped before they reached the buffet, keeping their discussion private. Ivy clung to him, with her painted face shining sweetly in the sun.

He said, "Our secret is different, Meagan. Ours is…"

Romantic, she thought. Sexual. Everything Max and Lizzie's wasn't. "You're right. It's not the same."

After a second of silence, he asked, "Are we on for tomorrow? Did you get Candy and Tanner to babysit for you?"

"Yes." She would be coming to his house, spending a portion of the day with him. "It's all set."

"Where did you tell them that you're going?"

"To a work meeting. I told them that I'm baking a pie for it, too. That people are bringing treats."

He lifted his brows. "Is that going to be a pumpkin pie?"

She smiled. "Why, yes, it is."

"That's awesome." He paused. "But how long is this meeting supposed to last? How long are Candy and Tanner expecting you to be gone?"

"I mentioned that some of us are staying afterward to reorganize the tack room, letting them know I would be gone most of the afternoon."

"Smart thinking."

"Thanks." It was as good a lie as any, and she wanted to make the most of her stolen moments with Garrett, when they could be totally alone.

Unlike now, she thought, as they resumed walking toward the buffet, immersing themselves in the crowd.

Busy as it was, the rest of the picnic went splendidly. After they ate, they took Ivy on a train ride, where she made choo-choo sounds the entire time.

Later, Garrett convinced Meagan to get her ankle painted. He suggested a blue rose and a yellow daisy twined together. She loved the significance of it, the language of flowers she'd told him about alive in the design.

During one quiet moment, after her ankle was complete, he whispered, "I wish I could kiss you. Here, in front of everyone."

His admission struck her as sweet but frightening, too. Her feelings for him were spinning like a top, and she'd already warned herself to keep their affair in perspective.

So she leaned over and said, "You can kiss me tomorrow when we're alone." She sucked in her breath, trying to keep herself steady. "As much as you want."

On Sunday afternoon, Garrett kissed the daylights out of Meagan—on every part of her body. They'd already had sex. Hot, mind-blowing sex. He wanted to do it again. But for the time being, they leaned against the headboard, balancing plates on their laps and eating the pumpkin pie she'd baked and brought to his house. He'd topped his with a mound of whipped cream, and it tasted delicious, as decadent as a dessert should be.

"I keep thinking about yesterday," he said.

She tucked her feet under the blanket. "In what way?"

"About how tough it was to keep my hands off you." He searched her gaze. "Maybe we should just start seeing each other openly."

She put her plate on the nightstand. Her pie was half-finished. "You want to break our secret?"

"We're both consenting adults." He didn't know how long they could pull this off, coming up with stories, lying to the people closest to them. "With all of this sneaking around, our families might suspect what we're up to, anyway."

"We can always deny it."

"We shouldn't have to deny anything. We have a right to do whatever we want."

She fidgeted with her hands, locking her fingers and then releasing them. "What about public perception?"

"You mean other employees at the resort?"

She nodded. "I don't want anyone thinking that I'm trying to profit from our affair. That I'm using you for your money or trying to find a way to embezzle from you again."

"We've already made our friendship public and no one is accusing you of that now. Besides, there are only a handful of people who even know about the embezzlement, and they haven't been gossiping about it."

"I'll bet they will if they discover that we're lovers." She fidgeted again. "And who knows how long we'll be doing this?"

"Long enough, I hope." He hadn't gotten his fill of her, not by any stretch of his imagination. "I'd be happy to see you—" he raised his fork in the air "—and your pie, every day."

Her voice turned soft. "Really?"

"Yes, indeed." Every day and every night—which sounded excessive, even to him. But he couldn't help it. He wanted to spend as much time with her as he could. "Here's an idea. If you're not comfortable about doing this openly, maybe you can just tell Tanner and Candy the truth. Then you can be with me without having to lie to them anymore." He pressed her to consider it. "Just think about what a relief that would be."

"Yes, but it could create other problems, too. Once Tanner knows what I've been up to, he's not going to like it. He'll probably worry about the effect he thinks it's going to have on me."

"I'm not out to hurt you, Meagan."

She sighed. "I know. But what about my track record and how easily I get attached? I'm already concerned about that."

"You've only had one relationship to speak of. That hardly constitutes a track record."

"It doesn't?"

"No." Not to him, it didn't. "And I'm nothing like Neil, so how bad can it be, getting attached to me?" He wanted her to care about him, just as he was beginning to care about her. "We've got something special going on here."

Meagan sighed again, only it was sweeter this time. "Yes, it's special." She angled her head, her hair spilling to the side. "If I decide to come clean to Candy and Tanner, does that mean you're going to admit it to your mom and brothers?"

"Yes, of course, I'd tell them. I don't think my brothers will say much about it. They don't poke their noses into my love life. Typically, neither would my mom. She rarely even meets the women I go out with. But since this involves you, she might want to discuss it with me."

"Do you think it will concern her?"

"She'll probably just want to be sure that this isn't some quickie thing that's going to hurt either one of us. But you already know that isn't my intention. If I had my way, I'd be taking you out on a proper date for the whole world to see."

She smiled, her skin flushing in the light. "Then what would you do? Get me naked afterward?"

He put his plate aside. He'd devoured his pie and now he wanted to gobble her up, too. "When you put it that way." He leaned over her. "Take a shower with me." He nuzzled her ear. "I want to get warm and sudsy with you."

She caught her breath. "I can't."

Garrett lifted his head. "Why not?"

"Because I can't go home and pick Ivy up with my hair damp and my makeup all washed off. I said I was going to a work meeting, not a pool party."

He skimmed her cheek. "See, now this is why you need to tell your family the truth."

There was another hitch in her breath. "So I can go home all a mess?"

"No. So you can sleep here and let me wash your hair and smear your makeup and do all sorts of sexy things to you." He kept leaning over her. "You should bring Ivy here to stay the night, too. You have a portable crib for her, don't you?"

"Yes, but my daughter isn't even sleeping at my house yet. As much as I want her to move in with me, I'm still new at being her caregiver. Sometimes I think she's ready, and other times I can't be sure. So I'm just tucking her into bed at Tanner and Candy's and waiting until the moment seems right."

Garrett looked into her eyes and saw her fear. "Why? Because you're afraid that she'll reject you if you try it again too soon? Do it this evening. Take her home with you."

"She might throw a fit and cry like she did before."

"And she might not." He placed his hand against Meagan's chest, stilling the choppiness in her breathing. "Isn't it worth the risk?"

"Everything seems like such a risk now. But I guess it always did. I wasn't even sure if I was going to keep Ivy."

Confused by her statement, he set his plate off to the side. "What do you mean?"

"After she was born and I saw how close she'd become to Tanner and Ivy, I tried to convince them to adopt her. I even tried to push them together before they were ready to become a couple, specifically so they could become her parents. I was terrified that I could never be the kind of parent that my daughter needed. Tanner and Candy were just so good with her—"

"You're good with her, too, Meagan. You're amazing, in fact."

"I wasn't amazing in the beginning. I was afraid to hold her or touch her. It was awful, being in prison and not being able to see her every day, so I withdrew from her instead." She pushed a strand of her hair out of her eyes. "I was treated for postpartum depression. It happens to a lot of women, and it's especially common with new mothers in stressful situations."

"That wasn't your fault."

"No, but plenty of other things were, like how I landed in prison to begin with. If I hadn't stolen the money, I wouldn't have—"

"That's over now."

"I'm still on parole."

Determined to comfort her, to make it better somehow, he kissed her. She moaned beneath him and deepened the kiss, taking what he offered.

Itching for more, he unhooked her bra. It was the kind that clasped in front, making his quest easier.

He rubbed his thumbs over her nipples, making them peak. If only he could lift her up and carry her to the shower. If only they were free to explore each other in every possible way.

"Next time," he said.

She didn't ask him what he meant. But she seemed to understand. If she followed his advice, next time would involve the commitment of her staying the night with him, of being honest about their relationship to their families, of bringing her child to his home, of this being more than just a clandestine affair.

"Doesn't what we're doing scare you?" she asked.

"No." He liked the feeling it gave him. "Being this close to you is exhilarating."

"For me, too, but it's changing so quickly."

"Nothing bad is going to happen."

"That isn't what you said when we first got together."

"I was just trying to protect you then."

Her gaze locked onto his. "And you aren't now?"

"It's a different kind of protection now. It's how a man and a woman should be together. Without lies, without secrets."

"I'm still scared of going this fast." Her words vibrated from her throat. "I've already had too many romantic notions about you as it is."

"Then we'll take it slow."

She shook her head, but she laughed a little, too. "Says who? The big bad CEO invading my dreams?"

He pushed his hand down her panties, and she swallowed the last of her laughter.

"Is that big and bad enough for you?" he asked, shooting her his best lord-and-boss smile.

"I should have known you'd do something like that." She pressed against his fingers, encouraging his dastardly foreplay. "You're making me crazy."

"Likewise." Garrett strummed her, this beautiful lover of his.

While he made her warm and slick, she clawed the sheets. He imagined her leaving nail marks on his bedding.

Or, better yet, on his back.

Anxious to have her, he stripped her completely bare. He ditched his underwear, too, and grabbed a condom.

He plunged deep inside, and when she clawed the hell out of his back, her nails biting into his skin, he couldn't think of anything except the way she came unglued in his arms.

Making him want her more than ever.

Ten

Meagan read a bedtime story to Ivy, just as she'd been doing for the past month. But the difference was that she'd brought Ivy to her house and put her to bed there, as Garrett had encouraged her to do.

And it was working! Ivy was in her crib with a boatload of cuddly toys, her eyelids getting heavy.

No tears. No fits.

Meagan felt like a real-life mom, and it was the most beautiful feeling in the world. Ivy looked so cute, too, in her pink pajamas and fluffy nighttime hair. She shifted onto her side and pulled one of her stuffed animals closer, as content as a two-year-old could be.

Once Ivy was asleep, Meagan put down the book and came to her feet. She turned off the main light, but she left a nightlight burning. Ivy was afraid of the dark. Meagan had been, too, when she was little. She liked the darkness now, the stars and the moon and the beauty of it.

She exited Ivy's nursery and partially closed the door.

Once she was in her own room, she listened for any sounds coming from the baby monitor in case her daughter woke up and needed her. She stayed that way for hours, even though Ivy was in deep repose.

Finally, she gathered her robe and headed for the bathroom, letting her little girl sleep like the princess she was.

Needing to unwind, Meagan filled the tub and added lavender-scented Epsom salts. Then, standing in front of the mirror, she removed her clothes and twined her hair around her head, securing the thick mass with large clips.

While she soaked in the tub, she thought about her dilemma with Garrett. She'd been prepared to keep their tryst a secret. But, for all of the reasons Garrett had pointed out, it made sense to reveal the truth. Still, it was going to be tough for her to admit to her family that she was intimately involved with him. She knew darned well that Tanner wasn't going to approve. What brother would feel good about his jailbird sister sleeping with one of the men she'd ripped off? It just sounded so…

…wrong.

Only it wasn't, Meagan concluded. The affair had been her idea, and she still wanted to be Garrett's lover, as much as ever. It was the speed with which their romance was unfolding that scared her. But she'd already explained that to Garrett, and he'd already told her not to worry about it.

So how wrong could it be?

She stayed in the tub until the water cooled and then slipped on her robe and returned to her room. She had a sudden urge to converse with Garrett, but since there was too much to tell him to put it in a text, she called him. She just hoped that he was available to talk.

When he answered, her heart jumped on the spot.

"What's up?" he asked.

She replied, "All sorts of things."

"Like what?"

She glanced at the baby monitor and smiled. Her child was making soft sounds in her sleep. "Ivy is with me tonight, snuggled up in her crib."

"That's awesome, Meagan. Was it easier than you thought?"

"Yes. She just dozed off, listening to a story I was reading to her, like she does when she's at Tanner and Candy's."

"Congratulations, Mama."

"Thank you." She got into bed and put the phone on speaker. "Know what else? I decided that I'm going tell Tanner and Candy about us." She wasn't going to drag it out, either. "I'm going to do it tomorrow after work."

Garrett's voice wrapped itself around her. "If you do it tomorrow, so will I. I'll talk to my mom and mention it to my brothers, too."

She touched the phone, tracing the shape of it, imagining him on the other end of the line. "We'll have to plan our next get-together at your house soon."

"For sure. I can't wait to be with you again."

She wanted that, too, more than anything. "Are you going riding tomorrow? Will I get to see you at the stables?"

"Unfortunately, I'm going to be tied up in meetings all day. But you can call me tomorrow night, and we can discuss what our families said and how they reacted to our news."

"Okay. Then I guess we should go now." It was getting late, and they both had to work in the morning.

"Night, Meagan. I'll be thinking about you."

"Me, too. About you." In her sleep, in her dreams.

When they ended the call, she removed her robe and got under the covers, with Garrett deep in her mind.

* * *

Meagan's talk with Tanner wasn't going well. Her brother was treating her like a child. She wanted to tell him that he wasn't her keeper, but after everything he'd done for her, she couldn't criticize him for reacting the way he was. Still, she wished that he would stop scolding her.

Meagan glanced at Candy in silence. Thankfully, her future sister-in-law was being supportive. Ivy didn't have a clue what was going on. Not only was she too young to comprehend the gravity of the conversation, she was out of earshot, throwing a bouncy red ball down the hallway for the dog to fetch.

"I'm not going to let you keep seeing him," Tanner said.

Before Meagan could respond, Candy came to her defense. "If she wants to be with him, it's not your place to stop her."

"The hell it isn't." He turned his cloudy gray eyes on Meagan. "Just because he gave you a job doesn't mean he can do whatever he wants with you. You've been through enough with Neil and how he controlled you. You don't need Garrett taking hold of you, too."

"He isn't taking hold of me." Except for her dizzying feelings for him, but that wasn't something she was going to elaborate on to her disapproving brother.

"Are you sure he's not using you?" Tanner asked.

"Yes, I'm sure. I made the first move to become more than friends."

"Dang, Meagan." He frowned. "Why would you do something like that?"

"Because I really like him." And because getting naked with Garrett was like orbiting the moon. It was that special. "You thought he sounded like a nice guy before I told you any of this. You were even interested in meeting him."

"And I want to meet him even more now. If you're determined to keep seeing him, then I think it's important for me to get to know him, too."

"He's a good man, like you are. Ivy certainly adores him." Meagan paused to glance back at her daughter. She was still playing with the dog. "He's going to tell his family about us. He's supposed to talk to his mother this evening, like I'm doing with you. It was his idea for us to tell our families and for me to stop sneaking off to see him and having to lie to you."

"That's good." Tanner calmed down. "That makes me feel better. Why don't you invite him for dinner here tomorrow night, if he's available to come by then?"

Candy chimed in, "I also think we should invite his mom. After all, she was instrumental in getting Meagan the job."

"That sounds good to me." Tanner looked at Meagan. "Does that work for you, sis?"

"Absolutely." She relaxed, grateful that it was getting resolved. "I'll talk to Garrett about it tonight. I'd planned to call him later, anyway."

Her brother blew out a breath. "I'm sorry if I overreacted. I just want the best for you."

"I know." She reached out to embrace him. "But everything is going to be fine. I'll let you know what Garrett says about dinner. I'll text you after I talk to him."

"Okay." Tanner held her in a big old bear hug, the way he used to do when she was a kid. "And just so you know, I'm proud of the mother you've become."

"Thank you." She hugged him tighter. Without him and Candy, she never could have come this far. "I should probably go home now. It's getting close to Ivy's bedtime, and I need to get her settled in."

Once Meagan was in her own little house, she gave Ivy a bath and got her ready for bed. Like the previous night, her daughter conked out without a hitch, listening to a story. For Meagan, it was a wonderful feeling of déjà vu.

And so was her phone call to Garrett.

"How did it go?" he asked her.

"It was difficult at first, but everything is fine now." She relayed her experience, explaining how Tanner had come around. She also extended the dinner invitation.

"I'll be there for sure. No doubt Mom will come, too, if she's feeling strong enough to go out. She was doing well this evening when I saw her."

"How did she react to you being with me?"

"She was surprised. She had no idea that you and I were attracted to each other. She was concerned about the outcome, the way I assumed she would be. But I assured her that everything was going to work out fine."

"That's what I told Tanner."

"Then we're on point."

"I'm glad that we don't have to pretend around our families anymore. You were right about coming clean to them."

"And now we can focus on spending time together. Could it get any better than that?"

Her thoughts soared, with visions of romantic days and sensual nights, of touching and holding and kissing. "It's making my heart pound."

"Mine is pounding, too. You're my come-to-life fantasy, Meagan."

"You're mine, too. My dream man."

"Then it's only fitting that I wish you sweet dreams."

"While I wish you sweet fantasies?"

"Definitely."

He cleared the huskiness from his throat. Or he tried to. She could still hear it.

Then, for a stilling moment, he went quiet and so did she, steeped in the heat of each other.

"I'll see you tomorrow at dinner," he finally said.

"You, too," she replied, still lost in the feeling of him.

Garrett's mother accompanied him to Tanner and Candy's house, but she kept stealing glances at him whenever he looked at Meagan. Clearly, Mom was trying to figure out just how serious he was about Meagan. She seemed interested in how close he was to Ivy, too. Garrett did his best to relax and not make too much of Mom's curiosity.

Everyone was gathered around a patio table, drinking coffee or sipping tea, depending on their preferences. They'd eaten indoors and had come out here to enjoy the night air.

Tanner and Candy were kind and caring people, and Garrett found them much to his liking. He sensed that they liked him, too. He and Tanner talked easily. They had a lot in common, with their Cheyenne roots and love of horses.

He'd brought Tanner a bundle of sage as a gift offering, and his mom had given Candy, the future bride, a tall white candle. She'd given Meagan a candle, too, only hers was red and smelled like strawberries. For Ivy, she'd brought a little rag doll dressed in early American Indian garb. Mom was handy with crafts. She'd made the doll specifically for Ivy, just that very morning.

"How are the wedding plans going?" Mom asked Candy. "Are you getting everything done?"

"We're trying, that's for sure. It's been hectic but fun, too." Candy glanced at her fiancé. "We're having the ceremony at Tanner's stables and riding academy. The land is so beautiful there, with a view of Griffith Park."

"So it's going to be an outdoor wedding?" Mom asked.

Candy replied, "Yes, but since it'll be winter by then, we're going to rent a tent to cover the altar and the aisle, in case it's rainy or cold that day. They make some really pretty ones, so it will add to the ambience, rather than take away from it. We don't need to worry about the reception. It'll be inside." She smiled at Garrett's mom. "I'd love for you to come." Then she turned to Garrett. "And you, too, of course. I'll send invitations to both of you."

"Oh, thank you." Mom spoke up first, accepting the offer. "We would be honored to attend. Wouldn't we, Garrett?"

"Absolutely." He looked across the table at Meagan. He wanted to see her in her bridesmaid's dress, carrying her blue rose. He wanted to see Ivy in her flower-girl finery, too, traipsing down the aisle with Candy's doga dog. "It sounds like it's going to be a spectacular ceremony."

"Thanks. We think so, too," Tanner said, joining the conversation. Ivy was seated on his lap, clutching her new doll. Every so often, though, she would shoot Garrett an impish smile.

The kid was an adorable flirt. Meagan, however, was behaving properly. But he knew how wild she could be in bed, tumbling the sheets with him. Not that he should be thinking about that now, especially in the company of his inquisitive mother.

Earlier, his mom had marveled over a photograph of Meagan and Tanner's mom that was perched on the fireplace mantel, saying that it brought back memories of having known her. Garrett was fascinated by the picture, too. Meagan looked a lot like her mom, with her long, straight dark hair, warm brown eyes and gentle smile.

Before the evening came to a close, Garrett said to Meagan, "Will you give me a tour of your house?" He'd yet to see it, even if he'd caught a faraway glimpse of it out back. "Maybe Ivy can come along, too?"

She smiled. "I'd love to. And I'm sure that Ivy—"

"Me, go." The toddler tried to wiggle out of her uncle's arms.

Tanner laughed. "Okay, little one. Hold on." He helped her down. "Go ahead."

Ivy dashed over to Garrett and reached for his hand. He stood and accepted her tiny palm in his. Garrett's mom was watching him again.

"Do you want to join us?" Meagan asked her. "And see where I live?"

"That's all right," Mom politely declined. "You three go ahead. I'm more than content to stay here and finish my tea."

Garrett understood that his mom didn't want to go trudging across the grass. But he figured that she was trying to give him and Meagan a bit of privacy, too. Nonetheless, he could feel her checking them out as they walked away.

He and Meagan crossed the lawn, heading toward their destination, with Ivy and her new doll in tow.

The area was well lit, with flowers, fruit trees and leafy vines crawling up trellises.

"This is a great piece of property," Garrett said.

"Candy's garden is the focal point. She spends a lot of time tending to it. I've been learning so much from her about plants and flowers."

"Have you been doing some gardening, too?"

"Not yet, but I hope to. Ivy likes digging in the dirt, though." She laughed a little. "So does Yogi. Sometimes she and Ivy get in there and play together."

"What a sight that must be." He laughed, too, and glanced down at Ivy, who was bouncing along between them. "Two loyal companions, with soil-smudged faces, hands and paws."

Meagan smiled. "They are a pair." A moment later, she stopped at the guesthouse and said, "Here we are."

Her home was surrounded by a picket fence. She opened

the gate, and Garrett glanced around. Her private yard sparkled, with a fountain out front.

"This is nice." Now he could envision her here the next time they talked on the phone. "It suits you."

"Tanner chose it with me in mind. He used to live in a bachelor pad above his office at his stables. But after I got pregnant and he agreed to take Ivy, he searched for a place that could accommodate all of us. He knows that I like fairy tales, so that's why he thought this guesthouse would appeal to me. It reminded him of the magic cottages in the stories I used to read." She gestured toward the exterior. "It's even called storybook architecture. Initially, it was too small, though. He remodeled it and added a nursery for Ivy."

They went inside. The kitchen was quaint and colorful, and the living room boasted an air of comfort, with a window that showcased the fountain.

Meagan's bedroom, rife with warm woods and brass accents, gave Garrett a thrill, simply because she slept there each night. Now he understood why she'd been so fascinated with his room, too.

Next up was the nursery, which was decorated to the hilt with all sorts of girlishness.

"Mine," Ivy said, letting him know this was where she'd been sleeping these past few nights.

Garrett smiled. "That's a nice bed you have, with all those stuffed animals in it." He pointed to another section of the room. "And look there, you even have your own rocking horse."

Ivy rushed over to the horse, proud to show it off.

"I just got that for her," Meagan said. "It's the first thing I ever bought her on my own, with money from my new job." She moved closer to him. "It felt good to give my daughter a gift that my brother didn't have to pay for."

"Maybe I should give you a raise so you can buy her even more things."

"My wage is just fine."

"Yeah, but the other money that's coming out of it—the restitution…"

"That's fine, too. It's my responsibility to pay it back."

Garrett touched Meagan's cheek, and she lifted her hand to cover his. Ivy came back over to them, wanting in on the affection. Garrett picked her up, and she put her head on his shoulder.

Meagan gazed at him with admiration. "My daughter has good taste in men."

"And I'm totally into her mother." A romantic impulse came over him, kicking him into high gear. "I want you to go out with me."

"Out with you?"

"On a date. Remember when I mentioned it before, that if I had my way, I would take you out for the world to see?"

She took a step back. "But I'm not ready for that. Telling our families was enough. We're supposed to be taking things slow, remember?"

"Yes, but, in theory, dating is taking it slow. That's what people typically do before they sleep together. We started off backwards."

"I know, but…"

"Men are supposed to take women out, to wine and dine them, to show them how special they are." He looked into her eyes. "And you're far more special than anyone else I've ever been with. Please, Meagan. Let me treat you the way you should be treated."

Her voice cracked. "How am I supposed to say no to that?"

"You're not."

She waited a motionless beat before she said, "Then my answer is yes. But that doesn't mean I'm any less scared."

"Scared of what? Being gossiped about?" He made the same case he'd made before. "We can't live our lives based on what others think."

"I know." She released a jittery breath. "But that's only part of it."

"And what's the other part? Getting attached to me? It's too late for that. Whatever feelings you have for me, I have for you, too, so what's wrong with exploring them?"

"And dating like normal people? You make it sound so simple."

"It can be, if we let it." He was still holding her child in his arms. But Meagan needed him, too. Intent on quieting her fears, he moved forward to kiss her, a light touch of his lips to hers—proving how good they were together.

And how much he wanted to make this work.

Eleven

Meagan kept changing her clothes, freaking out about what to wear on her date with Garrett. She couldn't afford to buy a new outfit, and she didn't want to ask her brother for the money. Her old clothes weren't out of style, so at least she didn't have to worry about that. Women's fashion hadn't changed that dramatically. But the fancy outfits were from her party days with Neil, and that made her uncomfortable.

Still, she didn't have a choice but to wear something nice. Garrett was taking her on an upscale date: dinner and dancing. She glanced at the clock in her room. She needed to get her butt in gear. He would be arriving to pick her up soon. Thank goodness her makeup and hair were done.

She went for a glittery red minidress, pairing it with strappy heels. For her jewelry, she chose a sterling silver squash blossom necklace and hoop earrings. She added a turquoise bracelet, too.

Ivy was with Candy and Tanner for the night. Meagan would be going home with Garrett later. She'd already packed an overnight bag.

This date was supposed to give their budding romance a sense of normalcy. But all she felt was anxiety. With each second that ticked by, her excitement mounted. And so did her nerves. This was a turning point in her life. Not getting attached to Garrett was impossible. She was falling for him.

Big time.

But he'd admitted that he was falling for her, too, that his attachment matched hers. And from now on, they would be seeing each other openly.

Heavens, this was scary. Beautifully scary.

Meagan checked her reflection in the mirror one last time as the doorbell rang. She dashed off to answer it, anxious to greet Garrett.

He looked incredibly gallant in a classic black suit, with a lavender-colored shirt and silk tie. No doubt he was sporting all kinds of designer labels. Yet he seemed completely enthralled with Meagan and her little red dress. He just stood there, staring at her. He also had a bouquet of bright yellow gerbera daisies in his hand. She could've melted on the spot.

"Wow," he said. "You're on fire."

"You wouldn't believe how many times I changed."

"Well, you nailed it." He turned over the daisies to her. "These are for old times' sake, but you probably already figured that out."

"Thank you. They're beautiful." She clutched the bouquet to her chest. "And you're as handsome as ever."

He smiled. "Invite me in?"

"Yes, of course." She was out of practice. Or maybe she'd never actually been on a date like this before. Neil never cared about taking her out, unless it was to hang out at clubs and try to rub elbows with the rich and famous. "Come in, please." She held up the flowers. "And I'll put these in water."

Garrett entered her house, and she searched for a vase, uncertain if she actually had one. Candy had stocked the kitchen before Meagan had moved in.

She found a lovely glass container in the cabinet above the fridge. But it was way in the back.

"I'll get that for you," Garrett offered. He was tall enough to reach the shelf without stretching.

He handed the vase to her, and she arranged the daisies. "When you bring me home tomorrow, these will be waiting for me."

He swept his gaze along her bare legs. "Too bad the flowers from the charity event are gone."

She felt her skin flush. He was talking about the body painting that had been done on her ankle. "It came off in the bath that night."

His gaze roamed over her again. "Are you all set for this evening?"

She nodded. "My purse and overnight bag are in my room. I just need to get them." Before she walked away, she asked, "So where are we going? What restaurant?"

"It's a private dinner club located in the basement of a nineteenth-century home. In the late 1920s and early '30s it was a Prohibition speakeasy run by Sally Sue Milton, the widow whose house it was then. I haven't been there yet. Jake told me about it and sponsored me to join. He said they serve French food and have a live band that plays jazz, blues and Latin ballads."

"It sounds wonderful."

"I thought so, too. I wanted to go somewhere with you that was new to me. And hopefully new to you, too."

"It definitely is." She smiled. "Sally Sue must have been a character."

He smiled, too. "So they say."

"If the club is in the basement where the speakeasy used to be, what do they do with the rest of the house?"

"It's used for private parties and special events. But it's only available to members."

She suspected that it cost a pretty penny to join. His billionaire status was showing, but she didn't want to think too deeply about that. She'd stolen from him, and now she was trying to separate herself from his money, to push it into the background.

But it wasn't easy. He owned a five-star hotel and resort and lived in a house on a hill, overlooking the ocean. She was exposed to his lifestyle every time she saw him. And tonight was no exception.

After she gathered her belongings, he escorted her to the chauffeured limousine that was waiting to take them to dinner.

Sally Sue's former residence was a fascinating place, and Garrett was glad that he'd brought Meagan here.

Patrons entered through the rear, taking a narrow stairwell to the basement before reaching the original speakeasy door.

The decor in the subterranean space was far more elegant than it had been during Prohibition, but the hidden vibe remained. Sally Sue's picture was on the cocktail menu, and Meagan seemed thoroughly taken with the strangely genteel old broad. Meagan had even ordered a drink named after the woman: a shot of gin served in a vintage teacup. It came with a bowl of sugar on the side that you stirred in yourself. The gin provided by the bootleggers in this area was too bitter for Sally Sue's tastes, so she'd sweetened hers right at the table, sipping it like afternoon tea. In those days, drinking out of teacups was common practice in case of raids.

Garrett chose a Gin Rickey, consisting of gin, lime juice and seltzer. It was a popular Prohibition-era drink referenced by F. Scott Fitzgerald in *The Great Gatsby*. To Garrett, that made it even more interesting. It tasted pretty good, too.

He and Meagan had already nibbled on appetizers, followed by marinated salads, and now they were waiting for their entrées. The band was just starting their set. Later, Garrett would sweep his date onto the dance floor.

He asked her, "Do you know how the term *speakeasy* came to be?"

She sipped her Sally Sue. "No. How?"

"Because it's what bartenders used to say to the patrons, reminding them to speak easy or quietly in public about the illegal places where they were gathering to drink."

"Oh, I like that."

And he liked the way the candlelight was playing off her eyes. Her shimmery red dress was enhanced by the flame, too. "They gave me a brochure about speakeasies when I joined this club."

"Then tell me more about what you learned."

"In order to gain entrance, you would have to say a password or use a specific handshake or a secret knock."

"I wonder what types of passwords they used."

"I don't know. But I doubt they were as complicated as what we're using for our computers now."

She laughed. "Can you imagine if they had to use upper and lowercase letters? And numbers and symbols?"

He laughed, as well. "They would've been standing there all night, trying to remember it." He glanced at the wax melting on the candle and then back at his gorgeous date. "Another interesting thing was how Prohibition changed the drinking habits of women. Prior to that, mostly they just sipped bits of wine or sherry. But then ladies like Sally Sue came along. In came the flappers, too, with their bobbed hair, ruby lips and short, sassy skirts. They flooded the speakeasies, smoking and drinking and being wild."

Meagan held up her teacup. "Here's to those old-time gals."

He joined her, lifting his highball glass. "And to the modern woman here with me tonight."

Her gaze locked on to his. "This is already turning out to be one of the most exciting nights of my life."

His heart punched his chest. "Then let's make it even more memorable and steal a kiss on the dance floor. Public displays of affection aren't usually my thing, but one slow, sexy kiss won't hurt."

"It won't hurt at all." Her delicately painted teacup rattled as she placed it back on the table. "It will probably feel…" She couldn't seem to find the words.

He understood. He couldn't think of anything else to say, either. He swigged the rest of his drink.

"Are you going to get another one?" she asked.

He glanced at his empty glass. "Sure." He signaled the waiter for another Gin Rickey. "But two is my limit." He wanted to be clearheaded for the rest of the night. "How about you?"

"I'm good. One Sally Sue is enough for me."

He suspected that Meagan's lips would taste nice and sweet from the sugar. "Too bad I can't kiss you right now."

"You're too far away." She graced him with a playful smile. "You'd have to climb over the table to get to me."

"Don't tempt me, dear lady. I just might do it." But he didn't, of course. He minded his manners.

His second cocktail arrived, along with their meals. They'd both ordered filet mignon with bordelaise sauce, accompanied by gratin potatoes and porcini mushrooms.

"This looks wonderful," she said.

"Yes, it does." His appetite was plenty strong, for his food and for her. He gazed at Meagan while they ate.

She moaned her appreciation. "This is like dying and going to heaven."

"I'll bet dessert will be even better."

Her eyes lit up. "We should share some pastries."

"Angel wings."

She blinked. "What?"

"If we've died and gone to heaven, then we should have angel wings. They're fried dough covered in powdered sugar and shaped into ribbons. They're thin and crunchy. But, in France, they make a soft variety, too, made with thicker dough. Those are called pillows. They might have that type here since they serve French cuisine."

"Angel wings. Pillows. It all sounds so pretty."

"I want tonight to be pretty."

"It is, Garrett."

"We're going to dance before we have dessert." He didn't want to wait that long to kiss her. The music was already calling to him.

"I'd like that." She swayed a little in her seat. "I wonder what Sally Sue would think of what became of her house."

"I think she would approve."

"I think so, too."

"There was some personal information about her in the speakeasy brochure." Not a lot, but enough to draw Garrett in. "They say that she loved her husband dearly and mourned him terribly when he died."

"Is losing him what led her to running a speakeasy?"

He nodded. "Supposedly, that was a big part of her motivation. Before he fell ill, he and Sally Sue would frequent other illegal drinking establishments. It was the highlight of their aging lives."

"Now I adore both of them." Meagan made a dreamy face. "Thank you again for bringing me here."

"It's my pleasure." The first of many dates, he thought, with the woman who bewitched him.

Garrett called the waiter over again, only this time he spoke quietly to their server, keeping Meagan from hearing what he was saying.

"What are you up to?" she asked afterward.

"I put in a request for a song."

"How will I know which one it is?"

"Don't worry. You'll be able to tell."

About ten minutes later, they finished their meals, just in time for the band to play "Could I Have This Kiss Forever," a duet recorded by Whitney Houston and Enrique Iglesias.

Meagan snapped to attention. "This is it, isn't it? What you requested?"

"Yes. This is what I chose."

"It's perfect."

He thought so, too. "I figured the band would be familiar with it since they played a few other songs by the same artists."

"Good call."

He stood and approached her. "May I have this dance?"

"You can have as many dances as you want." She looked up at him and whispered, "And kisses, too."

Garrett escorted Meagan onto the dance floor. They moved beautifully together, with the same sensual rhythm they shared when they were in bed.

He kissed her passionately, the lyrics of the song tumbling in his head. He was a teenager when it first hit the airwaves, but he remembered how some of the girls in school used to swoon over it.

Meagan pressed closer, and he slid his hand along the back of her dress, enjoying the feel of her body next to his.

They danced to four mesmerizing songs, and he kissed her during all of them.

"Are you ready for dessert?" he asked.

Yes." She spoke softly. "Angel wings."

"Or pillows," he reminded her.

They returned to the table and scanned the dessert menus that were given to them.

"Both types are available," she said.

"Then let's go for broke."

They agreed on a platter of each, eager to indulge in the powdered-sugar sweetness, no matter how soft or crunchy the pastries were. The waiter brought extra plates, so they could share.

Meagan ate her portion lavishly. "I can't decide which one I like better."

Garrett nodded. "I don't have a preference, either."

"They both remind me of Navajo fry bread but for different reasons." She studied him from beneath her next bite. "Maybe we should make fry bread together sometime."

"Sure. Why not?" He smiled. "I can make it with the best of them. But it's always fun to get at powwows, too. That's another thing we should do together."

She stopped eating. "Since we're going to keep dating and planning events, do you think you could spend some nights at my house?"

"Yes, of course. I'd love to."

"Thanks. It's nice to hear you say that. It will make Ivy happy to have you there. But I'll bring her to your place on other occasions, too."

"I'll be glad to have both of you as my guests." But tonight, it was only Meagan.

She returned to her dessert and then lifted her hands. "I'm making a mess."

So was he but not as much as she was. He gestured to the wet towels that had been provided. "That's what these are for." He went ahead and used his, shooting her a teasing grin. "But you can lick your fingers if you prefer."

"I wouldn't dream of doing that here." She lowered her voice to a discreet level. "But I just might need a shower when we get to your house."

Damn, he thought. Could she be any sexier, reminding him of how badly he wanted to get wet and soapy with her? He leaned in to the table and said, "Imagine that. I just might need one, too."

Still reeling from their date, Meagan stood in Garrett's luxurious bathroom, removing her clothes. She piled her jewelry on the counter and gazed at her lover.

"Aren't you going to get undressed?" she asked.

"Yes, but not until you do." He was watching her, like a hawk zeroing in on its prey.

Meagan suspected that she was going to get eaten alive, unless she took a big juicy bite out of him first. "This is as far as I go, until you take something off, too."

He cocked an eyebrow at her. "Are you giving me an ultimatum?"

"Yes, I most certainly am." She drew an imaginary man with his broad-shouldered, narrow-hipped body in the air. "It's your turn, Garrett."

"Fine." He took off one shoe.

She stifled a laugh. "Seriously?"

"Yep." He drew an outline that represented her, creating

all sorts of curves. He even dotted her imaginary breasts with nipples. "Now you."

Both of her shoes were already gone. "This isn't fair." It was like playing strip poker with half of your clothes already gone. All she had left was her dress and underwear.

"Go on." He prodded her.

Her dress didn't have a zipper. But, thank goodness, she managed to divest herself of the garment without it getting stuck over her head. That wouldn't have been very graceful. She doubted that Garrett would have cared. He was too busy checking out her bra and panties.

She turned in a slow circle, showing him every angle. She'd worn her very best lingerie.

He kept checking her out. "I'm a lucky man."

And she was a lucky woman, being admired by him. "You need to catch up."

"I will," he said, even if he just stood there, looking at her. "In due time."

She moved forward. "Maybe I better help you." She unbuttoned his shirt and then put her hand on his fly. When she toyed with his zipper, he sucked in his breath. She could actually hear air whistling past his teeth.

The game was over. Neither of them wanted to linger over their clothes anymore. He whispered "hurry" in her ear and they both got naked as quickly as possible.

He pulled her tight against him, and they kissed hard and fast.

She thought that he was going to take her, right then and there, against the sink. But he hadn't forgotten their original plan.

He released her and turned on the shower. Meagan stepped inside the stall while he produced a condom from somewhere in the bathroom and joined her.

"You're prepared," she said.

"Always," he replied. "Now you get wet first."

She moved to stand under the showerhead, letting the water pummel her. It soaked her hair and skin. She didn't need to worry about her makeup smearing too badly. Her lipstick was already eaten off, and her mascara was waterproof.

Garrett put his mouth against hers, and they kissed once again. He wasn't playing nice. He was fully aroused and groping the hell out of her.

She tried to get on her knees for him, but he wouldn't let her, telling her that if she went down on him, he wouldn't last.

Meagan found all sorts of power in that. He found power, too, in rubbing his big, hard body all over hers.

He pumped out a handful of liquid soap and lathered every part of her. She washed him, too. But mostly they were just doing it to feel good. This wasn't about getting clean. If anything, it felt dirty. So magnificently dirty. She reached for the condom, but Garrett beat her to it. He already had it in his hand.

He struggled to open it. The packet was downright slippery. She used the extra time to press the front of her body against the back of his. He turned and kissed her, biting at her lip.

Somehow, in the midst of the frenzy, he tore into the packet and put the protection on. Pinning her against the wall, he lifted her up, encouraging her to wrap her legs around him.

Three heartbeats later, he slammed into her.

Steam filled the glass enclosure, rising up to the top. She repeated his name, over and over in her mind. His stomach muscles flexed with every thrust. He was so dog-gone hot she could have screamed. By the time this was over and he quit manhandling her, she would probably have his thumbprints permanently imbedded on her butt.

She'd never had sex like this before.

Meagan came first. He soon followed, his climax bursting like a volcano. The water kept running, the sound of it shooting past her ears.

Good God.

They slumped into each other's arms, too spent to speak. If he hadn't been holding her, her knees would've buckled.

He rolled his forehead against hers, keeping his hands around her waist. Content to be with him, she closed her eyes, grateful that he wasn't letting go.

Twelve

As the weeks passed, Meagan couldn't begin to count how many times she'd awakened next to Garrett, breathing in the scent of his skin. They saw each other as much as possible, and each moment was as glorious as the last.

On this quiet Sunday afternoon, they were at her house, preparing to take themselves and Ivy out to lunch.

"Let's go to Burbank Billy's," Garrett said.

"Really?" Meagan fastened her daughter's shoes. "That's where you want to eat? A fast-food joint?"

"Heck yeah. I love Billy's. It was my favorite place when I was a kid. And Ivy can play there."

"Me pay!" Ivy said, obviously listening to what he was saying.

"See?" He grinned. "She's totally on board."

"Okay." Who was Meagan to argue with the majority? "I wouldn't mind a burger and fries myself."

"And a milkshake," he added. "It wouldn't be complete without a shake."

"Chocolate?" she asked.

"I'm kind of partial to the strawberry. Their apple fritters are good, too."

She laughed. "Do you realize that all we ever do is eat? And that there's always something sweet involved?"

"Yeah, but nothing is as sweet as kissing you." He reached down and picked Ivy up, twirling her in his arms. "Isn't that right, princess? You like it when I kiss your mama, don't you?"

The toddler nodded. "Garry kissy."

"Yep. Just like this." He moved toward Meagan and planted one right on her lips.

Ivy squealed and clapped.

"Show-off," Meagan said, nudging him away and then pulling him back again. He was darned hard to resist.

They left the house and piled into his truck. He owned several cars, but, on casual outings, he drove a big Ford pickup. He didn't look like a CEO today. He looked more like a California cowboy, with his blue jeans and scuffed leather boots. But Garrett was a chameleon of sorts. He could be highly polished or decidedly rugged, depending on his mood.

Funny, too, how things were moving right along between them. Everyone in their inner circle knew they were together. The other employees at the resort knew, too. Sure, it had caused a buzz at first, but the gossip had died down soon enough. Of course, Garrett had made it known that disloyalty among the ranks wouldn't be tolerated. Even his accountant, who owned the firm where Meagan had stolen money, accepted the status quo. Meagan figured it was probably just for the sake of keeping Garrett as a client. But at least no one was treating her like a leper.

When they stopped at a red light, she turned to look at

her lover, studying his handsome profile. Then she said, "I saw my parole officer yesterday."

He glanced over, a slight furrow between his brows. "Did you tell her about us?"

"Yes." She'd been nervous about coming clean to her PO, uncertain what the reaction was going to be. "She wasn't particularly happy about it, but since I'm not breaking my parole by dating you, she couldn't scold me for it. She did express her thoughts, though. Mostly, she was concerned about how it could affect my job if things don't work out between us."

"Your job isn't in jeopardy, Meagan, and neither is this romance of ours." He reached across the center console to put his hand on her arm. "It's just getting started the way it should be."

She smiled, pleased with his answer. They were doing their best to follow a normal path, to enjoy each other's company the way new couples were supposed to.

The light changed, and he crossed the intersection. "You're still my fantasy girl."

And he was still her dream guy. If she could have straddled his lap and kissed him senseless, she would have, even if he was behind the wheel.

When they got to Burbank Billy's, Garrett carried Ivy inside. After their order was ready, they sat at a table in the play area, so Ivy could nibble on her meal with the promise to play once she ate enough of it.

Finally, they let Ivy dash over to the plastic jungle gym, where she climbed inside and poked her head through an oversized hole, along with another little boy about her age.

Meagan was still picking at her food, but Garrett had already finished his double cheeseburger and extra-large fries. He'd drunk half of his shake, too.

"Hungry much?" she asked.

A silly grin stretched across his face. "Yeah, and now I'm going back for an apple fritter. Do you want one?"

"Thanks, but I'll pass." Her stomach would burst apart if she stuffed it beyond its capacity. "But you go ahead and have at it." Garrett and his hot-guy abs. It boggled the mind.

Before he left, he scooted onto the bench seat next to her. "You sure you don't want a fritter?"

"I'm sure." She laughed when he threatened to kiss her, the way he'd done at her house. The exaggerated kisses Ivy liked.

"You don't know what you're missing."

"You can catch me up later."

"I'd rather catch you now." He stole the kiss he was hankering for, leaving her hungry for more.

While he was gone, someone approached the table. Meagan glanced up to see Andrea Rickman, an emotionally troubled, hard-drinking blonde she knew from her old club-scene days with Neil. At the time, Andrea's boyfriend, Todd, had been one of Neil's best buds. For all Meagan knew, Andrea was still part of that reckless circle.

Meagan wanted to run and hide, but there was no escape.

Especially when Andrea said, "I noticed you earlier, but I didn't want to intrude. But now that you're sitting here by yourself, I thought it would be okay to come over and say hi. Truthfully, I didn't even know you were...out." She said the last part with trepidation, obviously referring to Meagan's prison stint.

Meagan hardly knew what to say. "I'm just having lunch." It was a stupid reply but the best she could do under the circumstances.

"Is that your daughter?" Andrea asked, glancing toward Ivy.

"Yes. She's mine." And Neil's, but that went without saying. Clearly, Andrea already knew that.

"That's my nephew she's playing with."

Meagan looked over at the little boy Ivy had befriended. She acknowledged the connection with a quick nod.

Andrea said, "I'm here with my sister." She motioned to a table on the other side of the play area. "She got married about the time you…"

Went to prison, Meagan thought. Andrea kept referring to that. But why wouldn't she? They hadn't seen each other since then.

"I broke up with Todd," Andrea told her. "My sister convinced me to get rid of him. He treated me like a doormat, like Neil did with you. I thought it was awful that Neil didn't want anything to do with your baby. Todd sided with him, of course. But it made me mad. Sometimes I still see him and Todd when I go out, but I never speak to either of them." Silence, then a concerned "Are you doing okay now?"

"Yes, things are good."

"Because of the guy you're with?"

Yes, Meagan thought. But she didn't say that.

Just then, Garrett returned with his apple fritter, and Andrea turned to look at him.

Before things got ridiculously awkward, Meagan said to him, "This is Andrea. She's an old friend of mine."

"Oh, hey. Nice to meet you." He offered a smile. "I'm Garrett."

His name didn't appear to ring a bell. But there was no reason for Andrea to know who Meagan's victims were. The blonde smiled casually at him.

Then she said, "I better go. It looks like my sister is ready to leave. It was good seeing you."

Meagan replied, "You, too."

After Andrea and her family left the restaurant, Garrett asked, "So how old of a friend is she? Did you go to high school with her?"

"I know her from Neil." She repeated everything Andrea had said to her. "It was weird, running into her like that."

"But you got through it."

Yes, she'd gotten through it. And now she was glad it was over. Ivy came back to the table to climb onto Garrett's lap and drink some of his leftover shake. He gave her a few bites of the apple filling from his dessert, too.

And suddenly everything was right with Meagan's world again, just the way it was supposed to be.

The following week, Meagan was hit with startling news from her brother. Neil had contacted Tanner.

"What did he say to you?" she asked.

"Nothing. He called me at the office, but I wasn't there. So he left a message, asking me to have you call him. He left his number, in case you didn't have it anymore."

She felt weak in the knees. Not the sweet dizziness that Garrett made her feel but the kind that came with fear and nausea. She sat on Tanner's sofa, fighting the sickness coming over her. "Did he say why he wanted to talk to me?"

"No. But I wouldn't trust that jerk if he was the last guy on Earth."

"He probably found out that I'm dating Garrett and wants to poke his nose into it."

"How would he have found out about you and Garrett?"

"I bumped into someone from the past, and I introduced her to Garrett." She explained the Burbank Billy's encounter. "I don't think she was aware of who Garrett was, though. Nor did she seem like a threat. She never even liked Neil."

"Maybe you should call him to find out what he's up to. If you don't, he might try to see you in person. And we don't need him sniffing around your door."

"You're right. It's safer to call him." Neil knew where her brother lived, and most likely he knew that she lived on the property now, too. "I'll bet he's going to try to use me to get some money out of Garrett."

"Whatever he's trying to pull, we won't let him get away with it."

"Thanks, Tanner. I'm going to go home and call him now. Will you keep an eye on Ivy?" Her daughter had crashed on his floor, with a blanket and a bunch of toys, but she would probably be waking up soon. "I don't want her anywhere near Neil, even if it's just when I'm talking to him on the phone."

"Of course. I'll let Candy know what's going on, too, when she gets home from her yoga class. Are you going to call Garrett and warn him that Neil surfaced?"

"Yes, but first I want to talk to Neil. Then I can give Garrett the full story." Whatever the twisted story was.

Tanner gave her Neil's number, and Meagan walked the garden path to her house, taking in the air, hoping the breeze would help. Her stomach was churning like a vat of spoiled butter.

She went inside and made the call.

As soon as Neil said, "Hello?" her stomach churned even worse, the sound of his voice horribly familiar.

"It's me," she replied. "It's Meagan."

"Well, if it isn't the billionaire's girlfriend."

She fired back, "I'm not anyone's girlfriend." She refused to give him the satisfaction of hearing her admit it.

"Who are you trying to kid? I saw Andrea the other

night. She was drunk as usual, stumbling around a club. She gave me an earful about how you'd moved on with some guy named Garrett. She hasn't talked to me since she dumped Todd, and then she comes at me, spouting off about you."

Of all times for Andrea to be brave, Meagan thought.

"Anyway," he said, "I got curious to know if there was even the remotest possibility that the Garrett in question was Snow. And sure enough, I discovered that's who he is. Apparently, you're working for him. And getting cozy with him in burger joints, too."

"What's this really about, Neil?"

"Our daughter," he harshly replied.

Oh, God. He was going to try to use Ivy as his pawn? Meagan's heart skipped a beat.

He continued by saying, "I'm well aware of my mistakes and how I did her wrong. But I want to make amends and be the kind of father she needs."

Meagan would rather die than let him get his hands on Ivy. "That's a load of crap and you know it."

He ignored her accusation. "Have you considered that Snow could be playing a game? Reeling you in to get back at you for ripping him off? I've heard that he has a ruthless streak." There was a long pause. "Unless it's you who's up to no good, trying to take him for whatever he's worth. Either way, I have concerns for our daughter being subject to that kind of environment."

"I'm not—do you hear me? not—going to let you see Ivy. So whatever game you're playing, you can end it right now."

"You can't stop me from getting to know my own child. I have rights as a father."

"I'll use the courts to stop you."

"Right. As if you're the poster child for motherhood, dating one of your victims."

"My relationship with Garrett is none of your business."

"If there's nothing shady going on, then why are you getting so defensive?"

"I'm hanging up now. And I meant what I said about you not seeing Ivy."

"Yes, well, we'll see about that."

He ended the call before she could, leaving her in a fresh state of panic, with a flood of tears running down her cheeks.

Garrett rushed over to Meagan's house when she told him about Neil. And now she was shivering like a half-drowned cat.

Garrett took her in his arms, determined to calm her frazzled nerves. She'd taken a long, hot shower before he'd arrived. He assumed that she was trying to wash away the grimy feeling talking to Neil had given her. Her freshly washed hair was still damp, and her tear-marked face had been scrubbed clean.

She peered up at Garrett with red-rimmed eyes. Earlier, she'd told him that Ivy would be staying the night with Tanner and Candy. But he understood that Meagan couldn't bear to let her daughter see her like this.

She said, "Tanner said that if Neil comes around here and hassles me to see Ivy, I should file a restraining order against him. But I don't think Neil is going to do anything to hinder his chances in court. He's not going to make himself look bad in the eyes of the law, not if he expects them to grant him visitations with Ivy."

Garrett smoothed a hand down her hair, catching some of the wet strands between his fingers. "I'll help you do whatever is necessary to keep him away from Ivy. I won't let that SOB come within breathing distance of you or your little girl."

"I think his main objective for now is to figure out exactly what my relationship is with you and use that to his best advantage. But the only way for him to infiltrate our lives is through Ivy."

A stab of guilt punctured Garrett's chest, forming a bloody wound deep in his soul. "If I hadn't pressured you to take our relationship public, none of this would have happened. He wouldn't even know about us."

"It's not your fault." She held both of his hands in hers. "You were right about us dating openly. I don't regret it, Garrett. Not for a minute. But I'm still terrified of the power Neil holds over me. I'm the one who's a parolee, who's dating one of her victims, who struggled with a severe form of depression. Neil has a lot of things to use against me."

"Your postpartum depression shouldn't be an issue. You recovered from that, and you're an exceptional mother. As for you and me, I'll testify on your behalf that our relationship is good and pure. I'll open up my entire life to them if I need to."

"What about the three counts of embezzlement I served time for? Neil probably doesn't even have a traffic violation. I lied to the police about how he wasn't involved in what I did. I can't go back now and say that he helped me plot those crimes. Sure, the detectives on my case suspected it. But there was no proof of his participation and there never will be. Neil got away with it, and if he gets away with this—"

"He won't," Garrett reiterated. "I'll talk to my attorney and have him recommend someone who specializes in family law. I'll make damned sure that you get the best lawyer money can buy."

Her hands went clammy. "I can't afford someone like that."

"I can."

"I can't let you pay my way."

"So consider it a loan."

"Oh, God." She squeezed her eyes shut, and when she reopened them, they were filled with another round of tears. "I never wanted my relationship with you to be about money."

"It's not about that. What I'm offering is to save you and your daughter from Neil." Garrett would do whatever it took to keep them from getting hurt, no matter what the cost.

Thirteen

Garrett sat on a bench in front of a gourmet coffee shop, located on the boardwalk near his resort. He was waiting for Neil.

Yes, Neil.

Garrett had already consulted his attorney about Meagan's situation, and although a top-notch lawyer specializing in family law had been recommended, Garrett and his advisor had also discussed another alternative. A quicker, easier, cut-and-dry way to keep Neil away from Meagan and Ivy, and that was the route Garrett had decided to take.

He hadn't talked to Meagan about it, though. He wanted to spare her the details until it was over, until he could hold her in his arms and assure her that Neil would no longer be a problem.

So here he was, wishing the other man would hurry up and get here. But Neil, the cocky bastard, was late.

Garrett gazed out at the beach. It was a chilly afternoon, with the wind kicking up sand and the ocean crashing onto the shore.

He'd chosen this spot because it was one of his favorite places on the boardwalk. Meagan had already gotten off work and taken Ivy home from day care, so there was no chance of her happening by.

Garrett shifted his gaze and saw a long-limbed, fair-haired man dressed in jeans and a leather jacket coming toward him. He knew it was Neil. Earlier, he'd checked out Neil's social media accounts to view his pictures, most of which were arrogant selfies. He was younger than Garrett, with blue eyes and pretty-boy features.

Neil plopped down beside him, making a smart-aleck expression, as if he found this whole damned thing amusing. Garrett wanted to ball his hands into tight fists and beat that smug look right off his face, but that wasn't on the agenda. He needed to stick to the plan.

"So did Meagan give you my number?" Neil asked.

"No. I got it on my own."

"Does she even know that you arranged this meeting?"

"No," Garrett said. "And you're not going to say anything to her about it. In fact, after today, you're never going to speak to her again."

"I'm not?" Neil raised his eyebrows. "And how do you propose to make that happen?"

"By giving you a shitload of money to stay away from her and Ivy." Garrett had no intention of beating around the bush. He wanted to get this done and over. "My attorney already drew up a document, where you'll be relinquishing all claims to Ivy. After you sign and accept the money, for all intents and purposes you will no longer be her father." Garrett slanted him an icy glare. "Not that you are, anyway, not where it counts. But legally, you'll be giving up your parental rights. There's also a nondisclosure agreement you'll need to sign, prohibiting you from speaking about this for the rest of your miserable, soon-to-be rich life."

"How rich?" Neil slyly asked.

Garrett removed a slip of paper from his pocket with the figure written on it.

Neil's head nearly swiveled on his neck. "Did you bring the documents with you?"

"They're at my attorney's office. I'll text you the place, day and time. But you'll need to bring your own attorney to read the legalese to you."

"I can read. I can—"

"Just bring a lawyer." Garrett wasn't going to let this conniving prick come back later and say that he'd been rail-roaded into this. Or that he didn't understand the fine print. Or any other cock-and-bull thing he might try to concoct.

"If I sign a nondisclosure agreement, what am I sup-posed to say to my friends?"

"About your sudden windfall? I'm sure you'll come up with a plausible story to tell them." Considering what a good liar he was.

Neil jerked his chin. "This better not be a scam to make me look bad in court later. Like you're filming this and are going to present it as evidence. Because that will create trouble for you, too, bribing me the way you are."

Garrett cut his reply to the quick. "This isn't a bribe. It's a business arrangement, and you'd do well to know the difference."

"Okay, hotshot. But what if I don't accept the terms you're offering? What if my attorney thinks I should hold out for more?"

"Then the deal is off." He shoved the paper with the figure on it back into his pocket. "And I'll never offer you another dime again."

"You've got it all figured out."

"Yes, I do." And Garrett wasn't wavering. "So you've got two options—take it or leave it."

And he was certain that Neil would take it, since Garrett was giving the lowlife exactly what he wanted.

Monetary wealth in place of a sweet, beautiful child.

Meagan was at Garrett's house, sitting in a patio chair beside his pool with her hands clutched to her chest, listening to him tell her about the deal he'd orchestrated.

He finished with "I spoke to Neil yesterday about it, and he signed the papers this morning. It's over. You won't be seeing or hearing from him ever again."

Speechless, she just sat there, his news swinging like a razor-edged pendulum, slicing her emotions in two. Neil was out of the picture, gone from her and Ivy's lives.

She could have wept from gratitude, cried from absolute joy. Except for the other part of it...

Garrett had given Neil money. He'd gone behind her back, using his power and influence to "fix" her problems, and that made her feel like his cheap-hearted mistress. An ex-con sleeping with a billionaire. A woman who would never live an honest or upstanding life.

When she finally spoke, her vocal cords rattled. "You shouldn't have done that, Garrett."

He gave her an incredulous look. "What?"

"You shouldn't have paid him off. You shouldn't have even approached him without talking to me first. The decision should have been mine."

"But I wanted to spare you the trouble of being involved. I just wanted to come to you and say that it was done." He shook his head. "And why does it matter, as long as he's gone?"

"Because I wouldn't have agreed to your method."

Her hands were still pressed to her chest, where a hollow cadence beat its way to her throat. "I just couldn't have gone through with something like that."

"You wouldn't have taken the easiest and quickest method of getting rid of Neil?" He looked at her with accusation in his eyes. "Why the hell not?"

"For so many reasons." She hated that this was turning into a showdown. That she couldn't speak her mind without him taking offense. "But mostly because I can't stand the thought of you giving him money and putting me and Ivy in the middle of it. As scared as I was about facing off with Neil in court, I would have stood tough when I needed to, fighting my battles the legal way."

"There was nothing illegal about the way I handled it," he shot back.

"Then why does it feel so criminal to me? I was already uncomfortable about hiring a pricey attorney and borrowing the money from you to pay the fees. That was already weighing on my self-esteem. But this goes beyond anything I could've comprehended."

"So what are you saying? That I did something that damaged you?"

"Not purposely. But you made a decision that wasn't yours to make. You controlled a portion of my life that wasn't yours to control."

"Like Neil used to do?" Garrett scowled at her. "How am I supposed to feel with you comparing me to him?"

"I wasn't doing that. I wasn't—"

"Yes, you were."

Meagan struggled to remain as calm as this discussion would allow, to keep from breaking down in confused and frustrated tears. "You're putting words in my mouth."

"Do you know how long a court battle could have taken? Or the anguish it would have caused you and your family?"

His scowl deepened. "Neil would have put you through the wringer, trying to finagle a way to make a buck out of being Ivy's dad. He would have been there at every turn, using you and your daughter to get to me."

"So you beat him to the punch? Why can't you at least try to understand my perspective?"

"And do what? Apologize for paying that bastard off? No way." He got out of his chair, pacing the poolside pavement. "No effing way will I ever be sorry for that."

"You rewarded him for his bad behavior."

He stopped pacing, turning sharply to face her. "At least you and Ivy will never be burdened by him again."

"I'm so incredibly glad he's gone." She couldn't pretend otherwise. "And for that, I'll be eternally grateful to you. I know you meant well." God help her, she did. "But, on the flipside, you can't just go around paying people off to make things easier for me. I already told you that I didn't want our relationship to be about money."

"I did what I thought was right."

"But it wasn't right for me. I've been working tooth and nail to be a better person, to complete my parole, to meet my obligation and pay the restitution I owe. But now I owe you for getting rid of Neil, too." And that was a debt she would never be able to repay. "I'm not like you, Garrett. I'll never earn that kind of money, not in an entire lifetime."

"Get real, Meagan. You don't owe me anything."

"So I'm just supposed to accept you paying him off?" She fought the tears she refused to cry. "How can I condone that?"

He tugged a hand through his hair, his movements tense, choppy. "Maybe we should stop seeing each other. Maybe being together isn't going to work."

His dismissal cut her to the core, and so did the stubborn pride in his eyes. Instead of trying to understand, instead of coming to an emotional compromise—he was ending what they had.

"I don't want—" *To lose you*, she thought.

He went as still as a statue. "You don't want what?"

She didn't reply. If she gave in, there would be nothing left of her, of the independent woman she was trying so hard to become.

He remained as motionless as before. Then he roughly said, "This doesn't change the status of your job. I'd never take that away from you. It's yours, for as long as you want or need it."

She held her breath, her lungs ballooning with air, filling her with pain. "Ivy is going to miss you."

"I'm going to miss her, too." He cleared his throat. He was speaking softly now. "I don't think I should stop by the day care to visit her, though. That might confuse her, if I'm not with you anymore."

"Will you still come by the stables when I'm there?"

"Yes, I'll still see you when I go riding. I just won't be able to…"

Touch her and hold her and kiss her? His unspoken words tore a hole through her heart. Neil was gone, but so was her romance with Garrett. That wasn't supposed to be the solution.

"I need to go," she said. She couldn't stay here a millisecond more. It was killing her to be this close to him.

Hurting worse than anything she'd ever known.

Meagan went home and told Candy what had transpired. But by now she was too distraught to keep her emotions under control, bursting into intermittent tears and drying them with the tails of her shirt. "I swear, I didn't mean to push him away."

Her brother's fiancée gently replied, "You were just being honest with him about how it affected you."

Meagan drew her knees up to her chest. She and Candy were in the garden, seated on the grass. Ivy was inside, playing with Tanner and the dog. Meagan was surrounded by family, yet she felt so horribly alone. "His intentions were good, but he shouldn't have taken his protection that far. Of course, that's what he does. Protect people, I mean. When he was young, part of his motivation to become wealthy was to have the means to take care of his mother. And when he was in foster care, he stood up for Max when he was being bullied."

"Those are amazing qualities for someone to have."

"Yes, they are." Garrett was the most amazing man she'd ever known, right up until the moment he'd let her go. "Before today, he kept reassuring me that it was okay for us to explore our feelings, and that he was as attached to me as I was to him."

"I'm sure he still he is, Meagan."

"Attached, but detached." She rubbed her swollen eyes. "I can't fathom not having him by my side. It's going to be unbearable waking up every day, missing all of those wonderful moments I used to spend with him."

"I wish I could make it better for you."

Only Candy couldn't do that. No one could. But the worst of it, the most difficult part, was the fear that was unfurling: the knee-jerk panic that Meagan had already fallen in love with him.

She didn't want to feel that way, but she didn't know how to stop it. Nor could she bring herself to admit it out loud. Yet it existed in the recesses of her broken heart, turning her life inside out.

It was painful. Too much to grasp.

"This shouldn't have happened," she said, talking in riddles, trying to make sense of it. "Not now."

Candy plucked at a blade of grass. "I'm sorry he hurt you."

"What am I going to say when Ivy starts asking me where Garry is? How do I tell her that he won't be coming to our house? Or that we won't be going to his? She loves curling up in front of the TV with him. He watches princess movies with her." Fairy tales, Meagan thought, with happy endings. "But I have to be strong for myself and my daughter. To make my own decisions, to be my own woman. That's what I was trying to explain to Garrett, what I was trying to make him understand."

"Maybe something will happen that will bring him around to your way of thinking. Or maybe you could discuss it with him again after the dust settles."

"It's a big issue for us to resolve." And now that she was fighting the ache of loving him, it seemed even bigger. "I can't make the first move. If I do, then I'll go back to being the girl I was when I was with Neil, desperate for a man's approval."

"However this turns out, at least you're free of Neil and any future damage he could've caused."

Because of Garrett, Meagan thought. Even as mixed up as all of this was, he'd acted on her behalf, protecting her and Ivy like the fallen hero he'd become.

Garrett plastered an upbeat smile on his face, faking his way through the happy occasion. Jake and Carol's beautiful new daughter had arrived today, and the hospital room was filled with love and cheer, with flowers and balloons and teddy bears.

Brightness. Life.

Carol was in bed, cradling the blanket-wrapped infant,

and Jake was seated on the edge of the mattress, beaming like a first-time father should be. Max was there, too, in full-fledged uncle mode. If only Garrett could feel their joy.

Five grueling days had passed since he'd ended his romance with Meagan, and he battled the loss every second of every hour. He hadn't even seen her at the stables, as he'd claimed that he would. He'd been taking his horses out when he knew she wasn't there, sparing himself the ache of being in her company. He'd tried to do right by her and Ivy, but Meagan had made him feel like an interloper instead. Were his actions wrong? Had he overstepped his bounds? He was too damned lost to even know.

He gazed at his foster brothers, cooing over the baby. He hadn't told them about his breakup. He hadn't told his mom, either. He'd been keeping it inside.

Finally, Garrett moved closer to the bed. "Can I hold Nita?" he asked. He'd yet to cradle his niece, to press her against his heart, to absorb her newborn warmth.

Jake proudly replied, "Of course." He removed the child from his wife's arms and the transfer was made.

Garrett looked down at the baby's chubby-cheeked face. She'd inherited Jake's golden skin and thick dark hair. Her eyes were shaped like his, too, except they were green like her mother's.

The baby made a cute and comical noise, a tiny snort of sorts, and Garrett smiled, this time for real. "Hello, funny bear," he said. "I'm your uncle Garry."

The infant gazed at him. Or he thought she did. For all he knew, she was staring into space, trying to get those Irish eyes of hers to focus.

Now he longed for Meagan and Ivy even more. He wished they were here, sharing this experience with him. "She's perfect," he said to both of her parents. "You created a wonderful little person."

He returned Nita to her mother. He couldn't hoard a baby who wasn't his.

When it was time for Nita to nurse, Garrett and Max left the room, leaving Jake alone with his wife and child.

Once they were in the hallway, Max said, "I'm going to grab some chow at the cafeteria. Want to come?"

"You go ahead. I'll just get a granola bar or something out of a machine."

"Then I'll see you in a bit." Max shot him a quick wave and headed for the elevator.

Garrett scanned the choices in the vending machines but decided to skip it. He was too preoccupied to eat. So he went to the nearest waiting room, an open area with pastel-painted walls and floor-to-ceiling windows. He was the only person there, alone with his scattered thoughts.

About five minutes later, he spotted his mom heading toward him, clutching a small gift bag. He stood and went over to her.

"I didn't know you were coming by today," he said. "I thought you were going to wait until they took the baby home."

"I was, but I changed my mind. So I called my driver, and he brought me over. I'm just so excited to see little Nita."

"She's a doll. But Carol is feeding her now, so we're just biding time until we go back in. Max went to the cafeteria."

"That's fine. I'll wait here with you."

Garrett resumed his seat with his mom by his side. "What did you get the baby?" he asked.

"I made her a pair of moccasins. I've been working on them for a while."

"I'm sure her parents will love them." He didn't doubt

the love and care that had gone into them. "You're going to be a terrific great-aunt. Nita is going to adore you."

"She's going to adore you, too. Just the way Ivy does. You've got a good thing with Ivy and her mommy."

His chest crumbled, right along with his heart, but he didn't say anything. He merely sat there, mired in his loss.

"Are you okay?" his mother asked, catching sight of his discomfort.

He tried to shrug it off. "I just have a few things on my mind."

"Do you want to talk about it?"

"Really, it's all right. I can handle it."

She tucked a strand of her gray-streaked hair behind her ear. "Are you sure?"

No, he thought. He wasn't. But he didn't want to burden anyone with his problems, least of all his mom. Yet keeping it to himself was starting to tear him apart, too.

Looking for an emotional escape, he glanced out the window that was behind him. The view was of the parking lot.

He turned back around to face her. "If I tell you, you might agree with Meagan and think what I did was wrong, too."

"Whatever it is, I promise I won't judge you, Garrett."

He relayed the entire story, and she listened patiently, her gaze trained on his.

Afterward he asked, "So what do you think?"

"Truthfully, my opinion doesn't matter. What happened is between you and Meagan. But I do think that there might be some other factors involved, things you haven't even considered." She adjusted the gift bag on her lap and the paper made a crinkling sound. "For example, why did you do it? Why did you go to such an extreme measure to get rid of Neil?"

"I already told you, to get him out of their lives."

"Yes, but why?"

"Because I couldn't bear to see Meagan and Ivy get hurt."

"Again, I'm going to ask you why."

Troubled by her tactic, he pulled back. "Why are you grilling me like this?"

"Because I want you to think about it. Not off the top of your head like you've been doing, but all way down—" she leaned forward, pressing a gentle fist to his gut "—from your soul."

Garrett flinched, feeling as if he'd just been shot. Suddenly, he knew exactly what she meant. Or maybe, fool that he was, he'd known it all along and just hadn't dealt with it properly. But the truth was there now, like a lead bullet piercing his already-frayed spirit. A gaping hole, he thought, that provided the answer.

For every lovelorn thing he'd done.

Fourteen

Eager to see Meagan, Garrett left the hospital. Since she was at work, he drove to the stables, preparing to unleash his heart.

But would she forgive him? Accept him? Love him? Want him? There was only one way to find out.

As soon as he arrived, he parked his truck, climbed out of the vehicle and searched the barn for her.

She was in the tack room, by herself, cleaning a stack of leather bridles. She was so focused on her task that she didn't even know he was there, standing in the doorway, watching her.

She looked pretty, as always, in her rough-hewn clothes and long shiny braid. But she looked troubled, too. Because of him, Garrett thought. The last time they'd talked, he hadn't listened to her reasoning. He hadn't respected her thoughts or feelings. He'd flown off the handle instead, destroying the bond they'd built.

And now he was trying to fix what he'd broken.

"Meagan." He said her name softly, so as not to startle her.

She glanced up, and their gazes met from across the space that stretched between them. He entered the room and closed the door behind him. But he didn't crowd her. He kept a cautious distance.

"What I did was wrong," he said, getting straight to the soul of it. "I can't lie and say that I'm sorry Neil is out of the picture. But I had no right to pay him off without your permission, and for that I am sorry."

She set aside the bridle she'd been oiling. In a bucket at her feet were the bits and chains that went with it.

She said, "I've missed you, Garrett. I've been waking up every day, thinking about you, wishing I could see you. And now you're here."

Yes, he was here and had a lot more to say. "Jake and Carol's baby was born today, and she's just the sweetest thing. And when I held her, it made me miss you and Ivy and everything we had. Everything I ruined."

Meagan seemed to sense that he wasn't done talking, so she remained quiet, allowing him to say his emotional piece.

He continued, "I didn't tell my brothers what was going on with you and me. I'd been keeping it inside. Then my mom showed up at the hospital and noticed that I seemed out of sorts. It wasn't easy, but I admitted it to her." He paused to ask, "Did you tell your family?"

"Yes," she replied. "Mostly, I confided in Candy. But my brother knows what's going on, too. They feel bad that I've been hurting, but they're grateful to you that Neil is gone."

"I don't want to be responsible for your pain anymore. I don't want to be *that* guy. Because that would make me like Neil, and I'm not him. I love you, Meagan. And I love your daughter. That's no excuse for what I did, but it's the reason I was so desperate to get rid of Neil. I couldn't stand for him to hurt you anymore than he already had, but then I ended up hurting you, too. I behaved horribly afterward, letting my pride tear us apart." He shook his head, chastising himself for it. "You were right to hold your ground, to show me the kind of woman you are." He took a step toward her. "The woman I love."

She moved forward, too, until she was walking straight into his arms.

"Does that mean you love me, too?" he asked, needing to be sure.

"Yes, I love you." She confirmed her feelings, saying it out loud, letting the words soothe him. "You just made me happier than I've ever been."

Garrett held her close. "I want to keep making you happy, Meagan, to marry you and adopt Ivy. But I won't push you to make it happen. The time has to be right for you."

She looked up at him. "I want to be your wife more than anything and have you become Ivy's father, too. But I do want to wait awhile. It's important to me to finish my parole and pay my restitution first."

"I understand." He truly did. He wasn't going to take her for granted. He'd nearly lost her, and he was never going to let that happen again.

She stayed in his arms. "Can I still work at the barn after we're married? I like it here."

He ran his hand down the length of her braid. "You can do whatever you want."

"Can we give Ivy lots of brothers and sisters?"

"Absolutely. I've always wanted a houseful of kids." He envisioned his home the way it should be, filled with love and joy. "Will you come to my house later and bring Ivy with you?"

"So we can tell her that I'm going to marry you and you're going to become her daddy?" Meagan smiled. "We'll be there with our bags packed."

Garrett grinned. "So you're going to move in with me, are you? This future family of mine?"

"If you'll have us."

He kissed her, giving her his answer, this forever lady who would someday be his bride.

On the day of Tanner and Candy's wedding, Meagan marveled at every splendid detail. The colors they'd chosen were silver and gold. There were bits of blue, too, like the dyed rose in Meagan's hand. She waited in the wings, preparing to walk down the aisle with the other bridesmaids. But, for now, she was watching Ivy.

Her daughter toddled toward the makeshift altar, with Yogi by her side. Ivy's dress was a puff of ruffles and lace, trimmed with delicate bows. She wore a crown of posies in her hair and sequined shoes. She was the cutest, brightest flower girl, hanging on to the dog's rhinestone leash.

Ivy kept glancing around at all the people. When she spotted Garrett sitting in the front row, she dropped the dog's leash and ran over to him.

Meagan's heart melted on the spot. Both man and child were the loves of her life.

Ivy climbed onto Garrett's lap, where she decided to stay. Yogi, the brilliantly trained Labrador, continued to the altar by herself.

Tanner stood like the elated groom that he was, dashing in his traditional tuxedo and white rose boutonniere. Ivy waved at him, and he smiled and returned her greeting.

When Meagan's turn came to walk down the aisle, she

took the arm of the groomsman she'd been paired with—her oldest brother, Kade. His wife and son were seated in the same row as Garrett, along with Garrett's mom. Shirley was already becoming a grandmother to Ivy.

The ceremony continued, and, finally, when the bride's song was played, everyone stood and turned to view her.

Meagan got a lump in her throat. Candy was more beautiful than she'd ever been, with her mermaid-style gown hugging her curves. She wore a single strand of pearls around her neck, and her hair was swept into an elegant twist and decorated with gilded combs. She carried a cascading white bouquet with a single blue rose in the center.

The vows Tanner and Candy took consisted of words they'd written themselves. During her oath Candy mentioned the unattainable dream that had come true, referencing the special roses she'd chosen for herself and the other women in her bridal party.

Meagan's eyes misted. Someday, in the near future, this would be her and Garrett, standing at an altar, professing their love and devotion.

By the time the reception was underway, Meagan was seated next to her man, enjoying a delectable meal. Garrett's foster brothers had been invited to the wedding, too, so they could meet Meagan's family.

Jake and Carol brought their new daughter. She was exactly a month old today. They didn't plan to stay long, considering how young she was, but they wanted to make an appearance and show her off. She was an adorable baby, all gussied up in pink.

Meagan was looking forward to having more children, not just for her and Garrett but for Ivy, too. So she could become a big sister. Already, she was crazy about little Nita. Earlier, she'd peered adoringly at the baby in her carrier.

At the moment, though, Ivy was chattering up a storm with Max. She'd grown quite fond of Max, or Maddy, as she called him.

After the meal, Garrett asked Meagan to dance and, as they swayed to the music, he said, "This is a wonderful gathering."

"Yes, it is. Everyone we love is here."

"Including each other."

She looked into his eyes. Truer words had never been spoken. "You're my heart, Garrett Snow."

"And you're mine, Meagan 'Winter Time' Quinn." He spun her around. The song had changed to an up-tempo tune.

They glanced over and saw that Max was dancing with Ivy, lifting her high in the air and rocking her back and forth.

"Me, fun!" she said.

They laughed, charmed by her enthusiasm. She was enjoying herself on this merry occasion, and so were they. Life was good, Meagan thought.

Beautifully, magnificently good.

After Garrett and Meagan got home from the wedding, they put Ivy to bed. She conked out right away, exhausted from the festivities. Garrett loved that Meagan and Ivy were living with him now. He loved watching his little princess sleep, too. On nights like this, his house really had become a castle in the sky.

He tucked the blanket around Ivy. "She had a big day."

Meagan nodded. "We all did."

"Are you ready to turn in, too?"

"With you? Anytime."

They went into his room—their room—and he unzipped her dress, a softly draped gold-tone gown with a jeweled neckline.

"You look gorgeous in this," he said. "But you look just as ravishing out of it." Her undergarments were sexy as sin. Wisps of silk and lace. If he wasn't careful, they would tear apart in his hands.

She smiled. "You're quite handsome yourself."

Garrett removed his tie and draped it over a chair. He'd discarded his jacket earlier. "I've been thinking about our wedding."

"I've been thinking about it, too, and how amazing it's going to be. But I still want to wait until my parole ends and my restitution is paid."

"I know." He wasn't going to hurry her. They'd made an agreement, and he was holding up his end of the bargain. He walked over to the dresser. "But I do have something to give you." He opened the top drawer. "I bought it a few weeks ago, but I kept it hidden in a safe until today."

She came closer to see what her gift was, and he handed her the ring-sized box. Then he said, "I want us to be officially engaged."

She flipped open the velvet-lined box and gasped. He'd shopped specifically for the diamond, choosing it for its flawless clarity and vivid blue color, much like the flower she'd carried today.

"Oh, my goodness." She looked as if she might cry. "I don't know what to say."

He'd designed the ring as a classic solitaire, simple in its elegance, assuming it was the timeless style she would prefer. But he'd still given her a piece of jewelry that spoke volumes. The diamond was as rare and beautiful as she was. "Just say that you'll wear it."

"Yes, of course, I will. It's stunning. More perfect than I could have ever imagined." She slipped it onto her finger, where the stone dazzled against her skin. "I'm going to have to use gloves when I'm at work to protect it."

"My stable-hand bride. I'm so proud of who you are."

"And I'm so honored to be your fiancée."

"I have a diamond for Ivy, too. It's a princess-cut pendant for her to wear on the day of our wedding. And anytime she wants to wear it after that, too."

"You're going to spoil us, Garrett."

"I can't help it. I'm excited about having you as my wife and Ivy as our daughter."

"Me, too." She kissed him, soft and sweet and slow.

He guided her to bed, and they finished removing their clothes. He caressed her bared body, and she arched and sighed. He knew just where to touch her, indulging in foreplay that pleased her.

She knew what he liked, too. She used her hands and her mouth, giving him wicked thrills.

Her hair was fixed in a long, wavy style, leftover from the wedding, with little crystals pinned into it. While she did wild things to him, he toyed with her ladylike coiffure, scattering the pins.

Finally, when he couldn't wait any longer, Garrett reached for a condom. Someday, when they were ready for more children, they wouldn't be using protection. But for now this was part of the process.

Once he was inside her, he pulled her tight against him, savoring the naked intimacy. He'd been waiting a long time to feel this way, to care about someone this much.

The sex overflowed with heat and passion. But so did the love. Garrett and Meagan were right where they belonged.

Together in every way.

* * * * *

MILLS & BOON®

Desire™

PASSIONATE AND DRAMATIC LOVE STORIES

MILLS & BOON®

Why shop at millsandboon.co.uk?

Each year, thousands of romance readers find their perfect read at millsandboon.co.uk. That's because we're passionate about bringing you the very best romantic fiction. Here are some of the advantages of shopping at www.millsandboon.co.uk:

* **Get new books first**—you'll be able to buy your favourite books one month before they hit the shops

* **Get exclusive discounts**—you'll also be able to buy our specially created monthly collections, with up to 50% off the RRP

* **Find your favourite authors**—latest news, interviews and new releases for all your favourite authors and series on our website, plus ideas for what to try next

* **Join in**—once you've bought your favourite books, don't forget to register with us to rate, review and join in the discussions

Visit **www.millsandboon.co.uk**
for all this and more today!